Could've FOOLED ME

Could've FOOLED ME

JENNY PROCTOR

*For the readers who've
read enough hockey romance to
turn into real life hockey fans.
I see you. (I am you.)*

A NOTE FROM THE AUTHOR

Hi, friends. Just a heads up. This book contains several characters who have lost loved ones to cancer or a car accident. There are also mentions of child abuse (in the past) and the impact it has on adult lives as well as conversations about mental health, postpartum depression, and panic attacks. There is a secondary character who has a healthy pregnancy and an uncomplicated delivery of a baby. I've tried my best to handle these topics gently and give you the happy, swoony, feel-good moments you want. (Plus the kissing. All. The. Kissing.) Happy Reading!

SARAH

After three weeks of living in Atlanta full time, I've decided the roads were planned by an angry toddler with a fistful of crayons. Roads change names with no warning, highways weave up and around and over themselves, and there are at least fifty different Peachtrees. Peachtree Road, Peachtree Boulevard, Peachtree Lane. Do they celebrate any other kind of fruit in Georgia?

I've eaten Georgia peaches, and they're admittedly delicious. But this level of obsession is ridiculous.

I slow my car and take a right into a restaurant parking lot so I can turn around. To be fair, it's on me for assuming I already know enough to get around without my GPS. But I only had to go to the art supply store, which is directly in between my new favorite coffee shop and the grocery store I've been to at least four times.

It shouldn't be this hard. And yet, I made the same wrong turn today that I made yesterday. And the day before that.

Across the street, Vortex Arena looms large, its glass walls gleaming in the late afternoon sun. I haven't been to the arena since I moved in, but the last time I was in the car with Anna and her girls, Poppy pointed out the window and said, "Aunt Sarah, that's where Daddy plays hockey! Now that you live here, will you come to games with us?"

I looked over and exchanged a glance with Anna.

"Sarah's pretty busy, Pops," my sister-in-law said. Then she launched into a list of the different restaurants Poppy and Olive could choose for dinner, and my oldest niece's question was forgotten.

I appreciated Anna's redirection, but honestly, I still haven't shaken the guilt that's been gnawing at me ever since.

Last year, my brother led the Georgia Jaguars all the way to the final round of the Stanley Cup playoffs. It was the closest he's ever come in the seventeen years he's been playing in the NHL, and I didn't see any of it.

As I ease back out onto the main road—one that is absolutely named after a peach—my phone rings from where it's sitting in the center console, and Anna's face pops up on my dashboard.

"Hey," I say, answering the call through the car's connection. "What's up?"

"Are you still out?"

"I am, but I'm almost home. I'm across the street from the Vortex."

She's quiet for a beat before she asks, "Did you get lost again?"

"It's an easy turn to miss," I argue, and she chuckles.

"Just use your GPS, Sarah. I still use mine, and I've lived here my entire life."

"Using it to avoid traffic is different than using it because you can't drive ten minutes to the art supply store without getting lost."

"You'll get there eventually," she says, and I hope she's right. I'm not sure why it matters so much. I'll only be here a few more months.

Two months, three weeks, and four days, to be exact.

And yes. I'm counting, but not in a good way. I'm the opposite of a kid crossing off the days until Christmas. Because the giant X on my calendar marking my departure only fills me with a sense of dread.

"In the meantime," Anna continues, "can you swing by Chick-Fil-A and pick up the platter of nuggets I ordered for the kids? I just called, and they confirmed it's ready. You can go through the drive-thru to pick it up."

"Sure," I say. "The one by Publix?"

"Yes, but I'll send you a pin for it. Don't try to get there on your own."

I breathe out an exaggerated sigh. "I have a reputation now, don't I? I'm always going to be your directionally challenged sister-in-law."

She laughs. "You have to have something to keep you humble. I sent the pin. Did it come through?"

"I've got it," I say as I pull up the location on my GPS. "I'll be home in a few."

"Thank you. Love you. See you soon!" Anna says, then the call disconnects.

My brother has done a lot of incredible things in his thirty-six years, his hockey career notwithstanding. But I'm not sure anything rivals convincing Anna to marry him.

Miles is ten years older than I am, so I was only sixteen when he and Anna got married, but she never treated me like I was just an annoying teenager. She loved me with her whole heart, which has made it easy to love her back. She's kind, funny, loyal. And honest in a way that people who love you should be honest, but not in a way that ever hurts my feelings.

Nine years later, the age difference is much less significant—we're as much friends as we are sisters. Best friends.

Which is why leaving is going to be so hard.

Twenty minutes later, chicken nuggets secure in the front seat, my GPS safely guides me back to my brother's ridiculously enormous house. The street out front is full of cars, so I'm guessing most of his teammates are already here. I pull into the second driveway and ease past the garage so I can park next to the pool house. There's a spare bedroom inside the main house that Anna and Miles offered to let me use, but it'll be Olive's room soon—as soon as they move her out of the nursery to make way for the new baby. So I'm living in the pool house instead.

It's dated—it wasn't renovated like the rest of the house was before Anna and Miles moved in—but it's cozy and private and I really like having my own space. The only downside is it doesn't have much natural light, so I still haven't figured out a good place to paint. I haven't minded too much—I've been so focused on spending time with my nieces—but I'm starting to feel twitchy, restless and ready to get back to it, so I'll have to solve the problem soon.

I climb out of the car just as an SUV pulls into the drive behind me. A couple gets out and walks together toward the front door, and I swallow a groan.

When Miles first mentioned the dinner, I considered faking a migraine to get out of having to attend. Not because I have a particular aversion to hockey players. It's watching the sport that's triggering—not being around the men who play it. But social situations are generally tough for me. Crowds are intimidating at best. Completely draining at their worst.

Anna posed the evening as an opportunity to meet someone—there's no shortage of single guys on Miles's team. But I'm moving in a few months. Seems dumb to start something when I won't be around. Plus, she's forgetting my brother would probably break his teammates' ankles before letting any of them date his sister, which is generally annoying but helpful in this case, because I have no interest in being a WAG.

I respect what my brother does for a living. And hockey Wives and Girlfriends are incredible women. At least the ones whom I've met—Anna most of all.

But I don't fit in that world.

I can't fit. Even if I want to.

Still, Miles has been in Atlanta for most of his career, and he talks about his teammates like they're brothers. Now that I'm living here too—at least temporarily—it feels rude to avoid them. Or maybe the guilt for missing all his games is starting to catch up with me. Finally meeting his teammates feels like a relatively low-risk way to support him.

I climb out of my car and move around to the passenger side to retrieve the large platter of chicken. It smells delicious and my stomach rumbles with hunger, prompting me to set it on the hood of the car and lift the lid on the tray so I can retrieve a couple of nuggets for myself. There can't be that many kids in attendance. Surely they won't miss a few.

The chicken is tender and juicy, and I let out a little groan as I sink back against my car. When was the last time I had anything to eat? I sketched all morning...which, honestly, I often forget to eat when I'm immersed in my work. I suddenly feel like I could eat this entire tray.

"Can I have one?"

I spin around, still licking my fingers, and find a little girl in the driveway behind me. She looks close to Poppy's age, around five or six, and has long red hair braided into pigtails. She's wearing fairy wings on her back, which feels like an odd choice considering she also has goalie pads on her legs. Either way, she's possibly the most adorable thing I've ever seen.

"A piece of chicken?" I ask.

She nods, eyes wide and serious. "The food is taking forever."

My mind flits back to a conversation I had with Anna when Poppy had a friend over who had at least a dozen dietary restrictions. Gluten, dairy, eggs. The poor kid was allergic to everything. It's making me nervous to offer food to a random kid, and my eyes dart to the back door, wondering if she has a parent nearby.

As if on cue, the door swings open, and a man steps out. "Charlie?" he calls, eyes on the backyard.

Even if I didn't know Miles's house was full of professional hockey players, I probably would have guessed this guy was an athlete just by the size and shape of him. Broad shoulders, tapered waist. Thighs straining against the seams of his pants. I can't see his face from this angle, but I don't mind the look of the rest of him.

I look at the little girl. "Are you Charlie?"

She looks toward the man calling her name. "Yeah. But that's just Uncle Carter. He won't mind if I have some."

"There you are," the man calls, finally turning this way and closing the short distance between us. Turns out, his face is even better than everything else.

Uncle Carter is really handsome. Light brown hair, a close-cut beard. And the most arresting blue eyes.

He offers me a brief smile, then zeroes in on the little girl—Charlie. "Your dad's looking for you. Did you tell him you were going outside?" His tone is gentle—more curious than scolding.

She shrugs. "I saw a bird."

"Yeah? What kind?" His answer surprises me, and it must surprise Charlie too because she perks right up.

"It was brown. With orangey-red on his belly."

"Sounds like a robin. Want to go see if we can find him?" Carter holds up a coat, pink with white hearts stitched around the hem.

Charlie nods. "Can I have some nuggets first?"

"It's not quite time to eat. But I think everything will be ready soon."

"She had some," Charlie says, turning her gaze toward me.

My eyes widen even as Carter gives me a playful look. "Did she, now?"

"Just a small sample," I say, though I have no idea why I have to justify myself to a six-year-old. Or a man I don't know.

Carter's lips lift into a small smile, those blue eyes flashing. "She must have been really hungry," he says without breaking eye contact.

There is nothing even remotely flirty about his sentence, and yet, the low rumble of his words sends a skitter of goosebumps racing down my arms. He isn't even talking directly to me—just *about* me. And my body is still reacting.

Then again, it's been a very long time since I've been around a man this handsome. I could just be out of practice.

"She can absolutely have one," I say, finally finding my

voice. "There's plenty. Anna asked me to pick them up for all the kids."

Carter's expression brightens. "Oh. You're Sarah."

My eyebrows lift. "Yes?"

"I was just talking to Miles about you moving to Atlanta." He lifts his hand and points at his eyes. "And you and Miles have the same eyes. Seemed like a safe bet."

I turn and lift the lid off the platter of chicken and motion to Charlie. "Is this okay? She doesn't have any allergies?"

He quickly shakes his head. "She's fine. Her dad won't care."

Charlie grabs a couple of chicken nuggets, and I replace the lid on the tray, then watch as she darts across the driveway toward the lawn with surprising speed, considering the cumbersome goalie pads.

"Charlie, your coat," Carter calls.

"I don't need it," she yells back.

It isn't exactly warm outside, not for January, and Charlie's nose was already a little pink. But it's not so cold that she'll freeze without it.

Carter looks at me and shrugs. "She was born here, but she's got Canadian blood. She probably thinks this feels like spring."

"Ha. Yeah. I can relate."

"Winnipeg, right?" Carter says. "How long have you been in the States? Did you come when Miles moved here?"

I remind myself that I'm Miles's sister, and Miles is Carter's teammate, so it makes sense he would know where we're from. But it's still disconcerting to have him know so much about me. Disconcerting—but not altogether unpleasant.

"No—I stayed in Canada until I was nineteen. Which

means it's been...almost seven years? I came for art school. I did my undergrad, then my master's and graduated last year."

"Yeah, Miles told me," Carter says. "I had a cousin who went to SCAD. Years ago, but she loved it."

Suspicion pricks at the back of my mind. This is more than just knowing we're from Winnipeg. Miles seems to have said a lot about me. Which is unusual. He's usually pretty protective of me when it comes to his teammates.

"I'm sorry. I should have introduced myself," Carter says, extending his hand. "I'm Carter Williamson."

"Right. Uncle Carter," I say, slipping my palm into his. His grip is strong and his hand is warm, making me suddenly aware of how cold mine has become.

"Not her real uncle," he clarifies. "But Holly's raising Charlie—Charlotte—on his own now, so we all pitch in."

He says this like I should know Holly, so I just nod. "Right. So she's got...twenty-two uncles?"

There's a sadness behind his eyes that makes me wonder who Holly is and why he's parenting alone. "Something like that," Carter says. He tilts his head in the direction Charlie ran and holds up her coat. "I should..."

"Right. Definitely. Canadian blood can only get her so far."

Before he leaves, he steps close and lifts the lid off the tray to steal his own chicken nugget. He holds my gaze as he pops it into his mouth. "It was nice to meet you, Sarah." He offers me a teasing grin, and it's all I can do not to suck in a gasp. Carter Williamson is handsome. But when he smiles, handsome turns into something else entirely. "Be sure to save some chicken for the rest of the kids," he says, then he turns and walks away.

I'm still flustered when I find Anna in the kitchen. I set the chicken nuggets onto the counter, then tug her into the large butler's pantry past the fridge, away from the small crowd milling around the island and picking at the appetizers.

She doesn't even flinch at the disruption, but she does grab a box of animal crackers off the pantry shelf. She helps herself to a handful. "I swear, this baby is making me so carb-hungry," she says before popping a cracker into her mouth. "What's up with you?"

"I want to know why Miles is talking about me with one of his teammates."

"He is? Which one?"

"Carter Williamson," I say. "He knew I went to SCAD, that I'm from Winnipeg, that I'm an artist..."

"You're Miles's sister," she says. "Of course Carter knows you're from Winnipeg."

"Fine. But you know how Miles is. He'd die before wanting me to date any of these guys. Why is he talking about me at all?"

She rolls her eyes. "He wouldn't die. He's only protective because he thinks you need protecting. You could always just tell him you don't."

I prop my hands on my hips. "Are you avoiding my question?"

"Of course not. I'm just sure it's nothing. Miles talks about you because he loves you and he's proud of you. Carter just pays attention more than most people do. That's probably what you noticed."

"That he pays attention?"

She waves her hand around like she's annoyed I'm not grasping her meaning. "He listens. And remembers stuff.

Like...he'll ask me about Poppy's dance recital if he hears me mention taking her to rehearsal. Or, after my mom died, the team got together and sent flowers, but Carter made a separate donation to the animal shelter because a year before, he met Mom at a team dinner, and she mentioned she volunteered there."

"Wow," I say. "That's legit."

"He's just that guy. Thoughtful. Kind. Super courteous."

I lean against the wall behind me, considering this new information. "It hardly seems fair," I say. "He's a pro athlete, he looks the way he looks, and he's a good guy?"

"I know, right? And here I thought your brother was the only one."

I reach over and steal an animal cracker. "Miles forgot your anniversary last year."

She frowns. "He did, didn't he? I guess it's lucky he's so good in bed."

"Anna, gross," I grumble, though I'm used to her making comments like this. My brother and his wife are disgustingly in love.

"The point is," Anna says, "you could do a lot worse than Carter Williamson. He's genuinely a great guy." She moves to the pantry door and looks across the kitchen to where it blends into the open concept living room. "He's also an identical twin. His brother is nice too, but Carter's my favorite because of how much my girls love him." She points. "Right there. Standing next to the fireplace talking to Holly. That's Carter's brother, Theo."

Sure enough, there is a man who looks remarkably similar to Carter standing on the opposite end of the living room. His hair is a little longer and he's clean-shaven, but everything else about him is pretty much the same.

"Holy genetics," I mutter under my breath, and Anna chuckles.

"Right?"

"And they both play professional hockey. What are the odds?"

"One of the most elite defensive pairings in the league. Carter is left-handed. Theo is right. They're pretty amazing."

"Who's Holly?" I ask. "Carter was outside with a little girl named Charlie."

Anna's face softens. "I told you about him, remember? He's the goalie. Beckett Hollifield. The guys call him Holly. His wife died of cancer last summer."

"That's right," I say, the goalie's full name triggering my memory. "Around the same time your mom—"

Anna nods, her eyes glazing the slightest bit. "They started scheduling chemo treatments at the same time so they could be there together," she says. "Claire's mom was out in California and couldn't be here as much, so Mom kinda took her under her wing. I think it made it easier on them both."

It's nice to think there was something good that came out of last summer. Watching Anna lose her mom to an aggressive form of breast cancer while she was busy raising two little girls was the worst. I tried to drive up from Savannah as often as my schedule would allow, but I was busy finishing up my master's degree and could only get away so much.

At least it was the off season, so Miles was around full time. And he had his own personal experience to lean on since we lost our mom to cancer when I was nineteen.

"Honestly, I think I've had enough mothers dying of cancer. Can we get a different script or something?"

Anna chuckles and dabs at the tears collecting in the

corners of her eyes. "For real." She eats another animal cracker and takes a deep breath. "Having this baby without my mom around would be a lot easier if I knew you were going to be here."

Her voice wobbles, making my heart squeeze painfully in my chest. "Anna, you know if there was anything else I could do to stay, I'd do it."

"I know," Anna says. "I just...stupid Canada." She sniffs. "Actually, just kidding. I love Canada. I just wish you didn't have to go back."

"Me too," I say. But it doesn't even come close to expressing the intensity of my feelings. I understand immigration laws. And I respect them. But it's been a very long time since Canada has felt like home to me—not since Mom died. Aside from my dad, whom I hope to never see again, the only family I have lives right here in Atlanta.

Miles, Anna, and their girls.

Living in their backyard the past few weeks has been bittersweet. Because now I know how amazing it would be if I lived here full time. Close enough to babysit. To surprise the girls with random outings to get frozen yogurt or go to the park. Even living in Savannah, I've always been close enough to drive. To be here for birthdays and Christmases and dance recitals and preschool graduations. But traveling from Canada—it will never be so simple.

"I'm going to do everything I can to get back," I say. "I just need a year or two to get things off the ground."

Anna nods, but I don't like the emotion brimming behind her eyes. I'm sure she doesn't blame me. She knows what I'm up against when it comes to getting a visa, but I can't help but feel like I'm abandoning her when she needs me most.

"I'm sure it'll all work out," she says wearily. "I've been

talking to Miles about hiring a nanny. So that's something good, I guess."

A nanny would definitely be helpful. The baby's due in late March, which is right before playoff season. If I'm lucky, I'll be here for the birth, but I'll leave shortly after, and Anna will be alone with three kids six and under. If her postpartum depression is anything like it was when Olive was born, she's going to need more than just a nanny. She'll need support from her friends. From Miles. From me.

Except I'll be fifteen hundred miles away.

Anna hands me the box of animal crackers and steps toward the pantry door. "I need to check on the girls." She shoots a meaningful look over her shoulder. She's putting on a brave face, and I can tell she needs me to let her do it. "But don't hide from Carter Williamson," she adds. "Trust me. He really is a great guy."

I look into the mostly empty box and reach in for the last few broken bits of cracker. I'm sure he is a great guy. But that hardly matters.

He's a hockey player. That's strike one.

He's Miles's teammate. Debatable, but that's probably another strike.

But most of all, I'm leaving. Looking for something new makes zero sense when I'm as good as gone. *Strike three.*

2

———

SARAH

As it turns out, I end up sitting with *both* of the Williamson twins at dinner, though not intentionally. We're eating buffet style, everyone filling up their plates and grabbing a seat wherever they can. Some people are in the living room, plates perched on their knees. Others are eating around the bar in the kitchen. I sit down at the dining room table while it's still empty, but Miles and Anna quickly join me, followed by Theo, Carter, Holly, and two other guys Miles introduces as Jordo and Fly.

Holly pulls up an additional chair for Charlie, who has taken off her goalie pads but still wears her wings, and Miles has his youngest daughter, Olive, sitting on his lap.

"Jordan Ewbanks," Carter says from beside me, "and Sebastian Cash. I know the nicknames can be tough to keep up with."

I look over at him and smile. I'm used to Miles using nicknames for some of his teammates, but I always get overwhelmed when I meet a lot of new people, so having the extra help feels good. I shift my gaze away, suddenly realizing

15

I'm staring at Carter's intense blue eyes. "Thanks," I say as I scoop up a bite of my potato salad. "It's definitely hard to keep up with who's who."

"Jordan is a center," Carter says. "Engaged to the woman over at the bar with the short, dark hair. Her name is Malia. Jordo is obviously short for Jordan."

"Got it," I say. "Jordan, Malia. And the other is Sebastian, but you call him Fly?"

"He's fast," Carter says. "That's why."

"I'll never understand Miles's nickname," I say. "Why call him Brick when his last name is *literally* Stone? Don't they basically mean the same thing?"

Carter tilts his head. "That's...a very good question. He had the nickname when I joined the team, so I haven't really ever thought about it."

"Do you *ever* call him Miles?"

"Sure," he says. "Brick is what I call him when we're on the ice or in the locker room. But if I'm calling his name when I'm standing in his kitchen, I'll probably call him Miles."

I like this answer, but I can't exactly pinpoint why. Maybe because my brother isn't just a brick wall of a hockey player, so I appreciate when people see him as more.

"What about you? Do you have a nickname?" I ask.

He's quiet for a beat before he says, "Just Carter. Or... Cars." Something about his tone draws my gaze to his. He almost sounds like he's disappointed to *not* have a nickname, though I could be completely off base. I don't know him well enough to truly tell. "The team calls my brother Sonny," he says. "Short for Williamson. Actually, did you meet Theo?"

"Not officially." I look past Carter to where Theo is sitting on his other side. This close, they look less alike than they did when I was looking at Theo from across the room. They're clearly identical, but there's something about Carter's eyes that makes it easy for me to tell them apart. There's a kindness there—a warmth that feels distinct.

"Theo, Sarah. Sarah, Theo," Carter says, doing a quick round of introductions.

"Nice to meet you," Theo says, offering me a handshake, but he quickly falls into conversation with the teammate sitting to his right. Sebastian, I think?

I'm never going to remember everyone's names.

"So how long will you be in Atlanta?" Carter asks. "Is this home for good?"

The sadness that seems to have taken up permanent residence at the back of my mind flits back to the surface. "Unfortunately, no," I say. "I was here for school, and since I graduated, I have to go back to Canada in a few months."

"You don't seem thrilled about that."

"There are definitely things I miss about Winnipeg, but it hasn't really felt like home in a long time. Miles and Anna—they're pretty much my only family. So...yeah. Leaving is going to be really hard."

"You can't get a work visa?" Carter asks. "Sorry. That's probably a dumb question. I'm sure you've explored all your options."

"Not a dumb question," I say. "But yeah. If I were a nurse or a teacher or worked in STEM, I'd have more options. But it's a little more complicated for artists. There's a visa designed for those with extraordinary talent, but that means you basically have to be a superstar."

"Wait. Are you talking about an O-1 visa? A few of my teammates over the years have had those."

"Exactly that," I say. "They aren't impossible for artists, but I haven't built that kind of career yet."

And now I'm out of time.

After my graduation, I managed to extend my student visa for what my immigration lawyer referred to as "optional practical training." It meant working as an artist-in-residence for a community arts center in Savannah, but it was mostly about buying me an extra twelve months to build the relationships I need if I want to stay in the States.

And I'm definitely getting closer. I've had a few smaller galleries express interest in my work, and I've sold enough to support myself, something I know a lot of artists can't say. But I need to go bigger, establish a presence in New York, possibly find an agent.

There's no way I'll manage all of that in the three months I have to work with.

"You haven't built it *yet*," Carter says. "But I'm sure you'll get there." He smiles, and a tiny dimple appears in his right cheek. The second it disappears, I feel an impulsive need to say something clever just so I can see it again.

"He says, having never seen my work," I say.

"Show me then." He takes a bite of his burger, his nonchalance making it seem like he didn't just make a monumental request.

"It's not like asking to see a picture of my dog," I say. "Showing you my work—that's a big deal."

"Is it? Couldn't I just google you?"

I bite my lip. Of course he could google me. I wouldn't be very serious about my work if I didn't have a website. Or at least an Instagram profile. But *asking* someone to google me is very different than finding out someone already did.

It's like that strange feeling when you give someone a gift and they ask if they can open it *right then,* while you watch. I mean, sure. Open it now. But it's also totally fine if you want to wait until I'm gone so I never, *ever* have to deal with the possibility of you hating it.

What's more, I feel weirdly concerned about what Carter will think of my work. I really, *really* want him to like it, which makes zero sense since I literally just met the man.

But it's too late to protest because he's already pulling out his phone. His thumbs fly across the screen, then he holds it up.

"This one?" he asks, pointing to the top search result. "This is you?"

I nod. "Yeah. That's it."

He hesitates, then he catches my gaze, his expression softening as he asks, "Can I click? I won't if you don't want me to."

His words are so sincere, I'm positive he would put his phone down and never pull up the website again if I asked him not to.

Which is exactly why I tell him he can.

"You can click," I say. "Just...don't tell me if you don't like something."

He lifts his eyebrows. "Do people actually do that?"

I grimace. "The internet is a very cruel place."

A look of understanding passes over his face. "True enough," he says. With such a public career, he probably gets it better than most.

I sit and wait while Carter scrolls through my portfolio, his eyes locked on his screen.

My website portfolio currently includes the collection of work I completed for my master's degree. I mostly paint people, hyperrealism blended with poetic abstraction. A lot of people find it fascinating to see paintings that look like they could be photographs, but that's not the most important part for me. It's more about the parts that aren't realistic. That's where the storytelling is.

Carter takes his time scrolling through, which makes me nervous. But I at least appreciate the chance it gives me to study him up close, to take in the angle of his jaw, the insanely long lashes that frame his bright blue eyes.

At one point, I glance over Carter's shoulder to see Theo studying me, a questioning look on his face, but the second we make eye contact, he looks away.

Finally, Carter looks up. "Sarah," he says, and my heart jumps at the sound of my name. "These are..." He shakes his head and lets out a little laugh, like he can't quite find the words. "They're incredible," he continues. "I can't think of anything that deserves the word *extraordinary* more."

Warmth sparks in my chest and spreads outward, climbing up to my cheeks. I lift my hands to cover the redness I'm sure he can see on my face. "You really think so?"

He nods. "I wouldn't lie to you."

"You would too," I say. "You're too nice to say something mean."

"She's got you there, man," Theo says, startling me when he joins the conversation. For a moment, it felt like Carter and I were the only ones in the room. "You are too nice."

Carter gives his brother an annoyed look. "But just because I wouldn't say something unkind doesn't mean I'm lying now. I'd maybe just say something...*less nice.*"

"Like when you told the poor kid at our last youth hockey clinic that he skated with a lot of heart," Theo says.

"He *did* skate with a lot of heart," Carter says.

"And that was about all he had going for him," Theo replies. "I'm just saying, it's a good thing you were giving him feedback instead of me. I'd have told him to find a different hobby."

"He was twelve," Carter says. "If every twelve-year-old who *isn't* bound for the NHL gave up hockey, the entire sport would fall apart."

It's fun to watch the brothers banter and interesting to notice what makes them distinct. Carter's entire demeanor is gentler than Theo's. He's a little more measured, a little more intentional with his words.

"Anyway," Carter says pointedly, "I did not tell you that you paint with a lot of heart—because these paintings are really amazing." He hesitates before adding, "Actually, I'd love to see something in person sometime. If you—if there's anything you have hanging somewhere."

"Look at you, Carter," Theo says slyly. "Making a move."

Carter elbows his brother without looking away from me, making my cheeks flush with embarrassment. Is that what Theo thinks Carter is doing? Making a move? Should I warn him that Miles might actually kill him if he is?

Either way, Carter is still staring at me—his eyes are so incredibly blue—so I have no choice but to respond. I clear my throat. "Actually, there's one hanging in Miles and Anna's living room."

Carter sits up a little taller. "The one of Poppy and Olive?"

I nod. The painting is one I did while I was still in school, so there's still a lot wrong with it, at least in my eyes, but Miles and Anna love it, so I'd never ask them to take it down. It's an overhead view of the girls sitting at the beach, waves lapping over their legs. Their faces are tilted up toward the sun, so you can just make out their wide smiles and see the freckles dotting their cheeks.

"When I first saw it, I thought it was a photograph."

Carter looks toward the living room, but the painting isn't quite visible from here. "But the way the water is moving and the way you can see their laughter—it's more than what a photograph could do." He holds my gaze for a moment, but then he quickly looks down. "Sorry. I don't really know how to talk about art."

"No, you're doing a good job," I say. "You saw exactly what I wanted people to see."

I have no idea how to explain what's happening right now. How to catalog the many, *many* feelings rushing through me all at once. Carter is handsome and kind and observant and charming.

He's also entirely off-limits. Geographically. Relationally.

I can't be into this man, but it would be so much fun if I could be.

He smiles. "See? Like I said. *Extraordinary.*"

Across the table, Miles asks Carter a question, and the conversation shifts to other things. Hockey and the game coming up next weekend and the fact that the Vikings likely won't get a playoff spot this year, despite having won the whole thing last year.

Jordo mentions his wedding in June and how much he really, *really* hopes it doesn't conflict with the playoffs. And Theo tells a very entertaining story about going on a date with a woman who had all of his hockey stats memorized. Just *one* date, though I'm sure it's one she'll never forget.

Through it all, my awareness of Carter doesn't diminish. I find myself paying closer attention to the things he contributes to the conversation, appreciating the way he responds to his teammates, noticing what makes him laugh.

I definitely feel drawn to him, which is a feeling I haven't experienced in a while. It's nice to notice if only as a reminder that I'm not entirely broken.

I barely dated at all through college, something my therapist helped me realize has everything to do with childhood. I'm very much into men, I'm just not very good at trusting them. I want to be. I've seen the way Miles is with Anna—and he grew up with the same father I did. If he can be better than what we had, it stands to reason I deserve the same.

But wanting to trust and feeling like I *can* aren't exactly the same thing.

Besides, I don't really have *time* to date. I'm kind of ridiculous about my work. I need to be if I have any hope of building a career significant enough to earn my way into a permanent home in the States.

I need a beat to rein in my unrealistic feelings, so once I finish my plate, I leave the conversation and head into the kitchen where I spend a few minutes cleaning up. After all the noise and the talking and the general hum of activity around me, completing a few mindless tasks proves good for my nervous system *and* my wayward heart, but I could still do with some *actual* solitude.

Anna is in the living room with Poppy and some of the other women, and Olive is still with her dad, so I grab a cupcake off a dessert tray on the counter and sneak into the butler's pantry.

This is definitely the most time I've spent in here in one day, but it makes for a perfect escape. It's quiet, it smells faintly of coffee beans, thanks to the espresso machine in the corner, and best of all, *I'm alone.*

It helps that the raspberry cupcakes someone brought from the bakery next to the Vortex are next-level delicious.

"Seems like a great place to eat a cupcake."

I am mid-bite when Carter appears in the pantry doorway, and I jump in surprise, smearing frosting all over the end of my nose.

"Oof. That was my fault, wasn't it?" Carter says. "I'm sorry. I didn't mean to startle you."

I wipe the frosting off the top of my lip, then, without a napkin nearby, lick it off my fingertips. "It's fine. I just needed a minute away from"—I motion a hand toward the house beyond the pantry—"the crowd, I guess."

"I'll leave you to it then. I just wanted to—" He pauses and takes a step into the dimly lit pantry. "Sorry, you just…" He lifts a single finger and wipes it over the tip of my nose. "You missed a spot." He pulls his finger away, looking around like he's not sure what to do with the frosting, but then, just like I did, he pops his finger into his mouth and sucks it clean. He lets out a little groan. "Man. I need to have one of those cupcakes."

Oh. Oh, my. I have no idea if he intended this conversation to feel like foreplay, but I suddenly can't stop thinking about raspberry frosting and what it would taste like on his lips.

I give my head a little shake. "Yeah, they're pretty good," I manage to say, my voice sounding unusually breathy.

Luckily, Carter doesn't seem to notice. Either that, or he's enough of a gentleman not to point it out.

"So, I'm actually headed out," he says. "But I wanted to say it was nice to meet you. And I really enjoyed our conversation."

"Yeah, I did too," I say, thankful my normal voice has returned.

He holds my gaze for another moment, then he takes a backward step toward the door. "I hope you get the visa situation worked out," he says. "I can imagine how much your family would miss you."

"Thanks," I say. "I hope so too."

"Bye, Sarah," Carter says, then he turns and leaves me alone with my cupcake and a whole lot of feelings.

At least when it comes to Carter, it's probably good I'm about to leave. There are too many reasons why I can't like him, and I'm pretty sure staying would make me forget what all of them are.

3

―――――――

CARTER

"SO THEN SHE ASKS ME IF I KNOW ANY NBA PLAYERS BECAUSE SHE'S never really been big into ice," my brother says from the bench beside me. He tugs his practice jersey over his head and tosses it into a laundry bin at the center of the room.

In every locker room, on every team we've played for, Theo and I have always been in neighboring stalls, our jerseys hanging side by side, the same last name printed across the back. I can't complain. I love the guy. But sometimes, I wonder what it might be like to sit opposite him instead. To be friends with my teammates as an individual and not as part of a matched set.

Theo scoffs before continuing. "Like being a pro athlete means I'm supposed to have a bunch of *other* pro athletes programmed into my phone."

I let out a chuckle and toss a ball of tape into the trash can at the center of the room. "What did you tell her?"

"That the sports world doesn't work like that," Theo says. "It's not like we're all in one big club."

"Sure we are," Fly says from across the room. "Haven't you gotten your invite yet?"

"I got mine," I say to Theo. "You didn't? Sad. Probably because you can't stop hitting the pole this season."

"And yet, I've still scored more goals than you," Theo says.

"*One* goal," I say. "You've scored *one* more goal than me. And the season isn't over yet."

Theo smirks. "For either of us." He stands and drops the last of his gear onto the bench of his stall. Once we've all cleared out, the equipment managers will be by to collect everything and get it onto drying racks. I have no idea how they manage to deal with how notoriously foul hockey gear smells, but I definitely think the equipment team are the unsung heroes of our sport.

"I'm going to shower," Theo says. "Don't talk about anything good without me."

"Are you coming to the Cave tonight?" Fly asks his retreating form.

"We'll be there," Theo says as he walks away.

We. Like it's a foregone conclusion if one of us goes, the other will too.

I lift my pads over my head, feeling a slight strain just above my left shoulder blade. I shift, trying to stretch out the muscle, and wonder why it irritates me that Theo answered for me.

It's not that I mind going to the Cave. It's a great bar with solid food and a chill vibe. And it would honestly be weird if Fly invited one of us but not the other. But the whole scene has been making me tired lately. The pressure of trying to meet people. The expectations connected to my job. The last few times we've gone out, I've found myself feeling lonely even though I'm sitting among friends in a room full of people.

Then there's the stuff that comes with being a twin.

Most of the time, when women meet us both, it's Theo they end up preferring. I'm the nice twin, but he's more fun.

Except, not with Sarah.

When I met Miles's sister at our team dinner last week, she didn't seem at all interested in talking to Theo. Despite sitting with us both through all of dinner, it was me she talked to the most.

When I left her in the pantry, I almost asked for her number. And I've stopped myself from asking Miles if he'll give it to me a dozen times since.

But she's leaving, and that feels like a good reason not to start something.

Then again, I play professional hockey, which means I could *also* be leaving at any point. At least during trade season. If I never started anything because I might end up having to move, I'd be alone the rest of my life.

My efforts do little to lessen the ache shooting up my trap muscles, so I move into the treatment room and climb into the ice bath to soak before I shower. Theo will have to wait on me, but he's used to it. We've been waiting on each other for years.

We don't always ride to practice together, depending on what we have planned for the rest of the day, but my car is in the shop, so I caught a ride with him this morning. Easy enough since we live in the same building in Midtown, on opposite sides of the top floor. He's got a great view of Grant Park, but I think I snagged the better apartment. On a clear day, I can see all the way to Stone Mountain.

Theo and I aren't the only set of brothers in the NHL. We aren't even the only brothers on the same team. But as far as I know, we are the only twins.

Even if it seems lucky we landed on the same team, it's not truly that surprising, considering our roles as defensemen. We skate best when we're skating together, so we've been a defensive pairing on every team we've played for. First in junior hockey, then for the Appies, the minor league team where we landed after the draft, and now the Jaguars, our home for the last six years. We've got two years left on our eight-year contract, and I think we'll both extend if given the opportunity. We like Atlanta. But more than that, we like playing together. Theo is as much my best friend as he is my brother.

Still, I think, as I lower myself more fully into the frigid ice bath, it might do us some good to establish a little autonomy. We play on the same team. Live in the same building. Have all the same friends.

Across the therapy room, a door opens, and Nico, one of our trainers, steps inside. He looks at me and pauses. "Theo? Wait. No. Carter."

"It's been six years, Nico," I say dryly. "It shouldn't still be this hard."

"It's easier when you're in street clothes," Nico says. "In here, I'm not sure I'll ever be able to tell."

Miles appears behind Nico, still wearing all his gear. "Carter's hair is always shorter," he says. "Plus his eyes are a lighter shade of blue. And he smiles more."

Nico looks at the Jaguars' team captain, his expression mirroring my own surprise. But Miles only shrugs. "What? You don't get to be captain by ignoring the little things."

"Fair point," Nico says. He looks back at me. "Are you going to need anything else?"

I'm tempted to ask for a little bit of muscle work on my shoulder, but Theo will already have to wait for me, so I shake my head no instead. "Nah, I'm good. Just the soak for today."

He nods, then looks over at Miles. "You? Anything hurting?"

Miles motions up and down his broad body. "I feel as good as I look." Nico rolls his eyes, but I can't help but smile. Miles's swagger is a part of his charm, and his confidence is what makes him such a good captain. He shifts his gaze over to me. "I do need you. You have time to talk after your shower?"

I sit up a little taller, sloshing the icy water around my shoulders. "Sure. You want Theo too?" Most of the time, team stuff relates to both of us as much as it relates to one of us, and I can't really think of something Miles would need me for that doesn't involve Theo.

But the captain shakes his head no. "Just you. Did you ride together? I can give you a ride home if you need it. This might take a minute."

A knot of trepidation tightens right behind my ribs. The first stupid thought that pops into my head is that Miles knows I've been thinking about his sister.

Could he know?

I haven't even told Theo I wanted to ask her out, though he's observant enough, he might have picked up on it at the team dinner.

But what else could it be?

"A ride would be great," I say. "I'll tell Theo."

Miles nods. "Good. Talk to you in a bit."

I hurry through my shower a little faster than I might after a typical practice, not wanting to keep Miles waiting. As soon as I'm dressed, I shoot Theo a text—he's probably in the dining room for our post-practice meal—to tell him not to wait for me after he's finished.

He texts back a row of question marks, but I don't have an explanation to give him, so I close out the thread and go in search of my captain.

I'm halfway down the hallway, heading toward the dining room, when he appears in the darkened doorway of Coach Kimzey's office. He's dressed just like I am, in joggers and a navy Jaguars pullover. He fills his out a little better. I've probably got an inch of height on Miles, but he's a solid six inches broader than I am. He comes by his nickname naturally.

He tilts his head into the office. "Coach said we can talk in here."

Another pulse of nerves pushes through me, Sarah's brown eyes flashing through my mind. I really have no clue what he could want, but I can't shake the feeling it has something to do with her.

Did he see me talking to her? Maybe he saw me go into the pantry and knew she was already inside?

"Is everything okay?" I ask as I follow him into the room.

To my surprise, he doesn't turn on the light. The wall between the hallway and the office is made of frosted glass, so we aren't completely in the dark, but unless someone was really looking, I doubt anyone passing by would notice us in here.

"Everything's good," Miles says. "Great. You want to sit?" He motions toward the leather couch and matching chair sitting at the back of the office.

This whole encounter feels so ominous, I can't even pretend to relax and just go with it. "I think I want you to tell me what this is about," I say instead, though I do sit, taking the seat on the couch perpendicular to his chair.

He runs a hand across his face. "I'm getting to it," he says. "But you shouldn't look so stressed. You aren't in trouble."

I hear Miles's words well enough, but something about his demeanor makes me think I shouldn't trust him. For a guy who handles the stress of high-intensity hockey games multiple times a week, he seems particularly nervous.

Maybe more nervous than I've ever seen him. Is he in trouble somehow? I read an article the other day about an NFL player who racked up enough gambling debt to wipe out two years' worth of salary. I don't *think* Miles is a gambler, but I guess a man can have his secrets.

"If I'm not in trouble, then why are you looking at me like you're about to ask for one of my kidneys?"

He huffs out a laugh. "It's nothing like that." Then he shrugs. "Well, not exactly."

"What is it then?"

He leans forward and props his elbows on his knees, then sits up again, rubbing a hand down his face. "Okay, here's the deal. You met Sarah last weekend, right? At the team dinner?"

"Sure," I say, trying to keep my voice casual.

"She has to go back to Canada—her student visa is running out—but we've been trying to think of a way for her to stay."

"Yeah, she said something about that," I say. "She told me she's trying to get an O-1 through her artwork."

Miles shakes his head, almost dismissively. "That's really a long shot. But I've come up with a better idea. If she gets her teaching credential in the state of Georgia, she'd only need to find a school willing to sponsor her employment."

I lift my eyebrows. I don't actually think it *is* a longshot for Sarah to get an O-1, but I'm not sure I'm in any position to argue with her brother. But I can't keep myself from asking, "Does Sarah *want* to be a teacher?"

Miles frowns. "Does it matter? She wants to stay, and this is a way she could do it. The only problem is she needs more time than she has to get certified. The program is nine months long, and she only has three."

I have no idea why Miles thinks this is a problem he needs to discuss with me, but I find myself brainstorming anyway, searching for possible solutions.

"Could she go back to Canada and finish from there? Then come back?"

He nods. "She could, but then she'd miss the baby being born, and…" His gaze drops to the floor and he's quiet for a long moment. When he finally lifts his gaze again, there's a seriousness in his expression that wasn't there before. "I don't know if we ever talked about Anna's postpartum depression after Olive was born."

I don't know a lot about postpartum depression, but I can infer that any kind of depression coupled with having a newborn would be tough to handle. "We haven't," I say. "I'm sorry she had to go through that."

"It was pretty rough," he says. "But she had her mom, so we got through it. I'm not sure we could have otherwise. That's the biggest reason why I'd really like to find a way to keep my sister here. We're all the family she's got, but more than that, Anna's going to need her."

They had Anna's mom—but now they don't.

I've sensed Anna wearing the loss of her mom on her

sleeve the past few months, something I recognize from personal experience. Theo and I lost our dad when we were seventeen.

"I'm sure," I say with a nod. "There isn't any way for her to extend her current visa? If they know she's working toward teaching?"

"We've looked into every possible avenue." He pauses for a long moment before adding, "There's really only one way to keep her here."

There's a weight to his words that makes me uneasy. "Okay?"

"She could get married," Miles says.

"Married," I repeat. "Is she dating someone?" A weird surge of jealousy flares behind my ribs. I'd like to think a boyfriend would have come up in all our conversations last week, but maybe not.

"For what I have in mind," Miles says, "she wouldn't need to be." He takes a deep breath. "Look. When I thought through all the guys on the team, you were the obvious choice."

He pauses, and I stare. The obvious choice for what?

"You're steady, you're calm, you're weirdly nice to everyone. And you're loyal. I've seen the way you watch out for your brother. Loyalty is important."

"Okay," I say slowly. "Thank you, I think?"

"You're also a solid hockey player who really fits with our system, which means you likely won't be traded anytime soon. That's important. That you aren't going anywhere."

"Still don't know what we're talking about here, Miles," I say.

He takes a deep breath, leveling me with a piercing look,

before he finally says, "I was thinking that maybe *you* could marry Sarah."

I freeze.

"You what?"

"Just hear me out," he quickly says. "You get married, but only on paper. We fake a few photos, create an online history of the two of you as a couple, keep up the facade publicly. But privately, you won't actually be in a relationship. As soon as she's licensed to teach, you can quietly get a divorce, and that's that. The whole thing would be over in nine months, a year, tops."

I shake my head, still struggling to process what he's asking. He wants me to *marry* his sister? Like, *marry* marry her?

"Miles," I say, not even trying to hide my shock. "If I married your sister just so she could stay in the country, we'd both be committing fraud. Is that honestly what you're asking me to do here?"

His jaw tightens. "I'm not necessarily asking, just... suggesting. I've done a lot of research—*all* the research—and I've got a solid plan mapped out. How long the marriage will have to last. How we'll convince everyone it's real. Convince Immigration it's real. It's completely airtight. It's not going to look like fraud."

"We just met for the first time," I say, "and multiple people were there when it happened."

Miles waves this away like it's no concern at all. "Trust me, it didn't look like it. The way you two were talking at dinner, you seemed like you were close. Close enough that I think people would buy you having some sort of secret relationship."

I lean back into my seat, suddenly uncomfortable with

the fact that Miles *did* notice my interest in Sarah. Is that why he's asking me?

Either way, it doesn't change anything. "Look, man. I like you, but this is—"

"I'm all she's got," he repeats. "Our mother is dead, and our father was a complete deadbeat we've fortunately been able to avoid since we live down here and he's still in Winnipeg. We don't have any other family up there." He pauses and takes a deep breath, his jaw tightening. "If she goes back to Canada, she won't know a soul. What's more, if she does go back, I'm not sure our father won't try to make contact. And that's the last thing she needs."

The thought of anything happening to Sarah forms a knot low in my gut. Even though I just met her, I would still hate for her to be at risk. I've heard bits and pieces of Miles's history, and a time or two, he's said something that's made me wonder about his dad.

But fraud is still fraud. Miles is asking me to put *myself* at a guaranteed risk—and her, too—just to avoid the potential of a different one. I'm just not sure the end justifies the means.

Miles leans forward in his chair, and his eyes turn pleading. "Just let me walk you through the plan, all right? Ten minutes of your time. And if you still believe it's something you can't do, you can walk. No questions asked."

I have seen a lot of expressions on my captain's face over the years. I've seen him determined, annoyed, angry. I've seen him relaxed and happy after a rewarding win and discouraged after a disappointing loss.

But I've never seen him like this.

I've never seen him look desperate.

Something tightens in the deepest corner of my heart, and I breathe out a sigh. "Fine. Ten minutes."

It's more like twenty minutes. But when Miles finishes outlining his admittedly thorough plan, I have to hand it to him.

He really did think of everything.

He has a social media plan for how we would soft launch the relationship, then a plan to appear in public together over the next couple of weeks. He has a place for us to live—or at least appear to be living—so it looks like our marriage is the real deal. He has a list of sample questions we'd have to answer in an immigration interview, with practical tips about how to prepare. Most importantly, he has a precise timeline regarding the steps Sarah would take to establish her own legal status. If everything goes as planned, it really shouldn't take more than nine months.

"I realize the one piece we haven't discussed is what's in this for you," Miles says, once he's talked me through everything. "But I don't want you to worry about that part. You won't spend a dime of your own money. And you'll be compensated for however much time all of this takes."

I raise an eyebrow. Neither one of us is hurting for money, but I know as well as he does that my contract is double what his is. He took less so he could stay in Atlanta, play out his career with the same team. Anna is from Atlanta. A higher contract wouldn't be worth uprooting his family, especially now that they have kids.

Not that it matters either way. Even if I felt like I could say yes, I wouldn't feel comfortable letting Miles pay me to do it.

I sigh and lean back in my chair. The one thing Miles *hasn't* said is that he noticed my interest and thought I might be a good match for Sarah, that maybe we would hit it off and find out we actually like each other.

He seems to think this will be all business, no real feelings involved. And that might be the biggest reason for me to say no. It feels like playing with fire to fake a relationship with someone I could see myself actually starting to like.

I suddenly wonder if this is why she seemed so interested in talking to me. Had she and Miles already hatched a plan, and she was just trying to soften me up?

"What does Sarah think?" I ask, suddenly desperate to know how she feels. If she had any clue this would happen when we met.

His jaw twitches. "She doesn't know yet."

My eyes widen even as relief courses through me. On the one hand, I'm so glad she isn't behind this conversation. On the other, I can't believe Miles is asking without her knowledge. "She doesn't know you're currently trying to *arrange* a marriage on her behalf? Did we just go back in time two hundred years?"

"It didn't feel worth mentioning if you weren't willing to do it," he says. "I didn't want to get her hopes up. She's really having a hard time with this whole thing."

I sensed a heaviness in Sarah when I met her, so this doesn't surprise me. And if there were an easier way to help her, I'd be all over it. But to marry her, to commit a felony and tie my reputation to a marriage and then a divorce...even if it only lasts nine months?

It's a lot to ask.

Too much to ask.

I shake my head one last time. "I'm really sorry, man. It sucks what your family is going through. I appreciate you trusting me enough to even ask. But there's too much at stake. My career—*your* career, if word got out you put me up to this. If there were anything else I could do to help, I'd do it. But I can't do this."

"Just take some time to think about it," he says. "You don't have to decide right now."

"I don't need time to think," I say, pushing myself to my feet. "It's fraud."

He's quiet for a long moment, but then he finally nods. "Okay. I understand, and I respect your decision. I was hoping you'd say yes, but you aren't the only guy on the list, so I'm at least grateful you made your decision quickly. The faster I can get something worked out, the better."

I pause, a twinge of discomfort making my gut feel tight. "You're going to ask someone else?"

"Of course I am," Miles says. "I'm out of options. Actually, Theo's on the list. Do you think he'd be willing?"

The discomfort in my gut turns into full-on nausea at the thought of Sarah and *Theo*. The most annoying thing is, he probably *would* do it. This is exactly the kind of impulsive thing he'd think was fun.

"I doubt it," I say, hoping Miles doesn't sense the uneasiness in my voice. "He's got a pretty active dating life. I don't think a marriage would really help with that."

He nods. "All right, well, let me know if you change your mind." Despite what I told him, it's not lost on me that Miles doesn't say whether he will or won't ask Theo.

He stands and follows me out of Coach Kimzey's office, and we fall into an awkward silence as we head toward the exit.

I suddenly wish I had my own car or had made Theo wait for me. After the conversation I just had with Miles, the thought of riding home with him feels painful.

I pull out my phone just as we reach the door. "You know what? I'm just gonna have Theo come back for me. No reason to make you drive into Midtown when you're heading the opposite direction."

Miles shrugs. "Fine by me. You're still living in Midtown? I'd hate all that traffic."

"It's worth it. I like the view."

He seems to consider this. "Are you still living with your brother?"

"Not with him," I say. "We're in the same building."

"So, *sort of* with him," Miles says.

"Nah, it's not like that. He's got his place, and I've got mine."

It's *mostly* not like that.

I don't often talk about the fact that when my dad was killed in an accident, Theo was the one who was driving the car.

It wasn't his fault—a drunk driver blew through an inter-section and t-boned him—but that didn't matter to Theo. He spiraled hard, and it was left to me to make sure he didn't completely fall apart. He only went to practice if I made him go to practice, only got out of bed if I was there to demand it.

If not for me, I'm not even sure he'd still be playing hockey.

Logically, I know he's fine now. An adult who takes care of himself. But there's a part of me that still thinks I have to stay close. Keep an eye on him to make sure he doesn't crash out again and throw everything away. I'm not sure how to break the habit of feeling like it's my job to look out for us both.

"Whatever you say, man," Miles says as he pulls out his keys. "You sure you don't need a ride?"

"Yeah. I'm sure. Thanks."

"Cool. Hey, don't say anything to Theo, all right? If I do ask him, I want to make sure he hears it from me." Miles pushes through the door without waiting for my reply, which is good, because I will absolutely be telling Theo about our conversation.

And making sure he understands that if Miles asks, he will not, under any circumstances, be marrying Sarah Stone.

If anyone's going to do it, it's me.

But I *can't* do it. And I have no idea where that leaves me.

4

CARTER

While I wait for Theo, I scroll through real estate listings and try not to think about Miles having the same conversation he just had with me...*with Theo.*

What is Miles even thinking? Talking about this like he can choose a guy at random and harness him to his sister for a year.

He made it clear the plan included *living* with Sarah. And he has a whole list of guys he's willing to ask? Not to mention the fact that he shouldn't be asking at all. It should be Sarah's choice. He shouldn't even be having the conversation without her explicit consent.

I grumble and send my brother another text.

CARTER

Are you close?

His reply pops up almost immediately.

THEO

Five minutes out.

I lean against the wall just inside the exit and flip back to real estate, and for a split second, it actually *does* distract me from my spiraling thoughts. A new listing just popped up, and I really like the look of it.

Big trees, a sweet pool in the backyard, and a long driveway that looks like it would provide a lot of privacy.

That's at least one good thing about living in the city. Our building has 24-hour security and a doorman who screens every single person who comes inside. Everyone on staff knows Theo and me by name—even if they sometimes mix us up—and are very protective of our privacy. Leaving that behind would mean having to consider things I've been able to take for granted thus far.

Still, if I want some autonomy from my brother, buying a house feels like a good way to get it.

My brother. Sarah. Miles. I groan in frustration.

I have got to be able to move on from this.

A minute later, Theo pulls up, shooting me a quick *I'm here* text.

I go outside and find him idling right in front of the door.

"Thanks for coming back," I say as soon as I'm in my seat.

"No prob," he says. "Say hi to Mom."

"How lucky am I that I get to talk to you both for once!" she says, her voice playing through Theo's speakers. He shoots me an apologetic look. *Sorry,* he mouths, but I wave away his concern.

It's been a minute since I've talked to Mom. I don't love the timing—I'd much rather talk through the last forty-five minutes with Theo—but she's already on the phone. I can't just tell her I'm not in the mood to talk. That will only make her ask why, and the why behind my current frustration is something I definitely can't discuss with her.

My mom is amazing, but she's also a big talker. She likes to process verbally...with *everyone*. Neighbors, friends, people in the checkout line at the grocery store. The woman never meets a stranger. Which is great. Unless those strangers are hockey fans.

Ask me how I know, and I'll point you to a Reddit thread in which the story of me wetting the bed at hockey camp when I was thirteen is described with a level of detail that could only have come from her. According to the original poster, he sat next to Mom at a Jaguars game and got the inside scoop.

"How are you, Carter?" she asks. "I've already gotten an update from Theo. But what's new with you?"

"Nothing new," I say. "Working hard, having a good season. Life is good."

"You sound like your brother. How's your dating life? Have you met anyone special?"

I should have anticipated this question—it's her favorite one to ask—but for some reason, tonight it catches me off guard. I clear my throat. "Maybe," I say, and Theo's eyes dart to mine.

Maybe? Why did I just say maybe?

Based on Theo's expression, he's wondering the same thing.

"What does 'maybe' mean?" Mom asks.

"Um, only that I'm not really talking about it yet, so..." I let my words trail off because *what* am I even doing?

I'm thinking about Sarah, but that doesn't make any sense because I'm not *dating* Sarah, and if Miles has his way, she might wind up married to someone else in the very near future.

Unless she's married to you.

The voice inside my head sounds an awful lot like my hockey captain, and I force it away.

"Oh, come on," Mom says. "You aren't going to tell me anything?"

"I promise you'll be the first person I call when I have more to say," I tell her.

"Wait, we aren't talking about Veronica, are we?" Mom asks, and Theo chuckles.

"No, Mom. I'm not back together with Veronica."

I haven't seen or talked to my ex-girlfriend in almost eighteen months, but my mother seems to have an abiding fear that I am always about to get back together with her. Maybe that's on me. I never have anyone else to tell her about.

Veronica wasn't a bad girlfriend. She was super into hockey, at every game, cheering me on. But that was part of the problem. She was *so* into hockey, I could never quite tell if she was truly into me or just liked having access to the team.

Theo never trusted her, and eventually, I grew weary of her constantly asking to "go out with the guys" or "hang with the team." It made me feel like hanging out with *just* me wasn't good enough.

"Well, good," Mom says. "You know I never trusted her."

"I know, Mom," I say because we've had this conversation at least twenty times.

I can tell she's hesitant to let the subject go, but I also know she won't push. She's good like that, which I appreciate, since the minute this phone call is over, Theo is going to push me until I tell him everything.

"Okay," Mom finally says. "Just remember my only wish is for you to be happy. That's the only reason I ask."

"I know," I say. "And I don't mind you asking."

We chat for a few more minutes about things going on in her life. Her gardening club, her book club, the recent training she completed to be a precinct worker in the upcoming primary election.

We finally end the call when we reach our apartment building, mostly because as soon as Theo pulls into the garage, we'll lose signal and the call will drop.

Theo doesn't say anything until we've reached his parking spot. When he pulls in, I notice my truck parked in the space beside his, washed, waxed, and looking good as new. I didn't expect the shop to deliver it until tomorrow, so it's nice to see it's back a day early.

Theo cuts the engine on his SUV and lets his hands fall from the steering wheel, but he doesn't get out. "Dude, what was that?" he says, and I breathe out a sigh.

I lean back into my seat and look over at him. "I don't even know what I was saying. After my conversation with Miles, I just...I don't know. My brain is all messed up."

"Are you saying there's a connection between your conversation with Miles and you telling Mom you've met someone? Am I making the right leap here?"

I lift my hands in a gesture of surrender, and Theo's eyebrows lift. "Maybe start at the beginning?"

I huff out a laugh. "You won't believe me if I do."

"Try me."

It takes about ten minutes to summarize the entire conversation, and Theo sits with his mouth hanging open almost the entire time. It's validating to know his reaction is the same as mine, so I'm surprised when he asks, "So, are you going to do it?"

I scoff. "Of course I'm not going to do it. Did you think I might?"

"I mean, not really. But you did seem to like her at the team dinner last week."

"Sure, I liked her. Enough to ask her out on a date, not to marry her."

"And you *did* just tell our mother that you met someone," Theo presses. "I'm guessing you were thinking of her?"

"I said I *maybe* met someone. That I wasn't sure what it was yet."

Theo rolls his eyes. "Which means you must be thinking about saying yes. Somewhere in the back of your brain, you're preparing Mom for the moment when you call her and say, *Surprise! I'm getting married.*"

I'm not sure I was consciously making the choice, but Theo's words don't sound entirely off base.

"Yeah, maybe," I say. "But that was impulsive. If I think logically for two seconds, it's clear I can't actually do it. I'm not going to commit fraud."

He studies me closely. "Because you don't break the rules."

I shoot him a look. "You broke enough for the both of us."

He grins. He knows better than to deny what we both know is true. "Maybe. But do you remember the one time you *did* break a rule?"

I lift an eyebrow, knowing he'll answer without more encouragement than that.

"When you pretended to be me and took my chemistry final senior year."

I *did* take his chemistry final, but only because he had to pass if he wanted to graduate, and he had to graduate if he wanted to play hockey.

"That was different," I say. "You were in no position to

take that test, but that wasn't your fault. It was less about breaking the rules and more about helping *you*."

He gives me a pointed look. "But you can't help Sarah because that would be fraud?"

I open my mouth to argue, but the words lodge in my throat.

"Honestly, I don't blame Miles," Theo continues. "His family has been through a lot. I'd probably try the same thing if I were in his shoes. And it's not like you'd be giving up some wildly active dating life. I can't even remember the last time you took someone out."

He's not wrong, but it's still not the reaction I expected from Theo. For the first time, he has me considering—truly considering—what it might look like if I actually said yes.

Nine months to a year isn't a very long time. But *no*. Marriage is a big deal. And immigration fraud is a felony.

"It's not the same thing," I say. "I'd be putting my career on the line."

"Only if you get caught. And come on. I saw the two of you together. It wouldn't be a struggle to pretend you're in love."

Heat spreads behind my ribs at the thought, but feeling a spark of attraction is not the same thing as pretending to be in love. No matter what my subconscious brain made me admit to Mom, this is a much bigger deal than Theo is making it seem.

I look over at my brother. "Miles said he had a few other people he was going to ask. He mentioned you. Asked me if I thought *you* would say yes."

Theo studies me carefully. "I think I know better than to even consider it."

"What's that supposed to mean?"

"It means you obviously like her, and I would never make you watch her pretend to love me."

I unbuckle my seatbelt and climb out of the car, grabbing my bag and tossing it over my shoulder before heading toward the elevator.

Theo quickly follows, jogging to catch up before falling in step beside me. "You mentioned other guys," he says. "Did he mention who? Other guys from the team, probably."

I flex my fingers at the thought, and Theo must see the gesture because he starts to chuckle.

"Dude. Come on. You're gonna have to just do it."

"I can't believe you would even suggest it," I say. "We shouldn't be having this conversation."

He presses the button for the elevator, and the doors slide open. "Then stand here and tell me you don't want to punch something when you think about her with Fly or Isakov or Watson."

"Watson's barely twenty. No one would believe they're actually in love."

"But they would believe *you're* in love," Theo says. "A lot of people probably already do. You *did* follow her into the pantry at the team dinner."

My eyes widen the slightest bit. "You saw that?"

"Everybody saw that."

Outside the elevator on the top floor, there's a small alcove with two doors. The one on the left is his apartment, the one on the right is mine.

Theo moves to my door, leaning against the wall while I pull out my keys.

"What are you doing?" I ask.

He shrugs. "We aren't done talking."

I sigh and push open my door. "I don't want to talk about this anymore."

"Not about that," he says, following me inside. "Though if you want my final answer, I think you should do it."

"I don't want your final answer." I collapse onto my couch and drop my phone onto the coffee table, feeling more annoyed than I should. This is exactly what I wanted to do when I climbed into Theo's truck. I just didn't expect him to challenge me. To make me think my decision to say *no* might not be the right one.

My cat, Gordie, jumps onto my lap, his tail brushing across my chin as he meows a hello.

Theo sits down on the chair perpendicular to me, and Gordie eyes him warily. If anyone can tell the two of us apart, it's Gordie. He loathes Theo as much as he loves me.

"Here," Theo says, looking into his phone. "I'm sending you something."

My phone buzzes from the table, but I don't reach for it. "What is it?"

"It's the contact info for a real estate agent I dated last year. Her name is Shelby. And she's good."

I freeze. "Why would I need a real estate agent?"

He rolls his eyes and reaches for my phone, using his own face to unlock it.

I lunge for my phone. "Dude. We have a rule about doing that."

He lifts his arms, holding my phone just out of reach while he clicks and scrolls, then finally tosses it onto the couch cushion beside me.

I look down to see the real estate listing I had pulled up right before he picked me up.

"Any reason you didn't want to tell me you're thinking about buying a house?"

5

SARAH

I STARE AT THE SCREEN OF MY LAPTOP, HARDLY BELIEVING THE invitation sitting in my inbox.

The Bainbridge Studio in New York has invited me to do a two-week residence as a guest artist. I did a residency in Savannah and one in Atlanta last summer, but never in New York. And Bainbridge has such an incredible reputation.

It's fairly last minute—someone dropped out, and they're hoping I'll fill the spot—but I don't even care. It's New York. It's almost impossible to break into the art scene in New York.

I quickly type out a reply giving them my acceptance, then head across the backyard to tell Anna and Miles the news.

I let myself in through the back patio door and find Anna on the couch in the living room, the girls crawling all over her like she's a jungle gym. She looks exhausted. Her brown hair is swept back in a ponytail, but half of it has fallen out, and there are dark circles under her eyes.

"Hey," she says when she sees me come in. "Oof. Olive, careful. You just stepped on my belly."

I glance at my watch. It's past seven, which means it's definitely late enough for the girls to go to bed.

"What are you doing here?" Anna asks.

"Nothing. Just came over to see if the girls want to do bedtime with Aunt Sarah tonight."

"I do, I do!" Poppy calls, standing up on the cushion beside her mom.

"Are you for real right now?" Anna says, hope in her eyes. "Miles said he would do it, but he's on the phone with an old hockey buddy, so it might be a minute."

"I'd love to do it." I reach down and scoop Olive into my arms. "How many books are we reading tonight, girls?"

"Three!" Olive says, bouncing in my arms. I turn around and let Poppy climb onto my back so I've got one girl on the front and one girl on the back.

"Hold on tight," I say to Poppy. We've done this before, but they're getting bigger, and it's getting harder.

"I want seven books," Poppy says.

"Seven? How about five?" I say.

"Hmm, how about eight?"

"That's not very good negotiating, Pops," Miles says as he walks into the room. "You can't up your own number."

Poppy giggles. "I want *ten* books!"

Miles reaches out and musses Poppy's hair. "Sorry, Sarah. Looks like you're negotiating with terrorists. Do you want me to take them?"

"Nah. I got it. But don't go anywhere. I have news to share when I come back down."

He nods. "Come here, girls. I need bedtime kisses."

The girls take turns leaning over to say goodnight to their dad, then I haul them upstairs, my thighs burning by the time we finally reach Poppy's room.

We'll read stories in here, then once she's settled, I'll take Olive across the hall to her room. Her room—for at least a few more months. Anna and Miles converted the crib into a toddler bed, but they'll need it for baby Fiona once she's born. Olive is *not* enthusiastic about this change and has been resisting her parents' attempts to get her to sleep in her big girl bed just like Poppy.

Last I heard, they were debating whether they should just cave and buy another crib, but I think Olive will get there eventually. She's quieter than her older sister. And usually takes a little longer to warm up to new situations.

I pick out pajamas for Poppy, then head across the hall to get Olive's before shepherding the girls to the bathroom. Once we finish with bath time, pajamas on and teeth brushed, we climb onto Poppy's bed and settle in for story time. Poppy finally agreed to seven books, the number she originally started with (clearly, she really *is* good at negotiating) but we only make it through four before both girls have fallen asleep.

I close the book and set it off to the side, enjoying the weight of Olive's bath-damp head against my chest.

I don't have very many memories of my mom when I was this young. Our lives were volatile in those days, and sadly, the traumatic moments are easier to call to mind than the happy ones. But I do remember reading books. Mom would come up to my tiny attic bedroom and snuggle under the covers beside me, and we'd read and read and read. Picture books, then chapter books as I got older.

It never occurred to me that all moms didn't spend more than an hour reading stories every night. I just thought that's what moms did.

In hindsight, I wonder if Mom just appreciated that with

his bad knees, Dad would never climb the stairs to my room, which made it a safer space than the rest of the house.

Olive shifts and nestles a little closer, and I wrap my arms around her back.

My mom would have loved being a grandma—she would have loved these girls. But she didn't even live long enough to see Miles get married.

Her cancer wasn't as aggressive, as insidious, as what Anna's mom dealt with. Anna's mom was healthy one month, then practically terminal the next. It all moved so quickly.

But my mom was sick for years. She was first diagnosed with ovarian cancer right before I turned six. It was an early diagnosis, and the doctors called it highly treatable, so after a year of chemotherapy, she was in remission.

But the cancer came back a few years later, then again a few years after that. By the time I was in high school, the doctors had shifted their efforts from trying to cure her to trying to prolong her life and keep her comfortable.

She lived long enough to see Miles drafted and to know I'd been accepted into the Savannah College of Art and Design. Then she died on my nineteenth birthday.

It's at least a comfort we didn't live through the hardest years of her illness with my dad around. Once Miles was drafted, he was able to get us out, away from Dad's emotional abuse.

Well, emotional for *us*. For Miles, it was a different story.

I shove the painful thought away and run a hand up and down Olive's back, comforted by the steady in and out of her breathing.

What I wouldn't do to give Mom the chance to see this. To see Miles's little family, to see what I've done with my art and know that despite Dad's best efforts to keep it from happening, we've done okay.

We're okay.

I'm going to miss seeing daily reminders of that fact. Whenever my memories start to haunt me, I can look at my nieces, see them happy and safe and thriving, and that makes the world seem okay again.

Poppy stirs, snuggling deeper into her pillow, and her legs push against where I'm sitting on her bed. She's clearly ready to have her own space, so I scoot over to the edge of the mattress and stand, careful not to wake Olive. I hoist her onto my shoulder and carry her across the hall to her room.

Once both girls are tucked in, covers wrapped around their shoulders and lights turned off, I head back downstairs, wishing for the thousandth time that I didn't have to move back to Canada.

Anna and Miles are still in the living room. A hockey game is on the TV, but the volume is muted. As soon as I sit down opposite Anna, Miles grabs the remote and switches off the game.

"You don't have to turn it off," I say, but Miles waves away my comment.

"It's fine. I can watch it in the bedroom. But not before you tell us your news."

I look from my brother over to Anna. "I just got an email from the Bainbridge Studio in New York. They've invited me to be a guest artist for a two-week residency."

"Sarah!" Anna says quickly, her face lighting up. "That's amazing!"

"What's a residency?" Miles asks, like I haven't explained this concept to him at least five times. Is he being intentionally obtuse? No matter how many times I explain how things work in the art world, it never seems to click.

"I explained when I had one in Savannah," I say. "Do you remember the studio you came to see?"

"Where you did the art classes?"

"Among other things," I say. "The classes were a small part of it, but mostly I just painted. Collaborated with other artists. The studio was open to the public, so people could come in and watch me work. That's what I'll be doing at the Bainbridge. Except it's New York. So the exposure, the interest it might generate...it's a really big deal."

Miles frowns. "How did they find you? Is this something you just...volunteer for?"

I narrow my eyes at my brother. "It's not volunteer," not even trying to hide how defensive I feel. "It's by invitation only. I could have been recommended by a professor at SCAD, or they could have organically come across my work. The point is, they only do this a few times a year, and they picked *me*."

"Sorry," Miles says. "I never understand all the art things. Good job."

I sink back into my chair. Miles *says* good job, but it doesn't really feel like he means it.

"When do you go?" Anna says.

"Soon. A week from Wednesday." I reach over and squeeze her hand. "I'm sorry. I know that leaves you without anyone around to help. But it's only two weeks."

She quickly shakes her head, squeezing my fingers right back. "Are you kidding? Do not apologize for chasing your dreams. I'll be fine."

"What about when I'm on the road?" Miles says, looking

down at his phone. "We've got a week of road games right at the same time."

Anna shoots him a look. "I'll be fine," she repeats, this time a little more pointedly. "Maybe it will make us get a little more serious about hiring a nanny since it's not actually your sister's responsibility to take care of them. Or me."

"You know I never mind helping," I say. "But that's the thing. This residency is exactly the kind of thing that will help level up my career. It will be great exposure and will make qualifying for my O-1 visa so much easier."

Miles breathes out a sigh. "I really wish you weren't hanging all your plans on literally the hardest visa to qualify for."

"Miles, don't," Anna says.

"Why not? I'm over here doing actual work to figure out a way for her to stay, and she's chasing a pipe dream."

As much as it stings to hear him question my entire career, that's not the thing that strikes me the most about his words.

"Wait, what does that mean?" I ask. "What do you mean you're doing work?"

Miles's expression shifts. "Nothing. It's nothing."

I look at Anna, who seems to be very intentionally *not* looking at me.

"Anna, what is he talking about?"

She looks at her husband. "If you don't tell her, I will."

Miles's shoulders drop, his demeanor a perfect combination of annoyance and resignation. He leans forward, propping his elbows on his knees, then he finally lifts his gaze to mine. "I'm pretty sure I found another way for you to stay. But I haven't said anything because I'm still trying to work out the details."

"What way?" I say. "I've talked to the attorney as many times as you have. There *is* no other way."

He tilts his head as if to concede the point. Then he says, "Unless you get married."

I scoff. "Unless I *what*?"

"You get married," Miles repeats. "But only for a year or so. Long enough for you to get your teaching credential. Then you can get a job with someone willing to sponsor you, and you get a divorce."

"Miles. Are you serious right now? Who would I even marry?"

"That's what I've been working on. I'm pretty sure I can convince one of the guys on the team to do it."

I immediately think of Carter, and a flush climbs up my cheeks. I won't deny feeling attracted to him, but that doesn't mean I'd be willing to *marry* him. Or anyone else on the team.

I sputter out a few disgruntled sounds, but the shock I'm feeling has left me utterly speechless. How do I even respond when Miles is being such a colossal idiot? It's bad that he's bringing up the teaching thing *again*, like it wouldn't completely derail the career I already have. But it's far worse that he thinks I would marry one of his teammates.

Miles and I get along pretty well, all things considered. But over the next ten minutes, we cover all the reasons why this is a terrible idea. Fraud. Felonies. Not to mention the fact that he's expecting me to live with a man I do not know for an entire year.

I understand he's coming from a good place. He's worried about Anna—I get that. But this is too much.

"So I guess you're saying you wouldn't do it," Miles says, the fight completely drained from his voice. "What if it wasn't a teammate? Someone totally separate from hockey."

It's a valid question. Miles knows better than anyone why my history with hockey is so complicated. But that's not the reason for my opposition.

"It wouldn't matter," I say. "I would never expect a man to put himself at risk for me. *Any* man."

"Told you," Anna says. She's been quiet for our argument, but now, she leans forward, pointing her finger at Miles as she adds, "This is why you should have talked to her first."

"First?" I ask, and suddenly neither of them will make eye contact. "What does that mean?"

Miles waves a hand in front of him. "Don't worry about it."

A wave of dread washes over me. "Miles," I say slowly. "Please tell me you haven't *already* talked to one of your teammates."

He breathes out a sigh. "Only one. But he said no. For a lot of the same reasons you did."

I close my eyes, afraid to ask. But I have to ask. "Who was it?"

Please don't be Carter. Please don't be Carter. Please don't be Carter.

"Carter Williamson," Miles says.

I sink into my chair. At least now I can say I know what it feels like to actually die of embarrassment.

6

CARTER

A week after my conversation with Miles, the Jaguars host their annual community food drive. It's a whole big thing, held in the parking lot at the arena, and as players, we're all expected to make an appearance. The signing table and photo station are mandatory for all of us, slotting us into a specific schedule so fans know when to show up to see their favorite players. Otherwise, we got to sign up for how we wanted to help.

Miles is manning a booth where kids can trade canned goods for a chance to take a shot at our mascot. Fly and Jordo are set up at a table where people can play "Pin the jersey number on the player," and Theo, Holly, and I are in an equipment sizing tent, helping youth players decide on the right stick length or helmet size. There are mountains of donated gear behind us, and if families bring in the requested pantry items for the premade meal kits being assembled in the neighboring tent, they're free to take home whatever gear we have that meets their needs.

I like the equipment tent. It's a lot better than where I

ended up at last year's event—running a spin-the-wheel-for-a-prize station. More than a few fans got a little too close for comfort. But in here, our purposes are a little more specific, so it doesn't feel like we're dealing with the masses in quite the same way.

The downside—or maybe it's an upside?—is that we're right next door to the tent where the WAGs are working with volunteers to assemble prepackaged meal kits.

The wives and girlfriends—*and Sarah.*

I find myself looking that way every time I have the chance. Sarah's wearing a dark pink beanie, so it's easy to spot her.

"What about this one?" The ten-year-old kid I'm trying to help, Jamison, holds up a hockey stick that's much too tall for him.

I force myself to focus and keep my eyes off the neighboring tent. "Maybe something a little more your size," I say. I swap the stick for a smaller one and hand it over.

"Shouldn't I have my skates on?" he asks, and I shake my head.

"Not for this. Just hold it right in front of you—good, just like that. You want the top of the stick to hit you here, somewhere in between your chin and your nose. Have you ever played before?"

He shakes his head no.

"Got it. Then I think this one is a good height for you. It's a little short, but that'll give you more control, which you'll need at first." I reach for the stick and turn it upside down, placing the knob at the top of the handle on the ground so the blade is in the air. "Okay, now I want you to take this and lean onto it a little."

"Like this?" Jamison asks.

"Yep. You've got it. Do you feel that flex? How the stick gives just the slightest bit? That's what you want."

Jamison's dad is standing off to the side, but he has his phone out, and it looks like he's taking notes. I look up and meet his eyes. "I think this one is a great fit for him. Do you have any questions?"

"I wrote down every word you said, so I think we're good," he says. "Hopefully, as he grows, I'll be able to help him pick out the next one."

On the other side of the tent, Holly fist bumps Jamison's sister, who's wearing a new set of goalie pads. "Thanks, Mr. Hollifield," she says.

"No, problem," Holly says. "You stay tough out there, all right?"

"I'm more than tough," she says. "I'm a brick wall."

Holly smiles and laughs, a sight I haven't seen in a long time.

It was the beginning of last season when his wife's cancer diagnosis turned terminal. He was out for almost five months, at first, just so he could be with her, and then, after she died, because he was in no mental state to play a hockey game.

He came back just in time to take us to the playoffs and get us all the way to the final game. But I rarely saw him smile, even when we were winning.

He was there because he had a job to do, but it didn't seem like he was taking much pleasure in it.

Theo steps up beside me as we say goodbye to Jamison's family. "It's nice to see him smiling," Theo says once we're on our own. He tilts his head toward Holly.

"I was just thinking the same thing."

Holly must sense us staring, because he looks up, his eyes

widening once he sees us. "What?" he says as he walks toward us. "Why are you staring at me?"

"No reason," Theo says. "Just talking about how ugly you are."

"So ugly," I agree. We only say this kind of stuff about Holly because the internet has very loudly branded him the best-looking guy on our team. We take our responsibility to keep him humble very seriously.

"Cool," Holly says. "For our next topic, can we discuss who Carter's been staring at all day?" He tilts his head toward the tent next door.

My face flushes with heat. I haven't been staring. At least not obviously.

Or so I thought.

Beside me, Theo starts to chuckle. "He's staring at Brick's sister."

Holly's eyebrows lift. "For real?"

"I'm not staring," I say. "And it doesn't matter."

"You want to know what Brick asked him?" Theo says, stepping a little closer.

I shoot him a look. "Dude. I doubt he wants everyone knowing about that."

"I'm not telling everyone. I'm telling Holly," Theo says. "It's *Holly*. We tell him everything."

"Well, now you have to tell me," Holly says.

I glance over my shoulder toward the volunteers at the front of our tent. The event is almost over, and there's nobody else waiting to see us, which means there's no one who could overhear. But I still drag them both to the very back of the tent, stepping outside to make sure there's no one anywhere outside it.

Once I'm sure we're completely alone, I fold my arms over

my chest and give Holly a shortened version of Sarah's circumstances and how Miles wanted to fix them.

"Are you going to do it?" Holly asks when I finally finish. His words are measured, like he's trying hard not to seem like he has an opinion on the matter. It makes me nervous. Outside of my brother, he's my closest friend on the team, and I care about what he thinks.

"Of course not," I say. "I already told him no."

"But you've still been staring at her all day," Theo says. "So...are you *sure* you're telling him no?"

"I was not staring at her."

"You really *were* staring at her," Holly says. "I saw you looking that direction at least a dozen times."

"It doesn't even matter," I say. "He's probably already asked someone else. Or maybe he realized it was a dumb idea and decided to let the whole thing go."

Holly clears his throat. "Either way, she's on her way over here right now, and I'm guessing she wants to talk to you."

I spin around and spot Sarah walking toward us, carrying a small square box. We make eye contact, and she lifts her hand in a wave.

"Hey, can you guys take one more?" a volunteer calls from the front of the tent.

Theo claps me on the back. "We'll handle this. You go talk to your fiancée."

I give him a playful shove as he walks away. "Theo, I swear..."

He laughs as he and Holly move forward to help a little boy wearing a Jaguars jersey with Holly's number on the sleeve.

"Hey," I say to Sarah as I approach.

"Hi." She pushes her free hand into her back pocket. Her

brown eyes are wide behind a pair of green glasses, her dark blond hair long and loose around her shoulders. The glasses are different than the ones she had on the last time I saw her, and they make her eyes look more hazel than brown. "Had a good day?"

"Great. It's a lot of fun working with the kids."

She nods. "Yeah, I *might* have spied on you a little bit. Seems like you're really good with them."

A burst of warmth spreads through my chest at her words. I shouldn't like the idea of her watching me quite as much as I do.

"Did your spying happen to catch the time I accidentally whacked a mom on the head with a hockey stick? If it did, could I convince you that was actually Theo?"

She presses her lips together like she's fighting a smile. "I must have missed that part. Shame on Theo."

"How was *your* day? Looks like you guys stayed busy."

"Yeah. It was amazing," she says. "I had no idea this was such a huge event. I'm really glad I got to be here for it."

Her eyes drop to the ground, and I wonder if she's thinking the same thing I am. That she's here now, but she won't be for long.

She clears her throat. "Anyway, I picked this up for you earlier today, and I just wanted to drop it off." She holds out the box. "It's an apology cupcake."

"An apology cupcake? What are you apologizing for?"

She bites her lip, her cheeks flushing with color, then she takes a deep breath. "My brother told me what he asked you to do."

It's the stupidest thought. But as soon as her words land, the first thing my mind does is wonder if I'm the only one she's apologizing to or if she has half a dozen cupcakes she's giving out to my teammates.

It shouldn't matter either way, but I find myself hoping I'm the only one.

I open the box and look at the cupcake. It's topped with pink frosting with a single fresh raspberry right in the center.

A raspberry cupcake.

"It's the same one you said you should…"

Her words trail off, but I remember the moment all too well. When I tasted the raspberry frosting that I wiped off the tip of her nose. I lift my eyes to her face. There are freckles on her nose that I didn't notice in the dim light of the pantry. Maybe they're more visible when she's out in the sun.

Sarah pulls her hair over one shoulder, snapping me back to the present. "Anyway," she says, "I was totally mortified when he told me and so, so embarrassed. I just wanted to make sure you knew it wasn't my doing. He concocted the whole wild idea on his own, and I'm so sorry he talked to you about it. He never should have put you in that position."

I close the lid of the cupcake box. "You don't have to apologize. I know how important you are to his family. I understand why he asked."

"But to expect you to give up a year of your life," Sarah says. "Not to mention the legal implications." She shakes her head. "It's ridiculous. *Completely* ridiculous."

"He said he was going to ask someone else. Were you…did he find someone?"

Her eyes widen. "Are you kidding? Absolutely not. As soon as he told me what he was doing, I told him he *couldn't* ask anyone else. I would never expect anyone to do such a thing. Not for me."

Something about the way she says this doesn't sit right.

Why not for her? If *anyone* is deserving of a little good fortune, she is.

Across the parking lot, a cheer erupts, and I look over to see a kid high-fiving the Jaguars mascot. When I turn my gaze back to Sarah, she's still looking that way. The wind has picked up, and a strand of her dark blond hair is blowing across her cheek. She lifts her hand and brushes it away as she looks back at me.

"Can I ask you something?" I say.

She nods. "Okay."

"Miles mentioned that staying for one more year would give you time to get your teaching credential. Then you would qualify for a different kind of visa."

Her face shifts as I speak, her jaw tightening as she looks away. She looks smaller somehow, like she's folding in on herself.

"But that's not what we talked about, is it? Do you want to be a teacher?"

It takes her a long moment to meet my gaze. I wait, because I sense this is a point of particular tension for her. "Miles and I have very different opinions about that," she finally says. "He thinks teaching would be safer. And he's probably right. It's just not what I want."

"So tell me this," I say. "If you had another year in the States, do you think you'd be able to qualify for the other kind? The visa you told me about?" I have no idea why I'm asking. But somehow, it feels incredibly important to know.

She looks up at me with those enormous brown eyes, questions flitting behind them I can't even begin to interpret. But then she nods, a fire sparking behind her expression that makes my chest tighten.

"Yes," she finally says, her voice steady, confident. "I really think I could."

"Hey, Sarah!" Anna calls from the neighboring tent. "You ready?"

She nods, then looks back at me. "I should go. And you really should eat the cupcake. It's delicious."

I hold her gaze. "I remember."

This pulls a small smile out of her, and I wonder if she's remembering the moment like I am. If she's been replaying our conversations the same way I've been.

"Bye, Carter," she says, then she turns and hurries back to Anna.

I stand and watch her for a long moment, trying to sort out what's happening in my brain. Miles reaches Anna at the same time Sarah does, and he has their girls with him. Olive reaches for her aunt, and Sarah takes her, then extends her hand to Poppy. I catch her profile as she does. She's clearly smiling, looking at her nieces with obvious affection.

I really *do* wish I could help her. But could I actually marry her?

I shake my head as I head back into the tent, not sure what to do with the fact that the longer I think about it, the less ridiculous the idea sounds.

By the time I make it back to Theo and Holly, they've finished with the last kid to come through and are picking up the remaining hockey sticks, slotting them into storage barrels that will be carted back to the Jaguars practice arena where the local youth hockey league skates.

"Have you set a date yet?" Theo asks as I crouch down and pick up a stick.

"Shut up."

"What did she want?" Theo asks.

"To apologize," I say. "Miles told her."

"Oh, man," Holly says. "I'm guessing she was mad."

"More just embarrassed," I say. "She wanted to make sure I knew it wasn't her idea."

"Well that's good of her, I guess," Theo says, then he narrows his eyes. "Wait. What's happening on your face right now?"

I lift a hand and wipe it across my mouth. "Nothing is happening on my face." I shove a handful of hockey sticks into his arms. "Put these away."

He takes the sticks, but he's shaking his head as he does. "Something is definitely happening. You're thinking about doing it."

"I'm not," I say, but there's no fire behind my response.

I can't explain why. Something about the way she sounded. Or how seamlessly she fits with her family.

I also don't love that her brother is pushing her to teach when she clearly wants something else. I was lucky enough to grow up with parents who always believed in me. Not in a way that felt like pressure, like I had to live up to *their* expectations. Just in that quiet, steady way that said they knew I could do it. And they were ready to cheer me on the whole way.

Everyone deserves that kind of cheerleader. I'm sure Miles thinks he's supporting Sarah by encouraging her to make the most practical choice. But I'm Team Sarah on this one.

Not that it matters. Neither option solves her problem fast enough to let her stay.

"So, wait," Holly says. "Do you actually like her? Like, *like* her, like her?"

I sigh and prop my hands on my hips. "I mean, I don't know her that well. But we definitely…"

"Have a vibe," Theo says. "They do. I saw it."

"She is really easy to talk to," I say.

"And?" Theo prompts.

"And…she's really talented. And obviously smart."

"And?" Holly this time.

"And insanely beautiful, with these eyes that just…" I take off the baseball cap I'm wearing and run a hand through my hair, then look at my two closest friends. "Could I really be thinking about doing this?"

Holly shrugs. "The way I see it, if you do it, you get to know her. Spend time with her. See if there's potential for something real to happen between you. Maybe it will. Maybe it won't. But at least you tried. If you don't, she leaves. Then you'll never know."

"Do you think Miles would actually be chill with you dating her?" Theo asks. "Like, if you went through with it and it turned into something? He has pretty intense big brother energy."

"If they're married, would he even have a say?" Holly says. "I never understand when guys are weird about their sisters dating. Do you want them to be happy or not?"

"I mean, Miles and Carter are teammates," Theo argues. "If things go south and someone gets hurt, it'd be hard not to let that impact team dynamics."

Holly shrugs. "I don't know. Seems like he gave up his right to be mad about anything when he asked Carter to marry her in the first place."

"Okay, but what if it's terrible? What if I marry her and three months in, I know it isn't going to work?"

"I mean, we're on the road half the time anyway," Theo

says. "You deal until your year is up, then you split and move on, knowing you still did a really nice thing for someone."

"On the flip side, what if it's great?" Holly says. "Maybe you really enjoy each other, and then you've got this great relationship you didn't even have to work for. I'm just saying, the right kind of love doesn't come along every day. If you feel even a fraction of potential with her, I'd do whatever I could to chase it." There's a weight to his words that lands differently, and I know he must be thinking about Claire. About the kind of relationship he had with her.

"Honestly, when was the last time you went on a date anyway?" Theo says. "Your life will barely change. You're already looking for houses. Now you'll have someone living in it while you're out of town. She could keep your cat alive. Seems like a win-win."

"You're buying a house?" Holly asks.

I glance over at my brother. He took the news better than I thought he would, probably because I only sort of hinted at the real reasons behind my decision. How do I tell him he's the most important person in my life while also admitting I really need some space?

"He thinks I'm a terrible neighbor," Theo says, and I'm relieved to hear the levity in his voice.

"You are a terrible neighbor. This morning, I found the remnants of *your* smoothie stuck to *my* kitchen floor."

Theo grimaces. "You're the one who gave me a key. It's not my fault your fridge is always way better stocked than mine."

"It's absolutely your fault," Holly says. "Just go to the grocery store."

"Thank you," I say, happy for the validation. If anyone has earned the right to call Theo out, it's Holly. When we were traded from the Appies and called up to the NHL, we lived with him and Claire for six months until we found our footing with the team. We stayed until right before Charlie was born.

"The point is," Theo says, "if you're getting a house anyway, I bet she could help you decorate the place. She's an artist. She probably has great taste."

"I'm not marrying her so she can decorate my house."

"And take care of your cat," Theo adds, like this will be the thing that tips the scales.

"But you *will* marry her so she doesn't have to move back to Canada?" Holly asks.

I can't believe I'm even thinking it. But I might.

7

SARAH

It's late on a very boring Sunday afternoon when I look out my living room window and see Anna flying toward the pool house. Well, maybe not *flying*. She doesn't move anywhere very quickly these days, but there's definitely a sense of urgency I haven't seen in a while.

I get up and meet her at the door. "What's got you moving so fast?" I say.

She doesn't answer as she barrels past me and into the living room. I shut the door and follow behind her. Her energy is almost frantic, and it has me worried something has happened.

She spins and looks me up and down. "This won't work," she says as she moves toward my bedroom.

I look down at my outfit. I'm in leggings and an oversized hoodie, but it's Sunday and I'm going nowhere. This is the perfect outfit for that kind of day. "What won't work?"

I hear my dresser drawer slide open and hurry after her. "Anna," I say from the doorway. She's already elbow-deep in my clothes. "Stop for two seconds and tell me what's going on."

She turns and tosses a sweater at me, then props her hands on her hips. "Carter Williamson is at the house."

My eyebrows shoot up. "Okay. Why does that mean I have to put on a sweater?"

She grabs a pair of jeans off the chair in the corner and shakes them at me. "Can you just hurry? He's waiting to talk to you, and you really can't go looking like this." She waves a hand in my general direction.

"What's wrong with how I look?"

"There's a weird stain on your hoodie and a hole in your leggings."

"Okay, fair." I pull the hoodie over my head, then slip on the sweater Anna picked out. "But why is he here to talk to me?" I say, voice muffled by the sweater which I can't seem to get over my head. When I finally pop through the right opening, hair flying from the static, Anna is staring at me, hands propped on her hips. There's a smile playing around her mouth, and her eyes are gleaming.

"You might want to sit down," she says, and my heart starts to race.

"Why? Why do I need to sit down?"

"Sarah, he said he'll do it," she says. "He's willing to marry you."

I lean back against my dresser, knees suddenly weak. "He did not."

"He totally did. He wanted to come back and tell you himself, but I convinced him you'd want a heads-up. Mostly because I fully expected you to look like this. But also—" She takes a step closer, holding my gaze. "You can still say no, Sarah. You know how much I want you to be here, but this was Miles's idea. We won't blame you if it's too much. I thought you deserved a minute to consider what you want for real before you face him."

I walk over to my bed and sink onto the corner of the mattress.

I have experienced a plethora of emotions since my conversation with Miles. At first, all I felt was anger. Then my anger turned into mortification. But the longer I sit with what happened, the more I recognize what's at the core of my brother's motivation.

We're all remaining hopeful that Anna won't have post-partum depression like she did before, but if she does, it will be doubly more difficult without her mom *and* me. I can't fault Miles for wanting me close, both for my sake and for hers.

But I never considered, even for a moment, that Miles's plan was actually a viable one.

"What made him change his mind?" I ask. My mind darts back to the exchange we had at the food drive yesterday. He looked good—*so good*—wearing a Jaguars baseball cap low on his forehead and a team-branded navy and white half-zip pullover.

I had to apologize—the thought of him believing I might have had something to do with Miles's proposition was keeping me up at night—but now I'm wondering if our conversation had something to do with him being here today.

"Who knows?" Anna says. She hands me my jeans, and I shimmy out of my leggings, then pull them on. "Does it matter?"

"Everything matters, Anna. We're talking about marriage here. Why would he agree to something like this? Did he say?"

"Not explicitly. But I don't think you have to worry about him having ulterior motives. Carter's a really nice guy. Like, nice enough that it wouldn't take much to convince me he's willing to do it *just* to be nice."

"But he wasn't willing at first," I say. "That's the point I'm making. He changed his mind."

"Maybe he really liked his apology cupcake?" she says. "Or he appreciated how hot you looked in those jeans because your butt looked totally amazing."

I look down at my jeans—the same ones I wore yesterday. "Really?" But then I give my head a quick shake. My butt, regardless of the jeans, is not the point of this conversation.

"That would actually be *bad* news," I say. "I don't want him noticing anything about me." Even as I say the words, a tiny pulse of doubt makes me question them, but I quickly squelch it. Liking Carter isn't an option. It can't be.

"Because he's a hockey player," Anna says flatly, and I shrug.

"It wouldn't be fair to him," I say. "You're a WAG. You know what it's like. Carter wouldn't want a wife who can't do anything to support him. Who never watches him play. At least, not a *real* wife."

She sighs. "Okay. Forget I suggested it. Let's just go with him being nice."

"He *is* nice," I say. I turn and look in the mirror, pulling my hair out of its bun and shaking it out around my shoulders. "But I still don't think that's enough reason." I turn to face her and adjust my glasses. "Better?"

She nods. "It's annoying that you can do *that* little effort and suddenly look like you belong on the runway."

I roll my eyes. "Hardly."

"You look great," she says. "So what are you going to tell him?"

"You mean am I going to do it?"

She nods. She isn't even trying to hide the hope in her eyes.

"No clue. What do *you* think I should do?"

She seems to consider my question. "Do you want me to answer as an objective third party? As your sister-in-law? Or as your best friend?"

I tilt my head to the side. "All three?"

"Okay. As an objective third party—definitely not. You don't know this guy. And the legal consequences of getting caught are *not* insignificant."

"Good. True," I say. "That's valid."

"As your sister-in-law, I desperately, with my whole entire heart, want you to say yes because I cannot imagine my life without you in it." Tears spring to her eyes as she speaks, and she groans. "This baby is making me so weepy." She sniffs and wipes at her eyes. "What was left?"

"Your best friend answer," I say, though honestly, that last one will be hard to override.

She's quiet for a long moment. "As your best friend, I think I'd tell you to tread carefully. Because pretending with a man like Carter Williamson feels very risky. If you don't want to fall for a hockey player, I'm not sure he's the safest bet."

I understand what she means. I liked talking to Carter. And I won't even begin to pretend I don't find him attractive. He's legitimately a level of sexy I've never experienced before.

But I can't have a real relationship with someone in his line of work. The thought makes my chest tighten, the familiar sensation blooming beneath my ribs and keeping my lungs from expanding all the way. For a split second, I'm at an NHL game in

Winnipeg, and the walls are closing in around me. The noises, the smells, the sound of bodies crashing against the boards.

I swallow and force air into my lungs, chasing the memories away. I lift a hand, running it across my sternum. "I won't fall for him," I say. "You know I can't."

"Okay," she says, not sounding at all convinced. "Then your best friend doesn't have any arguments against it and would really love for you to be around." She holds out her hand. "Ready to go talk to him?"

I shake my head no. "I can't believe this is happening. Is this really happening?"

She shrugs and gives me a hopeful smile. "Let's go talk to him and find out for sure."

Carter stands as soon as we enter the living room. He looks nice, wearing tailored pants and a button-down, and I wonder if he made more of an effort just for this—for our conversation.

Olive and Poppy are stretched out on the floor with an iPad, playing some sort of matching game, but as soon as Olive sees me, she runs over and holds up her arms, asking to be picked up.

I scoop her into my arms, suddenly grateful for her grounding presence.

"Hi, Sarah," Carter says. I like that he uses my name.

Wordlessly, Anna takes Olive out of my arms and nudges me more fully into the room. She calls to Poppy, then motions to Miles to follow her into the kitchen, leaving Carter and me alone.

Well, *sort of* alone. The kitchen isn't so far away that we can't still hear Anna's hushed instructions to the girls to give us some privacy.

Carter looks toward the kitchen. "Do you think we could take a walk?"

"Yes! Definitely," I say. "A walk sounds great."

We're quiet as he follows me to the front door. He pulls on his coat while I shrug into one of Anna's. She always has a couple hanging in the entryway, and wearing hers feels easier than going back to the pool house for one of mine.

Even though it's dark outside, Miles and Anna's house is in a well-lit neighborhood with sidewalks and plenty of streetlamps, so we head down the driveway and turn toward the park at the end of the road.

Carter looks over at me. "I'm sorry I didn't tell you myself," he says. "I wanted to, but Anna insisted you might need a minute to get used to the idea before we talked."

"She was right," I say. "I'm still not sure I believe this is happening."

"I can imagine," he says. "Are you wondering what changed my mind?"

I nod, grateful he's willing to guide the conversation because I still feel entirely upside down.

"It was a couple of things," he says. "First, I did some reading about postpartum depression and the importance of a good support network. Then I factored in the added stress of being a hockey wife, dealing with how much we're on the road. Hired help can only get you so far, and I respect Miles and his family. If you want to stay in the States to be close to them, that feels like something I ought to support if I have the means to do so."

My brain snags on the word *ought*, but I'm not sure why. Saying yes because he feels like he should is different than saying yes because he wants to. But then, if he were saying yes because he wanted to, that wouldn't sit right either because we aren't talking about a *real* marriage.

Ought to feels safer, even if it does feel less exciting.

"That's really kind of you to say," I say, forcing myself to focus on the kindness behind Carter's words. Anna *did* describe him as thoughtful, but reading about postpartum depression to better understand what it is feels next level.

Anna would hate it if she knew, only because she hates to be needy, to have anyone making any kind of fuss about her. But she has no idea how much she does for the rest of us. She deserves all the fuss.

"I understand how important family is, so I want you to be close to yours."

I pause my footsteps and turn to face him. "So you're saying you changed your mind because you're nice? I don't believe you, Carter. You have to have more reason than that."

"I didn't say I don't. But that's the biggest one, so I wanted to get it out of the way first."

A chilly wind blows past us, and I tug my coat a little closer. Even though it was almost sixty degrees today, it feels closer to thirty now that the sun has set.

"Okay. What are your other reasons?"

"A few things," Carter says as we start to walk again. "First, to make the marriage look as authentic as possible, I think we'll need to live together. Miles said the pool house has two bedrooms, but I'm hoping you might be open to a different option."

My shoulders fall the slightest bit. I hadn't heard that Miles wants us to live in the pool house. As grateful as I am for his and Anna's willingness to let me stay here for free, the pool house has zero room for painting. Which isn't a huge deal. I could always rent out some studio space somewhere.

But sometimes I paint at ridiculously weird hours. I don't truly have the right to be choosy, but it would be nice to have a studio at home.

"A different option like what?"

"Like...a house," Carter says. "I've been talking to a real estate agent lately. I thought we could move into it together. That's something married couples do, right?"

A knot of dread tightens in my stomach. "Wait. You aren't..." I swallow, then lick my lips. "You aren't looking to buy a house *just* for this, right?"

Carter quickly shakes his head. "Definitely not. It's more just convenient timing. I'm in an apartment in Midtown, living across the hall from my brother. I've been itching for something different for a while."

The certainty of his response is reassuring, but it also makes me feel a little silly for questioning his motives. People don't buy real houses for fake marriages.

Then again. People also don't get married when they aren't in love. So maybe I should stop trying to make *any* of this feel realistic.

"It's important to me that if we do this, we do everything we can to make it look legit," Carter continues. "I think the house will really help with that. Plus, it'll be a huge help to me if you move in."

"A help? Why is that?"

"Because of Gordie."

"Gordie?" I repeat, and he nods.

"My cat. The neighbor below me currently takes care of him when we're on the road. But if I move, I won't have anyone to check on him. So it would actually be a huge favor to me if you were around, keeping an eye on the house and taking care of Gordie."

I huff out a laugh. "Carter, you can't marry me just so I can feed your cat. You can hire a pet sitter."

"Gordie's a special cat. I can't trust him with just anybody."

I stop again, propping my hands on my hips.

"I don't believe you," I say. "You could buy a house without me. You could hire someone to watch your cat. These are not good reasons to marry someone."

He smiles, his dimple appearing and making my heart skip a beat. "I'm not done, Sarah. Are you going to let me finish my list or not?" His tone is light, teasing, and I have to wonder what his endgame is here.

The fact that he's trying to spin this as *me* doing a favor for him is incredibly sweet, but it almost feels too good to be true.

I shake my head, smiling despite the worry still pulsing in my chest. "Okay. Let's hear it."

He starts moving again, his hands pushed into the pockets of his wool coat. He's wearing a camel-colored scarf along with it, and the whole vibe is really working for me. I don't mind him in joggers and team pullovers, but I love this look too.

"I was hoping you'd help me decorate my place," Carter says. "As soon as I have one, anyway. Which—I want to qualify that by saying I'm not asking just because you're a woman or because I think it's something a wife would necessarily do. I'm only asking because you're an artist, which makes me think you probably have good taste. I don't have any experience decorating anything, so I could really use the help."

I don't point out that he could *also* hire someone to do his decorating, and if I were to actually help, I'd probably hire a professional just to make sure I didn't screw it up. Bare minimum, I would call my college friend, Emerson. He studied interior design at SCAD, and he's brilliant.

"That's all?" I ask because surely it can't be. "Take care of Gordie and decorate your house?"

"Not quite," he says. "There's one more thing."

I let out a little laugh. "You could name ten more things and I'd still be in your debt." Another sharp gust of wind cuts through the insubstantial fabric of Anna's coat, and I suck in a breath.

Carter looks over, pausing under a streetlamp, and unwinds the scarf from his neck. He lifts his arms and drapes it around me, tying it into a knot beneath my chin. "Better?" he says softly, and I nod.

He holds my gaze before saying, "I'd like a Sarah Stone original to hang in my house."

"A painting?" I ask.

He nods. "You don't have to do anything special—it can be one you've already done. I just want to be able to say *I knew her when* and have something to show off to my friends."

I suddenly understand Anna's *best friend* warning. It's going to be very difficult to protect my heart if Carter continues to be so charming.

But what else am I supposed to do? He's making it impossible to say no, especially when he's offering me something I desperately want.

He's offering me a ticket to stay.

8

CARTER

Monday night, I leave my helmet on the bench and skate a few laps around the Vortex. The stands are nowhere near full —not yet— but there's a good crowd just behind the glass, here to watch warmups before our game against the Denver Summit.

I look up into the stands to where players' families usually sit and wonder if I'll see Sarah tonight.

After our walk last night, we headed back to the house and spent the next two hours talking logistics. We came up with a timeline and discussed strategies regarding when and how we'll share our relationship, first with the team and close friends, then on social media with everyone else.

Miles was thorough in his research about what immigration will look for and how long it will take to file an adjustment of status for Sarah's visa. As long as we get married before her current one expires, she's free to stay in the country while her *new* status is processed, reviewed, and hopefully approved. But that approval will be contingent on them believing our marriage is legit. Which is why it's so important that we're living together, that we appear in public together, and that we know enough about each other to handle the interview questions with ease.

I already called the realtor Theo mentioned last week, and we've been to see a house I really like. She's confident if I make an offer, we'll be able to close quickly—especially if I'm paying cash, which is what I'd prefer.

Everything else we'll knock out a little at a time as Sarah and I get to know each other. We're getting together tomorrow night to take some pictures we can share on social media, but the point is to imply that even though we're only *now* going public, we've been seeing each other for months.

Considering my very public career, I don't think it's a hard sell. As long as we get all the details right, I'm feeling pretty confident we can pull this off.

What we didn't talk about is whether Sarah would come to tonight's game. Even though we aren't sharing anything explicit yet, we're supposed to be focusing on the team and the Jaguars' staff, teasing a relationship that exists, just not in the public eye.

I explained the situation to Theo, and he's on board to help sell things to the team, to fuel the fire, so to speak. And of course, Miles will contribute too. But it seems like Sarah being here would also help matters, so I'm surprised it didn't come up in our conversation.

For the rest of warmups, I find myself searching the stands, looking for any sign of Miles's family. Sarah never shows, but that doesn't necessarily mean she won't be here. It's still early.

Once we go public, it might seem weird if she doesn't come, and the prospect makes a tiny swell of excitement rise in my chest.

I like the idea of Sarah watching me play.

On my right, Miles skates by, and we make eye contact. He gives me a nod, and I wonder if things will be different for us now. We've always had a solid relationship. But I'm going to be his brother-in-law. Sort of brother-in-law?

Surely, that will change things.

Once the game starts, I can't afford to think about Sarah or wonder where she is. My team needs my focus. Denver plays dirty, and they spend a lot of time in the penalty box. Unfortunately, we go zero for four on the power play, so even though they give us every opportunity, we can't seem to get ahead.

Two minutes before the end of regulation, we're down one to two.

When Theo and I climb over the boards for our last shift, Holly is coming off the ice to the bench. We'll play empty net so Miles can join our line as a sixth attacker.

I settle in, dialing up my focus even more. We can do this in two minutes. We've done it before.

The puck moves into our offensive zone, then gets trapped on the boards, but I fight it out and chip it over to Fly, who circles wide, then sends it back to me. As the play shifts, I see a lane open up and make eye contact with Miles, who will have a clean shot if I can get him the puck. It's a clean pass, and Miles receives it easily before sending the puck soaring under the goalie's elbow and into the net.

The goal horn sounds, and the crowd explodes as Miles throws himself into my arms, followed by Fly and Theo. I pound Miles on the back, celebrating with him before he skates past the bench for his well-earned high fives. Twenty seconds later, Fly scores a second time, giving us the lead right before the final horn sounds. That's the game. We win three to two.

Miles looks into the stands, touching his glove to his heart once before pointing at his family. I follow his gaze to see Anna standing at the glass, Olive perched on her hip and Poppy beside her. I look behind them, around them, then up to where the families usually sit. But I don't see Sarah anywhere.

I push away the twinge of disappointment this triggers. It's been a long time since I've had anyone in the stands here just for me. That was the one good thing about my relationship with Veronica. She'd bring a whole cheering section. Posters. My face on homemade t-shirts.

It's a shame her enthusiasm didn't carry over to when I was *off* the ice.

"Second star tonight, Carter," Dave, our communications director, says as I head down the tunnel. "And post-game interview with Avery on the bench." I nod, then turn back toward the rink, stepping to the side so the rest of the guys can file past.

Theo claps me on the back on his way. "Way to get it, brother. I'll see you back there," he says, then he heads toward the locker room.

I wait beside Fly while the broadcasters announce the three stars of the game—the three players who, in their minds, had the greatest impact on the win.

Fly accepts the third star, skating onto the ice, then tossing a puck into the crowd for the cheering fans. I do the same for the second star. The fans are loud as I lift my arm and wave, but tonight, it doesn't feel as good as it usually does. There's a loneliness lurking right behind my ribs that's making the cheers of people I *don't* know feel shallow.

Usually, I'd head straight back to the locker room, but since I'm doing a post-game, I wait while Miles skates out and accepts the first star.

When he comes off the ice, he stops in front of me and makes eye contact. "Don't freak out over the question," he says. "We're just planting seeds. Smile, then deflect. That's all you have to do."

Before I can ask for clarification, Miles heads down the tunnel, and Dave ushers me onto the bench, where one of the Jaguars' broadcasters is waiting for me.

I have to wonder if Miles was talking about one of the questions I'm about to be asked *live,* in front of an arena full of people and broadcast to thousands at home. The thought makes my gut tighten with nerves.

Thankfully, Avery's questions are predictable. How do I feel about our power play? What went wrong? Did it feel good to make up for it by feeding Miles such an incredible pass? I give the answers she wants—accountability, focus, trusting the system—and I start to relax, thinking Miles must have been talking about something else.

But then Avery gives me a knowing smile.

"Just one more question," she says. "It seems like you had great chemistry with Stone tonight. He's such a force for the Jaguars, and he's told me the two of you have a pretty close relationship off the ice as well. What's it like for you, as a younger player, to have this kind of relationship with a player of his caliber?"

Okay, that's a little more specific than what I'm used to, but it's still on topic.

"Miles is a great captain," I say. "It's an honor to play with him and learn from him not just as a player, but also as a husband and a father. He's a great guy all around."

Avery smiles. "He also mentioned he's been giving you a lot of marriage advice lately. Are you taking notes for any particular reason?"

"I'm sorry?"

Her smile falters. "Just wondering if we should expect an announcement from you in the coming weeks?"

My jaw tightens. So this is what Miles meant. *Smile and deflect.*

I channel Theo's bravado and offer Avery what I hope is a convincing smile. "Did Miles put you up to that question? I'm going to go with *no comment.*" I add a wink at the end that feels much more like something my brother would do, and Avery laughs.

"Fair enough. Great game tonight, Carter. Thanks for chatting with us."

I stop in the tunnel on my way to the locker room and take a deep breath.

This is exactly what we talked about last night. But it definitely feels a little more real now.

I have to appreciate how quickly Miles thought on his feet. He had no way of knowing how the game would go, that I would get a star or be asked to do a post-game interview. That he managed to feed information to Avery—probably while I was accepting my star—is impressive.

I find Miles in the locker room already half out of his gear. I give his shoulder a playful shove as I walk by. "Way to put me on the spot, man."

He grins. "How did it go?"

I drop onto the bench at my stall, directly across from him. "I'm already regretting the nice things I said about you."

"Wait, what's happening?" Fly says. "Is there drama here? What did I miss?"

"No drama," I say. "Just an annoying post-game question I'm pretty sure Miles put Avery up to asking me."

"Dude. Is she asking what I think she's asking?" Theo says from the bench beside me. He has his phone out with the interview already playing. He must have pulled up the live broadcast and tracked backward to find it. He looks up and grins. "Look at Avery getting all personal. That's not usually her style."

Fly moves in and looks over Theo's shoulder. "What did she ask?"

Several other guys take an interest and crowd around Theo's phone.

I look over at Holly, who is sitting next to Miles and watching me closely. He's the only person on the team besides Miles and Theo who will know I'm not actually in a relationship with Sarah. Partly because I already told him what Miles asked and partly because even if I hadn't told him, he'd never believe me dating someone and not talking to him about it.

He lifts his eyebrows and tilts his head up the slightest bit, like he's asking if I'm okay.

I shrug and give him a nod. If I think too hard about what's happening, panic definitely threatens to creep in. But I went into this with my eyes open. We already started this ball rolling. I just have to ride the momentum and hope I land on my feet on the other side.

"So *is* Carter seeing someone?" Jordo asks. "Is that what she was implying? That he was taking notes on marriage because...he's getting *married*?" He sounds completely shocked, and I can't say that I blame him.

I keep my head down, eyes focused on unlacing my skates. At this point, it's all about the power of suggestion. If I don't say anything, they'll take my silence as an admission and fill in the blanks for me.

Jordo slaps my back as he moves past. "Dude. Are you holding out on us? What aren't you telling us?"

"I guess you'll know when I decide to tell you," I say.

A chorus of laughs and jeers and jokes erupts around the room, then I'm assaulted with a barrage of questions. Is it someone they know? How long have I been seeing her? Does Miles know? Is that why he tipped off Avery? Has Theo met her? Has Holly?

When Coach Kimzey finally comes in for a post-game debrief, I'm happy for the interruption, but I still find myself struggling to focus on his feedback. My mind keeps drifting to Sarah, wondering if she watched the game from home, if she maybe saw the post-game interview.

It's an odd feeling to know that my actions, my words—they're all tied back to her now. Whether I'm ready for it or not.

Once I'm showered and ready, I catch Miles on his way out. "Hey, did Sarah come tonight?" I ask, and something in his expression shifts, taking on a slight wariness that wasn't there before.

"Nah, man. She didn't come. She—"

"Daddy!" Poppy calls, cutting him off. We both turn to see Anna and the girls walking down the hall. Poppy runs and leaps into Miles's arms.

"Hey, kiddo," he says. He looks at Anna over Poppy's shoulder. "I thought you took the girls home."

Anna shrugs. "Poppy really wanted to wait and see you."

Poppy takes Miles's face into her hands and squishes his cheeks. "Good job on getting a star, Daddy." She looks over at me. "You too, Carter."

"Thanks, Poppy," I say. Standing here, watching Miles with his family, the loneliness I felt at the end of the game sharpens, the chasm inside my chest growing wider and wider.

Olive reaches for her dad next, and soon, he's so immersed in his family that he doesn't seem at all concerned with finishing our conversation.

Not that it matters. Sarah wasn't here, which is the information I wanted.

Theo appears behind me. "You ready?" he asks, and I nod.

We rode to the game together tonight, so we say goodbye to Miles and the rest of his family, then head out to the player parking lot.

"You probably feel like you've been thrown into the deep end," he says, and I let out a chuckle.

"Definitely. Thanks for backing me up."

"You know I've got you," he says. "Was Sarah at the game tonight?"

I unlock my truck as we approach. "No, she wasn't there."

"I wondered if she would be now that you're a thing."

"Maybe once we've officially gone public," I say as I toss my bag into the back of the truck. It concerns me how much I hope that's true.

As soon as we're both in the cab, I buckle my seatbelt and start the engine. "You good with a quick detour before we go home?"

Theo shrugs. "You're driving, so I'm not sure I have much choice."

"We won't be able to see much," I say as I pull out of the parking lot. "But I want to drive by anyway."

"Drive by what?" Theo asks. "A house?"

I nod. "I've been texting Shelby, talking about this one

listing. They're refinishing the floors, so I can't see the inside until next week, but I've been to see the outside twice, and I think this might be the one." It's the same one I found the night Miles first asked me about marrying Sarah. That was just over a week ago, but so much has happened since then, it feels like it's been a lot longer.

Theo shifts in his seat. "You already texted Shelby?" There's something like hurt laced through the question, and I look over at him.

"I mean, you gave me her number. Isn't that what you wanted me to do?"

"Of course it was," he says. "But then we didn't talk about it again. And now you're saying you've already found *the one*? And gone to see it twice? Just feels like you're making a lot of big decisions really fast."

I hear his words, but I also hear what he isn't saying. I'm doing it without him.

I don't want to hurt my brother. And I *do* care about what he thinks. But it's been nice to talk to Shelby and make decisions on my own without worrying about what it might mean for him.

I've never really done that before.

"I should have mentioned it to you," I say. "There's just been a lot going on the past few days."

He scoffs. "That's an understatement. Look, I already told you I don't care if you move. But I *do* care if you shut me out. You can't buy an ugly house, man. How can I make sure that doesn't happen if you don't tell me anything?"

"It's only been a week. And I'm taking you there right now."

"Good," he says.

"Good," I say right back.

We ride in silence for the rest of the drive, which only seems to punctuate Theo's obvious unease.

Our entire lives, every big decision we've ever made has always been a decision for both of us. Hockey has pretty much been our life since we were twelve years old, and now it's our career. Same team. Same position. Same city. Same apartment building.

I think we've both been aware it wouldn't always be like this, but knowing it and experiencing it are two different things.

And I'm ready to experience it. I *need* to, honestly. I think I'm at the point where my relationship with my brother depends on it.

I turn the truck onto a wide road flanked by sidewalks and dotted with streetlamps. On either side, enormous houses with immaculate lawns reach into the cloudy February sky.

A mile or so in, I turn right onto the driveway and wind my way up to the house. The house is vacant but all the exterior lights are on, so we can still make out a decent amount about the property. It isn't as big as the others I've looked at, but the house is on a larger lot with a long, winding driveway and a tree line running along one side that makes it feel private even though it's still in a neighborhood.

I stop my truck right in front, and I'm struck with the same sense I had last time I was here.

This is somewhere I'd really love to live.

"I like it," Theo says as he peers up at the porch. "Seems very you."

"In what way?"

Theo shrugs. "I don't know. It's nice but it's not flashy."

He shoots me a grin, reclaiming some of his typical levity. "Not half as nice as what I'll end up buying."

I open my car door and tilt my head toward the house. "Come on. No one's living here right now. Let's walk around and see the back."

Theo leads the way, and I follow him along a stone path that winds through a series of flower beds until it reaches a gate to the backyard.

The gate is locked, but Shelby gave me a key code, so I pull out my phone to retrieve it. Once I punch it in, the gate swings open.

"Whoa," Theo says as soon as we step through.

I can't blame him. So far, this is my favorite part of the house.

A covered patio with an outdoor kitchen is situated next to a huge pool, which, despite the chill in the air, is still clean and welcoming. It's probably heated. Beyond the pool, the expansive green lawn is surrounded by heavy woods. When I was here during the day, I could just barely make out the shape of another house through the trees on the far edge of the lawn, but in the summer when leaves grow in, I doubt I'll be able to see anything at all.

"I'd probably buy it just for this," Theo says, his hands pushed into his pockets. "And you've seen pictures of the inside?"

I nod. "Yeah, it seems great. At least from what I can tell."

He stares out at the water for a long moment. "You should do it, then."

"You think?"

He shoots me a look, one eyebrow raised. "You don't need my approval. You've already been out here twice. Unless you're asking me to live here too. In which case, only if I get to pick my bedroom first."

I push my hands into my pockets. "I'm sorry I didn't bring you the first time I came. I think I needed to do it by myself. And I maybe worried it would be weird for you."

He lifts his gaze to meet mine. "Weird that you're buying a house?"

"Maybe more that I'm moving away from you."

We don't say anything for so long, I wonder if the conversation is over. But then Theo shrugs. "It is a little weird. But that doesn't mean it won't be good for us." He's quiet for another beat before he adds, "You've been looking out for me for a long time, man. I've let you do it because you're the oldest. And you're good at it. And I've definitely had moments when I needed it. But I'm solid now. I can survive on my own."

"Survive? Yes. Get to practice on time..."

He scoffs. "You haven't had to wake me up for practice in years."

"What about the day after Thanksgiving?"

"Practice the day after Thanksgiving is criminal, so that shouldn't count. And I still would have gotten up. Just because I don't need thirty minutes to make my bed and iron my underwear before I leave the house doesn't mean I would have been late."

"That happened *once*," I say.

We were sixteen when I very nervously ironed every article of clothing I planned to wear before my first date—including my boxer briefs—and Theo has never let me forget it.

"Once is all it takes, man," Theo jokes. "But seriously. If you kept this to yourself because you were trying to protect me, stop. I'm fine. I'm happy for you. And maybe you'll inspire me to do the same thing."

I breathe out a sigh of relief. I maybe didn't realize I *was* protecting Theo, but it was pretty uncharacteristic that I came to see the house for the first time without him. He's the person I ask about everything.

But I guess that's about to change too.

Even if my marriage to Sarah won't be traditional, she'll still be my wife. Living in my house. Sharing my space. I already know she's easy to talk to, and we will be spending a lot of time together. By default, that probably means I'll talk to Theo less.

"So, when are you going to tell Mom?" Theo asks.

"The truth?" I ask. "Never."

"Obviously," he says. "I mean when are you going to tell her you're getting married? You know she follows your Instagram. You can't let her find out on the internet."

I breathe out a sigh. "I'll call her tomorrow."

"At least you already set her up for it," Theo says. "Even if it wasn't intentional."

I move to the edge of the pool and lower myself onto a deck chair. "I'm hoping she wants us to be married badly enough that she'll roll with the timeline as long as I promise I'm happy."

"Or she'll just think Sarah's pregnant."

My brain makes fast work of conjuring what it might be like to have that kind of a relationship with Sarah, and a sudden flush makes my cheeks warm. I clear my throat, forcing the thought away, hoping the low light might keep Theo from noticing, but based on his current smirk, he knows exactly where his words sent my thoughts.

He's annoying, but he's not wrong. Mom absolutely *will*

think Sarah's pregnant. But then, when the marriage happens so quickly, a lot of people will.

"You're probably right about that. But it's not like I can tell Mom the truth."

Theo chuckles. "No, you definitely can't. She'd tell half her neighborhood." He sits down across from me on a neighboring chair. "Are you going to make an offer?"

"I think so. Shelby says once the interior is open to showings, it'll sell quickly, so I don't want to lose it to someone else. We've got the first available appointment once the floors are finished."

"Will you let Sarah see it first?"

"She'll be in New York," I say. "She leaves this week for a two-week residency. If Shelby is right, it would be risky to wait for her to come back. I think she'll like it. There's a room above the garage that would make a perfect studio. Huge windows, tons of natural light. Hardwood floors."

Theo only stares.

"What?" I finally ask.

"Carter, are you buying a house because it has a good studio space for your *not-real* wife?"

"Of course not. I don't even know if it'll work. I just saw the picture and thought it might."

"Let me try this again," Theo says. "Have you been filtering properties based on whether they have good studio space for your not-real wife?"

"That's not—she also has to live in it," I say. "Paint in it. It's a very practical consideration."

Theo starts to laugh. "Oh, man, you are in so much trouble."

"I'm not," I say. "It's not like that."

"It is too like that. That's why you said yes—something

you can't deny because I was there when you decided. And so was Holly."

I can't argue with him. After we left the food drive, the three of us went out for a beer and outlined the three things I should ask for in exchange for saying yes to the marriage. At the time, fueled by their enthusiasm and one too many beers, it seemed like a perfectly decent list.

In retrospect, and especially after the game tonight when she wasn't there, I realize just how much of that enthusiasm is tied directly to my hope that eventually, I might have a relationship with Sarah for real.

"Okay, you're right," I concede. "But I'm trying really hard not to get ahead of myself."

"Smart," Theo says. "But I still think you should let Sarah see the house before you make an offer. Do a video call, send her the listing. Something."

"All right. I hear you. I'll call her. I'll give her a video tour before I make any decisions."

"Good," Theo says. He stands and offers me a hand. "See? You do need me."

"Don't let it go to your head," I say.

Theo grins like only a brother can. Then he turns and shoves me directly into the pool.

9

SARAH

IN THIS, THE AGE OF THE INTERNET, CARTER AND I DECIDED WE ARE unlikely to convince anyone we're actually in love enough to get married without photographic proof, so tonight, he's coming over for a photoshoot. Well, dinner first and *then* a photoshoot.

Nothing too fancy or professional. Just Anna and her iPhone. We only need them to work for Instagram, and she'll be able to handle that. But I'm still having a terrible time deciding what to wear. Anna said I need multiple outfits so it isn't obvious all the photos were taken at the same time, but I can't even come up with one.

Not to mention my hair. Should I wear it up or down? Glasses or contacts? These shouldn't feel like monumental choices, but I can't shake the feeling that if I get this wrong, this whole scheme will come crumbling down around me.

I reach into the back of my closet and pull out a box of sweaters I haven't touched since I got here. The one on the top looks decent, so I shrug it on.

Annnnd no, it doesn't look decent. I look like a square tomato.

I yank off the sweater and toss it onto the floor, then scoop up the pile of options I've amassed on my bed and carry it over to the main house in my jeans and tank top, my feet bare. The winter air nips at my exposed skin, but it's a short walk around the pool. Honestly, I'm surprised I don't fall in—I can hardly see over all the clothes I'm carrying—but I make it without incident and let myself into the kitchen, kicking the door closed behind me.

"I give up," I say as I drop the clothes onto the kitchen table. "I am completely incapable of making myself look hot enough to actually be married to a hockey player. He's going to look incredible, and I'm going to look like a bridge troll in glasses that are too big for my face. And do you see this?" I point at my forehead. "This beach ball of a zit showed up this morning because of course it did. The one time I actually *need* to look good in a photo, I look like I'm seventeen and struggling with my T-zone."

Anna bites her lip like she's trying really, *really* hard not to laugh. "Okay, maybe just take a breath," she says. "And..." She clears her throat. "Say hi to Carter?"

I freeze, mortification making me all but completely immobile. I give my head the tiniest shake. "Please tell me you're joking."

Anna grimaces. "Not joking."

I turn slowly, and there he is. Standing in the living room with Miles, looking every bit as gorgeous as I expected he would.

Heat spreads across my chest, and my heart starts pounding.

He's here.

And he just heard every single word of my rant right down to the mention of my T-zone.

"You're early," I say.

He glances at his watch. "Am I?"

I pull my phone out of my back pocket and stare at the screen. It's 6:40, which makes zero sense because the wall clock in my bedroom said it was 5:45 when I left the pool house.

Come to think of it, it *is* a little dark to still be 5:45.

Stupid clock. It must need new batteries. I've been so caught up in my own brain, I didn't even notice.

"Okay, so you're *not* early," I say. "But I am very much late."

Luckily, Anna comes to my rescue. "You know what? We're going to figure this out." She turns me toward the table and hoists the pile of clothes back into my arms before steering me toward her bedroom. "Miles, can you finish dinner?"

"I'll help you, Daddy," Poppy says. The last thing I see before disappearing down the hall is Carter lifting Olive into his arms.

"Well, that was a fun little freakout," Anna says as soon as we're alone.

I drop the clothes onto her bed, then faceplant beside the pile, groaning into her mattress. "I can't believe that just happened."

"If it's any consolation, you looked adorable through the whole thing."

I roll over and look up at her. "I doubt he even noticed. How could he notice anything but the giant zumor on my forehead?"

"Zumor?"

"A zit that feels like a tumor."

She chuckles, then pulls on my hands until I'm sitting up. "It can't be that bad," she says, but then she takes my face and tilts it upward to get a closer look. "Okay, it is that bad. But we can airbrush it out. I'm a whiz with Instagram filters."

"I don't want to be airbrushed."

"Do you want to look like a unicorn?"

I scowl at her, then drop back onto the mattress and pull a pillow over my face. "Can we just...cancel? Reschedule?"

"We cannot. You're leaving for New York tomorrow, and he's leaving the day after. It's now or never, kid."

I toss off the pillow and meet her gaze. "What if I'm really, *really* scared?"

Her expression softens. "Scared enough not to go through with it?"

I think about leaving Georgia, and my resolve hardens. "Not that scared."

She grins. "Good. Then let's put some makeup on that face and get this party started."

Fifteen minutes later, Anna has miraculously pulled four different outfit choices out of the stack of clothes that are cuter than any combinations I tried on my own, adding a wrap dress and a pair of heels she pulled out of her own closet. She's made my zumor almost undetectable with her exceptional makeup skills, and she's hyped me up to the point that I almost feel like I can do this.

"Just think," Anna says as she steers me toward the door. "You *aren't* going to miss Poppy's seventh birthday this fall. Isn't that exciting?"

"Good. This is good," I say. "What else?"

"Olive's first dance recital," Anna says. "And Fiona's first steps."

"I'll probably hear her first word," I say, hope springing in my chest, and Anna smiles.

"You totally will."

I slide my hands down the front of my dress—Anna's dress. "You're sure starting with the dress is the right choice?"

"It totally is. You look gorgeous. Absolutely worthy of a hot hockey player."

I groan as Anna nudges me out the door. I still can't believe Carter heard my ranting, but there's nothing I can do about it now.

Dinner is already on the table by the time we join everyone else. "You're sitting here, Aunt Sarah," Poppy says, motioning to a seat right next to Carter.

I glance over at him as I sit, and he offers me a small smile.

"Sorry about all that earlier," I say.

"Sorry about what?"

Is he really going to make me say it? I swallow against the nerves in my throat. "Just all my...ranting."

He gives me a quizzical look. "I don't remember any ranting. I just remember you walking in here wearing a great dress, looking really beautiful."

I gaze into his warm blue eyes, and something in my chest loosens, my whole body softening.

"Aunt Sarah?" Poppy asks, and I look across the table to meet my niece's eyes.

"What is it, sweetie?"

"Is Carter your boyfriend?"

My eyes widen at the question, but I do my best to reel in my shock. Of course Poppy would ask. She's always been observant, and Carter has been here twice in the last three days. Not to mention my freakout earlier, which Poppy witnessed.

I look over at Carter, who is watching me closely, eyes sparkling like he finds her question highly entertaining. "Um, yep," I finally say. "He sure is."

Poppy nods, like this is exactly the answer she expected. "Does that mean he'll be my uncle like he's Charlie's uncle?"

I look up to meet Anna's gaze. For all our talk of logistics, we didn't really cover how this relationship might impact the girls. Will they be sad when Carter's no longer around? I'm still floundering, trying to figure out how to respond, when Carter comes to my rescue.

"You want to know a secret, Poppy?" he says.

She nods, brown eyes wide and curious.

"I'm not really Charlie's uncle. But since I'm really good friends with her dad, she sometimes calls me Uncle Carter. Does that make sense?"

Poppy nods. "I think so. It's like my friend Kenya at school. She has seven aunties, but they aren't related. I told her that didn't make sense, and she told me sometimes family is family and sometimes friends are family."

"Right. Exactly," Carter says.

"Good answer, Poppy," Anna says, her voice soft.

Poppy scoops up a bite of her potatoes. "So can I call you Uncle Carter too?"

"If it's okay with your parents, it's okay with me," Carter says.

The conversation moves on, Poppy chattering about school and the book she read all by herself and her favorite teacher. But I can't stop glancing over at Carter, marveling at how easily he handled the exchange with Poppy.

And he doesn't stop there. For the rest of dinner, every time I get caught up in my own head, worried about what he's thinking or how things are going to go, Carter finds a way to put me at ease.

He tells a funny story about his brother. He pulls up pictures of Gordie on his phone. He even keeps the entire table enraptured with the story of how he found Gordie in a dumpster outside the Vortex when he was so tiny, his eyes were still closed.

"You wouldn't have believed it, girls," Miles adds. "Smallest kitten I've ever seen."

And Carter was the one who took it home.

Over dessert, he asks the girls to help him brainstorm what kind of painting he should have me create for him, something I sense is intentional. Like he's reminding me he's getting something out of our arrangement too.

Once Miles takes the girls upstairs to put them to bed, Anna leaves Carter and me in the living room with wine. "Drink," she says. "The next part of our evening will be easier if you're both relaxed. I'll be right back." She turns and heads into her bedroom, and then I'm alone with Carter for the first time all night.

I take a huge sip of wine. Several sips, actually.

Carter looks over and grins. "You okay over there?"

I give my head a little shake and set my glass on the fireplace mantel. "Just struggling to wrap my head around everything."

"Yeah, me too. I actually called my mom today."

My eyebrows lift. "To tell her about...us?"

He nods. "I figured she should know before she sees anything about it online."

"Right. Good call. How did she react?"

He shrugs. "She said she's happy for me, and she can't wait to meet you, and that was pretty much it."

I nod. "I guess that's good? I wish you didn't have to lie to her."

He winces the slightest bit. "Yeah. Me too. But she's too much of a talker. If she knew the truth, she'd definitely tell someone, even if just accidentally."

"Sounds like Anna's mom," I say. "She told the entire neighborhood Anna was pregnant with Olive before she'd had the chance to tell Miles. He was on the road, and she wanted to tell him in person, but then they went to a block party and her mom said something about a double stroller, and everyone figured it out."

"Exactly the kind of thing my mom would do," Carter says. "Nothing malicious. Just…"

"Misdirected excitement?" I say, and he nods.

"Yes. Perfect description. Or misdirected concern."

I feel my shoulders drop the slightest bit. I hate to think of his mom being concerned. But there's no way around it. She would be if she knew the truth.

Fortunately, Anna returns, phone in hand, sparing us from continuing our conversation. I pick up my wine glass and drain the rest of it, and Carter does the same. When he puts down his glass, he holds out his hand. "Ready to do this?"

I slip my fingers into his. "Ready as I'll ever be."

"Actually, don't move," Anna says. "You look good standing right there. Carter, can you put your arm around her?"

He looks down and meets my gaze. "If this ever gets weird or uncomfortable, just tell me, all right?"

I nod. "Right. Same," I say, then he slips his arm around my waist and tugs me into his side.

He smells good—like citrus and sandalwood, but the scent is light, not like he's wearing cologne. I never love it when a man's cologne lingers even after he walks away.

But this isn't that. It's subtle. Like I'm only going to notice he smells good if I get as close as I am right now.

There's something sexy about that. Like the scent is only meant for me.

Or. You know. Some other woman who isn't *pretending* to be in a relationship with Carter.

"Perfect," Anna says, looking up from her phone. "Now we only need to do it about fifteen more times."

My sister-in-law is a very good director, but Carter is the reason the whole photoshoot isn't horribly awkward. Mostly because the entire time we're taking pictures, with Anna directing us this way and that, he keeps up a running narrative of what our "date" is when each photo is taken.

"This is the night we played miniature golf for the first time," he says when Anna makes us put our coats on and pose on the front porch. "I won, by the way. Completely smoked you."

When we're standing by the stairs and he wraps his arms around me from behind, he leans close, his breath tickling the skin on my neck, and whispers, "This is the night we went to see a movie. Sadly, I stopped and bought myself a couple of chili dogs on the way and got sick, so you ended up watching most of the movie by yourself."

I stifle a laugh. "Did you just give yourself indigestion on one of our dates?"

"It made you smile, didn't it?"

"The smile is *perfect*," Anna says. "Whatever you're saying to her, Carter, keep saying it."

He absolutely *does* keep saying it. He talks about the time we spent his day off at the Atlanta Zoo. The night he discovered I have an obsession with nineties boyband music, which is weirdly specific and also—unbelievably—entirely true.

When Anna asks us to sit on the couch and snuggle up together under a blanket, he creates a ridiculous story about riding the Ferris wheel at the state fair and getting trapped at the top of the ride for so long that he had to pee in an empty water bottle to keep from wetting his pants.

"Carter, we can't have a pee story in our dating history. Not after the chili dogs."

Carter grins. "Just keeping it real. If we're getting married, there has to be at least one bathroom story."

"I appreciate you making all the embarrassing ones about you," I say.

I have to be grateful for Carter's strategy, because it absolutely works. In every single photo we take, my smile is completely genuine.

Somehow, with Carter's narration, the whole thing feels fun and a little silly instead of big and scary, which is what I expected going in. But more than that, I'm learning that Carter's presence just puts me at ease. Even though I fully expect it to, it never feels awkward to touch him, to let him wrap his arms around me or hold me close.

"What about a kiss on the cheek?" Anna says.

I look up at Carter, not wanting to push past any of his boundaries. As comfortable as he's seemed all night, I don't think he'll have a problem. "Is that okay with you?" I ask, and he nods.

"For sure."

I slip one hand onto his shoulder and push up on my toes. I've never dated a man this much taller than I am, and it's a nice change. I press a kiss to his jawline while he slips a hand around my waist.

I arch my back, my body curving into his as my lips hover just centimeters from his skin. Knowing Anna is taking photos, I stay where I am, breathing in the delicious scent of him.

His grip around my waist tightens, and my free hand lifts to his chest. He's warm and solid and he smells so good, and it's a good thing my sister-in-law is taking photos because I'm not sure I could be trusted otherwise.

"Oh, my gosh, this is perfect," Anna says. "Honestly, the two of you have really great chemistry. There's no way people won't believe this is real."

I immediately drop my hands and take a step back, Anna's words serving as a stark reminder that it *isn't* real.

It's not that I forgot. With Anna snapping photos, it would be impossible to forget. But I'm not sure I expected to enjoy it so much.

To enjoy *him* so much.

I take another step backward and adjust the brown V-neck I put on during our last wardrobe change.

"Good," I say, my voice sounding unnaturally high. "That's sort of the point."

Carter pushes his hands into his pockets. "Do you think we got enough?"

"Definitely," Anna says, scrolling through her phone. "We can totally make these stretch until you guys start spending time together for real."

I lift my eyes to Carter's. I wish I could read his expression.

Tonight has been fun. For me, anyway. And it seems like he's had a good time too. I'd like to think it will *keep* being fun. But after spending half an hour touching him, hugging him, feeling his strong arms wrapped around my body, I'm all too aware of how quickly this whole plan could go sideways.

That was Anna's concern—that I might have a hard time not blurring the lines. But relationships are about so much more than fun. And Carter is a man who, it bears reminding myself, agreed to marry me trusting that the marriage would not, under any circumstances, last longer than a year.

He's not expecting anything out of this, and neither am I.

Physical chemistry? Okay, *fine*. There's definitely a little. Maybe even a lot. But it doesn't have to mean anything. Not if we don't want it to.

And we don't.

Simple as that.

Simple. As. That.

After Carter says goodbye to Miles and Anna, I walk him to the front door. It feels like the least I can do considering what he's agreed to do for me.

"Are you excited for your trip?" he asks as he shrugs into his jacket.

In the dim light of Miles and Anna's entryway, his eyes look more gray than blue, and I find myself wondering what colors I would mix to get that exact shade.

I won't paint *him* for his Sarah Stone original, but that doesn't mean I won't paint him at all. It would be fun to see if I could truly capture the intensity of his eyes. I'm not sure painting him would qualify as *keeping it simple*. At least not when I consider what staring into those eyes seems to do to me.

"I think so," I say. "Maybe more nervous than excited."

"Why nervous?" he asks.

I shrug. "Um, I guess just because the Bainbridge is so well-connected with a lot of galleries in the area. It could mean a lot of exposure in front of people who have a lot of influence in the art world. I would love to get a show in New York, so it feels like there's a lot at stake, you know?"

Carter leans against the wall and folds his arms like he's in no hurry to leave. "Have you had shows before?"

"Lots. But mostly group things—or solo things at smaller galleries. But I have my first solo show here in Atlanta in March—over in Old Fourth Ward. It's a pretty big deal too, but New York would obviously be a step up from that."

He holds my gaze for a long moment. "I think it's really amazing what you do."

My chest warms at the compliment. They seem to hit differently when they come from Carter because they feel so sincere. "Did you write down all the ideas the girls gave you about what I should paint for you? I particularly liked the Bluey suggestion."

"I'm totally into Bluey," Carter says with a grin. "She's one of Charlie's favorites."

I smile at this. I really love how much he cares about Charlie. Holly is lucky to have him as a friend.

"Honestly, you can give me something you've already painted," he says. "I don't need you to create anything new. Or I could come to your show and buy something. That's the goal of these things, right? To sell everything?"

"No," I quickly say. "Absolutely not. I mean, yes, that's the point, but you are not buying anything at *any* of my shows. You're getting something custom. Something *free* and custom. And you aren't allowed to fight me on that because it's the only thing I'm truly giving you in this bargain."

His eyes lift as he smiles. "Don't forget the cat. You're also taking care of him."

"Of course! The cat. That makes *all* the difference."

Carter pushes his hands into the pockets of his coat. "The show that's here in Atlanta—will we be married by then?"

I do some quick math in my head. We haven't picked a specific wedding date yet, but we did say six weeks from now, which lands us somewhere in the middle of March. My show at Second Light Gallery is the last week of March, ten days before I was supposed to fly back to Canada.

It's wild to think that a few weeks ago, I fully expected to have that show and then say goodbye to Georgia for the foreseeable future. A wave of relief washes over me.

Not anymore.

Now I get to stay. All thanks to Carter.

"Um, yeah. It's at the end of March, so I guess we will be."

"Okay, then. I'll make sure it's on my calendar so I can come support you."

My eyes drop to the floor, even as heat climbs my cheeks. So far, my imaginings of life with Carter have been contained to our own individual interactions. I've thought about living with him, occupying the same space. But having him come to my show, introducing him to my peers, my friends, to gallery owners. Calling him my *husband*.

The idea has a certain appeal to it. I mean, *look at him*. Not to mention the general goodness he seems to radiate. But I don't want him to feel obligated. He's already going above and beyond; putting any further demands on him feels like too much.

"It's sweet of you to offer, but you really don't have to," I say. "I think as long as we're seen together *some*, you shouldn't have to worry about my art things."

"I don't know," he says. "Seems like it might seem suspicious if we aren't showing up for each other. I come to your shows. You come to the occasional home game. I'd be happy to support you in that way."

I wrap my arms around my middle and sink against the door, my stomach falling into my shoes. I especially can't expect him to show up for me when I can't do the same for him.

"Hey," Carter says gently when I don't respond. "Did I say something wrong? You went a little pale."

"No, I..." I clear my throat. "You're right. It's a perfectly reasonable expectation. It's only, I don't..." I pause and take a deep breath. "I guess Miles didn't tell you I don't go to hockey games?"

Carter lifts his eyebrows. "He didn't. So you don't go...just as a general rule?"

I nod. "It's complicated. And probably stupid. But I—" I close my eyes for the briefest moment and try to take a steadying breath.

"It's not that I don't *want* to be there," I say to Carter. "I just *can't* be there." I force myself to look up and meet his gaze. "And I would appreciate it if you didn't ask me why."

His eyes are troubled, his brow furrowed, but then he nods, taking on a more neutral expression. "Okay. I understand," he says. "I'm sure we can find plenty of other ways to be seen together."

Carter's words sound sincere, but there's definitely a distance between us that wasn't there before. It's my own fault, but there's no way I can talk to him about this. Not without digging into things I still struggle to talk about with my family, much less people I'm only just getting to know.

I was sixteen the first time I had a panic attack during a

hockey game. Miles was already in the NHL by then, playing for Boston before he was traded to the Jaguars. The team was in Winnipeg for a game, and Mom and I went to see him play. It wasn't the first time we'd been to games, but it was the first time Miles got into a *fight* during a game. Not just a hard hit against the boards, an actual fight. Fists flying, bodies scrambling.

In a flash, I was nine years old again, watching my father throw his fists into Miles over and over again.

I threw up into my popcorn bucket and white-knuckled it through the rest of the game. But the next time his team came to town, my body did the same thing. Reacted the same way even when he *wasn't* fighting.

The damage was done. I left before the end of the first period, and I haven't watched Miles play since.

"Thank you," I say, forcing my memories aside so I can give Carter my full attention. "And…I'm sorry."

"Don't apologize," he quickly says. "Going to hockey games was never part of our agreement. I assumed, but I didn't have a good reason to. It's really fine."

I take in his warm gaze, and some of the tension eases out of my shoulders. For a split second, I want to just tell him. Explain everything. But then my mouth goes dry, a sheen of sweat breaking out across my forehead, and I let the words die on my tongue. "You're too nice for your own good, Carter," I say instead.

He smiles. "Not the first time I've heard that one. But I promise I don't need you at hockey games to feel like I'm getting the better end of this bargain."

I roll my eyes. "You definitely are not."

"You haven't met the cat yet."

I stifle a laugh, appreciating that somehow, he's managed

to bring back a little levity to our conversation. "Should I be concerned?"

"Gordie's great," he says. "But he does like to chew through shoelaces, so you'll need to keep your closet door closed."

"Gordie," I repeat. "After Gordie Howe? I meant to ask before, but I didn't get the chance."

He lifts an eyebrow, like he's surprised by my hockey knowledge.

"I just said I don't *watch* hockey. Not that I don't *know* it. Miles is still my brother."

"Fair enough," Carter says. "So, when I come to New York next week, we'll just...meet after the game?"

The Jaguars' upcoming game schedule will take the team up to Montreal, then to New York, then finally to Boston before returning them home to Atlanta. The New York game hits in the middle of my second week in the city, so Anna suggested we get together for our proposal and make sure we're somewhere public, where a hockey fan or two might recognize Carter.

"I hope that's okay," I say. "Sorry I can't come to the actual game."

"Don't worry about it," he says. "I won't have a ton of time after, but I'll figure out a place we can go and text you the details."

"Sounds good," I say. "Thanks again for doing this. I'm still not sure I understand why you said yes."

Something I can't quite read flickers behind his expression, but then he smiles, looking a little chagrined. "I don't know what else to say. Your art is just that good."

"Stop it. It is not. And you have to promise you'll tell me if you decide to change your mind. If at any point you don't want to go through with it, all you have to do is tell me."

"I won't change my mind, Sarah," he says. "I gave you my word."

"Did you?"

He seems to think for a second. "I guess not officially. So here." He holds up his pinky.

"A pinky promise?"

He nods as I link my pinky around his. His skin is warm, and despite all the touching we've already done tonight, the contact sends a rush of sensation up my arm.

"You have my word, Sarah. You can trust me."

I may not understand how we ended up here or why he ever agreed to say yes. But for right now, wherever it may lead, I'm choosing to trust his pinky promise.

Here's hoping I don't regret it.

10

SARAH

I HAVE CARTER'S PINKY PROMISE ON MY MIND AS ANNA DRIVES ME TO the airport the following morning. That, and the text he sent me late last night, long after he went home.

At first, all that came through was a picture of Gordie, sitting next to a pair of what I assume are Carter's shoes, the shoelaces clearly chewed in half. Then his message popped up.

CARTER

Evidence of why you should be very concerned about living with Gordie. But also, I don't want you to keep score, Sarah. You have my pinky promise. We're doing this. No more talk about who owes who more.

I hearted his message and responded with a simple, *Thanks, Carter.*

"You okay over there?" Anna asks, and I drop my phone into my bag.

"Yep. All good. Just nervous."

"You're going to do great," she says as she pulls up to the curb outside of my terminal. "And you have the schedule for when and what to post next?"

"I've got it," I say. "Thanks for mapping it out for me."

"How's the post doing this morning?" she asks. "Have you checked?"

After Carter left last night, Anna helped me choose three of the photos we took. I wasn't sure about posting all three, but Anna suggested that posting multiple photos at once implies we've been seeing each other for a while. I added a caption that read, *Been spending time with someone special…* Then I tagged Carter's profile and hit publish.

"Six thousand likes already," I say. "And too many comments to read."

"Perfect. It's all happening according to plan!" She leans over and gives me an awkward hug, hindered both by her belly and the center console of her SUV. "I'm going to miss you."

"Same," I say. "Thanks for driving me."

Fifteen minutes later, I'm standing at the Delta counter, trying to figure out why my ticket says I'm sitting in seat 2A.

"I don't understand," I say to the ticket agent. "I didn't pay for first class. Did I just get lucky?"

She leans a little closer to her computer screen. "No, the upgrade was definitely paid for." That's all the explanation she offers before returning my boarding pass and passport. "Enjoy your flight."

I walk toward the closest security checkpoint, still scratching my head over who would have possibly upgraded my flight. Miles or Anna, maybe, but they know how fiercely I value my independence. Just because my brother makes millions doesn't mean I want him to spend any of it on me.

I step into line at the checkpoint, sighing as I look at the many, *many* weary travelers ahead of me. We're barely moving, so I pull out my phone to kill some time. I still haven't done the daily crossword puzzle, so I pull it up, but I'm only two clues in when my phone buzzes with a text from Carter.

CARTER

Here's the thing. If you really were my girlfriend, I'd make sure you flew first class anytime you traveled anywhere.

SARAH

It was you! I was just trying to figure it out.

CARTER

I hope you aren't mad. When I reached out to Anna for your flight info, she told me you like your independence. But if we're keeping up appearances…

Sneaky Anna. She drove me all the way to the airport and didn't tell me.

SARAH

I'm not mad. It was sweet of you.

CARTER

Enjoy your flight. I hope you have a great time in New York.

I heart his message, then switch back to my crossword puzzle, but I can't really focus.

I couldn't help but feel like I disappointed him last night, so to have him do something so thoughtful feels like a really big deal.

He can call it keeping up appearances, but to me, it just feels like kindness.

I pull up our text thread one more time. It feels like I should thank him somehow. Or at least show him I'm as concerned with his well-being as he is with mine.

I still wish I'd been able to tell him the truth about my panic attacks last night. I feel like if anyone would understand, he would, though I'm not sure *why* I feel that way. I don't actually know that much about Carter. He's mentioned his mom briefly, but I don't know anything else about his family or personal life.

It's wild that I trust him as much as I do—but Miles certainly has something to do with that. As annoying as my brother can be sometimes, he's a good judge of character. And he thought of Carter first when he hatched this entire plan. That has to mean something.

Finally through security, I settle in at my gate and pull up my Instagram post to look for any new reactions. There are hundreds of new likes and comments, but only one that Instagram has flagged as high priority, from a profile belonging to Kim Williamson. *So excited for you both!*

That has to be Carter's mom.

I click over to her account just to be sure. She only has one post—a picture of her standing between Theo and Carter in their Jaguars uniforms. Even though all three of them have the same eyes, her expression reminds me more of Carter, the same kindness and warmth I don't sense in Theo.

Back on my own profile, I heart her comment and follow her account—she already followed mine—then take a screenshot to send to Carter. He's tagged in my post, but I have no idea if he pays attention to his social media—I'm guessing he doesn't—and I think he'd like to see what his mom had to say.

Once the screenshot sends, I type out another message.

SARAH

Your mom is adorable. She just followed me on Instagram.

CARTER

She's pretty great.

SARAH

You have her eyes.

CARTER

We have her eyes.

SARAH

Maybe, but it's not quite the same. I see more of her in you.

CARTER

Tell that to everyone who can't tell me and Theo apart.

SARAH

Honestly, that baffles me. I could immediately tell you apart.

CARTER

Good to know we can't ever trick you by trading places.

SARAH

HAVE YOU ACTUALLY DONE THAT?!

CARTER

I'll neither confirm nor deny…

SARAH

Carter.

CARTER

Fine. Yes. But only once. It was right after my
dad died, and Theo had a chemistry final he
had to pass or he wouldn't graduate. He was
in no position to take a test, so…

My heart squeezes painfully in my chest. Carter lost his
dad? I had no idea.

SARAH

Okay. I rescind my judgment. That might be
the only acceptable use of twin powers.

I didn't know you lost your dad.

CARTER

Yeah. We were seventeen. Car crash.

SARAH

I'm really sorry. I was nineteen when my
mom died. Cancer.

CARTER

Man. What a terrible thing to have in
common.

SARAH

Yeah. The club no one ever wants to join…

But it's nice having people who understand.

CARTER

True.

SARAH

So, did Theo get an A on the test?

CARTER

Nah. I landed him a solid C-minus. Didn't
want to draw too much attention.

Actually, you're the only person I've ever told about that. Not even my mom knows. She would have been furious.

SARAH

Your secret is safe with me. I promise.

When he doesn't respond, I switch back to Instagram and scroll through the pictures I posted one more time. Fans are already having fun speculating as to whether the Sarah Stone snuggled up with Carter Williamson is related to the Miles Stone who captains his hockey team.

At the end of this week, I'll share a photo of the four of us, with a caption about hanging out with my brother and his wife, which should effectively end the speculation.

Then, after Carter and I go out after his game in New York, we'll announce that we're engaged. We'll have to take a new photo that night, featuring the ring that's currently tucked into an inside pocket of my carry-on. It's one of Anna's—a real diamond that I'm terrified of losing—but she insists the ring needs to look as real as the rest of our relationship. It's not anything like what I'd choose for myself—too gaudy, too showy, too heavy. But I'm not about to complain when she's loaning me something with so much value. I'm sure I'll get used to wearing it.

I read through the rest of the comments on the post, hoping I haven't missed any from people I actually know, but there are so many, it's hard to wade through them all.

I'm a little surprised by how many are from women mourning the fact that one of hockey's "favorite hotties" is off the market, but I have to laugh at all the responses pointing out that at least there's another one who looks just like him.

The only Instagram account I have is the one I use for my art, so at first, I debated whether it was the right platform for "relationship news." But my content is a pretty balanced combination of work and personal stuff, so ultimately, I decided it would be fine and my followers would likely enjoy hearing the news. If nothing else, they'll enjoy the view. Carter looks amazing in every single shot.

A few moments later, the flight attendant calls for first-class boarding, and I stand, feeling weirdly *aware,* like people might be looking at me, wondering what someone like me is doing flying first class.

But as soon as I settle into my very comfortable seat, I stop caring what anyone else might think. I could definitely get used to this kind of travel.

In the seat next to me, a boy around eleven or twelve is wearing a Georgia Jaguars jersey. I lean back, wondering if there's a player's name on the back, but with the way he's sitting, I can't quite tell.

It's not unusual to see team-branded gear or merchandise around Atlanta. Even down in Savannah where I was getting my master's degree. The Georgia Jaguars franchise is less than ten years old, so the fact they made it all the way to the Stanley Cup championships last season really amplified the team's local support.

Normally, I wouldn't pay attention to player names, but now that I'm pretending to be engaged to one, I find myself curious, even a little hopeful that it will be Carter's name I see printed across the boy's jersey.

It feels like such a ridiculous hope. But when the boy leans forward and tugs a pair of headphones out of his bag, I read the C. Williamson across the back of his jersey and feel a tiny twinge of victory.

I have no idea what I think I'm winning, but it feels like a good sign anyway.

It suddenly occurs to me that if I *were* dating Carter Williamson for real, I might handle myself differently if I found myself sitting next to a fan.

Or would I? Would I just ignore it? Would I say something?

What would Carter want me to do? I have no idea what protocol is when it comes to this sort of thing.

On the opposite side of the aisle, there's a couple also dressed in Jaguars gear. I make eye contact with the woman, and she offers me a polite smile. "I promise he won't be a bother," she says. "He's got a movie downloaded. He's a great traveler."

"I'm not worried," I say, returning her smile. "Did you come to Atlanta for a game?"

She nods. "His tenth birthday." She motions to her son. "It's his favorite team."

I look down at the boy. "And Carter Williamson—is he your favorite player?" This is so far outside of the norm for me. I don't talk to strangers. I get on flights and put on headphones and tend to feel resentful if I have to make eye contact with anyone.

I don't mind if someone talks to me.

I'm not horrible.

But I don't seek out opportunities to interact. And yet, here I am talking to a ten-year-old about hockey.

The boy's eyes widen. I doubt he expected me to know Carter's first name. "He's the best defender in the league," he says.

"Even better than his twin brother?"

He sits up a little taller, like he's more than ready to give me his reasons. "It's close," the boy says. "But I think Carter has a better eye for the game. He's a playmaker. He sets people up for shots that no one else can see."

The flight attendant appears, and the boy is momentarily distracted while his parents ask him about his menu preferences for dinner, so I take the opportunity to pull out my phone and text Carter. Something tells me he'd appreciate knowing I'm sitting next to a kid wearing his jersey.

SARAH

True story. I'm sitting on the plane next to a kid wearing your jersey. He came to Atlanta for his tenth birthday so he could watch a game.

CARTER

For real? That's awesome. Do you have a few minutes before you take off?

I frown at my phone screen, not sure why he's asking.

SARAH

I think so. People are still boarding.

I expect another message. Instead, I get a FaceTime call.

I accept the call and suddenly, Carter is filling my phone screen.

Well. More like Carter's torso. His *bare* torso. Something flutters low in my belly at the sight of all that toned skin, but then Carter's head pops through the top of his t-shirt, and he slides the fabric into place, blocking my view. As soon as I see his face, a knot of tension at the base of my sternum loosens and unwinds. He offers me a warm smile. "Hey, gorgeous."

My cheeks heat. My brain knows he's only pretending, but my body is clearly struggling to get the memo. "Hi," I say, proud of how normal I sound.

"Sorry," he says, offering me a sheepish grin. "I realized right after I hit call that I should probably put a shirt on."

I shift and turn my back to the wall of the airplane so there's no way the kid sitting next to me can see the screen. "What are you doing?" I ask, dropping my voice to a whisper. "What's happening right now?"

"Put the kid on," Carter says.

I turn down the volume on the call, glancing at the boy next to me. But he's still leaning over the aisle talking to his mom. "What?"

"The kid sitting next to you," Carter says. "I thought I could wish him a happy birthday."

Of course he does. Because he's Carter. And this is exactly the kind of thing he would do with his fans.

"Um, okay. Hang on," I say. I mute the call and set the phone face down on my tray table, then look over at the little boy. "So, listen, if it's okay with your parents, I've got someone on the phone who would like to say hello to you."

His eyebrows lift. "Who is it?"

I smile. "I don't think you'll be disappointed." I look up at his parents, and they nod their approval, though the dad's expression is slightly wary, like he can't quite decide if he should trust me yet. "What's your name?" I ask the boy.

"Aidan," he says, and I nod.

I pick the phone back up and say to Carter, "This is Aidan. And this"—I hand the phone over to Aidan—"is Carter Williamson."

"What's up, Aidan?" Carter says, his voice warm. "I hear you just had a birthday."

I make eye contact with Aidan's parents one more time and smile, then I listen to five minutes of the most adorable conversation I've ever heard.

Carter is *amazing*. Kind. Solicitous. Complimentary of Aidan. He asks him questions about hockey, then really listens, paying attention to every single word, like a ten-year-old's opinions on the game are vitally important. Eventually, another voice sounds through the line.

"Who are you talking to?" the voice says. It's similar enough to Carter's that it has to be Theo.

"Oh my gosh, oh my gosh, oh my gosh!" Aidan says, one hand gripping his hair like he can't believe what's happening.

"Hey, Aidan," Theo says after Carter explains the call. "What's this I hear about my brother being your favorite?"

"You're both amazing," Aidan says. "He's barely ahead. You're basically tied!"

"Hey, now," Carter says. "I liked being your favorite."

Theo laughs. "It's all right, Aidan. I'll let him have the win. He gets so few of them."

At the front of the plane, the flight attendant motions for me to wrap it up, and I nod.

"Time to say goodbye," I say loud enough for all participants of the FaceTime call to hear me.

Aidan says his goodbyes, then I take the phone. "That was amazing," I say, my voice a little quieter.

"It was fun," Carter says. "Text me when you land?"

I nod. "Okay."

His eyes shift, and he looks to his left before pulling the phone a little closer. "Fly safe. Love you."

My heart falls into my stomach as my entire body flushes with heat.

I *know* he's pretending. *Of course* he's pretending.

But somehow, every new situation we find ourselves in feels like a situation I'm not prepared for. I have no idea how to reconcile what my brain knows—this isn't real—with how my *body* reacts.

My gaze darts over to Aidan, who is watching with rapt attention.

So I guess we're doing this.

I look back at Carter. "Love you too."

The call disconnects, and I drop my phone into my lap, then shove my hands between my thighs to keep them from trembling. It's ridiculous that I'm reacting like this. But those words just felt so *real*.

A twinge of sadness pings around in my heart.

I've never said *I love you* to a man before.

It hurts to think that I just did for the first time...and I didn't mean it.

"Carter Williamson is your boyfriend?" Aidan asks from beside me.

I manage to smile at him. "He sure is."

"Best birthday present *ever*," Aidan says. "Thanks for calling him."

"That was all him," I say. "I texted him and told him you were sitting next to me, and he called me."

Aidan's parents pipe up next, offering their own thanks. The whole exchange really was so fun, but I'm too distracted to truly appreciate their gratitude. My own feelings feel too difficult to sort out. I feel oddly proud, which doesn't make sense because I'm not in a real relationship with Carter. But I also feel a little bit sad. This man is kind and generous and good. Am I taking advantage of that? Of his generosity?

When my phone buzzes in my hand, I scramble to open the screen. I don't realize I'm hoping for a message from Carter until I see one and immediately feel relief.

CARTER

I hope that was okay. I know we didn't talk about it, but it felt like a good way to end the conversation since I knew they were probably listening.

SARAH

Good thinking. They were listening, so it was the right call.

CARTER

It felt weird to say it. But it probably won't be the only time we do. Maybe it's good we got the first one out of the way?

SARAH

True. Do you think it will get easier?

CARTER

I'm sure it will. We'll get the hang of things.

SARAH

I'm trusting your confidence here.

CARTER

We're going to be fine. I promise.

SARAH

Okay. Turning on airplane mode.

CARTER

Text me when you land. Fly safe.

Another text pops up, this one from Anna. It's a picture of the girls sitting at the island in her kitchen, their hands and faces covered in rainbows of finger paint. Their smiles are wide and happy; I can just see the beginning of Poppy's missing front tooth growing in.

ANNA

> They miss you already! Forget New York and come home.

I love the image, then send a quick response.

SARAH

> Kiss them for me. Back in two weeks!

I sink back into my seat, thinking of how different leaving the girls would feel if I knew I wouldn't see them but a few times a year. There aren't words to describe my sense of relief. And that's all thanks to Carter.

11

CARTER

Shelby meets me at the house late on a Thursday afternoon. The Jaguars leave for a week on the road first thing tomorrow morning, so I'm glad it worked out that I can see it now. We've already got paperwork for an offer ready to go. If I like what I see today, I'll sign, and Shelby will have everything she needs to negotiate and work out the details while I'm gone.

Assuming Sarah *also* likes the house. Which is definitely an important piece of this.

She's been in New York just over a week, and I'm already itching to see her again. She's on my mind pretty much all the time, which somehow feels both reckless and inevitable.

We still don't really know each other—that makes it reckless. But we're about to announce our engagement, so how can I *not* think about her? I'll see her the day after tomorrow, and I'm already counting down the hours.

Since she posted about our relationship and tagged my account, I've been inundated with messages from family and old friends and former teammates.

The captain from my AHL team, Alec Sheridan, called and said I owe him a phone call with a very thorough update.

And Mom texted to say she was happy we'd finally gone public so she can talk about it with her friends. I honestly didn't expect her to wait, so I'm impressed by her restraint.

Even after eight years of playing professional hockey, I still feel surprised when people I know respond to news they hear about me...*not from me.* Instead, they read about it on social media or see a headline on ESPN. Generally, I try to avoid all the social media stuff. The team has people who will let me know if there's anything I should be concerned about.

But this time, I find myself itching to look, to see what people think of Sarah and me together, especially now that everyone knows she's Miles's sister.

I push my hands into my pockets and look toward Shelby's car. She's gotten out, but she's on the phone, leaning against her driver's side door. She looks up and makes eye contact, mouthing a *sorry* as she holds up one finger.

I wave to let her know I'm fine. While I wait, I pull out my phone and text Sarah, letting her know I'm at the house and that within the hour, I should be able to call her so she can look at the place with me.

We've been texting quite a bit since she left, not about anything in particular. Just casual stuff. How much she loves to read. My secret ability to identify all eighty-eight constellations in the night sky. She told me a little about growing up in Canada. And I outlined all the things I both love and hate about having an identical twin.

She shared the playlist she listens to when she's painting, and I've been playing it in my truck every time I drive anywhere. We have surprisingly similar tastes in music. Well, sort of. If you subtract the nineties boybands and add in a little bit of nineties country, *then* we'd be almost entirely aligned.

Everything that brought us to this point happened so fast, it's been nice to feel like we're getting to know each other. There's also a certain safety in texting. A distance that makes it easier to ignore how attracted I am to her.

The one thing we haven't talked about is her childhood. She's mentioned a few vague things about Canada, but mostly, she steers clear of anything that even hints at her life growing up.

I have to believe that has something to do with why she doesn't go to hockey games. I won't say I wasn't disappointed when I found out I'll never see her cheering in the stands. Having family support is a big part of hockey culture. Then again, she isn't my *real* family, so do I really have the right to be disappointed?

I don't know a lot about Miles and Sarah's history, but I know they went through some stuff. And I definitely got the sense her reason for avoiding hockey games runs deep.

I hope she'll eventually trust me enough to tell me, but she asked me not to ask, so I won't.

Still, it triggers something in me—some need to protect, to make sure she knows she will always be safe with me.

Finally, Shelby drops her phone into her bag and hurries up the driveway. "So sorry to keep you waiting," she says. "I've got another deal that's supposed to close tomorrow, and my buyers are getting cold feet, so that was me talking them off a ledge."

"It's no problem," I say.

She glances behind us, eyes scanning the driveway. "I wondered if you might bring Theo to give you an extra opinion."

Funny she should ask. I *did* ask Theo to come, but he declined, saying he thought it might be uncomfortable for Shelby if he did. I pushed him for more information, wanting to make sure he didn't play her in a way that would require me to apologize on his behalf. He swore he didn't. She just felt more of a spark than he did and was really disappointed when he called things off.

Shelby is beautiful and very much Theo's type. And she's been pleasant and easy to work with, so I'm not sure what Theo didn't see in her. But he's been cagey about relationships lately, talking less than he usually does. It makes me think he's hiding something, but I couldn't begin to guess what.

"No, he couldn't make it," I say. "He had somewhere else to be today."

She gives me a pointed look. "In other words, he just didn't want to see me?"

I respect her too much to lie to her, so I offer her a grimace. "Sorry. He said he thought it might make you uncomfortable."

She huffs out a laugh as she unlocks the house. "That man—I swear, one day he's going to make a woman very happy. But it might take a miracle worker to get him to open his heart."

I study her, not sure how to sync up this version of events with what Theo told me. Maybe she misread the whole situation, but knowing what Theo has been through, it wouldn't surprise me if he has a hard time opening up in romantic relationships.

I have no response to Shelby's comment—I won't utter a word against my brother in any circumstance—and she must realize as much because as soon as we're in the entryway, she claps her hands. "Okay! Let's look around," she says.

I walk through the entire house, but at this point, it feels more like a formality. The interior is great. And the room over the garage really will be perfect for Sarah.

Shelby has been trailing me, pointing out her favorite features as we move from room to room. "So what do we think?" she asks as we make our way back to the kitchen.

"Pretty sure I want it," I say. "I just need to call my girl-friend and make sure she agrees." To my surprise, the word *girlfriend* rolls right off my tongue, no hesitation.

Shelby's eyes widen. "Oh, fun! I didn't realize. She'll be moving in with you?"

"I hope so," I say. "I'm about to propose, so that's the goal."

"Yay!" Shelby says, looking genuinely excited for me. "That's seriously so great. I'm sure she's going to love it."

"Sarah's in New York for work or she would be here," I say. "But I'd like to FaceTime her so she can see it before we make an offer." I pull out my phone and hold it up. "Do you mind if I…"

"Go right ahead!" Shelby says. "I'm just gonna head back to my car and answer some emails. Should I come back in about twenty minutes?"

"That's perfect," I say. "Thanks, Shelby."

I pull up Sarah's contact info and initiate the call. Even though I texted and gave her a heads up and she told me this morning she'd definitely be available, when the phone rings three, then four times without her answering, I start to worry I've somehow missed her.

"Hey!" she finally says as her face pops onto my screen. "Sorry. I was painting, and I had to scramble for the phone."

"Sorry to disturb you," I say.

"No! This is great. I'm due for a break. How's the house? Do you love it?"

She must have the phone propped up on something, because her hands are both free. She's sitting on a stool, and I can see a palette of paint on a table beside her, so I'm guessing the phone is on her easel.

She lifts her hands to the small of her back and stretches. Her hair is up, a scarf tied around it, and she's wearing her green glasses. My favorite ones. Her eyes are bright, her face a little flushed, and she looks really, *really* beautiful.

"Where are you right now?" I ask.

"At the Bainbridge. Studio hours are over, but I was in the groove, and I didn't want to stop. And since I'm staying upstairs, I figured, why not?"

Her first night there, she gave me a video tour of her very tiny accommodations—a two-hundred-square-foot apartment above the art studio. Tiny bed, tiny couch, tiny bathroom, very tiny kitchen. Sarah went on and on about how charming it was, but it's so small, I'm not sure I would even make it through the door frames without having to duck.

"What are you working on?" I ask.

"You really want to talk about this now? I thought you wanted to show me the house."

"I'm not in a hurry," I say. "Tell me."

Her eyes shift, like she's looking past me. Likely at her artwork. "It's a piece for my show at Second Light. All the pieces will be demonstrations of mood, but I'm only using facial expressions. So people in isolation, no setting, no background. Just their faces with the rest of their head and shoulders dissolving into the background."

"Sounds...difficult?" I say, and she grins.

"Yeah, I've second-guessed my decision about ten million times. I've got a few done already that I feel really good about, but the woman I'm painting now is giving me trouble. I was going for curious, but...I don't know. What I *want* her to say and what *she* wants to say—they aren't lining up."

"Is this woman someone in particular?" I ask.

"No," she quickly says. "I mean, yes. But only inside my head. I made her up. I almost always make them up, and I usually have a pretty good idea of what their story is when I start. But this time—she isn't cooperating."

"Hmm."

"Hmm? What's that supposed to mean?" she asks, a playful fire in her eyes.

"It means I'm not an artist and won't even begin to pretend like I know what I'm talking about."

"But?" she prompts.

"But...I don't know. I was just thinking that in hockey, there's a certain rhythm to the game that's often the same. And when you play it a lot, you get good at reading it. At sensing where the puck's going to go. Where the play is going to happen. But sometimes my instincts will flare and tell me to do the exact opposite of what I would *usually* do. And suddenly, I'm going a different direction, or passing instead of taking a shot. I don't always know why that happens. I'm sure I'm reading the game, but sometimes it happens so fast, I don't always know what I'm reading. I'm just...*feeling*." I clear my throat, suddenly feeling a little sheepish. "I know it's not the same. But I think my point is that sometimes the exact opposite of what we usually do is the thing that works."

She bites her lip and gazes past me one more time. "So maybe I should stop trying to force her to feel how I want her to feel and let her tell *me*?"

"Maybe?" I say. "Or you could completely ignore me because I have no idea what I'm talking about."

"No," she says, cupping a hand around the back of her neck. "That's good advice. I can't force it."

"I'm sure you'll get there," I say.

She takes a deep breath. "Thanks. So...the house? How is it?"

Instead of telling her, I flip my camera around and show her. We walk through the bedrooms, then into the kitchen and around the rest of the house. Finally, I head down the hall and take the stairs that are just off the kitchen to the bonus room above the garage.

"So, I saved the best part for last," I say as I step into the room. I push the door all the way open and aim the camera at the large windows filling up the east wall. "I was thinking this could be your studio."

I slowly pan the phone around the large, open space. "You could paint over here by the windows where the light is best. The house has a southern exposure, but with the way the trees are situated in the backyard, you should get really good light pretty much all day long. Then back here on the opposite wall, there's tons of space for storage. I'm just brainstorming—you could use the space however you want. But you definitely have options."

Sarah is quiet for so long, I start to wonder if I've said something wrong. I quickly flip the camera around so she's seeing my face again.

"Hey," I say. "You can totally ignore my suggestions. And if you don't like the house or if there's another space you like better, we can—"

"Carter," Sarah says softly, cutting me off. "That's not it.

I'm just feeling a little overwhelmed. I've never had my own studio space—not like that."

I shrug. "Well, you should. You deserve it."

"Are you going to buy it?" she asks.

"I want to," I say. "As long as you like it too."

She bites her lip, and I can tell she's struggling not to protest.

She doesn't *want* me to ask her opinion on stuff like this, because she doesn't think she has the right to one. I'm not sure why. When it comes to her art, to her career, she is her own best advocate. But with everything else, I get the sense she's constantly trying to earn her keep and *not* seem like an inconvenience.

I see the value in being useful, and there's a lot of talk about her staying in the States because she'll be needed when Anna has her baby. But I don't think that's truly at the core of why they want her to stay. She's family. They want her around because they love her. Not just because she's willing to babysit.

"Don't make a big deal out of it," I say, and Sarah swivels her gaze from her painting back to me. "I would want your opinion even if you weren't going to live in the house. Just tell me if you like it."

Finally, she lets herself grin. "Fine," she says. "I really love it. Really, *really, really* love it."

"Good," I say, returning her smile. "That makes me happy. I guess I need to go sign some paperwork, then."

She lifts her hands over her head in a celebratory cheer that's completely adorable. "I'm going to see you in a couple of days, right?" she asks. "Is that still the plan?"

"Definitely," I say. "I'm looking forward to it."

Downstairs, it sounds like Shelby is back inside, so I turn and head toward the kitchen.

"Hang on," I say to Sarah. "I think the realtor just came in."

"I can just let you go," Sarah says, but I shake my head no.

"Not yet. Just give me a sec."

Shelby is standing at the kitchen counter, iPad turned on in front of her. She looks up and smiles wide as soon as she sees me. "Is she still on the call?"

Next thing I know, she's plucked the phone out of my hands and is saying hello to Sarah, gushing about the house.

"I just know you're going to love it," Shelby says to Sarah. "Trust me. The bathrooms are incredible. And the kitchen! You two will be so happy here."

"I already love it," Sarah says.

"Have you seen the pool?"

"Oh, um, not yet, but I'm sure I'll see—"

"I can show you right now!" Shelby says, standing and moving toward the patio door. "It's almost dark outside, but the pool lights are on, and honestly, I think it looks more beautiful at night."

I follow behind her, wondering what Sarah is making of this unexpected interaction.

"Okay, well, I'll give you back to Carter," Shelby eventually says. She eyes me, then looks at Sarah one more time. "You sure are getting a good one with this man."

Shelby hands me the phone, and I carry it inside and into the primary suite off the kitchen so I can say goodbye to Sarah without an audience.

"Well, she was...enthusiastic," Sarah says as soon as we're alone.

"Sorry. She just grabbed the phone. Didn't even really give me a choice."

"I noticed," Sarah says. "She seems nice."

"Yeah, she is. She's been helpful."

She presses her lips together like there's something else she wants to ask, but then she gives her head a little shake, and I sense the moment has passed. Sarah confirms as much by stretching her arms over her head and stifling a yawn. "Okay. I think it's time for me to call it a night. I need food. And my tiny sofa in my tiny apartment."

"No night on the town for you, huh?"

"Takeout and terrible television is more my speed these days."

"I wish I could join you," I say, "except I don't think your couch could handle both of us."

She laughs. "Definitely not."

"I'll see you in a couple of days," I say, and she smiles.

"Goodnight, Carter."

I say goodnight, then disconnect the call.

Two more days. Two more hockey games.

Then I'll see her again.

I've never looked forward to back-to-back road games quite so much.

12

SARAH

THE BAINBRIDGE STUDIO IS CLOSED TO THE PUBLIC ON FRIDAYS, SO I start my day without any idea of how I'd like to spend it. I could go downstairs to paint, but I need a minute away from my canvas before I fixate so much on changing it that I wind up ruining it instead.

At this point in the process, tiny changes can make a huge impact for good *or bad*. So I have to tread carefully. The best way to do that is to give myself some breathing room and not try to force it.

At least, if Carter's advice holds any weight.

Carter. Thinking of him stirs up all kinds of uncomfortable feelings. I'm well aware that my tiny freakout after our last phone call was unreasonable.

Too aware.

But I couldn't help it.

First, he walked me through a *stunning* house because for some ridiculous—possibly chivalrous—reason, he thinks he needs my approval to buy it. Then he showed me the most incredible studio space I've ever seen and talked about it like he'd already given serious thought to how I might use it effectively.

It was amazing. Generous, thoughtful—as kind as I have grown to expect Carter to be.

And then, we were back downstairs and I was face-to-face with his very beautiful realtor, and suddenly and completely irrationally, I wanted to jab my fingernails directly into her perfectly made-up eyeballs.

The jealousy that welled up inside me as soon as Shelby's face filled my phone screen was sudden and fierce, and I really did not like the way it made me feel. Mostly because it came completely out of the blue.

My phone buzzes from my nightstand and I reach for it, somehow hoping it both is and is not Carter at the same time.

It isn't Carter—the disappointment swirling in my gut makes my *true* feelings clear—but it *is* Emerson, my closest friend from SCAD, which is an unexpected surprise.

EMERSON

SARAH. You're in New York right now.

SARAH

Yes? Why do I feel like I've done something wrong?

EMERSON

You've done nothing wrong. I'm just stalking your Instagram. Your account AND the Bainbridge account. LOOK AT YOU GO.

SARAH

Aww. Thanks. It's been an amazing experience so far.

EMERSON

I'm glad, but that's not why I texted you. I texted to say…

I AM ALSO IN NEW YORK RIGHT NOW.

SARAH

Shut up. You are? Why?

EMERSON

Does anyone truly need a reason to be in
New York?

SARAH

In February? Yes. Yes, they do.

EMERSON

Fine. True. Do you remember me mentioning
Jeremy?

SARAH

The violinist?

EMERSON

That's him. He's from Long Island. We're
here for the weekend to meet his family.

Instead of responding to Emerson's message, I immediately call him.

He answers on the first ring.

"Um, we're just working that into a random text message like it's no big deal? You're meeting his family?"

"Do you like how I did that?" Emerson says.

"So this is pretty serious between you two," I say, sitting up and tugging my comforter around my shoulders. My temporary apartment is nice, but I've had the toughest time keeping it warm. Which is odd because it shouldn't be difficult to heat two hundred square feet.

"Yeah, it really is," he says. "Not that I have any desire to talk about me. I told you I've seen your Instagram, woman. You have *a lot* to tell me."

I've been posting pictures of my residency all week, so I'm

not surprised Emerson wants all the details, and he's exactly the friend I would love to share them with.

"Where are you?" I say. "Want to meet for coffee?"

"I was hoping you'd ask that," Emerson says. "Because I'm actually outside the Bainbridge and I already *have* coffee."

I practically squeal as I jump out of my bed. "Shut up! Are you serious? I'm coming down right now." I toss on a hoodie and fly down the stairway that leads into the studio. There's a side door into a narrow alley, and I prop it open with a loose brick that's left on the stoop for precisely this purpose and run up to the sidewalk to look for Emerson. It's absolutely frigid outside, so I'd better not have to look long. Thankfully, he's only a few yards away.

"Emerson!" I call, and he spins around. I haven't seen him in almost a month, and the sight of his lanky frame makes me so incredibly happy. He has a little more facial hair than he did the last time I saw him, but everything else is just the same.

"Have you lost your mind?" he asks as he walks toward me, two coffee cups in his hands. "Your feet are bare."

I reach up to give him a hug which he only partially returns because of his full hands.

"Please don't make me spill," he says as I squeeze his neck. "These lattes were ten dollars apiece."

"Are they dusted with gold?" I ask, dancing back and forth to keep my toes from freezing to the sidewalk. "Come on. Let's get back inside."

Once we're back in my tiny accommodations, I grab a pair of socks from my suitcase and a blanket from the bed. Emerson unwinds his scarf from around his neck, but I stop him.

"You should probably keep it on," I say. "I think my heat is broken."

"Your heat?" he says, lifting his thick black eyebrows. "That sounds like a Bainbridge problem. If you're cold, call them."

I wave a hand away. "They're letting me stay here for free. It's not a big deal."

"You aren't staying for free. You're painting. Bringing in patrons. This is a residency. Not a hostel."

"It's fine. I only have a few more days. It's really not a big deal."

He rolls his eyes. "Must you be so long-suffering? Complain a little! Make demands!"

I toss the blanket at him. "Stop it and give me my coffee."

We settle onto the couch with coffee and a couple of croissants Emerson miraculously pulls from his inside coat pocket. They are a tiny bit smushed, but they are no less delicious for it, so I cannot complain.

"This is the best surprise ever," I say as I take another bite of the buttery croissant. "How did you know I was here?"

"I told you. Instagram," he says.

"No, I know. But *here* here. Did you know the Bainbridge has living quarters attached?"

"I didn't. I actually thought I'd find you working. Is the studio closed today?"

"It's always closed on Fridays," I say.

"Then all of this makes more sense," he says, motioning to my pajama-clad self. "So how has it been? Amazing? I'm sure it's been amazing."

I can't help but smile. "It totally has been. Everyone has been so supportive, and I've met some incredible artists. I've loved every second of it."

"Was I correct in thinking I saw a photo of you with Calista Reinhart? Isn't she the gallerist from the Rooke?"

"She is, and I absolutely freaked out when she stopped by. She wants me to come by the gallery on Sunday morning for tea."

"Shut up. Is she going to offer you a show?"

"I have no idea. I really don't want to get my hopes up, but she had great things to say about the piece I was working on, and...I don't know. It was really good talking to her."

"You know she's *from* Georgia, right?" Emerson says. "She went to SCAD."

"She told me."

"I went to a guest lecture she did my freshman year—it was brilliant." Emerson studied interior design at SCAD, but it's totally like him to attend all the guest lectures no matter the department. "Anyway, I'm super excited that might happen for you, but that's not what I want to talk about right now."

"Right!" I quickly say. "You and Jeremy! I want to hear all about it."

Emerson stares at me like I've grown a third eyeball in the middle of my forehead. "Are you serious right now?"

"Of course I'm serious. Why wouldn't I be?"

"Sarah. We are not talking about my very boring, very normal relationship when you are dating a professional hockey player."

I press my lips together. Of course he wants to talk about Carter, but I'm not actually sure I *can* without telling Emerson the whole entire truth. That's the kind of friendship we have.

When Carter and I hashed out details of how this would work with Anna and Miles, we came up with a list of insiders who would know the actual truth about our relationship. I didn't put Emerson on it, but I should have. Now that we're together in person, lying to him feels impossible.

"Right," I say. "I guess you would want to know about that."

"You think?" he says. "Spill it. I need all the details."

I bite my lip, considering my options. I want to tell Emerson, but I can't do that unless I clear it with Carter first. We agreed on the list, and I won't violate his trust.

"Hang on one second," I say to Emerson. Then I reach for my phone and squeeze myself into my very tiny bathroom.

Carter answers almost immediately.

"Hey," he says, and I close my eyes, the sound of his voice already making me feel better. Steadier somehow.

"Hi. How are you?"

"At the airport about to take off," he says.

"Right. You play in Montreal tonight."

"And New York tomorrow." He pauses for a beat before adding, "I can't wait to see you."

I can tell by the sounds around him that he isn't alone. He's probably with teammates, so I shouldn't put any stock in his words. But it still feels good to hear them.

"Yeah. Me too," I say. "So, listen, I just ran into a friend in the city. An old friend from SCAD, and we're catching up and having coffee and I think...I'd like to tell him the truth." I pause and take a breath. "About us."

Carter is silent for a long moment before saying, "Okay. Do you..." He pauses and clears his throat. "Do you mind if I ask why?" His voice is almost strangled, like he's fighting really hard to get the words out.

"Um, I guess just because we're really close and it feels wrong not to be honest?"

He scoffs. "Hang on. Let me get somewhere private." I hear some shuffling, then a creaking door, then stillness. I'm struck by the image of him trying to cram his six-foot-four frame into an airplane bathroom just so he can talk to me, and I smile as I picture it, even if I am struggling to understand why he sounds upset.

"Sorry about that," he says. "I guess I just want to know what you mean by close. How close?"

Oh, my gosh. Suddenly, I know exactly why Carter is having such a hard time. And the thought makes me perfectly giddy.

"Carter Williamson," I say, my tone turning playful. "Are you jealous?"

"What? No," he quickly says. "I'm just...curious. And I've never heard of this guy, so I want to make sure you trust him."

"Uh-huh," I say.

"I'm not—" he says, but then he breathes out a sigh. "I'm sorry. I overreacted. If you trust whoever this is, then of course you can tell him."

"It's my friend, Emerson," I say pointedly. "We went to SCAD together, but he's currently in New York visiting his *boyfriend's* family."

"Right," Carter says slowly. "Emerson has a boyfriend."

"He does," I say. "And they're very much in love."

"I just made a fool of myself, didn't I?"

"Yes," I say. "But it's okay because I actually think it was kind of cute."

"I'm sorry," he says again. "There are parts of this...I know they aren't real, you know? But sometimes they feel real. I want you to tell me if I ever overstep."

A sense of relief washes over me that we're dealing with

similar struggles. "I get it," I say. "And I've had similar moments. Last night I felt a weird and totally irrational urge to leave Shelby a one-star review on Google. Just because of how pretty her eyes are."

"Shelby, who once dated my brother and is still hung up on him?"

"I didn't say it was valid," I argue. "Just that she was there, in the same room with you, with those gorgeous eyes."

"I guess we're even, then," he says. "So moving forward, no review-bombing innocent realtors?"

"And no stressing over very gay best friends."

"Done," he says. "But Sarah, I shouldn't have reacted the way I did. I trust you. You don't ever have to justify your choices to me."

"I appreciate that. And same. Side question: are you hiding in an airplane bathroom?"

"Yep," he says.

"Can you even stand up all the way?"

"I cannot."

I let out a giggle. "I'll let you get back to your seat. See you tomorrow?"

"I can't wait," he says, then the call disconnects.

I stand and stare at the mirror, fighting my smile. I made Carter jealous. I probably shouldn't be so happy about that, but I absolutely am.

"What was that all about?" Emerson asks when I return to the living room.

"Oh, nothing. Just me convincing Carter you and I aren't dating."

Emerson sits up a little taller like he's proud of himself. "Wait. A professional hockey player felt threatened by *me*? I need to write this moment down. I need to tell Jeremy. Was it my Instagram profile picture? I've been told it reads very straight."

"Stop it," I say through a laugh. "He's never seen your photo. But I told him I want to tell you the truth—the whole truth. And it made him wonder."

"Oh, this sounds dramatic," Emerson says.

I nod and toss him an extra blanket. "You'd better buckle up. I've got a lot to tell you."

IT TAKES a solid thirty minutes to explain everything. And I mean *everything*. From the first time I met Carter to every single interaction we've had since. When I get to the part about not going to hockey games, I end up unpacking even more, telling Emerson about my panic attacks and, at least in vague terms, the trauma that triggered them.

He reaches over and squeezes my hand. "I really wish I'd known. I had no idea how much you were dreading going back to Canada."

"I know. I didn't really talk about it. I think I was in denial. Which is why I really appreciate what Miles did for me. And Carter—I mean, he's my literal hero."

"Sure," Emerson says. "But you can appreciate both of them and also feel like this is really hard. You're having to navigate some very complicated emotions." He tosses me the last half of his croissant. "Here. You need more carbs."

"I *do* need more carbs," I say, then I shove the rest of the croissant into my mouth in one giant bite. "This is really good therapy," I say through a mouthful of crumbs.

"Best kind there is," Emerson says.

I lick the last of the butter off my fingers. "Can I ask you something?"

"Always."

"Do you think...it's fair for me to expect Carter not to date? Or even see other women while we're together?"

"I mean, you'll be married," he says. "Which means if he does, he'll technically be cheating. Which isn't a good look when you have a public career like he does. Or like you do, for that matter. Appearances matter for you both."

"But...no kissing, no dating, no anything for a year. That's what we're committing to."

Emerson gives me a look. "I mean, when was the last time *you* kissed someone?"

I give the question serious consideration because I can't actually remember. "Probably Diego," I finally say.

His eyes widen. "Diego, the one you met during our junior year? Sarah, you haven't been together for at least two years."

"What? I've been busy. I haven't had time for dating."

"Then you just made my point. One more year isn't going to kill you."

"I'm not worried about me; I'm worried about him. We haven't talked about this part, so I have no idea what his expectations are. For me or any other women."

"Did something happen to make you think he might *want* to be with other women?" Emerson asks.

"Not explicitly. But...I don't know. I saw his realtor on a video call, and she's really beautiful. Like, stop traffic beautiful."

"You just *saw* a beautiful woman? That's it?"

"Don't make me feel stupid," I say. "She was there with him, and she was looking at him with these big, beautiful eyes, telling me how lucky I was. And then *he* got jealous of you—"

"That one makes much more sense," Emerson interjects.

"Oh, my gosh, stop," I say. "I'm just saying. We probably need to talk about this, right? We need to be straight with each other about what the expectations are."

"Definitely," Emerson agrees. "You need dating rules about other people but you also need house rules just for the two of you. You're going to be living together, right? Is he allowed to walk into his kitchen to get his morning coffee with nothing on? Swim in the pool naked? Watch TV in his boxer briefs?"

"Why did you just make him naked in every example? Normal people don't do any of those things."

"Not at *your* house," Emerson says. "But how do you know they aren't normal at his house? You've never lived with the man."

"Fine. Fair," I concede. "House rules. And dating rules. About seeing other people—"

"Hopefully about *not* seeing other people," he says, and I nod, really hoping for the same thing.

"Right. Yes. Hopefully that."

"You also need rules about how you treat each other. Are you good with PDA? Is it expected? And how much? Hugs? Holding hands? Kissing? Will there be different rules when you're in public than when you're in private? I mean, bare minimum, you'll at least have to kiss him at your wedding, right? I recommend practicing at least a few times first to avoid the risk of it being totally awkward. Wait—are you having a wedding? Or will you just do a courthouse thing?"

My heart swells the tiniest bit at Emerson's stream of consciousness rambling. I've really missed seeing him on a regular basis. "We're definitely having a wedding. Next month," I say. "And you'd better be there. You should bring Jeremy."

"Count on us both," Emerson says. "Jeremy is actually a huge Jaguars fan, so he'd probably like that."

I raise my eyebrows. I've only met Jeremy once, but he was all black cardigans and careful diction. The kind of man who reads the New Yorker religiously and looks like he's never raised his voice in his life—least of all at a hockey game. "Your symphony-writing, violin-playing boyfriend is a hockey fan?"

"I know, right? I was shocked too. Shame on us for believing in stereotypes."

I breathe out a sigh and look over at my friend. "This is good advice, Em. I'm really glad you happened to be in New York."

He beams. "Me too. What a happy coincidence." He glances at his watch. "Sadly, now I've got to run. I'm meeting Jeremy and his sisters for lunch. I'm so glad we got to do this. And now that I know everything, you have to keep me updated."

"I will. Thanks for listening."

"Do we need to brainstorm some rules before I go? Write out a list?"

"No, go meet Jeremy. I can call Anna if I need help."

"Oh, she'd be perfect at this. How is she? Still pregnant?"

"For two more months," I say. "And she's good. She's been a huge help through all this."

"I'm sure. Tell her I said hi. Also remind her that Emerson would be a very cute name for a baby—boy or girl."

I chuckle. "How many times have you already texted her that?"

"Apparently not enough, seeing as how I still don't have a namesake."

"I love how you've decided it's *my* sister-in-law's job to do this for you."

"Actually, don't feel special," Emerson says. "I have this conversation with anyone I meet who's having a baby."

"I'm going to tell Anna you said that."

"You wouldn't."

"Sorry, Em. Baby Fiona already has a name."

"Ohhh, Fiona! I love that."

He stands and holds out his hands, tugging me to my feet. "When will you see your man again?"

"He'll be in the city tomorrow," I say. "He has a game, then we're going out after to officially get engaged. Wanna come? It might make it easier to follow the rules I haven't put in place yet."

"I wish I could just for the fun of watching you try," he says. "But I'll be at Jeremy's niece's school play tomorrow night."

"Look at you doing all these family-centered things," I say. "How *is* his family? Do they like you?"

"I think his mom would like me more if I could give her grandbabies. But his dad is a gem. And I love his sisters." He pulls me into a hug. "I know we didn't talk about your art today—clearly this was much more important—but I need you to know how proud of you I am. You're doing amazing work."

I squeeze him a little tighter. "Thanks. I've got a show in Atlanta at the end of March, if you want to come. I can text you the invite."

"A wedding *and* a gallery show in the same month? You are making my social calendar so much more fun."

"Oh! I almost forgot," I say, pulling back from the hug. "I'm also supposed to decorate Carter's house. That's part of the agreement. Want to help? We basically get a blank check."

"Um, do peaches grow on trees?"

"And on every road in Atlanta," I say.

Emerson nods. "Text me the details. And send pictures. I'd love to help."

I walk him to the door of the apartment, blanket still wrapped around my shoulders. I had no idea this was how I'd spend the first half of my day, but it's exactly what my heart needed. I look at Emerson one more time. "It's going to be okay, right?"

"What's going to be okay?"

I shrug. "Everything?"

As jokey as he's been all morning, I'm surprised to see his expression turn thoughtful. "It always is, isn't it?" he says. "Even when things turn out differently than we expect. Just take things one day at a time. And don't be afraid of what the next day might bring." He gives me a saucy wink that's much more in line with his personality. "Especially if it lands you a hot hockey player *for real*."

13

CARTER

AFTER OUR GAME AGAINST THE NEW YORK WARRIORS—WHICH WE lost in a shootout, three to four—I change quickly and duck out early so I have time to meet Sarah. At first, I wished she was at the game, but after the way I played, maybe it's better she wasn't. I let our public relations people know before puck drop that I wouldn't be available for any interviews after, but I shouldn't have even bothered. Nobody will ask, based on my performance.

I did the bare minimum, playing distracted, my brain already hours ahead, thinking about seeing Sarah again. Which would concern me if it was a pattern, but it was just one game. I'll lock in and get myself sorted in Boston this weekend.

Miles gave me a pointed look on my way out, yelling after me to tell his sister hi, and that got a reaction from the rest of the guys. They'll understand even more once they see the engagement news.

I book a driver to use for the night, and he picks me up

outside Madison Square Garden. The plan is to head to a private club where we know we'll be seen by at least a few important people in hockey. Maybe it won't matter, but if we can create a digital footprint of our engagement, get a few mentions in the news, it's only going to help build our story.

Still, it feels weird to be going out without Theo, especially outside of Atlanta. Then again, if he were coming along, I'd still be waiting for him. Despite the loss, he had a killer game tonight, scoring a goal and an assist in the second period, then a second goal in the third. Two goals in one night is great for any player, but it's rare for a defenseman. He's the guy everyone will want to interview tonight.

The driver has the address of the Bainbridge Studio, where I'm picking Sarah up, so I sit back and will myself to relax.

I'm excited to see her, but also *nervous* to see her. After our conversation yesterday when I freaked out over Emerson, I'm not sure how things will feel between us. I was obviously jealous, but she admitted having similar feelings about Shelby, so where does that leave us?

I don't think either of us would deny our chemistry, but when does chemistry turn into something more? And will we know when it does if we're so focused on pretending?

I lift my hand to my inside coat pocket and press against it, feeling the hard ridges of the ring box.

Sarah has a ring—one Anna gave her. But she didn't seem all that impressed with the design. Plus, if we're aiming to make this seem real, a purchased ring carries a lot more weight.

"Almost there, sir," my driver says.

"Thanks," I say, then I text Sarah a quick heads-up.

She's just stepping out of the building when we pull up to the curb, and the sight of her stops my breath. She looks stunning, giving new meaning to the phrase *little black dress*. The one she's wearing is hugging her curves in all the right places. Her hair is down, and she isn't wearing her glasses.

As I climb out of the car, she takes the coat draped over her arm and wraps it around her shoulders, slipping her arms through the sleeves. It hangs past her knees, but that still feels like a lot of leg exposed in this cold, and I'm struck with a sudden urge to wrap her up in my arms just to make sure she doesn't freeze.

"Hey," I say as soon as I'm standing in front of her. I take in her warm gaze, and something inside me settles. "You look amazing."

She leans forward and presses a kiss to my cheek, and I lift a hand to the curve of her waist, closing my eyes as I breathe her in.

"Thanks," she says as she pulls back. "You too."

I take a step toward the car and hold out a hand. "Ready?"

I help her into the SUV, then jog around to the other side to get in myself. She's buckled her seatbelt by the time I'm in my seat, her hands clutching a tiny gold bag like her life depends on it.

"Sorry about the game," she says, and I wave away her concern.

"Don't worry about it. We can't win them all."

"How did you play?"

"Terrible," I say. "But Theo had a great night, and he was due for one."

Sarah studies me for a second. "I maybe shouldn't ask this question, but I'm guessing people compare the two of you a lot. Is one of you…" She hesitates. "Actually, I don't think I *can* ask you that."

I smile. "Is one of us better than the other?"

She grimaces. "That *is* what I was going to ask, but then I thought better of it."

"Don't worry about asking. You're right. People do compare, but our stats are surprisingly similar. He scores more than I do, but I have more points overall because I get more assists."

"I read an article that talked about your *near telepathic* connection on the ice," she says.

It's not quite the same as watching me play, but I do like that she's looking me up. "So you're reading about me now?"

She shoots me a playful look. "Don't let it go to your head. You googled me first."

"And look at us now," I say.

She laughs. "I don't think I would have predicted where we are now in a million years."

"I might have," I say, watching her eyes widen, "but maybe not *exactly* like this."

She holds my gaze for a long moment, a question behind her eyes. I don't want to freak her out, but it's never been hard for me to imagine us in a relationship—not since the first day I met her.

A moment later, Sarah's phone buzzes, and she breaks eye contact, looking down to slip it out of her purse. I can't help but wonder what might have happened if the circumstances were different. If I were meeting her after a game just because I like her. Then again, I'm still not sure she would have agreed to go out with me, so maybe it's a moot point.

Would she have chosen me just because? Chosen me for *me*? It sucks that I'll never actually know.

"Everything okay?" I ask.

She nods. "Just Emerson." She turns her phone to show me a photo of a family standing in a theater, a little girl at the center of the group dressed like a tree. "That's Jeremy's niece. Tonight was her school play. And this guy on the end is Emerson."

"Looks like a nice guy," I say, the embarrassment over my stupidly jealous reaction triggered all over again.

"He really is. He studied interior design at SCAD. He's still in Savannah, working for a firm there. But he agreed to help me with your place, so you'll get to see his brilliance firsthand."

"Just as long as I'm paying for his brilliance."

"You will be," she says. "He'll give us a deal. But I'll be sure to keep track of everything." She puts away her phone, then looks out the window. "So where are we headed?"

"There's a place called the Lexington over in Midtown," I say. "Near the Garden, where a lot of the Warriors players are frequently seen. Also the guy who hosts the biggest hockey podcast in the country is known to hang out there after games. He was at the game tonight, so I'm banking on him being there. If he sees us, he'll definitely mention it on his show."

"That's great," she says. "Exactly what we need."

"It's mostly just a sports bar," I say, "but a little more upscale. And smaller. I didn't want to take you somewhere with a big, noisy crowd."

She lifts her eyes to meet mine. "Thank you," she says. "Thanks for thinking of that."

"No problem."

She opens her bag one more time. "I guess I should go ahead and put this on." She pulls out Anna's ring.

"Actually," I say, pausing to reach for the one in my pocket. I glance forward to our driver, a sudden swell of nerves making me sweat. I'm wearing too many layers for this kind of conversation. "Hey, can we get a little privacy?"

The driver nods, then a screen raises between us and the front of the SUV. I have no idea how soundproof it is, but I drop my voice to a whisper anyway, just in case it isn't. "I know we agreed Anna's ring would be fine, but the more I thought about it, the more I thought it would look better if I went ahead and purchased one, so..." I hold up the ring, hand trembling the slightest bit. "I got you this one."

Sarah stares, eyes wide, mouth slightly open. "You bought a ring?" she asks, her voice hushed.

"I wasn't sure what you'd like, so I made a guess. I hope it's okay." I hold it toward her. "May I?"

She gives me her left hand, and I slowly slide it onto her ring finger. The moment feels a little too real, and I force myself to remember we're only pretending.

She extends her arm in front of her, tilting her hand this way and that. Her voice is breathy when she says, "Ohhhh, wow. It's so beautiful."

A tiny pulse of victory pushes through my chest. Real or not, I really wanted her to like it. I'm glad that she does.

"How did you know what size to get?" she asks. "It feels perfect."

"Do you remember when I slid Anna's ring onto my pinky and almost got it stuck?"

She nods, biting her lip in a way I'm beginning to recognize as a sign that she's feeling particularly emotional.

"I used that as a gauge. Are you sure you like it? I won't be offended if you'd rather wear the other one."

"No, this one is so much better," she says. "I really love it."

"Well, you should. You have to wear it for a year."

Something flashes behind her eyes, but there's no time to ask what she's thinking because the privacy screen slides down as the SUV eases to a stop.

Outside, a security guard stands in front of a sleek black building with a minimal, low-profile entrance.

"Just let me know when to come back for you," our driver says. "I'll be close by all night."

Once we're both on the sidewalk, Sarah pauses under a streetlamp. "Here," she says, pulling her phone out of her bag. "Let's take a picture with the ring. I'm supposed to post something tonight." She holds up her phone. "Actually, you're the one with the long arms. If we're doing a selfie, you should take it."

I take her phone, then she steps in front of me, pressing her back to my front. Instinctively, I wrap an arm around her, clasping it around her shoulder. She relaxes against me, lifting her hands to curl them around my arm, and I'm struck with the rightness of how this feels. I felt the same way the first time we took photos together. With my free arm, I lift the phone and center us in the frame. The ring sparkles in the lights of the streetlamp. I take a couple of photos, then, when Sarah looks up at me, exposing the long line of her neck, I take one more.

She takes the phone and looks through the photos. "Perfect," she says. "We actually look really good."

I shoot her a grin as we head toward the entrance of the club. "You could take a photo next to a dumpster and still look amazing."

She smiles playfully. "I'll take your word for it because I'm definitely not testing that theory."

Once inside, we check our coats and find a cozy booth

with a round bench seat hugging the wall. The place looks busy, but not so busy that it's overwhelming. The vibe is chill, making me confident this was a good choice for Sarah. I take a minute to scan the room, looking for anyone I recognize.

To my surprise, the Jaguars general manager, Brady Norcott, is sitting a few tables over with his wife and the Jaguars team owner. Norcott is traveling with the team, but I hadn't noticed his wife was with him, though maybe she just met him here. Pretty sure the team owner lives in New York, so it makes sense they would want to meet while we're in town.

I make eye contact with Norcott, and he tilts his head up in acknowledgement.

I point them out to Sarah, but I doubt we'll spend much time talking tonight. I have a good relationship with Norcott. He's a great GM. But our team owner isn't very hands-on. I've only interacted with him once or twice, and that's after six seasons with the team.

Even so, it can't hurt Sarah's cause to have people from inside the organization see evidence of our relationship. Every person who remembers seeing us together or remembers the night we got engaged makes our case stronger.

"What about the podcast guy?" Sarah asks. "Is he here?"

I take another quick look around the room. "Right there," I say, pointing at the bar. "Sitting by a couple of Warriors players. That's Griffin Knox."

Theo and I have done interviews for Griffin's podcast, Hockey House, a few times before, and I would say we're on friendly terms. Enough that it won't be unusual for me to say hello to him, make sure he knows I'm here.

"Can I get us some drinks?" I ask, and Sarah nods.

"Should we have champagne?" she says. "We're celebrating, aren't we?"

"That we are. I'll be right back."

On my way, I stop and shake Norcott's hand, then say hello to the team owner. I make a point to mention celebrating with my new fiancée, then I excuse myself and head to the bar.

I lean against it right beside Griffin, glancing over at him before giving the bartender my order.

"Well, if it isn't one of the Williamsons," Griffin says as soon as he notices me.

I look his way and lift an eyebrow, giving him the chance to determine *which* Williamson brother I am.

"Carter?" he asks, and I grin.

"Lucky guess."

"Sorry about the loss tonight, man." He gives me a good-natured smile. "You played terrible."

"Yep," I say. "Thanks for pointing that out."

"You know I call it like I see it. Your brother killed it." He looks around. "Is he here?"

"Nah, not tonight," I say, making eye contact with the man sitting on Griffin's other side. It's the Warriors' team captain, a guy named Markham.

He lifts his drink like he's toasting me. "Tell Stone I appreciate him fumbling his last shot in the shootout."

I cock my head to the side. "Still got a point. And that puts us how many ahead of the Warriors?"

"Six," Griffin answers for me. "And three ahead of the second-place team in your division."

"Thanks for the stats, Griff," I say, patting him on the back.

"For now," Markham says. "We'll see who chokes in the playoffs."

I turn my attention back to Griffin.

"So you're flying solo?" he asks.

The bartender slides over two flutes of champagne.

"I guess not," Griffin says, answering his own question. He eyes the champagne. "Are you celebrating something?"

"My engagement," I say, proud of myself for not tripping over the words. "I just proposed tonight."

"No wonder you were off your game," Griffin says. "You were playing nervous. Hey, congrats, man. I'm glad she said yes."

"Yeah, me too," I say, and something turns over in my stomach. I've been pretty self-aware going into all this, but the deeper we get, the more I'm starting to wonder if I can handle it. If I can truly keep my feelings sorted.

I say goodbye to Griffin and pick up the champagne, then make my way back to Sarah.

"How did it go?" she asks as I slide into the booth beside her. I move her champagne a little closer, and she lifts it to take a sip. "Did you tell him?"

"I did."

Sarah scoots a little closer and slides her fingers through my hair just above my ear. Her hand lingers there, brown eyes on mine. I'm surprised by the sudden touch, but I'm not about to complain.

"Is he still watching?" she asks, her voice soft, and a twinge of disappointment pushes through me. I can't keep forgetting that this is all for show.

I glance toward Griffin. "Yeah. He is."

She drops her hand back in her lap and bites her lip. "So

what's our play here? Is seeing us enough? Or should we leave no room for doubt?"

If I had any sense of self-preservation, I would retreat. Instead, I lean in closer. "What do you have in mind?"

"I'm actually not one who's big into public displays of affection. But considering the circumstances, and since we have an audience..." Her eyes drop to my lips, and I smile playfully.

"Do you want me to kiss you, Sarah?"

"I mean, no," she says with a scoff. "Of course not. I'm just saying it might be helpful in our present situation. It would have to be natural. Chill. Like we've done it a thousand times."

I let out a little chuckle. "That's a high bar. Asking me to kiss you for the first time...and be chill about it."

"Right," she says, like she genuinely thinks I'm joking. "Because I'm honestly so intimidating."

"Clearly you don't see yourself the way I see you. Kissing someone as beautiful as you will always be a big deal no matter how many times it happens."

Her eyes drop to her lap, and she breathes out a laugh as she shakes her head. "I think you're just saying that. Like I'm one of your youth hockey players who's *skating with heart*."

Suddenly, it doesn't matter if we're pretending. I just want Sarah to believe she really *is* that beautiful. That she has no reason to doubt herself. "That's not what this is," I say. "Some things are just objectively true. You *are* beautiful, Sarah."

She holds my gaze, and I can tell she's fighting, like she just doesn't want to accept the words as true.

"I can tell you want to deflect," I say. "Don't do it."

She presses her lips together like she's fighting a smile.

"It's just easy to say that when I'm all dressed up. But you haven't seen me at my worst." She lifts her arms and wraps them around my neck, her fingers brushing against my hairline. "Bedhead. Giant glasses. The imprint of the book I fell asleep reading smooshed into my cheek."

I shift a hand to her hip and tug her a little closer. "Is that something that happens a lot?"

"More than I'm proud to admit," she says.

"I doubt it makes a difference. And I like your glasses. The green ones, especially."

Her eyes light up. "Those are my favorites."

I pick up her champagne and hand it to her, then grab my own glass.

"Are we making a toast?" she asks, and I nod.

"We are," I say. "And then I'm going to kiss you like I've done it a thousand times."

"Like kissing is old news," she says.

"Totally boring," I add.

She clinks her glass to mine. "To our exceptional acting skills," she says.

We both take a drink of champagne, then we set down our glasses.

Reminding myself not to hesitate, I gather my courage, lift my hands to cradle her face, then press my mouth to hers.

As soon as our lips make contact, it's all I can do not to forget the plan and pull her all the way into my arms. Her lips are warm and soft, and she tastes faintly of champagne, and I'm...*flying*.

The kiss is supposed to be familiar, so I fight to keep it simple, like something we've done countless times, but it's taking all my willpower to do so when what I want is to deepen the kiss, taste her, explore her mouth. Her hands lift to my chest, gripping my shirt as she tugs me closer. It doesn't feel like she's pretending—it feels like she's *hungry*. And I want to be the one who gives her everything she needs.

Sarah lets out a soft moan, and my desire sharpens just enough to remind me that we should stop. Here is not the place and now is not the time.

I pull back, and Sarah's eyes flutter open. My thumb brushes over the corner of her mouth, tugging at her bottom lip, and she sucks in a breath. "You look a little stunned for our one-thousandth kiss."

She blinks slowly, and I try to read her expression. She had to have felt the same thing I did. But then she gives her head a little shake.

"One thousand and *one*," she corrects. She glances toward the bar. "And...mission accomplished. Pretty sure podcast guy saw the whole thing."

I swallow my disappointment.

Right. Mission accomplished.

The rest of the night passes by in a blur. Griffin comes over to meet Sarah and buys us another round of champagne to congratulate us on our engagement. And Brady Norcott stops by on his way out so his wife can tell Sarah that after meeting Anna at a team event last summer, she's been following Sarah on Instagram and loves her art.

Sarah is flattered and clearly overwhelmed by the attention, but she's gracious and kind and even agrees to take a photo with the woman.

"Did that even just happen?" she whispers to me after the couple leaves. "You're the famous one. People aren't supposed to recognize *me*."

For my part, I've had just enough champagne to soften the edges of my defenses. To let myself fully enjoy holding

Sarah's hand or keeping an arm around her shoulder. Pressing a kiss to her temple whenever she leans close.

But not *so much* champagne that I've forgotten that all of this is temporary. I can touch her, treat her like she belongs to me because we have an audience. Something to prove.

But for how long?

It's jarring to be with her, to feel like this thing between us is real, but then keep getting reminders that it's not. That maybe my feelings aren't reciprocated and she's just really good at pretending.

Sarah reaches over and pats my knee. "We should go," she says. "You have to leave early tomorrow."

I nod. "Okay. Have you had fun?"

She smiles. "Yeah. I really have."

We get our coats, and I send a quick text to our driver, letting him know we're ready to leave. But I'm hesitant to let Sarah go. To say goodbye when I won't see her again for almost another week.

"Is your hotel far?" she asks, and I shake my head no.

"Just a few blocks."

She seems to consider this information, then she looks up at me and asks, "Can we just go there?"

I lift my eyebrows. "You don't want to go back to Soho?"

"There's actually something I was hoping we could talk about. I know it's late, but we're together, and I think it'll be easier in-person."

I can't begin to guess what she wants to talk about, and I'm suddenly nervous. Did I cross a line? Somehow make her uncomfortable?

"Hey," she says, stepping closer and lifting a hand to pat my chest. "You're not in trouble. I promise. It's truly not a big deal—just something that's been on my mind."

I nod. "Okay. Do you want me to come to your place? As late as it is, that would be easier. Then you'll already be home safe."

"My place is frigid," she says. "The heat doesn't work very well. It's fine if I'm in bed buried under blankets, but…"

"Hotel it is," I say. "But since it's so late, will you stay until morning? I promise I'll be a perfect gentleman."

"You don't have to promise me that," she says as our driver pulls up. "I know you will."

14

SARAH

Carter's hotel room is lovely. Mostly because it's *warm*. Considering how much the temperature has dropped in the last few hours, I think I would have been miserable back at the Bainbridge. Either that or sleeping on the studio floor downstairs. Pretty sure it's just my apartment that's stuck in the Arctic zone.

Still, I'm not sure I fully thought this through. Because now...*I'm in Carter's hotel room.* And I agreed to stay until morning.

All the more reason to figure out our rules and make sure we're both committed to them.

After spending the last two hours close to him, touching him, feeling the reassuring weight of his arms around me—I need all the help I can get.

Not to mention that kiss.

On the grand scale of kisses, it shouldn't have seemed like much. It only lasted a matter of seconds. But it still triggered something bone-deep, even visceral. I am very, *very* attracted to this man.

"Here," Carter says from where he's rummaging in his bag. He holds out some clothes. "They're going to swallow you, but it'll be better than nothing."

Of course, my brain immediately thinks of wearing *nothing* with Carter, and a flush climbs up my neck.

Behave, brain. Behave, behave, behave.

"Thanks," I say, my voice a little too breathy. "I'll just... change in the bathroom."

I step out of my heels and hurry that way, not fully taking a breath until I've clicked the door closed behind me.

I lift Carter's clothes to my nose. They smell like him, warm and woodsy and so delicious. I have no idea how I'm supposed to put them on my body and not lose my ever-loving mind.

I look at my reflection in the mirror, clothes tucked against my chest. I'm always a little surprised when I catch a glimpse of myself without my glasses. My contacts are fine, but for whatever reason, my glasses make me feel most like me—the me I'm most comfortable being.

Wait. I'm wearing contacts. Which means I'm going to have to sleep in contacts because I don't have any of my stuff with me. No lens solution. No case. I groan inwardly, but what choice do I have? Hopefully, since I didn't put them on until late in the day, I'll make it till morning without being too miserable.

I put down Carter's clothes and reach for the zipper of my dress. I manage to get it halfway down, but then it snags. I shouldn't be surprised—it was a struggle to get it on because it kept catching in the same place. I eventually got it to work, but not without significant strain.

Now, I can't get the zipper to move in either direction. Up or down.

I try reaching around my waist and up. Then I try reaching over my shoulder and down.

No luck. I am officially trapped.

I'm either sleeping in my dress, or I'm asking Carter for help.

I sigh, hands propped on my hips as I study my reflection. Then I turn and open the bathroom door.

Carter is just hanging up the hotel phone when I step into the room. He turns to look at me, and my throat immediately goes dry.

He's taken off his shoes and his coat, and his dress shirt is untucked and unbuttoned, hanging open to reveal his torso. His very muscled, very beautiful, incredibly *sexy* torso.

I saw Carter shirtless over FaceTime, but only for a split second. My memory of that moment does not compare to this.

I'm struck with a sudden impulse to cross the room to him, lift my hands to all that glorious skin...

"Are you okay?" Carter asks, and I snap my eyes upward to meet his. The look on his face makes me feel like a kid caught stealing Oreos from the pantry.

"Good," I quickly say. "Just stuck."

"Stuck?"

I turn around and look at him over my shoulder. "Can you help?"

I face forward, but there's a floor-length mirror on the wall in front of me, so I watch him approach and stop directly behind me. His gaze down, he uses one hand to sweep my hair to the side, pushing it over one shoulder, then he uses his big hands to wiggle the zipper free.

Slowly, he slides it down, his fingers barely brushing along my spine until he reaches the small of my back. I watch him through the mirror, and I swear it looks like he's leaning in, but then he closes his eyes for a moment and takes a step back, letting his hands fall from my body.

I hold the dress to my front—it has a built-in bra and I'm suddenly feeling the lack of support—and slowly turn around. My eyes catch on a necklace looped around Carter's neck. It looks like a penny—an actual penny—with a hole drilled through it so it fits on a chain.

I want to ask him about it, but I'm not foolish enough to start any kind of conversation when I'm this close to being completely undressed.

I lift my eyes to meet his. "Thank you," I say.

He licks his lips, his voice low as he says, "No problem."

Those lips...it would be so easy to step forward, let my hands graze over his chest as I—

"You should get dressed, Sarah," Carter says, his expression almost pained.

"Right. *Yes.*" I take an enormous step backward. "I really should."

I take my time in the bathroom. I think we could both use a minute to regroup.

The conversation about rules—we cannot have it quickly enough.

Carter has given me a pair of soft flannel pajama bottoms and a long-sleeved Jaguars t-shirt. Fortunately, the pants have a drawstring waist so I'm able to cinch them up, even if I do have to roll the waist down three times to keep the hem from dragging on the floor. The t-shirt really does swallow me, but it's soft and comfortable and smells incredible, so I'm not complaining.

I'm running my tongue over my teeth, wishing I could brush them, when a soft knock sounds on the bathroom door.

I open it to find Carter standing on the other side, a small bag in his hand. He's fully dressed now, in a pair of gray sweatpants and a plain white t-shirt.

"I wasn't sure what you might need," he says, holding the bag open, "so I just had them send up everything that was available. There's contact lens solution, a toothbrush, toothpaste, some face stuff, I think?"

I take the bag. "This is perfect," I say, touched that he even thought to try. "Thank you. That was really kind of you."

"It wasn't a big deal. It might all be terrible."

"I'm sure it isn't. It's probably exactly what I need."

He lifts his lips into a small smile. "Good."

I close the door and manage to get ready for bed mostly like I would at home. I take out my contacts, which feels amazing, and wash my face and brush my teeth. I squint at my bare face—I'm a little blurry without contacts or glasses—and wonder if I made the right call. This is the most dressed-down Carter has ever seen me. But maybe that's exactly what I need.

To feel as unattractive as possible so I stop contemplating the possibility of forgetting the rules and just throwing myself at him.

I emerge from the bathroom to find Carter leaning against the headboard, legs stretched out in front of him and crossed at the ankles, phone in his hand. As soon as he sees me, he sets it on the nightstand.

"Did you have everything you needed?" he asks.

"Yes, totally. Thanks again."

He's quiet for a beat before he says, "So, what was it you wanted to talk about?"

I look around the room, my eyes catching on a pad of hotel-branded stationary sitting on the desk. I walk over and grab it, as well as the pen sitting beside it, and carry them over to Carter.

"I think it's time for us to talk about our rules," I say. I hold out the paper and pen. "And I need you to take notes because I currently can't see well enough to do it myself."

He takes the writing tools, then retrieves a pillow from the other side of the bed and sets it on his lap to use as a desk. "You're farsighted?"

"Horribly. I've been wearing glasses since I was seven."

"Maybe you can talk to Charlie. She just found out she needs them, and she's not happy about it."

I sit down in the armchair across from the bed. "I'd be happy to. It's a big adjustment when you're a kid."

He uncaps the pen. "So...rules," he says. "I'm not entirely sure I know what you mean by that."

I hesitate, suddenly wondering if he's going to think this whole thing is dumb. Maybe I'm making a big deal out of nothing. But then I think about seeing shirtless Carter on the regular, and my self-preservation kicks in. Dumb or not, we have to have this conversation.

"I just mean we're going to be living together," I say. "But since this isn't a real relationship, we need to figure out what our boundaries are so we're both comfortable with everything."

"Got it," he says, a little hesitant. "That makes sense."

"Also, what's expected when we're out in public," I say. "Will we always hold hands? Hug? Are we comfortable with kissing? That sort of thing."

He tilts his head to the side. "I think we managed okay tonight."

"Right. We totally did. But I still think it would be helpful to talk about it." I gnaw on my lip for a second before adding,

"We need to be careful, you know? We clearly have…" I pause, suddenly nervous to finish the sentence. I was going to call out the attraction between us, but maybe I'm wrong and it's all one-sided.

"Chemistry?" Carter finishes for me, his flirty smile making my face flush hot. "Does that embarrass you? I'm not going to pretend like I don't find you attractive."

"No, I—" I swallow, my throat suddenly feeling very, *very* dry. "I was going to say the same thing. That's what makes the rules so important. I don't want either one of us getting hurt. Or…getting real feelings involved."

He holds my gaze for a long moment, his scrutiny so intense, I have to fight the urge to look away. A huge part of me wants to forget the rules. Chase whatever this is just because of how good it feels.

But I don't want to hurt him. And I'm nearly certain that in the end, I will *definitely* disappoint him.

The reality is, if Miles hadn't put him up to it, I'm not sure Carter would have chosen me. And simply because of his profession, I wouldn't have even considered him, no matter how charming I found him the day we met. But throwing ourselves into situations where we're pretending has the potential to confuse us both. Make us feel and think things we might not have chosen otherwise.

I don't want either one of us to fall into something simply because it's convenient.

"Fair enough," Carter says, left hand gripping the pen. "Where should we start?"

15

———

SARAH

"Let's start with our house rules," I say, tucking my legs under me in my chair. The movement sends a whiff of Carter's scent up to my nose, and I fight the urge to lift my shirt to my face and take another deep breath. "Obviously, our relationship at home will be purely platonic. We'll have separate bedrooms, of course. Outside of that, I'd say respecting closed bedroom doors, staying out of private spaces. And making sure we're always fully clothed whenever we're in shared spaces."

He nods, then looks at the paper. "So no helping you out of your dress when your zipper is stuck," he says as he writes.

I scoff, and he looks up and grins.

"That was an extenuating circumstance," I say. "And I was never unclothed!"

"You didn't have the same view I did," he teases.

"Carter!"

"I'm kidding!" he says, laughing. "I'm kidding. I totally get it. Clothes on in public spaces. Respect private spaces. It's all written down."

"That means you can't even be shirtless," I say.

"What if I'm swimming? We do have a really great pool."

I try not to dwell on the way he said *we*. Like the house he's buying belongs to both of us. "Obviously swimming is fine," I say. "But no strolling around the house without a shirt on. It's not fair."

Carter's lips twitch like he's fighting a smile, but he keeps his head down as he makes a few more notes. "Got it. Shirt on at all times. What else?"

"Probably there should be no touching," I say. "Just to make things simple. Unless it's like...necessary for survival or something."

"For survival? So...CPR?" Carter says, eyes sparkling. I know he's teasing me, but somehow it doesn't feel hurtful. There's no bite to it, no real criticism.

It makes it easy for me to add, "Obviously. Also the Heimlich maneuver. And if you ever see a spider anywhere on my person, you have my permission in advance to touch whatever part of me is necessary to remove it."

He presses his lips together, and I can tell he wants to laugh, but he keeps writing without breaking. "No touching," he says slowly, his words in time with his pen. "Exceptions: Spiders, choking, stopped hearts." He looks up. "Is that it for house rules?"

"I think so. Can you think of anything else?"

"Yes. You aren't allowed to wear my clothes."

I sit up a little taller. "Why not?"

"You tell me why you don't want me to go shirtless, and I'll tell you why I don't want you to wear my clothes," he says, a playful challenge in his eyes.

I huff out a sigh. "Fine. Just write it down."

He nods as he writes. "Probably the dress you wore tonight should also be off the table."

"Stop it," I say, laughing, because once again, Carter is doing what he seems to do best. This conversation could be so uncomfortable, but he's making the whole thing feel so much easier than it would with anyone else.

"What about when we're out?" he asks. "Like we were tonight?"

"I'm comfortable with everything that happened tonight," I say. "As long as we're communicating, checking in to make sure we're both okay."

He nods. "So, touching, holding hands, kissing if it feels like it's something a married couple would do. That's all good?"

My mind tosses me back to the moment Carter's lips touched mine. I half wonder if I'll start dreaming up reasons to take him out in public just so we can do it again.

"Sounds great," I say. "All good."

"Good," he says. "So basically the opposite of *no PDA.* We're *only* into PDA."

"*Reasonable* PDA," I say.

"Naturally," Carter says. "What about friend touching?"

I lift my eyebrows. "I need clarification because that statement sounds kind of questionable."

He grins. "I just mean...like if I haven't seen you in a week and it feels like I should hug you hello. Is that allowed? I have a lot of friends I might hug if I haven't seen them in a while."

"So...hello hugs?"

"Sure," he says. "Or, I don't know. A pat on the back if you've had a hard day or a helping hand if you trip. Just friendly stuff."

"Right. No, that makes sense. I think we can handle friend

touching. But can we call it something else so it doesn't sound like we're randomly accosting our friends?"

"Friend...ly touching?" Carter says.

"That's better."

He nods as he writes. "Adding the -ly now." He puts down his pen. "Okay. Is that it?"

"Almost," I say. This is the part of the conversation I've been dreading the most. I pull my knees up to my chest, wrapping my arms around them. "We still need to talk about expectations regarding other people."

His brow furrows. "Other people?"

I shrug. Why does this feel so incredibly awkward?

"Seeing them," I say. "I think it's important that you have the freedom to...I mean, obviously, you would have to be careful, but I'm just saying, I don't think it's fair for me to stop you should you want to—"

"Wait," he says, cutting me off. "Obviously we can't date anyone else publicly, so when you say *seeing people,* are you talking about sex?"

I close my eyes, scrunching my forehead up in embarrassment. The truth is, I really don't like the idea of him sleeping with other people. But he won't be sleeping with me, so it feels like something we should talk about just in case.

"Sarah," Carter says, his tone firm but gentle. "Look at me."

I squint one eye open, then force myself to open the other.

"That's not going to happen," he says.

I bite my lip. "It won't?"

He quickly shakes his head. "Not for me. I have too much respect for you and too much respect for marriage to let people think I would ever sneak around behind your back."

Honestly. Every time I talk to this man, it's more and more obvious why Miles picked him.

He's just so good.

"I feel the same way," I say. "Especially with you having such a high-profile career. But if you were to ever change your mind, I wouldn't judge you for it. A year is a long time."

He smirks. "If a year without sex was going to kill me, I wouldn't be alive to have a conversation about it. Monogamy is the only look I'm going for. Nothing is going to change that."

I can't truly quantify how much I like his answer. But the relief washing over me is as potent as it is powerful. Not just that Carter wants to honor the marriage but that he isn't the kind of guy to have casual relationships in the first place. It wouldn't have disqualified him—I'm in no position to judge people's choices. But I like that we align in this way.

"What about you?" Carter asks. "Are you shutting down an active dating life so you can marry me?"

I laugh even as my face flushes with heat. "Not even close. I haven't dated anyone in almost three years. Maybe if I were better at dating, I wouldn't need my big brother to browbeat a teammate into saving me."

He smiles. "No browbeating has happened, I promise."

I hold his gaze. "But you are saving me."

He reaches over and puts the pen and paper on the night-stand, then lifts his arms, propping his hands behind his head. "Three years is a long time. Will you tell me about your last boyfriend?"

I stifle a yawn. Now that we've finished the rules conversation, which went so much better than I thought it would, the emotions of everything are catching up with me. Plus, it has to be close to two, possibly even three, in the morning.

Carter pats the bed beside him. "Come on. Tell me from over here."

He doesn't have to ask me twice.

I walk to the foot of the bed, then crawl up to the other side, keeping a healthy measure of distance between us—easy in such a giant bed.

"My last boyfriend was a guy named Diego," I say. "I met him junior year of my undergrad and we dated until right after I graduated."

"What happened?" Carter asks.

"We just grew apart, I think. I was staying in Savannah to do my master's, and he wanted to move home to Boston, and neither of us seemed to care about being together enough to either make long distance work or change our plans. It became very obvious very quickly that we were not meant to make it."

"I get that. But seriously, *no one* since then?" he says, his tone light and teasing.

"Don't judge," I say. "I've been busy." I yawn again, which is surprising. Wearing Carter's clothes, snuggling into a bed when he's less than three feet away, I might have guessed I wouldn't be able to relax. But it actually feels like the opposite. I almost feel *more* relaxed simply because he's here. "I've tried a few times. But..." I hesitate, not sure I want to admit this next part.

"But?" he prompts.

"I don't know. I think I'm scared. Scared to love someone I might lose. Or trust someone who might hurt me..."

Carter looks over at me. "You've been through a lot," he says gently. "Losing your mom. And then dealing with your dad..."

I tuck my arm under my head and look up at him. "What did Miles tell you about our dad?"

"Nothing specific," Carter says. "Just that he wasn't a great guy."

His tone is so gentle, so full of understanding, I'm half-tempted to tell him everything. But I don't want to ruin the night we've had by digging into my childhood. And I don't want him to look at me differently once he knows.

"What about you?" I ask instead. "Who was your last girlfriend?"

He pauses for a second, but then he seems to accept the subject change and scoots a little lower on his pillow. He turns to face me, stretching out on his side with his head propped on his hand. "Her name was Veronica. We broke up... maybe eighteen months ago? She was super big into hockey, and that was fun for a while, but then it just started to feel like it was more about hockey and less about *me*. Like I could have swapped myself for any other guy on the team and she wouldn't have cared."

"Ouch," I say, and he huffs out a laugh.

"Yeah."

"I'm sorry that happened. It must be hard when you don't know people's motives. If they're looking for money or status or whatever else."

"Theo's gotten good at looking for the signs," Carter says. "He dates a lot more than I do, so he has more practice."

"Why is that?" I ask.

"Why does he date more?" Carter asks, and I nod. "I don't know. He's chasing something, I think. But also...it's probably not so much that he dates *more*, but that I date *less*."

"Why is *that*?" I ask.

He shrugs. "Sometimes I think it's my own fault. When I

go out with Theo, it's hard to compete with him. Even though we look the same, he's funnier, more charming, better at flirting. And I never go out without him, so I'm not giving myself much of a chance."

A tiny piece of my heart breaks at the thought of Carter ever feeling like he's *less than* his brother. I recognize Theo's charm, but Carter is steady and good and thoughtful and just as charming in his own way.

I suddenly feel a pressing need to help him see that. To show him that he's just as dateable as his brother, even more so in my eyes. I open my mouth to tell him, but then I swallow the words. I'm not sure I can say them without it sounding like a confession of feelings.

"You should sleep," Carter says. "It's been a long day."

I let my eyes fall closed. "Yeah."

Carter gets off the bed and heads to the bathroom while I fight to stay awake. If I sleep, the night will be over, and it's been a really, *really* good night. We got engaged, we had champagne, we *kissed...*

Wait. We got engaged! And I never posted the photo.

I sit up and scramble across the bed to get my phone. I don't have much battery left, so I hope whatever charger Carter uses for his phone will fit mine too. I look through the photos, grabbing the one that makes the ring most obvious, then upload it to Instagram. I tag Carter's account and add a caption that reads *forever with @c.williamson starts now.*

The bathroom door squeaks open, and Carter reappears.

"I forgot to post the engagement photo," I say. "But it's up now. I tagged you."

"Wow," he says, pausing midstride. "I guess it's really real now."

I nod, holding his gaze. "Should I have waited to make sure you were still good to move forward?"

He quickly shakes his head. "Nah. You have my pinky promise, remember?" He steps to the side of the bed and holds out his hand. "Do you need to charge your phone?"

"Will it mean you can't charge yours?"

He quickly shakes his head. "I've got an extra charger. It'll be fine."

I hand it over and snuggle back down under the duvet. "Are you even for real right now? You got me toiletries even though I didn't ask for them. You gave me pajamas. You have an *extra* phone charger. Are you this good at taking care of *everyone*?"

"Not everyone," he says softly, and my heart skips a few beats, loving the thought that maybe it's just me who gets this kind of treatment.

Once my phone is plugged in, Carter climbs into bed and turns off the light. We've been on the bed together for a while now, but the darkness suddenly makes me hyperaware. Exactly how far away is his body from mine? If I roll over in my sleep, am I going to kick him? Will I snore? Wait. *Do I snore?*

"You okay over there?" he whispers into the darkness.

"Totally. Just having a small existential crisis trying to remember if I snore."

He chuckles. "I doubt I'll hear you if you do. I shared a bedroom with Theo for too many years. I'll sleep through anything."

"Are you just saying that to make me feel better?"

"I swear I'm not. I really do sleep like the dead."

I push up on my elbow. "Hey, can I ask you a question before you fall asleep?"

"Sure."

"What's with the penny?"

"For being so close to sleep two minutes ago, you sure do seem wide awake now."

"It was the panic of realizing I forgot to post," I say. "I'm still buzzing from the adrenaline."

"You know it would have been fine if you'd posted tomorrow. Technically, it already *is* tomorrow."

"Are you kidding? And risk Anna's wrath? She has the whole timeline planned."

"Fair," Carter says.

"So tell me about the penny. Help me get sleepy again."

He's quiet for a beat, long enough that I start to wonder if it's too personal.

"You don't have to tell me if you don't want to," I say.

"I don't mind," Carter says. "It's just been a minute since I've talked about it."

I wait, sensing that whatever the story is, he doesn't need me to yank it out of him.

"The penny I'm wearing is one Theo gave me," he finally says. "But it's significant because of my dad."

Without saying anything, I scooch over on the bed until I'm close enough to find Carter's hand, then I slip my fingers into his. "This is friendly touching," I whisper into the darkness. "Just FYI."

He squeezes my fingers once, then holds on. "Have you ever heard the saying 'penny for your thoughts'?"

"I don't think so," I say.

"It's just something people used to say. When you look thoughtful or contemplative, someone might look at you and ask, *penny for your thoughts*? Instead of just saying what are you thinking? So I don't remember this part, but I guess the story is that I was sitting outside on the front porch, maybe five or six years old, and my dad came out and sat down beside me and asked, penny for your thoughts? And I guess I looked at him, real serious, held out my hand and said, 'okay.'"

I chuckle. "Smart kid."

"So he gave me a penny, and I told him what I was thinking, and it started this whole thing between us. I remember being in high school and having a rough time about something, usually something hockey related, and he'd come in and toss a penny on my bed." Carter shifts, changing his position so his voice gets closer, but he doesn't let go of my hand. "I don't know why it worked, but whenever I saw that penny, it felt like permission to just say whatever I was feeling, trusting that he wouldn't judge me for it."

"He sounds like a really good dad," I say, and Carter breathes out a sigh.

"Yeah. He really was."

"Did he do the same thing with Theo?"

"He didn't," Carter says. "It was just our thing. I think he sensed that was important. That he single us out sometimes. I think Theo resented it. I mean, he had plenty of other things that only he did with Dad, and he never said anything to me about it. It was just something I sensed."

"I can't imagine how much you guys had to balance. Looking alike, playing the same sport. Did you fight a lot?"

"All the time when we were really young," he says. "But it was mostly out of our systems by high school."

"I worshiped Miles when I was young," I say, fighting off a yawn. "He was so much older than me, we didn't really have much to fight about."

"Hey, there's a yawn," Carter says. "My goal to bore you is working."

I smile into my pillow. I would fight sleep all night if it meant getting to talk to him. "It's not boring at all! I love it. So why did Theo give you a penny? If it was a thing with your dad?"

Carter spends the next ten minutes telling me the story of the night his dad was killed. How Theo was driving. How Carter wasn't with them because he'd stayed late after hockey practice for speed drills Theo *didn't* have to do. He'd clocked times fast enough not to need them. So the two of them had gone out to grab dinner, with a plan to circle back by the rink to get Carter.

Theo was a good driver. He'd had his license over a year. Followed the rules. Didn't speed. But none of that mattered. The other driver was drunk, speeding, and ignoring the red light that was supposed to keep all of them safe.

Carter tells me how hard Theo spiraled after the accident. How hard he had to fight to keep his brother on the ice, committed to the goals they were so close to achieving despite how much they were both grieving.

My heart aches for them. That at such a young age, they had to deal with such a sudden and tragic loss. My mom was sick for years, so sick that by the time I was seventeen, I'd already grown used to the idea that at some point, she wasn't going to be around anymore. It wasn't better—in a lot of ways, it was probably worse. Living with death hanging over us all those years.

But at least I was prepared when it finally happened.

I rub my thumb over the back of Carter's knuckles, grateful for the point of contact. For some small way to remind him he isn't alone.

"Anyway," Carter continues, "there was one night when I was just so frustrated with Theo. We'd already been drafted and were playing for an AHL team in North Carolina. He'd had too much to drink and was picked up by the cops for drunk and disorderly conduct, and I was just so angry with him. Our team captain had to come pick us up, and it just felt like...everything was slipping away."

"I can imagine," I say. "Especially when your success was so closely tied together."

"After he sobered up," Carter continues, "I pretty much iced him out. I was done trying. Done taking care of him. Being the older brother."

"Are you older?" I ask.

"By seventeen minutes," he says. "And I always acted like it. But then I decided if he wanted to throw his career away, I wasn't going to stop him. Not anymore." He pauses, and for a long moment, all I can hear is the low hum of the central heat. Somewhere down the hall, a door opens, then shuts. "Then one night after a home game, he came into our room and tossed a penny onto my bed."

I suck in a tiny gasp. "Because he knew then you'd have to talk to him."

"Exactly."

"This is a really good story, Carter."

"You're supposed to be getting sleepy over there," he says.

"I can't. I have to know how it ends."

"That's pretty much the end. We talked, and for once, I didn't hold back. I told him exactly how I felt about everything he'd been doing. He listened, nodded, then a week later, he showed up with two pennies, one for each of us. Said they were to remind us to never stop talking. That's what Dad would want."

"Geez, are you serious right now?" I ask, tugging my hand away from his so I can wipe at my tears. "You could write a book with this story."

"It's not that big of a deal," he says. "It feels a little cheesy."

"It's not cheesy. It's perfect. And honestly, it makes me like Theo a little more."

"You didn't like him before?"

"No, I did," I quickly say. "Theo is fine. But I've never liked him as much as I like you."

Carter shifts again, his foot brushing against mine. Somehow, our conversation has migrated us closer and closer to the center of the bed. For once, all this touching really does just feel friendly. Like it's more about being present with each other. "Can I have a three- to five-paragraph essay detailing the many reasons why? As this is the first time in history anyone has ever preferred me to my brother, I'd like written evidence."

I laugh. "You aren't giving yourself enough credit. Anna likes you more. And she says her girls do too."

"I liked it better when we were talking about why *you* do," he says.

"Let's see," I say. "One, because you're nice enough that you aren't going to freak out when I use your very warm leg to thaw my frozen toes."

"I'm not, huh?"

"Nope." I shift my toes, pressing them up against his calf.

"I think this counts as *unfriendly* touching," he grumbles, and I dig my toes under a little deeper. "This should earn me at least three more reasons."

"You're real," I say. "And thoughtful. You pay attention and listen with your whole face."

"My whole face?"

"Yes! You don't look at your phone. When you're talking to me, you're only talking to me. You have no idea how rare that is."

"This is a fun game," Carter says, and I reach over and nudge him in the side.

"You shouldn't ever feel less than your brother. Truly. You're going to make someone very happy one day."

The words hang in the air between us, silence stretching for so long, I start to wonder if I said something wrong. But then Carter's voice cuts through the silence.

"Thanks," he says softly. "You said some really nice things about me."

"They're all true." Another beat of silence passes before I say, "I'm glad we're friends, Carter." As soon as the words are out of my mouth, I wonder if the word *friends* feels like enough.

Carter takes a deep, audible breath before adding, "Yeah, me too."

16

CARTER

I wake up to my alarm at seven a.m. with Sarah's arm draped across my midsection, her head resting on my shoulder. I have no idea how we got here—but I know the four hours of sleep I just got were the best I've had in a long time.

I manage to retrieve my phone from the nightstand and turn off the alarm without disturbing Sarah, then I drop it onto the mattress beside me and take a second to enjoy having her so close.

Pretty sure the leg she has draped over *my* leg wouldn't qualify as "friendly touching," which means we're breaking her rules right now, and as soon as she wakes up, she's going to realize it. But I can't bring myself to push her away. Not yet. Not until I absolutely have to.

Sarah stirs, snuggling in a little deeper, and I let myself wrap my arm around her shoulders as I think back on the last eight hours.

The night was not what I expected. At least not entirely. I expected her to look amazing. I expected us to get engaged. But I didn't expect how easy it would feel. How kissing her would feel like the beginning of something much bigger than a marriage of convenience.

I've never clicked with anyone like I click with Sarah, which is why it was so hard to hear her outline all the ways she wants to protect her heart...*from me.*

I almost asked her, right before we fell asleep, why we needed the rules at all. She admitted she's attracted to me, and I'm definitely attracted to her, so what if we just see what happens?

But I couldn't do it. In the end, I didn't want to ask because I didn't want her to tell me that for her, it's only physical. I didn't want to hear her say she wouldn't have chosen me if her brother hadn't put her up to it.

She's the one who asked for the rules, so she must have a reason. And there's not a whole lot I can do about that.

Which sucks. Because holding her like this feels *really* good.

Maybe I can convince her to give me a chance or at least figure out why she's resistant. She *did* mention she's not great at trusting people. So maybe she needs time to realize she can definitely trust me.

Sarah lets out a small moan. "Mmm. Is it time to wake up yet?"

I lift my head to look at her. She looks beautiful. Peaceful. So comfortable. I hate to make her move. But even if she doesn't have anywhere to be, I've got to be on the team bus in less than an hour.

I reach up and brush her hair away from her face. "Yeah, it is," I say softly.

Her eyes flutter open, and I wonder when she's going to realize just how much of her is touching me. She blinks once, twice, then slides her hand over my chest before sitting bolt upright in bed.

There it is. Reality hitting her.

"Did I—were we...?" She glances behind her and looks at the other side of the bed. "Did I accost you in the middle of the night?"

I let out a chuckle. "You did not. I think we both shifted toward the middle while we were talking, then we fell asleep and just..."

"That's not like me. I'm not usually much of a snuggler." She looks up and meets my gaze. She looks sleepy, a little disheveled, and completely adorable. "I'm sorry if I made you uncomfortable."

"You didn't. Not at all." I tilt my head toward the other side of the room. "You want the bathroom first?"

She nods and scrambles off the bed.

I don't have much to do to get ready. Sarah comes back out, giving me a quick turn in the bathroom, then I yield the space back to her while I pack up what little stuff I take with me when we're on the road. We're traveling today, so once I pull on a pair of navy joggers and a team hoodie, there isn't much else to do.

I respond to a text from Theo asking me if I want a breakfast burrito—*yes, please and thank you*—but ignore the five others he sent wanting an update on how things went last night. Then I skim over at least a dozen different texts from people congratulating Sarah and me on our engagement. Some teammates, a few friends back in Texas, my mom. I'll eventually respond to them all, but it feels like too big a task for right now.

Sarah comes out of the bathroom with her dress back on, and my mind flashes to last night when I helped her take it off. Well, *sort of* take it off. All I know is it was almost physically painful to see all that skin and not be able to touch her.

Now, she has her hair pulled over one shoulder and woven into a braid. She can't have any makeup on, but she still looks beautiful. Bright brown eyes. Pink lips. Freckles on her cheekbones.

"Thanks for letting me borrow these," she says, handing me my clothes.

I almost tell her to keep them. I like the idea of her having something of mine—*wearing* something of mine—but that would break the rules, so I take them and tuck them into my bag. "What do you have planned for today?" I ask.

"Open studio hours at the Bainbridge," she says. "And a conversation about getting the heating fixed in the guest apartment. Though I've only got a couple of nights left, so I might just endure."

"Don't endure," I say. "I'll pay for a hotel if you need it."

She holds up a finger and points it at me. "Listen, mister first class upgrade, I can afford a hotel if I need one."

I grin. "Sure. But it's more fun when someone else is paying."

She purses her lips like she's considering. "A true statement. Still, I think I'll be okay. I spend most of my time downstairs in the studio anyway, and the heat works perfectly fine down there. Oh!" she says, her expression brightening. "I forgot to tell you my most exciting news."

"Let's hear it."

"Earlier this week, the head gallerist from a gallery called the Rooke came by the studio. I've been a huge fan of hers for years. We chatted about my work, and she looked at what I was working on, and then she invited me for tea tomorrow. At her gallery."

"That feels big?" I say, hoping she'll explain because honestly, I have no idea. I've been googling a lot of art terms lately, but my research hasn't covered gallery shows and what those mean to artists.

"It could be," she says. "There's no guarantee this will go anywhere, but even just having her acknowledge my existence is a big deal."

I loop my bag over my shoulder, and Sarah pulls on her coat. I take one last look around the room, making sure I didn't miss anything.

"What about you?" she asks. "Just travel today?"

I glance at my watch. "Yeah. A bus to the airport in twenty minutes, then a flight to Boston. Probably a team meeting, some game tape. Then I'll crash early before our day game on Sunday."

"Three games in four days? Does that happen a lot?"

"They try to avoid it, but yeah, sometimes." I open the door for her. "Can I get you a cab before I go?"

She nods. "Yes, please. That would be great."

I'm surprised we don't see any of my teammates in the hallway or on the elevator downstairs—I'm cutting it pretty close timewise. As far as Coach Kimzey is concerned, if we aren't fifteen minutes early, we're late.

"So, the Rooke—the gallery you mentioned, are you hoping she'll invite you to do a show? Would that be a bigger deal than the one you have in Atlanta?" I ask after we step onto the elevator.

"Definitely. The Atlanta gallery is amazing, but the Rooke is career-defining. It would be a huge step up. Not that anything has happened yet. But..." She shrugs. "Maybe?"

"It'll happen," I say. "I really believe it will."

The elevator doors slide open, and I lift a hand to the

small of her back, guiding her forward and through the lobby. Outside the hotel, the bus is idling, Theo and Jordo waiting outside to climb on. Jordo sees me first, then he nudges Theo who turns, eyes widening when he sees Sarah and me leaving the hotel together.

I shoot him a look that hopefully makes it clear he'd better not react beyond that, then I steer Sarah to the curb in front of the bus. I hail her a cab, then open the back door for her.

She turns to face me, taking a deep breath before offering me a smile. "So I guess this is goodbye for now." She bites her lip in that way I love. "I had a really nice time last night."

"Yeah, it was nice." I glance back at the bus, noticing several teammates standing toward the front, obviously watching us. I sigh and turn back to face Sarah, suddenly feeling a little sheepish.

She must see them too, because there's a smile playing on her lips.

"So what do the rules say about this particular situation?" I ask, running a hand over my hair.

"Good question," she says. "We *are* in public, and since your whole team is watching...I think you probably have to kiss me goodbye."

I look at her and shake my head. "The sacrifices I make..."

She grins, then I lean forward, slipping a hand inside her coat to grip her waist. I brush the tip of her nose with mine. "See you next week," I say softly, then I press a kiss to her lips, ignoring the cheers and jeers of my teammates coming from inside the bus.

She leans into the kiss just long enough for it to feel like more than a peck, then she pulls back, eyes sparkling. "Bye,

Carter," she says, then she smiles one last time and ducks into the cab.

I close the door, then watch as the driver pulls away from the curb. When I turn to head to the bus, I find myself face-to-face with Miles. I'm not sure if he was on the bus and got off or if he just exited the hotel. Either way, he doesn't look happy.

I hand my bag to one of the equipment managers, then push my hands into my pockets, trying to look casual, despite the nerves suddenly making my stomach tight. We can't look like we're having a confrontation—why would we be?—but Miles's body language is anything but chill.

"You want to explain to me why my sister was in your hotel room last night?" he practically seethes.

"It's not what you think," I quickly say. "We were out last night, getting engaged, *being seen* getting engaged, and by the time we got back, it didn't feel right to send her back to Soho. But nothing happened."

He grunts. "It looks like something happened."

I lift my eyebrows. "That's the point, right? We're engaged."

"You weren't supposed to hook up," he says. "Even if you are engaged."

"We didn't," I say. "I *wouldn't*."

He holds my gaze for a long, uncomfortable moment, like he's peering all the way into my brain. I hope not, because I've had more than a few thoughts about his sister I wouldn't want him to see.

He finally sighs. "Fine. But did you have to kiss her good-bye? You aren't really together."

I glance past him, looking around to make sure no one could have heard him. "Can you be a little more careful, please?" I say. "Sarah and I have talked about this. We came up with rules to handle our public relationship in ways that we're both comfortable with. That part of this is not your concern."

His jaw tightens, but he doesn't say anything else.

"You need to get used to this," I say. "Sarah and I will be living together. Looking like we're together to everyone else. You can't freak out if you see us kiss. It will only make it harder for us to sell this."

He gives his head a little shake. "You're right," he concedes, his shoulders relaxing the slightest bit. "Sorry I freaked out."

I reach forward and clap him on the shoulder. "No problem. Now, can you smile like you don't want to murder me so our team doesn't think we're in the middle of a family fight?"

He tugs my arm off his shoulder and pushes me to the side with a good-natured shove. "Get off me and get on the bus." I grin and step to the side to move past him, but then he stops with a hand on my forearm. "Just stick to the plan, all right? Don't make things more complicated than they need to be."

I lift my eyebrows. "I don't know what that means."

His jaw tightens, his brown eyes an uncanny reflection of his sister's. "Kiss her because you have to," he says. "But don't kiss her because you want to. That way nobody gets hurt."

With those parting words running circles in my brain, I climb onto the bus and step into the aisle. My teammates erupt into applause and cheers as soon as I appear, slapping me on the back and offering their congratulations as I pass by. I nod and smile, taking it like I know I should, but when I finally drop into the empty seat next to Theo, I feel a strange twinge of sadness I can't quite shake.

All these things I'm experiencing, the engagement, the celebration—it's all happening for the first time. I'll never get any of these firsts back, and I don't like feeling like it's all based on a lie.

Theo hands me the burrito I completely forgot he was bringing me. "Dude, we got a lot to talk about," he says, and I shake my head.

"Not here, we don't."

He lifts his hands. "Come on. At least give me the condensed version."

"We're engaged," I say. "That's pretty much all there is to tell." I look around pointedly at the many, *many* ears that might overhear our conversation.

"Fine," Theo says. "But don't think I won't bring this up again." He pulls his headphones over his ears and leans against the window, leaving me with my own thoughts.

Twice now, I've had Sarah and then her brother tell me that *real* feelings aren't a good idea. That's the safest way to keep anyone from getting hurt.

I can't decide if they're more worried I'll hurt Sarah or more worried that she'll hurt me.

17

CARTER

"Come on...three more." Theo's hands hover under the bench press bar in Holly's garage, but he doesn't touch it. He knows I'll tell him if I need his help. I let out a groan, arms trembling, but I manage to crank out three more reps before finally letting Theo help me rack the weights.

"Good work," he says as he adds a few more plates to either side of the bar.

"Dude, why are you adding more? I'm maxed out."

He grins and motions for me to get out of the way. "But I'm not."

I grumble as I get up and switch places with him. He's always been able to bench more than I can, which is annoying. We have identical DNA, and I swear I train as hard as he does. Unless he's sneaking in workouts in the middle of the night, there's no logical reason why he can do more.

Holly walks in from the kitchen, a protein bar in his hand. It's rare for any of us to train outside of the Jaguars' practice facility, but after a win at home on Tuesday night, we have a rare Wednesday off, and since Charlie is out of school for a teacher workday, we brought the party to Holly.

He has a decent amount of equipment in his garage, but we're really here for him more than for the weights.

Him...and me, apparently. Since I'm all Theo and Holly want to talk about.

I'm surprised they haven't gotten it out of their systems already. As soon as we landed in Boston, the two of them cornered me in my hotel room and demanded to know everything that happened with Sarah.

I did not hold back. From buying a ring to our first kiss to the conversation about house rules. I even told them about my confrontation with Miles when he accused me of hooking up with his sister.

In retrospect, I hate that I let Miles intimidate me. Like he's the big brother warning me not to get handsy on prom night. He asked me to do this. Now he has to trust me enough to let me.

"I just don't understand," Holly says, his mouth full of protein bar.

"Why I'm so much stronger than my brother?" Theo says from underneath the bar, which he is lifting with annoying ease.

"Why Miles seems to think Carter is a bad idea," Holly says, completely ignoring Theo. "And Sarah, too. He's, like, the perfect guy to take home to your parents."

Theo racks the weights on his own and sits up. "Boring. Reliable. Perfectly respectful. I see what you mean."

I tug the towel off my shoulder, tossing it at Theo's face.

He tosses it right back. "I don't think it's about Carter," Theo says. "We're talking like the people are the problem. But what if it's the situation?"

"Explain," Holly says, and I nod.

"Yeah. Explain."

"We're assuming Sarah doesn't want to be with Carter because he's Carter," Theo continues. "But what if it doesn't have anything to do with him? Nobody wants to be the convenient choice. The default. People want to be chosen. You and Sarah didn't pick each other. So, you move in together, you get comfortable, you think you're into it...but then you realize you were only into it because she was right in front of you, not because you would have picked her. Know what I mean? It's not the same thing."

"But he *would* have picked her," Holly says. "He was into her before all this happened."

"For, like, twenty minutes," Theo argues. "He met her once."

"Twice," I say.

"That's not any better," Theo says. "You were *interested*. That doesn't mean you were *into* her. Or that you would have been had you just dated her normally instead of diving head-first into engagement photos and house shopping."

"I get what you're saying," I say. "But I've spent enough time with her to know that I would have been into her. Even if we'd just dated normally."

"All right," Theo says, his expression turning resigned. He lifts his shoulders in a shrug, like he's sorry he has to say this next part out loud. "But maybe she can't say the same."

It's the same conclusion I keep coming to, and it doesn't suck any less to hear someone else say it.

"Still," Holly says. "Just because she's trying to protect herself doesn't mean she doesn't like you. Or *wouldn't* like you. Nothing about this situation is traditional. And it's not like you've put yourself out there, right? So she doesn't know you aren't just pretending. It makes sense she would want to be careful."

"I've told her I find her attractive," I say.

"Not quite the same thing as *I'd like to build a life with you,*" Holly says.

"I think you're playing the long game here," Theo says. "You know you have chemistry, so just...be yourself. Show her how good things could be for real and hope she comes around."

I move over to a rack of weights and pick up a set of dumbbells for bicep curls. "But that goes back to what you were saying earlier. Do I want her to just come around? If she never would have dated me in the first place?"

"That's your ego talking," Holly says.

"It isn't," I say. "If she has reasons to resist, I don't want to pressure her just by being available all the time. I want her to want me because I'm me. Not because I agreed to do this or because she's living in my house."

"But now you sound like you don't trust her to know her own mind," Theo says. "If she falls for you, she falls for you. Who cares how or why your relationship started?" He lies back down on the bench and motions for Holly to spot him. "If you're good together, you'll know, and she will too. I think you have to trust that."

Holly nods. "I agree."

We *are* good together. We're only just getting to know one another, but I already feel more comfortable with Sarah than I ever did with Veronica. That has to mean something. Even when we're not together in person, we're texting. She messaged me about her visit to the Rooke, I texted her after I played a great game in Boston, then again last night when we were back at the Vortex. She already feels like a friend. I just want her to be more than that. "So in the meantime, I just…?"

"Follow the rules," Theo says in between reps. "That says you respect her. Then woo her in all the ways that *don't* break the rules."

"Has she said anything else about hockey?" Holly asks. "About why she doesn't go to games?"

I push through two more reps before I have to put down the weights. "She hasn't," I say. "But I don't think it's just a preference thing."

"Meaning?" Holly asks.

"That she isn't skipping them because she doesn't like hockey. There's more to it than that."

"Like what?" Theo asks, still cranking out reps. The fact that he can talk while he's lifting that much weight makes me want to drop a dumbbell on his toe.

"Maybe something happened at a game?" I say. "I don't know. I get the sense she's really been through something. I don't see how it's all connected, but I feel like it has to be."

Holly's expression shifts, like he's considering how much he wants to say, but then he shakes his head like he's thinking better of saying anything at all. I watch as he helps Theo rack his weights—sometimes Holly takes a minute to formulate his words—but he never says anything.

"What was that?" I finally ask. "What were you about to say?"

He loops a hand around the back of his neck. "It's nothing. Or…maybe it was nothing. Either way, I'm not sure it's my story to tell. This is your fiancée's family we're talking about."

"Sort-of fiancée," Theo clarifies. "And the *sort-of* means

you should say whatever you're thinking because our man here is trying not to get his heart broken."

"Whoa, hearts are not involved yet," I say. "Let's not get ahead of ourselves."

"I don't believe you," Theo says to me. "But I do want to hear what Holly has to say."

Holly drops onto a weight bench, propping his elbows on his knees. "It's not much," he says. "It might have been nothing. But when I played junior hockey with Miles, he came to practice more than a few times with bruises I don't think he got on the ice. I mentioned it to our coach once, and he said he'd look into it, but nothing ever happened. I don't *know* that it was happening at home, but that's definitely what it seemed like."

My stomach tightens into a knot. The thought of Sarah growing up in a home with a father like that—it makes me feel ill. She hasn't talked about it. Doesn't really seem like she wants to. But even just the possibility makes me want to burn the world down just to keep her safe.

"Miles told me their dad was a deadbeat," I say. "So that fits."

"Daddy?"

All three of us turn to see Charlie standing in the garage doorway, her new glasses perched on her nose. Holly gives Theo and me a look, and we both understand our conversation is over. At least for now.

"What's up, Char?" he asks.

"Is it time for me to go to my playdate with Poppy?"

Holly pauses, his face saying he has no idea what Charlie is talking about. "Right. Your playdate," he says. "It might be. Let me text Anna really quick."

Charlie nods. "I'm gonna go pack a snack. Can I take an

extra Rice Krispies Treat for Poppy? And another one for Olive? Okay, good, thanks!"

She runs away before he can answer, probably on purpose. Charlie is absolutely crafty enough to turn silence into permission.

"I can't take her to Anna's," Holly says, staring at his calendar app. "A guy is coming to fix the water heater. I have a four-hour window when I'm not supposed to leave the house." He runs a hand through his hair. "I don't even have a playdate on the calendar."

"Are you sure she didn't make it up?" I ask. "Or… remember it wrong, maybe?"

He stares at his phone for another few seconds. "No, it's in my texts with Anna. Since they're out of school, she set it up. I just forgot." He breathes out a frustrated sigh. "All I do is forget stuff."

"Let me drive her over," I say. "I need to see Sarah about something anyway. I'll just take her with me."

Holly nods. "Yeah, that would be good. I've rescheduled the plumber twice because of team stuff, and we haven't had hot water for almost a week."

"Dude. What are you doing without hot water?" Theo asks.

Suddenly, I feel bad that we've been spending all this time talking about me when we clearly need to be talking about Holly. Most of the time, he seems like he's doing okay. But when stuff like this happens, I'm reminded of just how much he's trying to juggle on his own.

He shrugs. "Taking cold showers? I warm up water on the stove to add to Charlie's bathtub."

"Definitely don't leave your house," I say. "You gotta get that fixed. I'll take care of Charlie this afternoon."

"Are you forgetting you're also my ride?" Theo says.

I shoot him a look. "What else do you have to do?"

Theo frowns. "Not go to a playdate," he grumbles.

Charlie comes back into the garage, a pink backpack tucked over her shoulders. "I'm ready," she says.

"What did you pack?" Holly asks. "Can I see?"

She stops in front of him and spins, and he unzips her bag. "Charlotte, is this the entire box of Rice Krispies Treats?"

"Yep," she says without a shred of hesitation.

Holly nods, then slowly zips the bag closed again. "Right. Good sharing," he says. "Are your glasses *also* in the bag?"

Charlie studies her dad. "Possibly," she says slowly.

"Charlie," he says, and her eyes turn pleading.

"I lost them, Daddy. I promise. I have no idea what happened to them."

"In the five minutes since you were out here last?"

"Maybe you should check the Rice Krispies Treats box," Theo says under his breath, and Charlie shoots him a death glare that makes me fight a laugh.

"Charlie, you have to wear them," Holly says. "You remember your headaches? You'll keep getting them if you don't wear them."

"I haven't had a headache all week," Charlie says.

"Because you've been wearing your glasses," Holly says patiently. "If you want to go to Poppy's, you have to wear them. That's the rule."

She huffs, folding her tiny arms across her chest. "Fine. Then I won't go."

Holly tilts his head. "Are you sure about that?"

She stares him down for a long moment. I gotta hand it to her. The kid has grit. Finally, she turns and stomps into the house, returning a minute later with her glasses back on her face.

"Good girl," Holly says. "So what would you say if Uncle Carter and Uncle Theo drive you over to Poppy's for me?"

"You can't come?" Charlie asks.

"I have to stay home so the plumber can fix our hot water."

"Finally!" Charlie says, and Holly grins.

"Will you be okay going with these two?"

She looks up at me and pushes her glasses up on her nose. "Will you stay for our picnic?" she asks me. "Poppy is bringing the juice boxes, and I'm bringing the snack. We'll have extra."

Holly grimaces over Charlie's head, like he's realizing he just signed me up for a lot more than giving Charlie a ride, but I shake my head.

"I'm always down for a picnic," I say.

She nods. "Okay. Then it's okay if you drive me."

"Thanks, man," Holly says as he pulls Charlie's booster seat out of his car. "I owe you one."

"Why do the kids always like you best?" Theo asks from the passenger seat as I back out of Holly's driveway.

"Kids?" I ask.

"At youth clinics." He tilts his head toward the back seat. "Charlie. Even that kid on the airplane."

"Because I talk to kids about them," I say. "You talk about you."

He rears back the slightest bit, like he wasn't quite expecting a serious answer. "Dude. That was brutal. Insightful. But brutal."

"Uncle Carter, do you like horses?" Charlie asks from the backseat.

"Who doesn't like horses?" I say, and then she talks for the rest of the ride to Anna's.

I listen with one ear, but I'm mostly thinking of Sarah. It's been four days since I kissed her goodbye in New York, but she didn't get back to Georgia until late yesterday, so I haven't seen her yet. We've texted a few times, but we haven't made any plans to see each other, leaving me wondering what the protocol will be between now and the wedding.

Since we aren't really in a relationship, we could go days, even a week or more, without needing to see each other, not unless we have some public event to attend. But that feels weird when we're getting ready to live together. Shouldn't we at least be spending some time in each other's company? Getting to know one another?

Then again, my motives aren't exactly pure. I really just want to see her.

I'll follow the rules. I'll respect every boundary she puts in place.

But I can't stop myself from wanting to be around her. It's too late for that.

When we pull into the driveway at Anna and Miles's house, Poppy and Olive are in the front yard using sidewalk chalk to decorate the front walkway. Anna is sitting on the porch, but I don't see Sarah anywhere. Her car is here—I can see it parked by the pool house—so I'm hoping that means she's somewhere close by.

"Uncle Carter to the rescue," Anna says as I approach the porch. "Miles is inside if you're interested in watching a hockey game."

I glance at my watch. "Right now? There's one on?"

"He's rewatching the 2008 Winter Classic," she says dryly. "He watches it at least three times a year."

"Dude. Is that the one where Crosby wins the shootout in the snow?" Theo says from behind me. "Can I go on in?"

"Be my guest," Anna says, then she looks back at me. "How are you? Congratulations on your *very* realistic engagement."

"Yeah. Thanks," I say. "Everything went pretty well."

"Griffin Knox had a lot of really nice things to say. That was well-played, going somewhere you knew he'd be."

"I'm glad it worked out." I push my hands into my pockets. "Is Sarah here?"

"Yeah," Anna says. "Back in the pool house. Working, last I saw."

"Do you think she'd mind if we went back to say hello?"

"Not at all," Anna answers. "The girls have interrupted her fifty times already. You'll probably be a welcome surprise."

"I'm gonna steal Charlie for a minute and take her with me," I say. "She's been having a hard time getting used to her glasses."

"Ohhh," Anna says. "Good thinking. I'm going to sit right here and enjoy the tiny bit of winter sun we're getting without moving a single inch in any direction."

I laugh. "Sounds like a good plan."

"Is Miss Sarah the lady who had the chicken nuggets?" Charlie asks after I explain where we're going.

"That's her."

"She's pretty," Charlie says. "Is she your girlfriend? Is that why you want me to say hello?" Honestly, it's nice to have Charlie's barrage of questions as we make our way through the backyard to the pool house. I'm more nervous than I should be, and she's giving me something to focus on besides whether I'm supposed to hug Sarah hello when I see her again.

Pretty sure that would qualify as the "friendly touching" we talked about, but is it what she would want? I don't want to assume.

"She's my fiancée," I say, "which means we're getting married soon. And I want you to say hello because Sarah wears glasses just like you do."

"Really? I don't remember her glasses."

"She does. And she started wearing them when she was your age."

We finally reach the pool house, and I knock, palms sweating, but then the door opens and…there she is. Looking more beautiful than ever. Her hair is up in some kind of knot on her head, and a pencil is sticking through it. Or maybe the pencil is holding it? Her fingers are tinted gray, and there's a smudge of what I'm guessing is charcoal along her cheek, just below the frame of her green glasses.

"Carter!" she says, and then she's leaning in to give me a hug.

A *friendly* hug, I remind myself, but I can't stop myself from breathing her in. It feels so good to have her back in my arms. "Hey," I say as she pulls back. "Welcome home."

"Thanks," she says. She lets her gaze drop to Charlotte. "Hi, Charlie," she says. "Do you remember me?"

Charlie nods. "You gave me chicken nuggets. And Uncle Carter says you wear glasses just like me."

"Sorry to interrupt your work," I say. "I was just telling Charlie that you guys were the same age when you started wearing glasses."

Sarah's expression brightens as she looks at Charlie.

"That's right! Except mine were not nearly as cute as yours. You want to see a picture?"

Charlie nods, and the three of us make our way into the pool house. The space is tiny. A living room, a kitchenette, and what I'm guessing are two bedrooms on either side of the living room. It looks like Sarah has been sitting at the small table in the kitchen, working on some sketches.

Sarah grabs her phone off the kitchen counter, then makes quick work of pulling up a couple of photos. She and Charlie move into the living room and sit down on the couch, but I linger in the kitchen.

The table is covered in Sarah's work. There are at least six different sketches in various stages of completion. They look like ideas, mostly, like she's brainstorming. On one sheet of paper, there's a hand with two fingers bandaged together. On another, there's the curve of a woman's neck, her hair pulled up, a string of pearls looped around then hanging down her back.

They're incredibly realistic, but I love that in her finished work, she always makes it about more than that. There's one on her website of a face and shoulders that look real enough to be a photograph, but then the rest of the person just...falls apart. Arms blur, hands dissolve into streaks of color and light. They aren't all as abstract as that one, but so far, it's my favorite. I won't pretend to be an art critic, but it feels like she wants people to notice what she *doesn't* include on the canvas as much as what she does.

She told me via text that her meeting at the Rooke went as well as she could have hoped. The owner, who is from Georgia, is coming to her show in Atlanta at the end of March. If she likes what she sees, she wants to have a conversation about showing Sarah's work at the Rooke.

I could tell from her message that Sarah's trying to stay chill and not get her hopes up, but I think she has every right to reach for the stars.

She's that talented.

I pick up the sketch of the hand and look a little closer. It could be a hockey player. Or any athlete, really. The roughness. The bruising. The wrapped fingers.

When I move to put it back on the table, my eyes catch on another sketch, one that was covered up before. My heart starts pounding as I swap the one in my hand for this one.

Sarah once told me she makes up the people she paints. But this sketch—*it's me.*

My eyes. My jawline.

"Snoop," Sarah says, her tone gently scolding. My eyes dart up, heat flooding my face as she gently tugs the paper from my hands.

"Sorry," I say. "I didn't mean—"

"Don't worry about it," she says. "I left it out, so I can't be mad you saw it." She looks down at the sketch, then sets it back on the table. "I was just messing around. I really want to try using oil. See if I can capture the color of your eyes."

"Are they different from other blue eyes?"

"They're totally different," she says. "They almost look translucent in some light, but then, when you're wearing navy blue—like, Jaguars navy blue—they shift into looking more like...ocean blue. So the goal would be to capture all the different shades they can look at the same time."

"Sounds like you've spent *a lot* of time thinking about my eyes."

She grins. "In a *strictly* professional sense, I have."

She holds my gaze for a long moment, and I suddenly feel like I'm tumbling down the side of a hill, gaining momentum so quickly, there's no stopping where I'm headed. I love talking to this woman. I love what she does. I love how she makes me feel. I love that she has charcoal on her cheek right now, and it only makes her more beautiful. More *real*.

I told Theo my heart wasn't involved yet, but right now, I'm not so sure that's true. I'm at least on my way there.

That realization might have worried me five minutes ago. But those are my eyes she's sketching, and that has to mean something.

She clears her throat. "Anyway, I'm going to show Charlie my glasses collection. Are you going to be around a while?"

"I've got a picnic date, actually."

Sarah's expression falters the slightest bit.

"With Charlie and Poppy," I add.

"Ah," she says, something like relief passing over her expression. "That sounds fun."

"I get a juice box," I say. "I'm totally stoked."

"Miss Sarah?" Charlie asks. "Did you draw these pictures?"

"I sure did," Sarah says. "And you know what helps me do it? Wearing my glasses."

Charlie looks at the drawings for a long moment, then she nods, like she's finally decided something. "Do you want to come to our picnic?"

Sarah smiles up at me. "Do I get a juice box too?"

"I can ask Poppy if she has an extra," Charlie says. "But if she doesn't, you can share with Uncle Carter."

"Fine by me," I say, and I mean every word. I'll share my juice box...and anything else that Sarah wants.

That thought doesn't terrify me nearly as much as it probably should.

18

SARAH

THE NEXT SIX WEEKS FLY BY IN A FLURRY OF PAINTING, WEDDING planning, and moving my things into Carter's new house. *Our* new house? In any case, things moved way too quickly, and now I'm standing in the tiny hall bathroom in Anna's house in a wedding dress, my hands pressed against the cool porcelain sink. Anna insisted I let her hire professionals for my hair and makeup, and the effect is pretty extraordinary. I've never felt quite so beautiful.

Plus, this dress.

It's beyond gorgeous. Strapless, with a sculpted bodice and asymmetric pleats and a flowing full skirt. It's simple and romantic but somehow still showstoppingly beautiful.

At first, I was determined not to stress about finding the *perfect* dress. My timeline was ridiculously short, which meant I couldn't afford to be choosy. I needed something white and nice enough to convince our audience it was one I loved. There was no reason to go all out.

But Anna talked me right out of that notion.

"If life has taught me anything," she said in the middle of the bridal boutique, "it's that every time you get the opportunity to wear a gorgeous dress, you take it."

When I tried to argue that I should save the *most* beautiful dress for my *real* wedding, her scolding only grew more intense.

"You have to stop calling it a fake wedding, Sarah. You're exchanging real vows. Signing a *real* marriage license. That means you get a *real* wedding dress. End of discussion."

And so I did. A real dress. Real hair and makeup. Real jewelry.

I glance down at my left hand. *Real engagement ring.*

And tonight, my *real* husband will drive us home to the real house I've been living in without him for the past three weeks. That was his idea. As soon as he closed on the house, he suggested I move in so I could make use of the studio. I tried to protest—it didn't feel right since he's the one who bought it—but he insisted, and honestly, I *needed* the space.

I've been overwhelmed trying to finish my pieces for my gallery show in a few weeks. Now that it might lead to something at the Rooke in New York, I'm even more determined to make sure everything is perfect. Having a studio large enough to work and display the entire collection together has been such an amazing gift.

Being in the house has also made it easier to decorate. Emerson has been up from Savannah three different times, and we've made excellent progress. The main living areas are all finished, as well as Carter's room and the guest room where I've been living. I've had a million *this* or *that* conversations with Carter trying to gauge a sense of his style, and I'm pretty sure I nailed it. He likes simple and clean but with a distressed comfort that reminds me of his Texan roots. His living room is full of soft brown leather and muted throw pillows and natural fabrics. I've kept the whole thing hidden from him—I want it to be a surprise when he officially moves in tonight. He knows I've been working, but he hasn't seen the inside of the house in two weeks.

I take another slow, calming breath, but when I lift my hands from the sink, they're still shaking. But I'm supposed to be nervous, right? It's perfectly normal to be terrified on your wedding day.

"Honey?" Anna calls from the other side of the door. "It's been a minute. Are you sure you don't need any help?"

It isn't the first time she's checked on me, and I can tell she's starting to worry.

I move over to the door, but instead of letting her in, I lean my forehead against it. "Can you just get Carter for me?" I say. I'm not sure what makes me say it. I just know I want to see him before I go out there and marry him.

Anna's quiet for a beat before she says, "Are you okay?" I'm probably stressing her out, something she doesn't need so close to when her baby is due. Not to mention how hard she's worked over the past month and a half. She basically spearheaded the entire wedding—in the middle of hockey season. In the weeks right before playoffs.

She even transformed her house. All of her living room furniture is currently in the garage so there's room for a ceremony and a reception after.

We never should have been able to pull this off. And we only did because of her.

"Yeah, I'm good," I say. "I just want to see him."

"Okay. Hang on."

Less than a minute later, another knock sounds on the door.

"Sarah?" Carter's voice calls.

I unlock the door, then take a step back, making room for him to enter.

I sometimes forget how big a guy Carter is, but in this small space, it's impossible not to notice. There's no way to be in this room together and not be close enough to touch.

His eyes move over me, then his expression softens. "Wow," he says so softly it almost seems more like he's talking to himself. "*Wow.*"

"You look really nice, Carter." This is the first time we've seen each other today, and he's so handsome, I can hardly catch my breath.

"You look like you need a drink," he teases.

I chuckle. "I'm sure."

Carter takes a step forward and holds out his hand. "Friendly hug?"

I nod and slip my fingers into his, letting him tug me into his arms. I breathe in his familiar scent, letting his solid presence ground me.

Despite all the painting and decorating and Carter's very busy game schedule, we've still managed to spend quite a bit of time together over the last six weeks. We've eaten meals together, watched movies together, spent time with Poppy and Olive while their parents got much-needed alone time.

I've gotten to know his brother and FaceTimed with his mom. I've attended two different events with his teammates and the other Jaguars wives and girlfriends.

In all that time, we've gotten to be really good friends.

Just friends, apparently. Turns out, establishing the ground rules of our relationship really helped knock us onto the same page, though I'm beginning to think I was the only one who needed the reminder. Carter is *very good* at following the rules. Almost too good.

I, on the other hand, have to remind myself regularly to ignore how steady he makes me feel. How he always seems to say exactly the right thing. Not to mention how incredibly handsome he is.

"I'm kidding about the drink," Carter says, lifting his hand to brush a strand of hair away from my face. "You're stunning." His hand lingers on my cheek for a long moment before he lets it fall. He tilts his head toward the living room on the other side of the wall. "Is it all the people? If it is, I can tell half of them to wait outside."

I manage a smile as I shake my head. "Don't make anyone leave."

He nods. "Are you having second thoughts?"

I look up into his earnest blue eyes. "That's not it either."

"Okay." He says this with zero judgment and zero sense of urgency. It's clear he'll stay in this bathroom and talk to me all day if that's what I need. "Do you want to tell me what it is, then?"

I drop my eyes to the floor, smoothing my hands down the front of my dress. "I'm not sure it's one particular thing. I just...got really overwhelmed, all of a sudden. Things are feeling very...permanent, you know?"

He waves a hand like it's no big deal. "Nah. You'll be on your own in no time. I've seen what's going into your gallery show. You aren't going to need me for long, not once you're famous."

Ha. Famous. Famous in the art world doesn't come close to *actually* famous, but I appreciate his vote of confidence anyway. "You make it sound so easy."

"You're *making* it easy," he says. "I'm only buying you a little time."

Of all the things Carter has given me in the past six weeks, his belief in me as an artist might be the most significant. While Miles is still dropping not-so-subtle hints about teaching, Carter hasn't mentioned it once. He talks like qualifying for an O-1 visa is a natural next step for me, like the requirements aren't a big deal at all. Even though he's the one who has every right to urge me to pursue what would get me a visa the fastest, he doesn't seem concerned.

He keeps using that word. *Extraordinary.* Like it's a foregone conclusion I'll get there without any trouble.

Like always, Carter's presence works wonders on my nervous system, and after a few more moments of deep breathing, I feel calm enough to leave the bathroom. "Okay. I think I can do this." I look toward the door. "Should we go?"

"Actually, since we're here..." His words trail off, and I sense a new trepidation that wasn't there moments before.

"What is it?" I quickly say.

He shakes his head like he's reconsidered. "Actually, just forget it. It's nothing."

"It's not nothing. You can't stand in here and talk me out of an anxiety attack and then dismiss your own feelings like they're nothing."

He runs a hand across his face, leaving his hand over his mouth like he's afraid to speak. "It's dumb," he says, his voice muffled by his fingers.

"I'm sure it isn't."

Finally, he sighs and drops his hand. "I was just...feeling a little nervous about kissing you in front of so many people. I know it's not the first time, but it's been a minute since our last kiss, and they're all going to be watching us so closely. I want it to be convincing."

My eyebrows lift.

The last time we kissed would have been the morning after we got engaged. We've done a lot of holding hands and snuggling when we've been out with other players and their wives or at hockey events, but we haven't had a reason to kiss again, especially since we've been following the rules so closely. But he's right. The wedding kiss isn't exactly optional.

Right now, Anna and Miles's living room is full of our family and friends. Emerson and Jeremy and a few others from Savannah have driven up. Carter's mom, Kim, is here, as well as his former captain from his AHL team, not to mention all his current teammates. Even Coach Kimzey and the Jaguars GM are here.

And all but a handful of those people currently believe we're in love.

"Right," I say. "It should be convincing. Were you thinking we should...practice?"

He gives me a sheepish look, but then he shrugs his shoulders. "It might make it easier out there if we do." He leans forward and hooks a gentle hand around my waist. "Can we break the rules in the name of practice?"

Carter has a playful air about him, but under the surface, I sense a vulnerability I don't always see in him. He's done so much to make *me* comfortable, coming to my rescue over and over again. So this time, it feels like I should be the one who rescues him.

"I think this definitely feels like an extenuating circumstance." I lift a hand to his face, my fingers wrapping around his jaw, then I push up on my toes and press my lips to his.

Carter's breath stutters at first, but he quickly stills, settling into the kiss as he lifts a hand to my face, his fingers grazing across my cheek.

The first time I kissed him, we were in a room full of people, making the whole thing feel a little like a performance. It was still amazing—I've been dreaming of that kiss for weeks—but this time, we're the only two people here, allowing my focus to zero in on Carter. *Only Carter.*

And the difference is significant.

His body is warm and solid in front of me, his lips soft, his grip firm, and *oh,* I really, *really* like kissing him.

Carter tilts his head to deepen the kiss, and somewhere in the back of my mind, it occurs to me that there's no way we'll kiss like this in front of our friends and family. A kiss like this —it's the kind that sparks hunger, a craving for more. More of this. More of *him.*

I should stop, but I can't bring myself to pull away.

Not until a knock sounds on the bathroom door. "Are you two ready?" Anna asks.

Carter pulls back, his expression stunned enough that I'm pretty sure he fell as deeply into that kiss as I did.

I press a hand to his chest as if to calm him and clear my throat. "We'll be right out," I say to Anna, then I wait until I hear the swish of her dress as she walks away.

I look back at Carter.

"I'm sorry," he says. "I think I got carried away."

"I kissed you, Carter."

"I know," he says. "But I...I shouldn't have done that."

I study his face, trying to read his expression. For once, I can't tell what he's thinking, if he regrets kissing me for my sake...or for his. Either way, the fact that he regrets it at all pricks at the tenderest places in my heart. I've done a pretty good job of compartmentalizing over the past six weeks, convincing myself that I am not, nor can I ever be, the supportive wife Carter deserves. But I don't like the reminders that at some point, I'm going to have to give him up. And the look on his face right now—that's what it feels like.

"We've had a lot going on," I say. "A lot of emotion. A lot of change. I think we can give ourselves a pass on this one. And, hey—at least now the wedding kiss won't feel like a big deal."

He lets himself smile the slightest bit, but it doesn't reach his eyes. "True," he says. He straightens his jacket, and I reach up to adjust his tie.

"Should we do this?" I ask, letting my hands linger on his chest, and he nods.

"Let's do it," he says. Then I slip my hand into his, and we head out the door together.

FIVE MINUTES LATER, Miles walks me down the aisle, then I'm standing with Carter, promising to love and cherish and care for him until death do us part. He adds a wedding band to the engagement ring I'm already wearing, and I slide a ring onto his left hand. There's a scar that runs up the side of his finger I've never noticed before—probably a hockey injury—and it suddenly feels startling to me that I don't know the story.

There's still so much I don't know.

"Breathe," Carter whispers, and I lift my eyes to meet his. His gaze is warm, steady like always, and my nerves immediately settle.

And then I'm officially Mrs. Carter Williamson, and a

room full of our loved ones is cheering us on while Carter presses the sweetest, tenderest kiss to my lips.

The post-ceremony celebration starts almost immediately as friends and family move in to congratulate us and wish us well. "I'll be right beside you all night," Carter says, slipping an arm around my waist and giving me a squeeze.

I love that he knows I need the reminder.

He stays true to his word, never leaving me as I greet his teammates and hug his mom. I meet former Appies players and former coaches. And Carter meets Emerson's boyfriend, Jeremy, who is just as much a Jaguars fan as Emerson promised.

"I already love you," Jeremy says as he gives me a hug, "just based on how highly Emerson speaks of you. But the fact that I'm currently sharing a room with the entire Jaguars team has definitely earned you some bonus points."

"What about me? Do I get bonus points?" Carter asks from beside me.

Jeremy's face flushes as he looks up at my husband. *My. Husband.* I wonder if I'll ever get used to saying that.

"Oh, you definitely don't need them," he says. "But if you want some anyway, bonus points are easily bought with gifts. A jersey signed by all your teammates, maybe?"

Carter grins. "I'll see what I can do."

Theo gives me a big hug, welcoming me to the family, and I must get at least five different hugs from Poppy, Olive, and Charlie, who is delighted to tell me she's tripled the size of her glasses collection. The ones she's wearing tonight are purple with pink hearts on the sides.

The other hockey wives and girlfriends are lovely and welcoming, many encouraging me to come to the next game just so I can sit with them. I smile and nod and promise I'll try, hating that I'm going to disappoint them all.

I wonder how long they'll want to include me if I only go to the events that don't have anything to do with playing actual games.

"Don't worry about it," Carter says, his voice close to my ear. "There are a lot of other ways you can support the team."

I give him a grateful smile, but I still can't shake the sense of disappointment in myself. This isn't just about letting down the other hockey wives. It's about letting him down too. That's the worst part.

Across the room, Theo and Holly are having an animated discussion with a few other Jaguars players, and Theo calls over to his brother.

"Carter! Come give us your opinion," he says.

Carter looks down at me. "Will you be okay for a second?"

I nod. "Go. I'm good."

"I'll keep her company," Kim says, moving in beside me.

Carter leans down and presses a kiss to my temple, then he moves across the room to stand next to his brother. I watch him go, feeling a strange mix of happiness and sadness at the same time. Happiness because I like him so much— and because I'm incredibly grateful he's the guy who said yes to this wild scheme. Sadness because I desperately wish I could be what he wants. What he *needs*.

"How are you holding up?" his mom asks. After multiple FaceTime calls, it already feels like I know her, but Kim Williamson is even better in person. She's warm and maternal and vivacious, and I really, really like her.

"It's a little overwhelming," I say, "but it's been a good day. It's nice to have so many loved ones together at once."

She nods. "So true. And teammates too. This team has

been such a good family for the boys." She looks over at me. "You'll need that family. I'm sure you know just from your brother, but being a hockey wife is not for the faint of heart."

I force a smile, even as my gut tightens the slightest bit. "Yeah, I've gotten that sense."

"With how much they travel and the potential for injuries or sudden trade deals, I'm not sure I could do it." She looks over at me. "Carter will make it seem worth it though. He's been ready to love someone since he was fifteen."

A knot forms in the back of my throat. "Yeah, he's pretty special."

"Honestly, I wasn't even surprised when he told me y'all were getting married," she continues. "I admittedly thought you might be pregnant at first, with how fast the wedding happened, but when he explained you wanted to get married before playoffs, I understood. And I could tell just by his words how much he loves you. I always knew with him that once he fell, he'd fall hard and fast."

A twinge of guilt makes my heart feel tight. I don't like that we're being dishonest with so many people today, but Carter's mom is the one who hits me the hardest. He clearly gets his earnest nature from her, and she seems genuinely happy for us. It's been hard enough having these conversations with her on the phone, but it's so much more difficult in person.

She would be so disappointed if she knew we were only pretending.

"Mrs. Williamson, will you excuse me for a moment?" I say, then I hustle across the hall and duck into the home office that's off the kitchen. Well, sort of home office. Anna treats the space more like a library. It has floor-to-ceiling shelves packed full of her paperbacks. Novels and books of poetry and memoirs. There's a desk in the middle of the room that the girls use for coloring or other art projects while Anna stretches out on the chaise lounge to read. She might be the only person I know who reads more than I do.

At least for right now, the room is blissfully empty, so I take a second to breathe, to let the quiet soothe my frayed nerves.

I know Mrs. Williamson didn't mean anything by her words, but they still triggered a sense of guilt that stings deeper than anything I've felt so far.

It feels like I've taken something from Carter. Some opportunity to fall in love—to have his mother see him get married for real.

He's been ready to love someone since he was fifteen.

I see it in him. The way he's so kind and gentle and good.

And now he's married to me.

I sink onto the chaise.

Carter Williamson is my *husband*.

A moment later, Miles steps through the door. He wore a dark blue suit for the ceremony, but he's already lost the jacket and tie, his shirt sleeves rolled up to his forearms to reveal a plethora of tattoos. We haven't talked since right before he walked me down the aisle.

"I thought I saw you come in here," he says. "How are you feeling?"

I take a deep breath. "I'm married," I say simply, and he chuckles.

"Yeah. Pretty wild." He clears his throat, and I get the sense he followed me for a very specific purpose. "So, listen. I know we don't talk about it much, but none of the guys on the team know how things were with Dad."

I sit up a little taller. Miles rarely even *mentions* Dad. He definitely never talks about the abuse.

"The way I see it, Carter is going to be my teammate longer than he's going to be your husband. So I would appreciate it if you'd help me keep it that way."

His words are pragmatic and factual. Carter and I only committed to a year. But they still feel like a punch to the gut—like a very callous reminder that all of this is temporary.

Still, the root of his request is that he doesn't want Carter to know, and I can't judge him for that.

"Okay," I say gently. "But Miles, I don't think it would change the way your team—"

"It would," he says, cutting me off. "I'm their captain. I don't want them to look at me differently."

"They wouldn't," I say. "They respect and love you so much. I can see that just from how they interact with you *off* the ice."

"But it's different on the ice," he says. "They need to know they can trust me. That I'll always keep my head. I set the tone out there."

"Which is exactly why it wouldn't matter," I say. "How Dad treated you doesn't define you, Miles. Your life is evidence of that. And so is how you lead your team."

He pushes his hands into his pockets. "Just promise me, all right?"

I hate promising to keep secrets from Carter, but I also understand that this isn't really my secret to tell. "Okay," I say. "I promise."

He nods and breathes out a sigh, visibly relieved. "Good," he says, finally letting himself smile. He's quiet for a beat before he says, "Big day, huh? I can't believe we actually pulled it off."

Something about his tone chafes against my already frayed nerves. There's no awe in Miles's voice. No true sentiment. Just relief. A sense of completion.

"You don't have to sound so heartless," I say, and his brow furrows.

"Heartless?"

"Sorry," I say, shaking my head. "I just...you're making it seem like a scheme. Some giant ploy to fool everyone."

He moves into the room and leans against the desk, feet crossed at the ankles. "Isn't that what it was?"

"Yes. But..." I shake my head. "It's fine. Just forget I said anything. I was talking to Carter's mom, and she went on and on about Carter being ready to settle down and love someone, and it just made me sad. That's all."

Miles's expression softens. "He didn't go into this blind, Sarah. Neither of you did."

"I know," I say. "But the lying part is still hard."

There's a bowl of Poppy's crayons on the table, and Miles takes a few out, lining them up on the table in a neat row. "It'll all be behind you soon," he says. "Now you just have to get certified and find a job. The hardest part is behind you."

I close my eyes. I really, *really* don't want to have this conversation with Miles right now. Not today.

"Speaking of which," he continues, "I talked to the principal at Poppy's school the other day. They already have an art teacher on staff, but he mentioned a few other private schools in the area where he has connections. He said he'd be willing to make some introductions whenever you're ready."

I shouldn't be surprised that Miles is networking on my behalf. Despite the many ways I've tried to protest, he always circles back to teaching.

But have I really been explicit with Miles? Have I told him outright that I don't want to do it?

I don't love confrontation generally, but I particularly don't love it with my brother. But after all the success I've had the past two months, it feels callous for him to throw this at me like it's the only option on the table.

"I don't want to teach, Miles," I say, my voice barely audible.

He scoffs. "Do you want to stay in Georgia?"

"Of course I do. But that isn't the only way. I keep telling you that—showing you the many ways I'm finding success—and you keep dismissing it like it's never going to work."

"Because it might not," he argues. He scoops up the crayons and dumps them back in the bowl. "I don't understand why it has to be one or the other. You can still paint if you're working as an art teacher."

"Not really," I say. "Not like I need to. Teaching is a full-time job. It's also about the optics—about wanting to look like a professional artist."

He folds his arms across his chest and levels me with his most big-brother stare. "I'm just saying. It seems like a lot to hang your hopes on when Carter has only promised you a year."

I lift a hand to my neck, massaging at the stress suddenly building there. "I know that," I finally say. "But I can't turn myself into someone I'm not."

For a moment, neither of us speaks, tension hanging heavy in the air. I realize I'm being idealistic. For Miles, who has always lived grounded in pragmatism, it probably seems naive, even childish for me to resist the most practical and obvious solution to my dilemma.

But somehow, deep in my gut, I *know* that teaching isn't

the answer. That what I would be giving up by pursuing that route would outweigh what I would gain. Even if it means going back to Canada.

Footsteps approach the doorway, and I look up to see Carter leaning into the room.

"Hey," he says cautiously, clearly clocking the tension between Miles and me. "Everything okay?"

I look at Miles, at the worry etched into his face.

Then I look at Carter, his expression open and easy. No expectation. No pressure.

"Yeah," I finally say. "But do you think we can go? I'm suddenly feeling really tired."

"I was just thinking the same thing," Carter says. His eyes dart over to Miles, and his jaw tightens, making me wonder what look my brother is giving him. Whatever it is, Carter shakes it off easily because when he crosses the room, his eyes are warm and focused entirely on me. He holds out his hand. "Ready?"

As I slip my fingers into his waiting palm, my brother clears his throat. "We aren't done talking about this."

Carter squeezes my fingers, giving me the strength to look over at Miles.

"We are, Miles," I say. "It's not your concern anymore."

Carter's hand settles on my back, warm and reassuring as he guides me through the crowd, through all the well-wishers sending us off with one last *Congratulations*.

We smile and wave as we make our way out the front door where Theo is waiting in the circle drive, leaning against Carter's truck.

The crowd spills out of the house behind us, cheering as Theo tosses his brother the keys, then steps to the side.

Carter opens the passenger door for me, then offers me a

hand while I hoist myself up, wedding dress and all. He leans in and presses a quick kiss to my lips, eliciting another whooping cheer from the watching crowd, then circles the truck and climbs in beside me.

My situation isn't any different now than it was five minutes ago, when I was talking about it with my brother.

But something about having Carter beside me makes the whole thing feel easier. Not like everything is solved, but at least like I can breathe again.

And for right now, that has to be enough.

19

CARTER

It feels weird to leave our wedding and just...drive home. I'm still in my suit, which isn't a big deal, but Sarah's in her wedding dress. She looks too beautiful for the night to be over already, but I'm honestly relieved we don't have to navigate a honeymoon situation. It's hard enough keeping her at arm's length on a normal day. Toss us into vacation mode, then heap on all the expectations of being a newlywed couple? I'm not sure I could do it.

Though we are, as of tonight, living together. Which can't be much better. I'm probably doomed no matter what.

I turn up the driveway—*our driveway?*—and glance over at Sarah.

There aren't words to describe how good it felt to pull her into my arms and kiss her like I've been dreaming of kissing her the past six weeks. The moment we were alone before the ceremony—it delivered, and then some. And then watching her interact with my friends, my teammates, my mom...it all felt so *right.*

I've tried to keep myself in check. It would be easy to get

swept up in the moment, to let momentum and the significance of the *event* propel me into feeling things we haven't truly earned. Sarah and I haven't had to do any of the work involved with figuring out a relationship because we don't have a real one. We've gotten to ignore the uncomfortable stuff.

Why doesn't she talk about her dad? Why can't she go to hockey games? Why do I need to be needed so much that I immediately swapped taking care of my brother for taking care of someone else?

It was Holly who threw that last question at me, and I've been ruminating on it ever since.

But then I look at Sarah and I just...want to be with her.

It's that simple.

And that complicated. Because Sarah is already my wife.

"How has Gordie settled in?" I ask as I park the truck in front of the house. I'm sure Gordie is fine, but I'm grasping for anything that might realign my brain, get me back to a place where I can coexist with Sarah without obsessing over how much I wish we were together for real.

"He's a dream," Sarah says. "We're already best friends."

When my lease ended a week ago, I moved Gordie into the new house with Sarah and crashed on Theo's couch until tonight.

Technically, I could have moved into the new house too—it's not like living under the same roof will change the nature of my relationship with Sarah—but she's been excited about surprising me with the decor, and she wanted another week to get everything perfect.

Across the truck, she takes a deep breath in, like she's willing herself to stay calm. It's comforting to know I'm not the only one feeling nervous, but I wish there was something I could do that might make us both feel better.

"Should we go in?" I ask.

"Yes?" she says, and I let out a little chuckle.

"Way to convince me you really want to."

"I do," she quickly says, "I'm just...scared. What if you hate your house? What if I've picked a bunch of stuff you think is ugly and you don't tell me because you're too nice?"

"I'm not going to hate it," I say.

"You don't know that."

"I do. You've asked me a million questions about what I *do* like. And most of the time, I was fine with either option, and I only picked one because you wanted me to."

"Shut up," she says. "Is that true?"

I shrug. "I mean, I really didn't like the blue velvet or the cow skin rug. But otherwise..."

"Carter Williamson, I never showed you blue velvet anything."

I look at her and grin. "My point exactly. I'm sure I'm going to love whatever you picked out."

With the truck turned off, the temperature is quickly dropping. Spring is fully upon us in Georgia, but the nights are still cool, and in her wedding dress, Sarah's shoulders and arms are exposed. "Come on," I say. "You're going to freeze if we stay out here any longer."

When we reach the front porch, she makes me close my eyes while she opens the door, then she takes my hands, guiding me across the threshold. The touch reminds me that now that we're home and no longer in public, I can't touch her like I have been all night.

Those little touches—a kiss to her temple, a squeeze of her fingers, her palm grazing across my shoulder or slipping under my suit coat to hook around my waist. They were some of my favorite parts of the night.

Second only to the kiss we shared before the ceremony.

And the tiny hitch in Sarah's voice when she said her vows. The emotion felt so incredibly real. Over and over—it all feels *so real*.

"Okay," Sarah says, a slight tremble in her words. "You can open your eyes."

We're standing in between the main living and dining areas, and I have to blink as I take in the transformation. The house looks...*amazing*. To my left, the living room is anchored by a low-profile leather sofa and a pair of matching chairs. The gas fireplace on the back wall is lit, casting a warm glow into the room. The only other light is a lamp, making the whole space feel cozy. Like home. On the wall opposite the couch, there's a collage of artwork, and I look closely, wondering if any of it is Sarah's. It doesn't appear to be, though it's all stuff I like. Warm tones, landscapes, trees. Things that feel like they're bringing the outdoors in.

"That big one is the TV," she says from beside me. She picks up a remote and changes the landscape filling the TV screen. "It looks like art when it isn't on."

"I wouldn't have known had you not told me," I say. I look over at her. "Sarah, this is amazing. I can't believe you did all this."

She takes my hand and tugs me toward the dining room. "I really love the table Emerson found. It's walnut and so beautiful, and even if Emerson might have sold a tiny piece of his soul to get it delivered in time, I really think it completes the space."

"It's incredible," I say, and I'm suddenly struck with a vision of sitting at this table across from Sarah, eating breakfast, watching the sun filter in through the windows. It's so easy to imagine a life with her, to see her here, filling up these spaces with her energy and her vision and her art.

She's already turned this place into a home for me. It's hard to imagine ever occupying the space without her in it.

I lift our entwined fingers to my lips, pressing a kiss to the side of her thumb before I even realize what I'm doing.

Our eyes meet, and the question in her gaze makes me drop her hand and push *my* hands into my pockets. An awkward second passes before I clear my throat. "Thank you," I say. "I really love how everything turned out."

"Come see your bedroom," she says. "It might be my favorite room in the house."

She's killing me here—she cannot tell me my *bedroom* is her favorite room in the house—but I follow her anyway. She stops at the door and spins, putting a hand on my chest to stop my entrance.

"Wait right here," she says. "I want to turn the lamps on. And close your eyes again."

I dutifully obey, waiting while she moves into the room ahead of me.

"Okay," she finally says. "Ready."

I open my eyes and step into the room, immediately sensing the calming vibe she's created. The bed is *my* bed, but she's updated the bedding and created a clean, masculine space that still has the same cozy feel as the rest of the house. Nightstands anchor the bed on both sides, and a low bookshelf under the window has several plants on top.

I told Sarah once that I love real plants, but I'm afraid to have them because of how much I travel. But I guess now, she'll be here to water them and keep them alive.

Gordie wanders out from the bathroom and weaves

between my legs in greeting before jumping onto the bed, flopping onto his side like he owns the place.

Sarah sits down beside him and scratches under his chin, and he immediately starts to purr. But I'm staring at the art hanging on the opposite side of the bed. I'm pretty sure this *is* Sarah's work.

I slowly walk across the room, stopping in front of the canvas, my heart suddenly racing.

Because it's...*me*.

Or I think it's me. You can't see my face, but seventy-four is my jersey number, which she had to have done on purpose. I'm in a knee slide, moving across the ice, like I'm celebrating a goal. Around me, the ice is shifting, moving, crystallizing into swirls of navy, light blue, and white—Jaguars team colors. Above me, the colors shift into an outline of the team logo.

I turn and look at Sarah. She's watching me from where she's sitting on the edge of the bed, her hands fiddling with the folds of her dress. "I was just messing around," she says, her cheeks flushed with color. "I don't know if you really want to have a painting of yourself hanging in your room, but I was hoping it more encapsulated the spirit of your entire team. Also, this isn't the painting. The one I'm doing for you as a part of our deal. I've got something bigger planned for that. This is just...this was just for fun."

I walk over and offer her a hand, pulling her to her feet. "I'm going to give you a purely platonic, very friendly hug now."

She slides her arms under my suitcoat and grips my waist, and I wrap my arms around her shoulders, leaning down to breathe her in.

"So you like it?" she asks, her cheek pressed against my chest.

"I love it," I say. "All of it. The painting, the house. It's all amazing." For a split second, I almost tell her I don't want to pretend anymore. That this—all of this—is exactly what I want, and I don't want an expiration date. We did things out of order, but that doesn't mean we can't still have a life together.

But then she breathes out a relieved sigh. "I'm really glad. I wanted you to love it. You're doing such a big thing for me—you deserve to love it."

Her words call our agreement to mind, and my confession dies on my tongue. Thinking I deserve it isn't a bad motivation—it's the situation we're in whether I like it or not. But it's not the same thing as doing things for each other because we want to.

Which means every action, every word we say to each other, has a question mark hovering over it.

I must be a glutton for punishment because I hold onto her anyway. Long enough that we definitely shift past friendly hug territory.

And then Sarah's stomach rumbles.

She sucks in a gasp, shifting back as she moves her hands to her belly. "Oh my gosh. That was embarrassing."

I chuckle. "Are you hungry?"

"Honestly, I don't even remember the last thing I ate. I didn't eat anything at the reception. Did you?"

"Not much. I didn't even have any cake."

"Anna packaged that up for us, at least. You want some?"

Across the house, the doorbell rings. "I do," I say. "But I think we should eat Thai food first." It was Holly who suggested

I order us some food to eat after the reception. He said when he and Claire got married, they had to stop for burgers on their way to the airport because they'd both forgotten to eat.

"Shut up," Sarah says. "You ordered Thai food?"

"I figured we'd be hungry. Wanna change and meet me in the living room?"

"Carter Williamson, you are the best human I know," she says. She reaches down and slips off her shoes, picking them up with one hand, then gathering the skirt of her dress with the other before hurrying toward her room.

Ten minutes later, we're together in the living room, both changed into sweats, drinking the very expensive wine Emerson gave us as a wedding gift and eating Pad Thai and Pad Krapow. It took a little bit of sleuthing and stealing Emerson's number from Sarah's phone, but between him and Anna, I've accumulated a pretty solid list of Sarah's favorites.

Thai. Margherita pizza. Glazed donuts with chocolate frosting. Blueberry scones. Lady Grey tea. I logged each thing in my brain, tiny puzzle pieces that make up who Sarah is and what makes her happy.

Gordie has followed us into the living room and is curled up on Sarah's lap—the traitor.

"Should we watch something?" I ask, reaching for the remote.

"Yes. Definitely. But nothing scary or traumatizing. I need happy feel-good TV."

"So we should watch *Ted Lasso*?"

"Thai food and *Ted Lasso* and vanilla bean wedding cake with raspberry frosting and Gordie in my lap?" She scoops up a bite of Pad Thai with her chopsticks. "Are you trying to give me a perfect evening?"

I turn on the TV and find the show. "It's not quite a honeymoon, but hopefully it'll still feel like a nice night."

Three episodes later, we've polished off the Thai, eaten way too much wedding cake, and opened a second bottle of wine. I've got a mandatory skate in the morning that's probably gonna be painful, but if there's ever a night to justify celebrating, it's your wedding night.

Coach Kimzey made it clear I'm still expected to be there, but I don't think he'll do anything but rib me when I'm dragging. Which I definitely will be.

Next to me, Sarah lets out a little groan as her head falls onto my shoulder. "Mmm. I definitely drank too much wine." As the night progressed, we ended up moving closer and closer, finally settling directly beside each other in the name of sharing a blanket. It's the most incredible kind of torture to have her so close—a masterclass in self-restraint.

The credits roll on *Ted Lasso*, and I reach over and use the remote to turn off the TV so another episode doesn't start.

"I'm a little tipsy, I think," Sarah whispers. "And very sleepy."

I shift, lifting an arm and wrapping it around her shoulders. "Let's get you to bed, then."

She burrows into my chest, wrapping her arms around my midsection. "Can I just sleep here? You smell so good."

I almost consider it. The couch is comfortable enough, but sleeping this close to Sarah when we've both been drinking feels like playing with too much fire.

I force myself to shift away from her and stand up. "Come on," I say gently. "You'll be more comfortable in your bed."

She flops onto the couch as soon as I'm out from under her. Apparently, she wasn't kidding about the *sleepy* part. It only takes a little effort to crouch down and scoop her into my arms. She wraps herself around me, her head resting on my chest, and lets out a moan that makes my blood heat. "Mmm, I like it here," she says.

Sarah's room is on the main level of the house at the end of a short hall off the living room. There's a lamp on in the corner, illuminating a space that already feels very Sarah, even in the short time she's been living here. There are three different bookshelves, all crammed full of books, and the top of the dresser is littered with half a dozen pairs of glasses, hair ties, and three empty mugs—probably from her tea.

The room smells like her, and it makes me wish I had a reason to stay longer.

I move to the bed and lower Sarah onto her pillow, but when I try to stand up, she tightens her grip around my neck. "Don't leave me," she says, her voice soft and sleepy.

"You need to rest," I say, and her eyes flutter open. She gives her head a tiny shake.

"Let's play truth or dare instead."

Oh, this woman is killing me.

She reaches up and brushes her hands over my jaw, her thumb touching my bottom lip. "I dare you to stay with me," she says, then she pulls me down for a kiss.

Her mouth is soft and warm, her lips pliant against mine, sending a heady wave of desire crashing over me. She's my wife, and she's telling me to stay, but I can't do it. Not when I have no idea how much of this is the wine talking. Not when I can't be sure that *she's* sure this is exactly what she wants.

I make myself pull back, then I lift my hand to trace the side of her face.

Her eyes are already closed again, making me even more certain the best thing I can do for her right now is to walk away.

"I want nothing more than to stay," I say. "But not yet." Not ever is more like it—unless we're torching our agreement. Which isn't a decision either of us is capable of making right now.

She takes a breath and sinks a little deeper into her pillow. I lean down and press one more kiss against her forehead, then I stand upright, turn off her lamp, and leave my wife to sleep.

2 0

CARTER

Sarah and I quickly fall into an easy routine. If I'm not on the road, we do dinner together, either something one of us has cooked or takeout of some kind. We finish watching the first season of *Ted Lasso*, then move on to the second, and to my surprise and horror, we both become totally addicted to a reality dating show.

In the mornings, we're usually up at the same time, having coffee before she heads up to her studio to paint or over to Anna's to help out with the girls, and I head to the complex for practice or training. According to her, she paints best in the morning, so when I get home in the afternoons, she's usually stretched out on the living room couch reading a book or listening to an audiobook while she bakes.

She's on a sourdough kick and has been taking full advantage of having a kitchen at her disposal. I'm not complaining, but I'm definitely having to pay closer attention to my macros.

As for Gordie, he seems to have completely forgotten he ever belonged to me. He sleeps in Sarah's room, follows her

263

around the house, and sits on the steps outside her studio when she doesn't let him inside.

She's close enough to her gallery show now that keeping the cat out is probably a good idea. She has all the pieces on display so she can study them as a group and, according to her, find the inspiration she needs to finish the last piece. Gordie is much too sneaky to risk him getting into trouble when the stakes are so high.

Two weeks after the wedding, the Jaguars are back in the Vortex for a three-game homestand after five days of away games in Florida and North Carolina. We only have ten more regular-season games before playoff season, but since our spot in the playoffs is already secure, we're pretty much coasting. Taking it easy to avoid injuries, trying to stay in the best shape possible. We're happy to have an entire week at home for a change, but I'd be willing to bet I'm looking forward to it the most.

"What about you?" Fly looks at me like I've been listening to the conversation he's having with Theo and not totally zoning out. We just snagged an easy win, and the locker room is buzzing with energy, but my brain is already on the way home.

"What about me?" I ask.

He rolls his eyes. "Are you up for going out?"

"He's only been married two weeks, man," Theo says. "And they didn't get a honeymoon. Let the man get home to his wife."

I glance over at Miles, who's watching me as he peels off the last of his gear. I won't say things have been *bad* since the wedding. But they've definitely been different. I worried it might be stressful trying to convince everyone the marriage was real, but with Miles around to back me up, my teammates took everything in stride like it wasn't a big deal at all. To them, it seemed less like we met and got married really fast and more like we got married not long after telling people about a relationship that already existed.

But I *didn't* worry about Miles treating me like I've done something wrong, and that's exactly what he's doing. Every practice, every game, he watches me like I'm his kid sister's screwup boyfriend, and he's just waiting for me to make a wrong move. It's really starting to piss me off.

"Yeah, I'm heading home," I say to Fly. "Y'all have fun."

"You could bring her," Fly says. "Is she here? Jordo is bringing Malia."

"Nah, Sarah's got her art show tomorrow. She's barely left her studio in days, which means she won't want to go out tonight."

It's an easy excuse, and it's mostly true. But at some point, my teammates are going to wonder why my wife has never watched me play. And I have no idea what I'm going to tell them because I don't know either. This is one of those areas Sarah and I very carefully avoid in conversation.

I shower and get dressed on autopilot, my mind on Sarah the whole time. She was painting when I left for the game, totally absorbed in her work.

She's probably barefoot, probably wearing one of my old t-shirts—she's developed a habit of stealing them out of the dryer despite our rule that she not wear my clothes. Her hair is probably piled on top of her head, a paintbrush stuck through the back, and she'll definitely be wearing her glasses.

I'm guessing she'll have a mug of tea sitting next to her easel. And she'll have no idea where her phone is. I've called her at least a dozen times in the past two weeks just so she can follow the sound of the vibration around the house until she finds it again.

I make eye contact with Miles one last time before he heads out for post-game interviews. Based on his glare, you'd think he was staring right into my brain, seeing how frequently his sister is filling my thoughts.

I'm only half dressed, still shirtless and barefoot, but instead of looking away, I glare right back. If Miles has an actual problem with me, he can own it and tell me what it is. I won't let him intimidate me when I've only done exactly what he asked me to do.

"What was that about?" Holly asks after Miles leaves. Coach Kimzey wanted our backup goalie to get some ice time, so Holly didn't play tonight, but he still geared up for the game just in case. As a result, he looks a lot less tired than the rest of us.

"No clue," I say. "He's been looking at me like that since the wedding."

"Have you told Sarah? What does she think?" Holly asks.

"Nah, I don't want her to worry about it," I say. "If it starts to affect our gameplay, I'll bring it up with Miles myself. But I don't think it will come to that."

Holly grabs his shoes and sits down to put them on. "He's probably just trying to intimidate you. Make sure you're behaving." He shoots me a look. "Which...are you?"

I retrieve my wallet and keys and shove them into my pockets. "You'd think the rules were tattooed on my eyelids for how closely I'm following them," I grumble.

Holly chuckles. "Hang in there, man." His phone buzzes, and he pulls it out of his pocket, frowning when he glances at the screen.

"Everything okay?" I ask.

He nods. "Yeah. Just—Charlie's with her grandparents for spring break. She's not having a very good time."

"With Claire's parents?" I ask, and he nods. Charlie loves Holly's parents, but it's been rockier navigating their relationship with his in-laws since Claire died.

"I flew her up to Montreal on Sunday," Holly says. "My parents will get her on Thursday, then keep her until Sunday when they'll fly her home. She'll be all right, but I've never been away from her this long."

"That sucks, man," I say. "I'm sorry." I hesitate a beat before asking, "Do you want to grab a beer? Talk about it?"

He gives me a knowing look. "You don't mean that."

"Of course I do."

He pats me on the back as he moves to the door. "Go home to your wife. I'm turning into an old man anyway. Once it gets this late, I don't want to go anywhere but home."

I'm surprised by how much I relate to his comment. But my desire to go home has everything to do with who will be there when I arrive.

On my way out of the arena, I pass by the family room. The doors are open as people spill in and out, teammates searching to find their people. Jordo is just inside the door, arms around his fiancée, and a twinge of jealousy pulses behind my ribs.

Jealousy I can never admit to, because as far as anyone else is concerned, I'm going home to a wife. Even if it's just on paper, it still chafes that she's never here. That in this one aspect, she isn't willing to pretend.

Theo comes up beside me and claps me on the back, and I realize I've been staring at Jordo. "You all right?" he asks, and I quickly nod.

"Yeah, I'm good."

Behind him, Fly is waiting. I guess just the two of them are going out.

Theo narrows his eyes at me, like he can sense I'm not telling the whole truth, but there's no reason to get into it here. Talking won't change anything about my situation.

It's been weird spending less time with Theo. We obviously still see each other when we're with the team, but living across the hall from each other, we were together almost constantly. That meant if one of us was feeling off, we never made it very long before the other beat the truth out of us—figuratively, if not literally.

It takes more of an effort now—checking in with each other.

"What if I don't go out with Fly and just come over?" he says. "Are you and Sarah doing anything? We could just... hang out."

I quickly shake my head. "Don't change your plans," I say. "I promise I'm fine. But we need to do something with Holly this week. Charlie's in Canada with her grandparents."

He nods. "Got it. I'll call you tomorrow, and we'll figure something out." He gives my shoulder another squeeze, then turns and jogs toward Fly.

It's late enough when I pull into the driveway that I can't be sure Sarah hasn't already gone to bed.

I drop my keys into the bowl by the door and toe off my shoes, moving quietly just in case she has. The house smells faintly like paint and tea, a scent that already feels familiar. Like home.

At the end of the hall next to the kitchen, I peek up the stairs that lead to Sarah's studio. The door is closed, the light still on, so she must still be awake. I make my way up, knocking when I reach the top. Sometimes she doesn't hear my knocks—if she has her AirPods in and she's actively painting, I'm not sure she'd hear the smoke detector going off. But tonight, she calls a soft, "Come in," and I push the door open.

Sarah is standing in front of the final piece she's been working on, arms wrapped around her middle. The rest of the pieces for the show aren't here anymore, so she must have taken them to the gallery while I was out of town. The space feels bigger without them.

Sarah looks at me over her shoulder. "Did you win?"

I lean against the door jamb. She usually keeps an eye on scores, but with how distracted she is, I'm not surprised she hasn't tonight.

"We did," I say, and she smiles.

"Good." She's barefoot on the hardwood, her toes a navy blue that matches the Jaguars logo on the t-shirt she's wearing. *Mine.* Just like I guessed. She has it knotted at her waist, and I spend a little too long noticing the curve of her hips, the way her leggings make her legs look a million miles long. There's a streak of blue paint running down the side of her neck, disappearing into the collar of her shirt.

"Everything else is already at the gallery?" I ask.

She nods. "All but this one. I only finished it tonight. Which, Second Light wasn't thrilled when I told them. And it definitely isn't ideal to hang something so fresh. But I had to get it right."

"They're worried about it being fully dry?"

She nods. "I did this one in acrylic, so it should be fine. But ideally, it should sit here for three weeks before I move it anywhere."

The piece she's studying is one I've seen her working on a

lot since the wedding. I can't pinpoint what's different about it now, but I'll never question Sarah's eye.

It reminds me of reviewing game tape—replaying the same sequence over and over again until the mistake finally reveals itself. An untrained eye might never see it. Never recognize the moment things went wrong.

Sarah stretches, propping her hands on her hips as she arches her back, then she tilts her head toward the canvas. "How does she look to you?" she asks.

"How does she look?"

"Her mood," Sarah clarifies. "What does it look like she's feeling?"

I study the painting, suddenly nervous that I might disappoint Sarah if I don't see what she wants me to see, but then she nudges me with her shoulder.

"Stop stressing," she says. "There's no right or wrong answer here."

Easy for her to say, but I keep my eyes on the painting, reading the emotion etched onto the woman's face. "She looks...resolute," I say. "Like she isn't trying to hide how she feels anymore." Like the rest of Sarah's work, the woman's face is photorealistic and fills up the middle third of the canvas. But her hair is a sea of rippling, shifting color.

She turns toward me, her shoulder brushing my arm as she does. It's completely accidental—a totally harmless touch. But it still sends a sharp pang of awareness through me, and I feel a sudden craving to step closer, to pull her into my arms. We've been so good since the wedding. With the exception of all the t-shirts she's stolen, we haven't broken the rules once. But every time I'm around her, it feels like the tension keeps ratcheting up, tighter and tighter. I'm starting to wonder which one of us is going to crack first.

"That was a good answer," she says, looking up to catch my gaze. We're standing close enough for me to see the flecks of gold around the edges of her irises, the freckles dotting the bridge of her nose. "It took me long enough, but I think I'm finally happy with it."

"It's amazing," I say, my voice low. "You should be happy with it." My eyes move to the streak of paint on her neck, and I can't keep myself from smiling.

"What?" she says. "Why are you smiling?"

I lift my hand and slide a single finger down her neck, tracing the paint until I reach the hollow above her collarbone. "Blue paint," I say. I hook my fingertip around her collar and tug it down just slightly, revealing the rest of the smudge. "It's the same color as your shirt." I lift an eyebrow. "Or should I say *my* shirt?"

She bites her lip. "Sorry. I know I said I'd stop stealing them. But they're just so soft and comfortable. And I only paint in this one because you said I could."

"Wear them all, Sarah. It doesn't bother me."

It should bother me. If I had any sense of self-preservation, I'd ask her to follow the rules we made for a reason. But I like the idea of her thinking of me whenever she wears one. Probably too much.

"It's your own fault," she says. "If you didn't smell so good..."

"She says when she pulls them straight out of the dryer."

"It doesn't matter!" she says. "They still smell like you."

I grin down at her. "You aren't so bad yourself."

"Whatever. I smell like paint and varnish."

"Okay, true. But also...honeysuckle? Sometimes oranges. And sometimes roses."

"You're taking notes, huh?"

I shrug. "Just noticing. I notice everything about you."

Her eyes drop, and for a split second, I wonder if I pushed too far. Made the flirting a little too pointed. But then she looks up again, this time with new purpose in her eyes.

"Are you off tomorrow?"

I nod. "Yeah. We have another game on Wednesday, and we won tonight, so we get Tuesday off."

"Want to help me take this to the gallery?" She tilts her head toward the painting. "They sent a courier over to pick up the others earlier this week, but I promised I'd get this one to them since I begged for extra time."

"I'd love to help."

"Good." She licks her lips. "And you're still coming to the show?"

"Of course I'm coming. I wouldn't miss it." A tiny prick of pain pinches the back of my heart. I *wouldn't* miss her show, and I'm really looking forward to being there. But it's hard to ignore the reminder that she can't show up for me in the same way.

I know she has her reasons. Nothing about Sarah is selfish —the entire reason she wanted to stay in the States was so she could be here to help her family. They're at the center of her life, so I don't think she isn't coming because she just doesn't care.

But my brain is having a hard time coming up with a reason that makes sense. And that's the frustrating part. As much as I would love to have her at a game, I don't like feeling like there's a piece of her that I don't understand and can't ask about.

"We'll be out in public," Sarah says, pulling my attention back to her. Her eyes flash with something that looks like hunger. "At the show. That means the rules will be different."

"They will be," I say slowly, heart rate quickening the slightest bit. "We'll have to touch a lot more. Are you ready for that?"

"Touching," she echoes, but then she leans forward the slightest bit, her eyes dropping to my lips as she almost whispers, "Kissing."

She wants it. I *know* she wants it. So why are we pretending that we have to keep following the rules? I'm about to ask her, but then she takes a deep breath and a *giant* step backward.

"I should go to bed," she says, the words fast. "And you should too. You're probably really tired after your game."

I swallow my sigh. "Yeah, I am."

We walk down the bonus room stairs and down the hall together, stopping when we reach my bedroom door. Gordie appears, and Sarah leans down, scooping him into her arms and holding him in front of her like a shield.

She gives me one last look over her shoulder. "Goodnight, Carter," she says, then she heads across the house to her room, taking my cat with her.

I move into my room and close the door behind me, smiling into the darkness.

I haven't forgotten the earlier reminder of Sarah's secrets, but it's stinging a little less now. Sarah Stone just told me she wants me to kiss her again.

And I don't plan on disappointing her.

SARAH

By the time the gallery doors open, I've adjusted the sleeves of my black dress at least fifty times and texted Carter twice, begging him to bring me something else to wear. Why did I think I could handle long sleeves? I have long arms, so long sleeves stress me out, hitting me an inch higher on my wrist than they do anyone else. Which is why I keep tugging on them.

Emerson steps up beside me and presses a wine glass into my hands, but I quickly shake my head and try to hand it back.

"I can't drink this. I haven't eaten anything. And I can't eat anything because then I'll throw up."

"Then just hold it," he says through gritted teeth, refusing to take it. "Because if I see you adjust your sleeves one more time, I'm going to rip them off your dress altogether."

"Actually, that might help," I say. "Do you think we could get a clean tear? Right at the seams?"

"Stop it," Emerson says. "Your dress is perfect. You look

like a million bucks." He takes me by the shoulders and spins me around. "Just look for a second. Look at what you did."

I take a deep breath and look around the space. It looks perfect—even the late addition the gallery didn't hang until this morning. The lighting is exactly right, the energy is good, and the gallery owner, a man named Bradley, says he's had a wonderful response to his marketing efforts and expects a full house tonight. There's already a small crowd milling about, wine glasses in hand as they study my work.

I have sixteen pieces for sale, all hung in the main room of Second Light. The rest of the gallery is open too, but so far, most people seem drawn to this space, drifting from one wall over to the other.

Selling all sixteen pieces would be a dream. Selling half would be a solid showing, enough to convince the gallery to work with me again. Less than that, and this might be the last time I get a solo show here.

"You did good work, Sarah," Emerson says, giving my shoulders one last squeeze. "Now just breathe and enjoy it."

"I'll breathe once Calista Reinhardt has come and gone," I say as I glance toward the main entrance of the gallery. It's hard not to dwell on how big it will be if the head gallerist at the Rooke is impressed tonight. I told Carter a show at the Rooke would be career-defining, and it would be. It would also all but guarantee an O-1 visa. But that's not the real reason I keep glancing at the door.

As comforting as it is to have Emerson with me, I'm not sure I'll *truly* relax until Carter is here.

Despite having a day off, he ended up having to go into the practice facility for some maintenance physiotherapy on his shoulder. He'd forgotten about it, but this close to the playoffs, the head athletic trainer wouldn't let him skip, so he begrudgingly headed into the practice complex late this afternoon. He promised he'd be finished in time to get here, so I'm trying not to freak out that he hasn't arrived yet.

"Jeremy was furious he couldn't come with me," Emerson says. "He's still waiting on his signed jersey. Did I tell you I've finally figured out why he loves hockey?"

"You didn't, but I'd love to know," I say, at least grateful to have Emerson as a distraction.

"It's the thighs," he says. "I can't believe it didn't occur to me sooner."

I laugh. "You can't even *see* their thighs. They wear too much padding."

Emerson's eyes widen as they lock on something over my shoulder. "No, but you can in a pair of nicely tailored suit pants."

I turn and see Carter, all six-foot-four of him, stepping through the entrance. My eyes drop to his legs, and Emerson is not wrong. Carter knows how to wear a pair of pants, his muscular frame filling them out to absolute perfection.

Carter scans the room, clearly looking for me. When we finally make eye contact, he smiles, and the tension in my shoulders eases the slightest bit.

He turns a lot of heads as he makes his way through the gallery. It's hard for him not to—he really does have quite the presence—but some people seem to recognize him, their eyes following him all the way to me. It occurs to me that so far, whenever we've been out in public, we've been with his team. In environments where everyone present fully expects to see a bunch of professional hockey players. But tonight, he's the only hockey player here.

To his credit, Carter seems very good at ignoring the attention. He probably has a lot of practice. I'm used to people recognizing Miles, but something about being the *wife* of a pro player hits different than being a sister. There's a sense of ownership, a pride that takes me by surprise, but there's also a sense of trepidation. I don't exactly love attention, and my husband is someone who's going to get it everywhere he goes.

"Hey," he says as soon as he reaches me. He slips a hand around my waist and tugs me into him. His eyes flash, and I think of the moment we shared last night when I all but begged him to kiss me.

He doesn't waste another moment before his lips are on mine in a hello kiss to rival all hello kisses.

"Sorry I'm late," he says as soon as he pulls away. "You look beautiful."

I smile, lips still tingling. I really do need to plan daily outings with this man, just so we can do this on a regular basis. But mostly, I'm just so incredibly happy to have him next to me. "I'm glad you're here."

He holds my gaze. "Is Calista here yet?"

"I don't think so," I say. "Honestly, she might not even show. Her plans could have changed, or she could have decided she isn't actually interested—"

Carter silences me with another breath-stealing kiss.

"What was that for?" I ask, though I'm not about to complain.

"It just seemed like the smartest way to shut you up," he says.

I huff out a teasing scoff, but he only grins, then he takes both my hands in his, giving them a gentle squeeze.

"She'll come," he says. "Don't psych yourself out."

I channel his easy confidence as Bradley approaches with

a look in his eye that tells me the schmoozing part of the evening is about to begin.

Carter leans over and takes the still untouched wine out of my hand. "I'll bring you some water," he says, his voice close to my ear. "You've got this."

For the next thirty minutes, Bradley guides me around the room to meet all of his VIP guests. I smile and say thank you and answer questions and try to talk about my "inspiration" in a way that feels both interesting and accessible. But on the inside, I'm mostly just thinking about not tugging on my sleeves. Or not guzzling the entire bottle of water Carter gave me all at once.

Carter stays close by, not a part of my conversations, but near enough that if I needed him, it wouldn't be hard to make eye contact and send him a distress signal. I'm also watching him. Noticing how easily he talks to people.

At one point, he's pulled into conversation with a couple of men who look up at him with obvious admiration. One of the men pulls a pen out of his pocket and offers it to Carter. I could be wrong, but it looks like he's asking him to sign the show brochure.

Carter holds up a hand and gives his head a quick shake, then looks over at me. The man nods and pockets the pen, then shakes Carter's hand. They all laugh together, and I can't help but marvel that even after he declined signing an autograph, assuming that's what he did, he still managed to make everyone feel comfortable and end their interaction on a positive note.

He's honestly *so good* at this—at talking to people. He's warm and engaging and interesting and he's a good listener, and he does it all so *naturally*.

I'll be fine tonight. I'm talking and smiling, engaging like a pro. But that doesn't mean I won't have horrible sweaty armpits the entire time. Or that I won't need at least three days to decompress once all this is over.

Eventually, I manage to sneak away from Bradley and duck into a recess near the gallery offices for a moment of peace and privacy.

But not solitude because Emerson follows me in. "Hi! How are you?" he says. "And by how are you, I mean are you aware that your husband is legitimately in love with you?"

My heart climbs into my throat at just hearing Emerson say the words out loud. It *does* feel like Carter's been looking at me differently lately, but I can't be sure I'm not making it up. It's hard because I've always had good chemistry with Carter. And because he *is* so good at communicating, it's hard to tell what's special treatment and what's just Carter being Carter.

"He is not," I say.

"Honey. Yes, he is," Emerson says. "He walked into this gallery and immediately found you like you're his oxygen. And that kiss...are you kissing like that all the time? Because if you are, I don't know how you aren't pregnant yet."

"Can we please not have this conversation here?" I say, even as a blush crawls up my cheeks. "I need to network. To focus. I need to sell paintings, and this is not going to help me."

"Answer my question, and I'll buy one myself," Emerson says.

"You can't afford me," I tease. "But *no*, we only kiss in public. When we're at home, we follow the rules you told me I needed to have."

"Rules, schmules," Emerson says. "I've changed my mind. You need to lock that man down."

It's a ridiculous suggestion, seeing as how we're already married and living together. Can you get more locked down than exchanging vows to love and cherish until death do you part?

But I fully understand Emerson's meaning because nothing about my relationship with Carter feels locked down. It feels more like a ticking time bomb, three hundred and fifty days away from going off.

Across the gallery, Carter looks like he's hunting for me, so I step out of the recess, dragging Emerson with me, and lift my hand to catch his eye.

He smiles and heads over.

"Did those guys ask for your autograph?" I ask as soon as he arrives.

Carter nods. "They did."

"But you didn't give it to them?"

He shrugs. "I told them tonight was about you."

"I wouldn't have minded," I quickly say. "If you want to—"

Carter lifts a hand and presses a finger to my lips, gently silencing my words. "I just want to be your husband tonight." His hand shifts, grazing along my cheek until he's gently holding the back of my neck, his eyes locked on mine. "Nothing else."

I swallow against a sudden knot in my throat, my heart pounding in my chest.

I want this.

I want *him*.

But is that even fair? He's here supporting me, showing up in a way I'll never be able to do for him. No matter my attempts to reason with myself—and I have, for my brother's sake, more times than I can count—my body remembers the trauma even if my brain is willing to forget. My mouth goes dry, my limbs lock up. I don't know how to get past the trigger. I want to believe it's been long enough that maybe I would be okay. That it might be different if I have Carter to motivate me.

Then again, maybe it wouldn't matter.

Does love always have to look symmetrical?

Maybe, if I explained, if Carter knew what I was up against, he would understand.

Maybe I could support him enough in other ways.

As the night moves on, I meet so many people, hear so many names I'll never remember.

Carter stays close, always available to fill an awkward silence or give my hand an encouraging squeeze. He also makes it his personal mission to keep track of how many red dots appear next to paintings indicating they've sold. Each time he gives me an update, he looks like a kid who just watched his favorite team win the Stanley Cup.

"Only four left," he says when the night's almost over. "That's good, right?"

I take a deep breath. Only four left is *very good*.

"Miles and Anna just got here," Carter says next. "I didn't know they were coming."

"I didn't either," I say. Anna's due date is only three days away, so I told her she didn't need to make the effort. She said she might try anyway, but I didn't truly expect them to come. I know how much of a hassle it is to get a babysitter on a weeknight—especially since their go-to babysitter is *me*.

I turn to see them approaching, Anna looking stunning in a black wrap dress stretched tight over her belly, Miles in a suit beside her. "You came!" I say, reaching out to give them each a hug.

"Of course we did," Anna says. "This is a big night for you. Besides, I thought I might lose my mind if I didn't get out of the house. The girls drove me up the wall today."

"I'm sorry I haven't been over more," I say. "But with the show behind me, I totally will be. As often as you need me."

"So you're moving in?" Anna jokes, then her expression turns more serious. "Is the New York lady here yet?"

I fight to hide my disappointment. "Not yet. And this late, she probably won't be. But you know who is here? Emerson. And he'll die if you don't say hello."

I walk with Anna to where Emerson is chatting with Bradley and roll my eyes over their baby name conversation—he's still campaigning, the big dummy. Carter is talking to Miles near the door, and I keep glancing that way, distracted by the obvious tension between them.

At a break in the conversation, I loop my arm through Anna's. "Hey, why do our husbands look like they want to kill each other?"

Anna's quiet for long enough that I'm guessing she and Miles have talked about it, and she's trying to figure out how much to say.

But I can't wait around for her to respond because Calista Reinhardt just walked through the door.

I suck in a gasp. "Oh my gosh," I say. "She's here."

Anna follows my gaze. "Oh, she's stunning," Anna says. "Very New York."

She *does* look stunning. Her gray hair is pixie-cut short and perfectly curly, just long enough to frame her face in a way that makes her cheekbones pop. Her dark brown skin is ageless and glowy, her outfit somehow looks both flowy and chic, and I really, really want to be her when I grow up.

Carter moves up behind me as Calista checks her coat. "Is that her?"

I nod. "I think I'm gonna throw up."

"Breathe," he says. He sweeps my hair off my shoulder and presses a quick kiss to my neck just above my collarbone. "You've got this."

"We're rooting for you!" Anna whispers, then I leave them and move to the door to welcome Calista.

"Sarah," she says warmly. "I'm so sorry I'm late. It's a ridiculous story that doesn't bear repeating. But trust that I'm so happy to be here now."

"It's lovely to see you, Calista. Truly, it's an honor you would take the time to be here at all."

"Are you kidding? I've been looking forward to this for weeks. Now, I won't make you endure the awkwardness of staying with me while I peruse your work. So you just leave me to it, and I'll be back in a bit."

"That sounds perfect," I say. "I'll be here."

"How's the wine?" she asks before moving away.

"The white is terrible," Carter says, stepping up beside us. "But the red is good." He offers her a glass, and she takes it, giving him an appraising look.

"Calista, this is my husband," I say. "Carter Williamson."

"Charmed," she says, and she really looks it. "Thank you for the wine."

As she moves into the gallery, I breathe out a sigh, and Carter slips his arms around my waist from behind. I let myself sink into him, not realizing that I need the support until I have it. I press my arms over the top of his and look around the room. The crowd is finally starting to dwindle, but there's no way to call the night anything but a success.

I catch sight of Anna out of the corner of my eye. She's

watching us, clearly waiting to finish the conversation that was interrupted by Calista's arrival.

I'm reluctant to let go of Carter, but I do want to know what Anna was going to say. "Hey, can you let me talk to Anna for a sec?" I say, giving his arm a quick squeeze.

"Of course," he says, letting me go.

"Don't go far," I tell him.

Miles is on the opposite side of the gallery now, talking to the same two men who stopped Carter earlier. After the chilly conversation I watched them have right after Miles arrived, I'm not surprised when Carter steers clear of my brother, heading the opposite direction to talk to Emerson.

Anna comes up beside me, one hand pressed against the bottom of her belly.

"You gonna make it?" I ask, and she nods.

"I swear, just walking makes me tired these days."

We're quiet for a beat before I say, "So you were going to tell me why our husbands don't seem to be friends anymore."

She breathes out a sigh. "I don't think that's it."

"Then what is it?" I ask. "He was so excited about Carter —so sure he was the perfect guy to do this."

"It's not really about Carter," Anna says. "Not entirely."

"Then tell me what it is about."

She glances over at Miles like she wants to make sure he's not heading this way anytime soon. "Miles told me about your conversation after the wedding," she says.

At first, I'm not sure what part of the conversation she's talking about—Miles asking me not to tell Carter about our dad or Miles trying to force a teaching career down my throat. I'm not excited to talk about either subject.

"He says you really don't want to do the teaching thing."

"I really don't," I quickly say without a shred of hesitation.

She holds my gaze, like she's considering my words. I know her loyalty will almost always be to Miles first—but I appreciate that Anna always listens and tries to be a voice of reason for us both.

"He's scared, Sarah. He feels such a responsibility for you. He always has." She winces a little bit, like she's hesitant to keep going.

"And?" I prompt. "Why do you look like there's something you don't want to say?"

"*And* he's made up his mind that Carter is the one encouraging you to pursue the O-1 without worrying about teaching. He thinks he might have ulterior motives."

I furrow my brow, struggling to truly wrap my head around what she's suggesting. "What does that mean? What kind of ulterior motive?"

She gives me a pained look. "If you try for the visa you're less likely to get, then you'll have to stay married to him."

Her words mostly just make me angry, but then a tiny flicker of doubt sparks inside my brain.

Carter wouldn't. *Would he?*

As soon as I give even an ounce of oxygen to the thought, a wave of certainty washes over me and douses it right out.

He wouldn't. I *know* he wouldn't. Carter is a lot of things. But he is not manipulative. He's the exact opposite. He's completely guileless. And he would never do anything so underhanded.

"It's sad Miles would believe something like that of his own teammate," I say.

Anna nods. "I know. I told him the same thing. But Miles truly feels that if you have to go back to Canada, it will be his fault. He has nightmares about the possibility of your father finding you again." She pauses, shifting her weight and leaning forward, like she's trying to stretch her back. "I don't mean to make excuses for him," she continues, "and I definitely don't want you to do anything you don't want to do. But would it be so bad to just talk to a couple of schools? Make Miles *think* you're considering both options?"

I understand why she's asking. It has to be tough to be both Miles's wife and my friend without feeling like she's caught in the middle. But there's no way I can say yes. "I can't do it, Anna. It's not the path I want. And if Miles would actually listen to me when I talk to him about my art, he'd understand why. I feel really good about where I am. I've already checked so many of the O-1 boxes. I'm not there yet—but I *am* getting closer. And I'm only two weeks into this marriage —I'm so much farther ahead of my timeline than I thought I would be. Especially if this thing at the Rooke works out."

She nods, but there's still hesitation in her eyes. "What does Carter think? Does he have opinions about the visa situation at all?"

"He's incredibly supportive," I say. "He has been from the start. Even before we got married, he talked like it was basically a done deal. That I'd qualify for an O-1 in no time. He's always said the wedding just bought me a little time."

She holds my gaze for a long moment. "That has to feel good."

I breathe out a little laugh, relieved that she finally seems to understand. "Yeah. It really does."

"Okay," she says. "I trust you. And I believe you."

I reach out and take her hands. "Thank you. But I also need you and Miles to believe *in* me. It's not the same thing."

"Oh, honey, you know I believe in you." She squeezes my

hands. "And I'll do my best to help your boneheaded brother see what I see."

I lean forward and give her a hug. "Thank you."

When I pull back, she doesn't let go of my hands. She turns and looks at Carter. "Do you think you're falling for him?"

Carter's arms are folded, his focus wholly on my friend. "I don't know," I say. "Maybe."

It's the closest I've come to admitting anything out loud, which feels big, but Anna doesn't respond. She *does,* however, squeeze my hands with a sudden intensity that turns the tips of my fingers white.

"Anna, are you okay?" I slowly ask.

She nods a little too quickly. "Yeah. Totally fine. The baby is just—really digging into my back."

I study her closely, noticing a thin sheen of sweat on her forehead.

She drops my hands, then grabs a cocktail napkin off a table behind us and dabs at her forehead. "Do you think he's falling for you?" she asks. I get the sense she's trying *really* hard to distract herself—and me—from whatever is happening inside her body.

"Maybe," I say, still watching her closely. "But I can tell he wants to ask me about hockey. About not going to his games. Which I understand. But if I tell him, I have to tell him everything, and I told Miles I wouldn't do that."

She frowns. "He asked you not to?"

I nod. "But even if he didn't, I'm not sure I'm ready for that level of sharing."

"Ignore your brother's request. He shouldn't have asked that of you. If Carter is the guy I think he is, it isn't going to change anything," Anna says. "And being honest might make it easier for you to work through this. When they're on the road next week, just come over. We'll try to watch a—" Her words cut off as she sucks in a breath, both hands moving to her stomach.

"Anna," I say. "Honey, what's going on?"

"Nothing," she says, almost impatiently. "Tell me something else about Carter. What's it like living together?"

"It's fine," I say pointedly. "Now answer my question for real."

She presses her lips together. "So help me, Sarah, I will not go into labor at your art show. I will not make tonight about me."

I look over my shoulder and make eye contact with Carter. The look on my face must indicate the urgency of the situation because he comes right over.

"What's wrong?" he asks.

"Nothing at all," I say. "But can you very calmly go tell Miles that his wife is in labor?"

His eyebrows shoot up. "For real?"

Anna looks down at her feet and lets out a little gasp. "Um, pretty sure my water just broke."

"That would be a yes," Carter says before heading after Miles.

Anna reaches out to squeeze my hands. "I'm sorry. I'm so sorry. My timing is terrible."

Tears spring into my eyes. "Your timing is perfect. I'm going to go explain to Calista why I'm leaving. Then let's go have a baby."

2 2

CARTER

"I'm just going to say it, man," Theo says as he walks into the waiting area on the labor and delivery floor of Atlanta General. "For not actually being in love with her, you really know a lot about your wife's clothes."

He drops a bag of food on the seat beside me, then adds one of the canvas grocery bags Sarah keeps in our pantry. I look inside to see the jeans, hoodie, and sneakers I had Theo grab from Sarah's closet.

Sarah and I have been at the hospital for almost an hour, and we came here straight from the art show. She told me I could head home and come back for her later, but then, Anna's labor progressed so quickly, I decided it'd be easier to stay. That way, I'm here whenever Sarah's ready to go. Plus, I might get to meet the baby. Assuming Miles will let me anywhere near the hospital room.

"It's not a big deal," I say, reaching for the bag of food and sorting through what Theo brought. "I folded her laundry yesterday." I look up to see his dubious expression. "And

291

don't say anything about me folding her laundry. It was in the dryer, and I needed the dryer."

"Uh-huh," he says. "I'm sure that was your only motivation."

I ignore him and text Sarah, letting her know her cheeseburger and fries have arrived. We were planning on grabbing some food after her show, but then we came here instead. When Theo texted and said he'd dropped by my house and wanted to know why I wasn't there, it seemed like a perfect opportunity to see him, feed us, and get a change of clothes for Sarah, since she's still in the heels she wore to her show.

I toss Theo his burger, then pull out my grilled chicken wrap. Because my brother apparently has both superior pectoral muscles *and* a faster metabolism, I can't do a cheeseburger this late.

Seconds later, Sarah drops into the seat beside me.

"How's everything going?" I ask.

"It's going," Sarah says. "Anna just got her epidural, so she's feeling pretty good now. And she's already at eight centimeters, which is awesome."

I look down at her. "I have no idea what half those words meant."

Sarah grins. "She's drugged, meaning she's numb from the waist down, and she'll probably be pushing within the hour."

"I appreciate the translation. Are you hungry?"

"Starving," Sarah says, and I hand over her food. "Can you believe that had we not gotten married, I'd be leaving next week? One week with baby Fiona. That's all I would have gotten."

"I'm really glad that isn't happening," I say, and I genuinely mean it. For all kinds of reasons—even the ones

I'm not willing to admit out loud. "Also, I had Theo bring you some clothes."

Her eyes widen. "Shut up." She takes the bag and looks inside. "This is perfect."

"I figured you were probably ready to get out of your heels."

"You're officially my new favorite person." She leans over and kisses me on the cheek. "Thank you."

"What about me?" Theo says. "Do I at least get bonus points for being the one who actually went to get them?"

Sarah stands, patting Theo on the arm as she walks past. "You can have all the bonus points, Theo. Whatever your ego needs."

He frowns. "Why do I feel like she was making fun of me there?"

I chuckle. "Because she was making fun of you."

"I'll allow it," Theo says. "But only because I think you really *are* in love with her." He takes an enormous bite of his cheeseburger, watching me like he's waiting for me to respond.

I'm not sure what to say. It's too soon to admit it. It's probably too soon to even be thinking it. But the thought has definitely crossed my mind.

"You know," Theo says, "denying your feelings won't make them go away."

"I didn't deny anything," I say. "I just didn't *confirm* anything either."

"Fair enough," he says. "So, how's it been with Miles? Holly told me he was basically murdering you with his eyes after the game last night."

"We barely talked tonight," I say, opening my wrap. "He

was civil at the art show, but I could tell he didn't really feel like talking to me."

"But why?" Theo asks. "It doesn't make any sense. He can't be pissed at you for doing the very thing he asked you to do."

"No clue," I say. "I can't think of anything I've done that might have made him mad."

Theo takes another bite of his burger. "Oh, man. Is there bacon on this thing? I didn't know about the bacon. That's good."

"You're going to regret that on the ice tomorrow," I say.

"Probably," he says. "But right now I really can't bring myself to care."

I hold up my wrap. I'm waiting for Sarah to come back before I eat it, but I'm happy to use it as a prop to make my brother feel guilty about his choices.

"I'm not going to regret anything," I say. "Because I respect my body. And I follow the rules."

"You know what's going to be funny?" Theo says. "When I skate circles around you tomorrow night, and you don't have a cheeseburger to blame it on."

"Who's skating circles around who?" Sarah asks as she comes back in, letting her fingers skim over my shoulders as she passes behind me. She looks much more comfortable now in her jeans.

"Mr. Righteous is making me feel guilty for my food choices," Theo says before shoveling in a handful of fries.

Sarah looks over at me and grins. "He *does* get a little pious about his food."

"I do not," I say.

"Then eat some fries," Theo says.

Sarah pulls a couple out of her container and holds them

up. "He won't do it," she says to Theo, and I frown as I look between them.

I hold up a finger, pointing from one to the other. "You two are not allowed to gang up on me."

Sarah grins. "Eat the fries, Mr. Righteous."

She moves them a little closer, still taunting me, so I lean over, eating all three fries out of her hand. My lips brush over the tips of her fingers before she draws her hand back. For a split second, I think about grabbing her wrist and licking the salt right off her fingertips. If she were teasing me like this at home, I might do it, but I'm keenly aware of Theo's eyes on me and his certainty that I've already fallen in love.

"Happy now?" I ask instead, and she bites her lip, gaze dropping to *my* lips just long enough to make me wonder if she had the same thought.

"Look at you," Theo says to Sarah. "You made him break a rule. Might be the first time ever."

"Why did you come here again?" I joke, looking at Theo.

He throws a French fry at me, which I retrieve from my sleeve and pop into my mouth, just to prove a point. "Because my brother got married and is too busy to hang out with me anymore, so I decided I had to go to where he was. Also, we need to figure out what to do about Holly. I was thinking we golf on Thursday? He needs the distraction."

"We can't golf this close to playoffs."

"The driving range, then," Theo says.

"What's the matter with Holly?" Sarah asks.

"Charlie's in Canada with her grandparents," I say. "He doesn't love it when she's gone."

"He tends to mope and think about Claire when he's alone," Theo says. "Which I get. We just try to keep him busy."

"Hey, Sarah?" A nurse appears at the edge of the waiting room. "She's gonna start pushing soon. She wanted me to come get you." The nurse's eyes move from me to Theo, then back to me again, widening the slightest bit. Sometimes I forget how truly identical we are until things like this happen.

Sarah crams the last bite of her burger into her mouth. "I'm totally coming," she says. "I'll be right there." She makes quick work of cleaning up her trash and wiping off her hands. "I'll text you updates," she says to me. "But it shouldn't be long now." She reaches over and takes my hand, giving it a quick squeeze. "Thank you for being here with me."

"I wouldn't be anywhere else," I say.

She stands and moves to the edge of the waiting area. "Thanks for the food, Theo."

He lifts a hand in acknowledgement, then I watch as she hurries down the hall, not realizing my brother is watching me the entire time.

"You really do seem like you're married," he says as soon as she's gone. "You're just...easy with each other."

"It's always been like that," I say. "From the very start. Even before we got married."

When Theo finishes his food, he stands and gathers up the last of the trash. "I'm gonna go wash my hands and find something to drink. You want anything?"

"I've got water," I say. "I'm good."

I watch as he steps into the hall, but then he immediately turns and comes back into the waiting area, swearing over and over again.

"What is it?" I ask. "What happened?"

He looks around the room, then moves into the back corner, stepping into the foot of space in between a snack machine with an Out of Order sign taped to the front and the wall. There's a fake plant sitting a few feet away, and Theo grabs it, pulling it in front of his hiding spot. For being such a big dude, it's surprisingly effective.

But why is he hiding?

"Theo?" a woman says from behind me.

I turn, and suddenly I'm face-to-face with a woman in navy blue scrubs, a nurse's badge looped around her neck. I haven't seen Rebecca Bradley since high school, but there's no mistaking her. I could never forget the only woman my brother has ever loved.

"I'm Carter," I say, and her shoulders drop the slightest bit, maybe from relief, maybe from disappointment. "Hi, Rebecca."

"Hey." She looks around the room. "He is here, isn't he? My friend said there were two of you. I thought there was no possible way, but then she said her patient was married to a hockey player and some of his teammates were here and..." She shakes her head. "I mean, there aren't that many hockey players who are identical twins."

"Yeah, we're the only ones," I say, wanting to punch my brother for hiding instead of just facing this woman. "At least, in the NHL."

She lifts her hands to her cheeks. "So, he's here? My friend wasn't seeing things?"

"He's here," I say. "He just...stepped out for a minute."

She nods, then lets out a little chuckle. "I knew he played in Atlanta, but it's such a big city. I just didn't think..." She shakes her head. "Anyway. It's good to see *you* again."

"You, too. I'll tell Theo I saw you."

She nods, then turns like she's going to walk away. But then she spins back around again. "Actually, you don't have to tell him. I came down here because I honestly didn't believe he could be in the building, but seeing you again, which feels a lot like seeing *him* again, I'm not actually sure I want him to know." She scrunches up her face. "I mean, obviously I know you're still going to tell him. But don't—I don't want him to come find me. I work on a different floor. He shouldn't—not that I think he would." She closes her eyes and takes a breath. "You know what? I'm just going to walk away now. Goodbye, Carter."

I sink back into my chair, waiting until she's a good distance down the hallway. Then I stand and slowly move to the back corner of the waiting room.

"She's gone," I say to the plant, but Theo makes no move to come out. I slowly push some of the branches aside, enough to see Theo's face. He's pale, just two bright spots of color on either cheek, and his eyes are hollow. Like he's seen a ghost. I'm surprised by his reaction—I wouldn't have guessed he still cared about Rebecca, but he's clearly feeling something, and the sight makes my heart ache the slightest bit. "You okay?" I ask.

He runs a hand over his face. "Yeah. But, uh—I'm gonna go."

"Okay," I say, knowing better than to try to stop him. When he wants to talk, we'll talk. But I won't get far if I try to force him into it now. "Thanks for the food."

He nods once, then drops a hand on my shoulder before heading down the hall in the opposite direction from Rebecca.

I drop back into my seat and exhale a disbelieving breath. Rebecca Bradley moved to Texas when Theo and I were freshmen in high school. She seemed nice enough to me, but Theo fell hard and fast. By the start of our junior year, they'd danced around being together but never fully committed. But then she asked him to be her date to homecoming, and they never looked back.

They were together nonstop. At least as much as our hockey schedule allowed. They drove everyone crazy with how stupid in love they were.

And then Dad died.

When Theo shut everyone out, he shut Rebecca out too.

I did my best to do damage control, but she didn't need answers. She knew what Theo was doing and why he was doing it. She just wanted to help.

And he wouldn't let her.

Half an hour later, Sarah is back in the waiting room, eyes damp, a huge smile on her face. I stand, and she steps into my arms like it's the most natural thing in the world.

"She's here?" I ask.

"She's here," Sarah says. "And she's perfect. Anna is so happy, and Miles can't stop crying, and I'm just really happy for them."

"Big day," I say. "For all of you."

She lets out a little chuckle. "Honestly, it feels like my art show was a hundred years ago." She looks up at me, arms still around my waist. "Did Theo leave?"

I nod. "Yeah. A while ago."

"It was really nice of him to come," she says, then she gives my waist a little squeeze. "Do you want to meet the baby?"

"Can I?" I ask. "Do you think Miles will mind?"

She looks at me, her expression curious. We still haven't talked about the way her brother has been treating me, but she doesn't look all that surprised by my question.

"He won't," she says. "He's a big softy right now. It'll be fine."

She threads her fingers through mine, then we walk together to Anna's room. Anna is propped up in her hospital bed, looking exhausted but happy, baby Fiona tucked into her arms. Miles is sitting in a chair beside her bed, phone in his hand. He looks up when we enter, and for once, he doesn't look like he wants to kill me.

Sarah leaves me by the door and walks over to Anna. She says something I can't hear, then smiles and lifts Fiona into her arms.

The sight of Sarah holding the baby triggers something deep in my gut. Something visceral—*inevitable*. She looks beautiful, but it's more than that. It's her looking so...*maternal*. It feels like some kind of evolutionary part of my biology just clicked on in my brain. I've seen her with her nieces and with Charlie, and she's great with them. But this feels different somehow.

In the back of my mind, I've always assumed I'd be a dad eventually. But I haven't given it any real thought.

I'm thinking about it now though. *Wanting* it in a way that feels both surprising and terrifying.

I'm about to walk over to Sarah, but then I make eye contact with Miles and stop, feet rooted to the floor. I'm annoyed that he's turned me into his enemy, but tonight isn't about that. It's about him, and if he doesn't want me here, I'm not going to fight him over it.

But then Miles gives me a quick nod, tilting his head toward Sarah.

It's a small concession, but I nod back, letting him know that whatever temporary truce this is, I'm grateful for it. I make my way over to where Sarah is standing. She looks up and meets my gaze. "You want to hold her?"

"I don't—I don't know how."

Sarah chuckles. "You'll be fine. Here." She tilts her head toward a wide bench that runs underneath the window. "Sit. That'll make it easier."

I do as she says, then she very gently lowers the bundled baby into my waiting arms.

Fiona is asleep, swaddled so tightly, the only part of her I can see is her tiny little face. She isn't much bigger than a football, but holding her is *nothing* like holding a football. She's warm and malleable, a living, breathing thing, and I'm suddenly overwhelmed with the thought of having to keep something this tiny alive.

Maybe I'm not ready to be a dad after all.

"She's so small," I say, and Sarah drops down beside me, tucking one leg under her as her arm rests on my shoulder. She leans close so she can look at Fiona, and I breathe in her familiar scent.

"Look!" Sarah whispers softly. "She's opening her eyes."

I shift my gaze back to Fiona's face and sure enough, she's looking up at me with wide, brown eyes that remind me of Sarah.

"She's got your eyes," I say.

"She's got *Miles's* eyes."

"They're your eyes, too," I say. "Besides, she's already prettier than Miles is ever going to be."

Fiona starts to fuss a few minutes later, and Sarah takes her back to Anna. I notice Miles watching me, the temporary compassion I saw in his eyes when I first came in already replaced with the stony glare I've come to expect.

"Hey, congrats, man," I say, stepping close enough to offer

him a handshake. For a long moment, he doesn't take it, and I almost pull my hand back. But I don't do it. He doesn't have to shake my hand, but I won't make it easy on him.

Finally, he grunts and takes my hand. "Thanks," he says, gripping my hand so tightly it takes a concerted effort not to react. I don't know what he's trying to prove, but it triggers my ire, and when I step back to Sarah's side, I look pointedly at Miles, then I lift my hands to his sister's face and kiss her right on the mouth.

"You ready?" I ask.

Her eyes are wide, slightly stunned. "Yeah," she says slowly.

I reach down and take her hand, eyes on Miles the entire time Sarah is making plans to relieve the babysitter and be with Poppy and Olive tomorrow. Then we say our goodbyes and head out to my truck.

"I just realized we left your car at the gallery," I say once we're pulling out of the hospital parking garage.

"We can pick it up tomorrow," she says through a yawn. Then she looks over at me. "Do you want to tell me what that was about? Right before we left?"

I glance over at her, suddenly feeling a little sheepish. "The kiss?"

She nods. "And all the glaring."

"I'm sorry if I made you uncomfortable."

"You didn't," she says. "You never do. I just wasn't sure what triggered it. Was it Miles?"

I nod. "I'm getting really tired of him looking at me like I'm doing something wrong."

She grimaces. "I was wondering if you'd noticed anything different. Was it bad in the hospital room? I didn't notice."

"Not at first," I say. "But then..." I'm not sure I want to tell her the details of everything that went down. I'm not sure she noticed, since she was talking to Anna, but I'm not entirely proud of how I acted. Miles was in the wrong first, but I probably didn't have to intentionally provoke him. "It wasn't great," I say.

"Is it messing with the team dynamic?" Sarah asks.

"Not yet. But the other guys are starting to notice something is up. Any idea why he's upset? Or...annoyed? I don't even know what he is. I just know he only glares at me now."

She's quiet for a long moment before she says, "I *do* know why Miles is mad. But I don't want to say it out loud because it's going to make you hate him."

"Okay," I say, trying to keep my tone level. "But I shouldn't hate him?"

"No, you probably should a little bit," she says. "It makes *me* hate him a little bit. But it's also complicated because I know he's coming from a place of love and also a place of fear, and sometimes we do crazy things when we're trying to deal with our past." She takes a steadying breath. "Especially when that past involves quite a bit of trauma."

I spare her a quick glance before forcing my eyes back to the road. She isn't admitting much, but she's telling me more than she's told me before. "I get that," I say, thinking of Theo and how badly he hurt Rebecca even though that was never his intent. Or maybe it *was* his intent, but not because he didn't love her. He just couldn't let *her* love him, so he had to push her away the only way he knew how. "I'm willing to give him the benefit of the doubt if you want me to."

She nods, biting her lip. "He thinks you're only encouraging me to get an O-1 visa because it's less likely to work, and as long as I can't get my *own* visa, I'll have to stay married to you."

I grip the steering wheel a little tighter. "Why would I do that?"

"He thinks...you're in love with me, I guess? And now you're doing whatever it takes to keep me here."

I choke out a disbelieving laugh because the idea of doing something like that is so completely ridiculous. Who would want to be married to a woman who didn't choose it?

"Marriage by coercion isn't really my style, Sarah." I force myself to keep breathing, but it's hard not to rail against the misjudgments Miles is making right now.

"I know. I absolutely know that. He's just angry that I'm refusing his help," Sarah says. "He doesn't think I'm making a practical choice, and I guess it feels easier to blame you for that than me."

I'm angry that he thinks I would ever manipulate his sister like that. I'm *more* angry that he has so little faith in her skill that, despite her continually showing him evidence of her success, he keeps harping on the teaching thing. I'm angry that he doesn't respect me enough to just talk to me, man to man, so he can *ask* me what I think of Sarah's art. That instead, he's choosing to intimidate. To throw his weight around as Sarah's "big brother" and my team captain.

But none of that is as important as making sure Sarah knows I would never do such a thing. I would never lie to her or push her to do anything that wasn't in *her* best interests. Honestly, I would love for her to have her own visa. At least then, if we were together, I would know it was only because she wanted to be. Not because I was her ticket to staying with her family.

I can't tell her that part, but I *can* reassure her that I would never do what Miles is suggesting.

"Sarah—"

"I know," she says, cutting me off.

My eyebrows lift.

"I know you would never do that," she continues. "When Anna told me, I was immediately certain it wasn't a possibility. That's not who you are, and I know that."

Her words immediately diffuse some of the tension coursing through my body. "I'm glad," I say. "Because I would never—"

"I know," she says, more gently this time. "You don't have to explain anything to me. I'm not worried that any part of what he said is true."

This trips me up the slightest bit. Because one part of what Miles said might be true.

I might be in love with his sister. Or at least on my way there.

And it's getting harder and harder to deny it.

23

CARTER

SARAH SPENDS A LOT OF TIME AT ANNA AND MILES'S HOUSE OVER the next week. Which is great because that's one of the biggest reasons she wanted to stay in the States in the first place. To support her family.

The downside is that I'm left with a lot of time to miss her. With the exception of one quick away game in North Carolina, I've mostly been home. And somehow, I've started measuring time in segments of how long it's been since I saw Sarah last and how long it's going to be until I see her again.

When I'm at the driving range with Theo and Holly, I'm wondering if she's still at the hospital with Anna or if she's returned home.

When I'm at the rink for practice, I'm imagining her at the park with Poppy and Olive or sneaking into Anna's pantry for a moment of solitude.

I'm leaving for nine days on the road tomorrow, so tonight, I'm making her dinner. I'm not an amazing chef by any stretch. But the chicken scallopini I'm making is one my mom used to make all the time, and it's pretty much

307

foolproof. Add in some roasted broccolini and the sour-dough Sarah made yesterday and it should be a decent meal.

Down the hall, the door to the garage opens and closes, then Sarah appears in the kitchen.

"Hey," I say as I take in the sight of her. Her hair is up—I love her hair up—and she's wearing a cropped t-shirt that reveals a tiny sliver of skin above the waistband of her leggings. She looks beautiful, like always, but she also looks a little frayed around the edges. It could just be that she's tired. She's been going nonstop the past few weeks, first, with her gallery show, and now with all she's doing for Anna and Miles.

"Hey," she says as she drops onto a barstool. "What are you making?"

"Dinner for you if you're hungry for it," I say over my shoulder. "Have you eaten?"

"Not yet," she says. "But you didn't have to cook for me."

I take the sauce for the scallopini off the heat and turn off the stove.

"I cooked for *us*," I say. "You've been working so hard to take care of everyone else. Let me take care of you for a change." I move to the cutting board and slice off a small piece of the sautéed chicken, dipping it in the sauce before carrying it over to Sarah and offering her a bite.

She takes it, her lips brushing against my fingers before she closes her eyes, letting out a little moan as she chews. "A man of many talents," she says. "That's delicious."

"Don't get too excited," I say. "It's one of about three things I know how to make well."

She rubs her hands over her face like she's trying to wake herself up. "Is there anything I can do to help?"

"It's all done," I say. "I'm plating everything now. But are you okay? We don't have to do this if you—"

"No, I definitely need to eat," she says. "And I want to. I'm just tired." While I plate our food, she moves around the bar and pulls two glasses out of the cabinet, filling them with ice and water. "I kinda got into it with my brother right before I left, so I'm still feeling a little off."

I carry our plates to the table. "Do you want to talk about it?"

"It's just more of the same. He practically cornered me on my way out the door and tried to make me talk to this guy, some teacher he found who also happens to be from Canada. The poor man was already on the phone, so then I had to very politely extricate myself from a conversation I never wanted to have in the first place." Sarah drops into her chair and looks down at her food. "This is amazing, Carter. Thank you."

I sit down across from her. "He shouldn't have put you on the spot like that," I say. But that's really only part of it. He shouldn't be pushing her. Insisting that he knows what's best for her when she's been perfectly clear about what she wants.

"He'll figure it out eventually," she says. "But it's really starting to feel less like he wants me to be pragmatic and more like he's just refusing to see what I do as something real. Like, do I need to show him my bank statements for him to accept that I already have a real job?" She gives her head a little shake. "Let's talk about something else. I don't want to give him any more of my headspace tonight."

"Okay, how about an update on the Rebecca situation?"

Sarah's eyes widen. "Um, yes, please. Have you gotten Theo to talk about it?"

Since my run-in with Theo's ex at the hospital last week, Sarah has been fully invested. "No," I say. "But I did talk to

Nico. He's the Jaguars head trainer, and he has a sister who works at Atlanta General. She asked around, and I guess Rebecca is a travel nurse. She travels with her best friend, who was one of Anna's nurses. That's what she was doing on the labor and delivery floor. Anyway, she works in surgery, she's only been here a couple of weeks, and she could stay anywhere from three to six months."

"Have you told Theo any of this?"

"I tried, but he shut me down pretty quickly," I say. "He doesn't want to talk about it at all."

"Poor Theo," Sarah says.

"For real. I genuinely had no idea she ever even crossed his mind. He's never talked about her."

Conversation is easy for the rest of dinner as Sarah grows more and more relaxed. By the time we're finished, she looks more like herself again. She's smiling a little more easily, laughing as she tells me all the adorable things Olive has had to say about the new baby.

It's such a simple thing, but there's something intoxicating about being the one who makes her feel better. I want that job.

Sarah told me once that I was rescuing her, but the truth is, she really isn't the kind of woman who needs to be rescued. She's stronger than she thinks and more talented than she knows. I might be buying her time, but she's rescuing herself. She's doing the work.

Still, even if I don't *rescue* her, if there's anything I can do to make the burdens she carries feel lighter, I'm all in.

After we finish, I carry our empty plates to the sink, but Sarah follows, nudging me out of the way with her hip. "You cooked," she says. "That means I'm doing the dishes."

"I don't mind doing them," I say, stepping to the side to

open the dishwasher. "You're the one who was on your feet all day."

"Didn't you have practice this morning?"

I shrug. "Yeah, but that's just practice."

"*Just* practice for a professional athlete is never *just* anything. You can sit and keep me company, but you aren't touching a dish."

She plants herself firmly in front of the sink, arms propped on her hips like she's guarding her territory and has no intention of moving.

I lift an eyebrow, then reach over her shoulder and pull a plate out of the sink. I load it into the dishwasher—what's she really going to do about it?—then reach for another.

Sarah's eyes narrow, then she moves lightning fast, grabbing the hand sprayer and aiming it at me, her other hand poised on the faucet. "Don't think I won't do it," she says, a smile playing around her mouth. "You move one more inch, and I'll soak you from head to toe."

"You wouldn't," I say as I reach for another dish.

She presses her lips together, then she shoots me with a two-second blast of ice-cold water that hits me square in the chest. Her eyes widen like she can't quite believe she actually did it.

"Oh, you're getting it now," I say, reaching for her, but she's too fast. She turns the water back on, and this time she doesn't hold back. She drenches the front of me, squealing and laughing as she out-maneuvers me, jumping this way and that to stay out of my reach.

I stand perfectly still, water dripping off the tip of my nose and trickling down my chest. As close as we're standing, I have no idea how she managed to stay so dry, but there's hardly a drop of water on her. The woman has excellent aim.

She looks at me, silent laughter shaking her shoulders, and I can't help but grin. She reaches for a dish towel sitting on the counter beside the sink and holds it out to me. "Here. It looks like you need this. You have a little water right here." She touches the tip of her nose.

"Very funny," I say, taking the towel. I use it to dry my face, then I toss it onto the counter and reach for the hem of my shirt, pulling it up and over my head. It's dripping all over the floor, so my decision is mostly practical. But that doesn't mean I'm not hoping to get at least a little rise out of Sarah.

I toss the shirt onto the counter beside the towel, watching as her eyes dip to my torso.

I step closer, crowding her against the sink, setting my arms on either side of her. "Do you know what I think?" I say, my voice low.

She licks her lips, eyes glassy as she asks, "What's that?"

"I think you did that on purpose."

She lifts her hand to the penny hanging around my neck, picking it up then letting it fall as her fingers graze down my chest to the top of my abs. My eyes close as goosebumps break out across my skin. I don't even know what we're talking about anymore, I just know I don't want her to ever stop touching me.

"Did what on purpose?" she asks, her voice much too innocent. It's that little bit of sass in her tone that snaps me back to the moment.

"You won't distract me out of doing the dishes," I say. It's taking all my willpower to make that statement true.

Both her hands are on me now, skimming up my chest and over the tops of my shoulders. "Are you sure about that?" she asks, and it's all I can do to stay on my feet. She has no idea how much she's killing me.

"Okay, you're done," I say, then I crouch and pick her up, tossing her over my shoulder and carrying her around the island and into the living room.

She laughs and squeals and beats against my back, but she's not truly fighting me. I deposit her on the couch, flat on her back, then I hover over her, my hands resting on either side of her head. "You're disqualified for not playing fair," I say.

Her eyes darken as her gaze drops to my lips. "I don't know," she says softly. "I think...maybe some rules are made to be broken."

She's asking me to kiss her, and not for the first time.

I *want* to kiss her.

But a part of me is still scared to do it. I've already kissed her enough to know that if I let myself have her because I want her, there's no coming back from that. I'll be all in—all the way.

Even if she never comes to a game. Even if I never understand why. Even if I'm never quite certain she would have chosen me *for me*. I'll be in too deep to care, to want any life but one that has her in it.

Slowly, Sarah lifts her hands to my forearms, her thumbs tracing circles on my skin. "I'm scared, Carter," she says, a new vulnerability in her tone. And that's what pushes me over the edge. What makes me realize it's already too late.

I'm in love with her. Wholly. Completely.

And then the doorbell rings.

Sarah grips my arms a little tighter, a question in her gaze. "Are we expecting anyone?" she asks.

I lean back and shift, pulling my phone out of my pocket. "Not that I'm aware of," I say. I pull up the app for our doorbell camera and check the live feed. "It's your brother."

"What's he doing here?" Sarah moves to sit up, and I scoot back, giving her a little more room.

"No clue," I say. "Should we just ignore him?"

Miles rings the doorbell a few more times.

Sarah sighs. "We can't ignore him. I just—really don't want to talk to him right now."

"Then I'll talk to him," I say. "If you don't want to see him, you don't have to."

She bites her lip. "Are you sure?"

I reach over and give her hand a quick squeeze. "Of course I'm sure. You just stay hidden." I take a slight detour to my bedroom to grab another shirt, then I make my way to the front door, glancing over my shoulder to make sure Sarah is nowhere in sight.

Then I swing open the front door and make eye contact with Miles. "Hey, man," I say, trying to keep my voice casual. "What are you doing here?"

"I need to see my sister," he says, his voice a little gruffer than usual. He's been off the last week, so I haven't seen him since I was at the hospital, and he looks exhausted. I don't think he's shaved since then, and there are dark circles under his eyes. I guess that's to be expected when he's got a newborn in the house.

Miles steps forward like he's coming inside, but I lift an arm, bracing it against the door jamb to stop his entry.

He hesitates, rocking back on his heels, then lifts his eyes to mine.

"Now isn't a great time," I say, and his gaze narrows.

"What do you mean it isn't a great time? You can't tell me I can't talk to her."

"I just did," I say slowly.

He huffs out a laugh. "What are you doing here, man? She's my sister."

"She might be your sister," I say calmly, "but she's *my wife*."

His jaw hardens, and for a fraction of a second, I wonder if he might hit me. He looks like he wants to. But then he shoves his hands into the pockets of his hoodie. "Your wife, huh?"

"She doesn't want to talk to you, Miles. Not tonight."

He rolls his eyes. "Can we stop with all this? You've got a lot of nerve, man. Acting like any of this between the two of you is real. Just let me inside so I can talk to her."

He moves to the side to step around me, but I move with him, blocking him with my whole body this time. "*My wife*," I repeat, "and *my house*." I level him with what I hope is my most intimidating stare. "And I said not tonight."

Something shifts in Miles's expression, some of the fight draining out of him, and he takes a step back. "You'll talk to your captain like that?" he asks, and my jaw tightens.

"Not on the ice, I won't," I say. "Out there, you know I'll follow you anywhere—do whatever you ask me to do. But this is bigger than hockey."

He studies me for a long moment. "I can't let her go back, man," he says. "I'm just trying to protect her." Something like hurt flashes behind his eyes. "I guess she's got you for that now, huh?"

"That's the thing, Miles. She doesn't need my protection. Or yours. Not anymore. She's stronger than you're giving her credit for. All she needs is for you to believe her when she tells you she's good enough to do things her way."

"It's not that I don't think she's good enough—"

"But that's what it sounds like. Every time you try to force her into teaching, that's how you make her feel."

He sighs and rubs a hand over his face. "I just know how few people actually qualify. I'm trying to be practical here."

"You know what else few people qualify for?" I say. "The NHL. Is that what this is really about? Your ego only has room for one person in your family to be great? To perform at an elite level?"

He frowns, eyes dropping to the concrete under his feet.

"Go home, Miles," I say. "Get some sleep. You look like you need it." I close the door before he can say anything else, then lean against it, adrenaline making me lightheaded.

I'm not sure where I got the courage to talk to Miles like that, and I might regret it the next time we're on the ice together. But I'd do it again if I had the opportunity.

Because this *is* bigger than hockey. Which is a weird realization. Nothing outside of my immediate family has ever been bigger—more important—than hockey.

But Sarah is. I'm sure of that now.

I slowly make my way back toward the kitchen, but I pause when Sarah steps out of the shadowy dining room. Her eyes are damp with tears, and a pulse of fear rushes through me. Did I say something that made her upset? She might not have wanted me to fight her battles, and that's exactly what I did.

"Did you hear…?"

She steps forward and wraps her arms around my waist, pressing herself against me and silencing the rest of my question. I let my arms wrap around her back and hold her against me, bending down to press a kiss against her hair.

She leans back, lifting her hands to my face, grazing her fingers over my jaw before pushing up on her toes and kissing me on the cheek, just shy of my mouth. "Thank you," she whispers, then she turns and heads to her room, taking my heart with her as she goes.

24

SARAH

I GLANCE UP AT CARTER, CHECKING TO SEE HOW CLOSE HE IS TO finishing his crossword puzzle. We've done the daily cross-word at the same time at least a dozen times, and every single time, I've finished before him. Not that we've been racing, exactly. But I've watched him watching me, sneaking peeks at my screen to see how close I am. Hazards of being married to a professional athlete. The man turns folding his socks into a competition.

Now, he's totally focused, which I love because it means I can sit here and stare at him without him noticing. Which— I've *always* enjoyed staring at Carter. But it feels different this morning.

After last night, *everything* feels different.

It was bad enough last week, when I saw Carter holding Fiona right after she was born, smiling down at her with a look of sheer wonder on his face. I'm not sure I've ever been so aware of my ovaries or thought so seriously about having a baby.

But not just any baby. In my alarmingly realistic fantasy, I was having a baby...*with Carter.* It felt like the world tilted off its axis, and I'm still not sure I've recovered.

But then Miles showed up on our doorstep last night, and Carter defended me, standing up to my brother with steel in his voice. I know how intimidating Miles can be, but Carter was firm, steadfast. Completely supportive. When I wrapped my arms around his waist right after, felt him lean down and press a kiss to the top of my head, I was filled with an overwhelming sense of certainty. A rightness I've never experienced before.

I reposition myself on my barstool and try to focus on my puzzle. I've finished all but one clue, but I must have spelled something wrong because the answer I want to use doesn't fit. I could ask Carter, but that would really spoil the fun of beating him.

I glance at the time on my phone, hating how close we are to him leaving. He's dressed for the road, ready to head to the airport, where he'll leave for the last four away games of the regular season. Nine days on the road, then the team will arrive back just in time for one last home game at the Vortex. After that, they'll get a couple of days off, then the playoffs start with the first two games of their opening series here in Atlanta.

I've practically lived at Anna's since Fiona was born, helping with Poppy and Olive, so I've already been missing him. Now he's leaving, and that's just going to get worse.

Not that I can truly complain. The whole point of all this was so I could be here for Anna, and I'm so glad I am without the threat of my impending departure looming over me.

Anna is doing great, but she's nervous about her postpartum depression returning. She's judging every little shift in her mood, watching for signs to make sure she's taking care of herself as well as taking care of Fiona, who, to her credit, is pretty much perfect. She's a good sleeper, a good eater. Everyone in the house is absolutely in love with her. But I'm glad I've been there anyway. Olive and Poppy still need a lot of attention, even a little extra while they adjust to the fact that now, they're sharing their mom with a new baby.

Miles is back with the team this week, so it'll be even more important that I support Anna. Even though I'm presently furious with my brother and don't feel like giving him *any* credit, he's been incredible with the baby, maximizing every second of time off the Jaguars gave him. He's changed diapers and made dinners and rocked Fiona so Anna could nap. He's been endlessly patient with Poppy and Olive, reading books and doing puzzles and taking them for ice cream when he senses Anna needs a break. We'll both feel his absence this next week—the girls too.

It's been a nice reminder that while he's definitely being an idiot when it comes to *me,* he's so good when it comes to everything else. I see the way he's actively trying to be everything our own father wasn't, and I have to give him grace for that.

"Finished!" Carter says, pulling me back into the present. He raises his hands from his phone like I might take away points if he touches it again.

"You are not."

He grins. "Did I actually win this time?"

I press my lips together, fighting a smile. "Did you *win?*" I say. "I wasn't aware we were racing."

He grins. "Did I say *win?* I just meant, did I incidentally, with no meaning attached at all, happen to finish before you did?"

I finally let myself smile. "Shut up and come over here and help me figure out what I've gotten wrong."

He moves around the kitchen island, setting his arms on the granite, one on either side of me, and looks over my shoulder. He's close enough that I feel the warmth of his chest against my back and the tickle of his breath moving through my hair. I feel a sudden impulse to lean into him, to soak up his solid presence for a little while longer before he leaves.

I probably could. We've both been lax about the rules lately. Finding random reasons to touch each other, to lean into "friendly hugs" just a little bit longer than we normally would.

Carter leans forward and taps his pointer finger on the corner of my phone screen. "This is an *a* not an *e*," he says. "You've got the right word. It's just spelled wrong."

"Ah—cedar with an *a*. We spell it with an *e* in Canada."

Carter chuckles. "You do not."

"Then we should." I spin around on my barstool to face him. He's wearing soft joggers and a Jaguars team pullover that brings out the blue in his eyes. "An *e* makes more sense."

His hands are still on the counter which means I've got Carter on all sides, and the effect is almost dizzying.

His eyes gleam as he says, "Just accept defeat. You're already the best artist in the city. You don't get crossword puzzles too."

His words send a warm fizzle of heat shooting through my chest. "Pretty sure with an eleven to one record, I actually *do* get crossword puzzles."

"Says the woman who *wasn't aware* it was a competition." He reaches up and taps my forehead right between my eyes. "You get this line right here when you're really focused. And you're only really focused when you're trying to be faster than me."

I purse my lips to the side. He's not wrong, and something inside me loves that he's watching me so closely. "I'll regret that line in my forties," I say, but Carter shakes his head.

"Don't. You're beautiful now. You'll be beautiful then."

His words almost sound like he'll be *around* then. Available to tell me I'm still beautiful, even in my forties. The thought brings a sharp yearning to my chest.

Carter lifts one hand to my cheek, slowly brushing my hair back, his fingers lightly grazing over my skin. He looks like he wants to kiss me, and I desperately want him to, but I know him too well.

He might fudge the boundaries of "friendly touching," but he won't break this rule even if he wants to.

Unless I ask him to.

The voice in my head sounds like Emerson, urging me on, willing me to own what I want and go for it. But I can't bring myself to say the words.

What if I'm wrong about how he feels? What if he doesn't want to kiss me? What if I ask him for more and it ruins everything and we still have to stay married for a year?

Carter's watch buzzes with a message, and he glances down, then takes a step back and lets his hands fall from the counter. "Theo will be here any minute."

I nod, swallowing against the sudden knot in my throat. I'm really, *really* going to miss having him around. I bite my lip. "I wish you didn't have to go."

"Yeah, me too." He holds out his hand, and I scoot off my barstool, letting him tug me into an enormous hug.

It's not a kiss, but it's a close second. I will never get tired of the magic that is being wrapped up in Carter Williamson's arms.

"Nine days," he says, his voice close to my ear. "It'll go by fast." His hands move to my face, and he presses his forehead to mine. His eyes are closed, his breathing shallow, and I get the sense he's fighting the same pull that I am.

I tilt my face up until my nose brushes against his, waiting, *willing* him to just *do it. Kiss me.* His lips part, his fingers pressing into my scalp, but then a car horn honks outside, and he breathes out a sigh. "That's Theo."

I swallow my disappointment, as well as a million curse words I wish I could yell at his brother.

I should have done it. I should have just pushed up an inch more and kissed *him.*

Carter takes a step back, letting his hands move to my shoulders. "Take care of yourself while I'm gone."

"I will," I say. "Travel safe."

He lifts his duffel bag and hoists it over his shoulder. "Nine days," he repeats, as he slowly backs away, then he turns and disappears out the door.

I stand there, my body still fizzing with unreleased tension. I lift my hands to my cheeks and feel the warmth there, then breathe deep, trying to slow my racing heart. I hate that he's gone, hate that he's—

The front door opens again, and Carter steps inside. He quickly crosses the foyer to where I'm standing in the kitchen and suddenly, I'm in his arms again, my back pinned against the wall.

Before I even know what's happening, his mouth is on mine, his fingers sliding through my hair. I wrap my arms around his back, hands gripping his sweatshirt as I pull him closer, *closer*. His lips part, the kiss deepening as I taste him, breathe him in.

I have never been kissed like this. Even my other kisses with *him* pale in comparison. There is nothing careful about what's happening now. Nothing scripted. Nothing that makes it fit for public consumption.

This is real and raw and desperate and *perfect*.

Carter pulls back, his breathing heavy, and presses both hands against the wall behind me. "We're going to talk about this when I get home." There's no question mark at the end of his sentence. It comes out more like a command. A little growly. *A lot* sexy.

"Talking is good," I say, my voice barely above a whisper. "But kissing is better."

I pull him down and find his lips again. The kiss is softer this time, more tender than the first.

"You're killing me, Sarah," he says against my mouth. "Because I have to go, and I really don't want to."

He leans back, blue eyes sparkling as he looks down at me, the sweetest expression on his face. "Here," he says, and then he shrugs out of his pullover, revealing a plain gray t-shirt underneath. The penny he always wears around his neck is resting against his sternum. "Keep this for me," he says, handing me the pullover. "I don't know how I'm going to make it nine days without touching you, but it'll help to know that at least something of mine is against your skin."

"This and all your t-shirts," I say.

He grins. "Those don't count because I already consider them yours."

Outside, Theo honks the horn so many times in a row, I know our time is up for real.

Carter kisses me one last time. "Nine days," he says. "Then we'll talk."

I nod. "Nine days."

I clutch Carter's pullover to my chest, breathing in his scent, already missing him with an ache rooted deep in my gut. I can hardly process what happened. But then, it feels like we've been building to this for weeks, cranking the tension up higher and higher, daring each other to be the one who breaks first.

I have no idea what's going to happen when he comes back. What we'll talk about. How things will look moving forward.

But I know I'm probably going to wear this pullover for nine days straight. And I dare anyone to tell me I shouldn't.

25

SARAH

I'M BEHIND ON A BUNCH OF ERRANDS I NEED TO RUN—A MEETING with my accountant, a trip to the grocery store, an appointment with my eye doctor—so it's after dinner before I finally make it to Anna's.

I'm still floating when I get there—it's only been eight hours since the kiss to rival all kisses—but all thoughts of Carter are pushed from my mind as soon as I reach Anna's front porch. I can hear Fiona crying from all the way out here. The sound makes me hurry a little faster.

I let myself in and kick off my sneakers before following the sound of Fiona's cries to the living room.

Anna is pacing in front of the fireplace, Fiona cradled in her arms. She's trying to get her to take a bottle, and Fiona doesn't seem very enthusiastic. The older girls are on the couch, watching an episode of Bluey, though I can't imagine how they're hearing it over Fiona's crying.

"Hey," Anna says when she sees me come in. "I'm trying to get her used to bottles, but she's really not having it."

"Here. Let me try," I say. "I might have more luck since I don't have boobs full of milk."

She sighs. "Please. But if she doesn't figure it out fast, I'll just nurse her."

I sit down on the couch with Fiona and the bottle and slowly brush it against her lips. Fiona fights it at first, but only for a moment before she manages to latch.

"Finally," Poppy says as Fiona gulps down the breastmilk.

"Good work, Fi," I say as I look down at her perfect little face. She's bigger than she was the last time I saw her, but I remember feeling that way about Olive and Poppy too. They grow so fast when they're tiny.

Anna drops onto the couch beside me. "I'm surprised it worked," she says. "It's a little early to introduce a bottle, but she's already such a good nurser, I hoped she'd figure it out."

"What's the reason for waiting?" I ask, and Anna shrugs.

"Some people say it can impact your milk supply if you aren't breastfeeding regularly or interfere with the baby's ability to latch. But I'm not worried. I have enough milk to feed an army of babies. Her taking a bottle isn't going to matter. Plus, this way, maybe I'll be able to go to the last home game."

I lift my eyebrows. "Are you serious right now? You want to go to a hockey game three weeks postpartum?"

"I mean, I won't take *her*," Anna says. "Assuming you'd keep her for me. But Miles plays better when I'm there."

Something about her statement makes my heart pinch. I love that she loves watching Miles play. And that she's so willing to be there for him, even so soon after having a baby.

It just makes me wish I could do the same thing. Be there for Carter enough that he feels like he plays better when I'm watching.

"Of course I'll watch her," I say. "You know I will."

"Mommy, can we watch another episode?" Poppy asks.

Anna tosses Poppy the remote. "Just one more," she says. "Then it's bedtime for you both." Anna shifts her attention back to me. "What was that face for?" she asks.

"What face?"

"The face you made when I said I wanted to go to a game. Are you thinking I shouldn't? I really don't think it's a big deal. It's not like I'll do anything but sit there."

"That's not it," I say. "I was just..." I scrunch my eyes closed, then peek one open to see Anna looking at me, expression curious. "I think..." I start to say. I look down at Fiona, readjusting the bottle. She's almost finished, and her eyes are getting heavy. "I think I'm ready to work through my panic attacks. I want to watch Carter play. I want to show up for him like he shows up for me."

Anna's expression softens. "I wondered if you might wind up here. The fact that you have—I think it means you love him, Sarah."

My face flushes with heat at the thought. I put the bottle down and lift Fiona to my shoulder, patting her on the back to help her burp. "Maybe I do? That feels like such a big word. I just know I can't stop thinking about him. Also, he kissed me this morning before he left and...Anna, I've never had a kiss feel like that. I think...he might be really special. And suddenly the sadness I feel over *not* being there for him feels worse than the fear making me stay away."

"That's a really big deal," she says softly. "And I'm really, *really* happy for you."

"Yeah?"

"Of course! He's a great guy. And the two of you seem

really good together," she says. "So what are you going to do?"

"No clue," I say. "Call my therapist? Practice watching games at home? I don't even know where to start."

"I think your therapist is a *great* place to start," Anna says.

"Yeah. I just feel like it shouldn't be this hard. Intellectually, I understand that Miles is fine. Fighting is a part of the game—"

"But not every game," Anna adds. "I think they play more games *without* fights."

I nod. "Right. I totally get that. But even when they *do* fight, I know Miles is never actually out of control. It's not the same as..." My voice cracks, and I close my eyes, suddenly grateful to have the grounding presence of Fiona in my arms.

"As it was with your dad," Anna says, finishing the sentence I can't finish on my own.

I nod. "If I know that, why can't I get through this?"

"Because your nervous system doesn't care what you think you know," Anna says gently. "Triggers don't always make sense. Especially when they're rooted in trauma. And Sarah, your childhood was really traumatic. Don't berate yourself over this. It's honestly a miracle that this is the worst of what you're dealing with."

Tears spring to my eyes. "But how is Miles okay? Dad never hit *me*. It was always Miles. He's the one who really suffered."

Anna reaches over and squeezes my knee. "That doesn't mean it wasn't also traumatic for you. Besides, Miles hasn't always been okay. You were too young to really see or understand, but he had a hard time when he first joined the league. He struggled to keep his anger in check, had terrible impulse control. Eventually, it started to impact his play. If not for Coach Kimzey, I'm not sure he would have made it through."

"Coach Kimzey? The Jaguars coach?"

"He was a player then. Captain of Miles's team in Boston."

I sniff. "How did I not know that?"

"I didn't for a long time," Anna says. "This was all before we met, and it's taken me years to pry all of the details out of him. But the long and short of it is that Kyle—Coach Kimzey—pulled Miles aside and told him if he didn't get himself into therapy and take care of his mental health, he'd never pass him another puck again."

"And it worked?"

Anna nods. "Yeah. It did. Miles was barely twenty years old, trying to live on his own, sending seventy percent of what he earned back to Canada for you and your mom. I think he understood that if he threw away his career, he was also throwing away his ability to take care of you."

"So he went to therapy?"

"For years," Anna says. "The team set him up with someone, and it truly changed his life. It's why he was committed to making sure *you* were seeing a therapist once you moved to the States. Because he knows it works."

I lean back into the couch cushions, one hand rubbing up and down Fiona's back. "When I was little, he told me he had special powers," I say. "That the hits didn't hurt him—like he was some kind of superhero."

"That sounds like something he would say," she says. "He's only ever wanted to protect you."

I breathe out a long sigh. "I know. That's what makes it easier for me to forgive him for how boneheaded he's being right now."

She gives me a commiserating look. "Did he try to make you talk to the Canadian teacher he found?"

"He all but called him for me." In my arms, Fiona wiggles, arching her back as she stretches and lets out the cutest tiny baby grunt. "Should I lay her down?" I ask Anna.

"You can try, but she'll probably wake up if you do." She stands. "You keep her. I'll take the girls up and put them to bed."

"Are you sure? I was going to do it to give you a break."

"You *are* giving me a break. And giving Poppy and Olive some much needed Mommy time. What do you say, girls?" Anna says to her two oldest daughters. "You want to do bedtime with me tonight?"

They immediately jump up and cheer, clearly thrilled with the idea.

While the three of them are upstairs, I pull out my phone and take a selfie, the top of Fiona's head just visible at the bottom of the photo.

I send it to Carter, a pulse of nerves pushing through me as I do.

If not for the kiss this morning, I might not have had the courage to send it. A text, yes—but not a selfie.

That kiss. I've replayed it in my mind at least a thousand times, and it makes my skin prickle with awareness every single time. Carter didn't just kiss me—he kissed me like I belong to him. Like there was no possible way he could pull out of the driveway *without* kissing me.

My phone vibrates beside me, and I grab it, my heart already pounding in anticipation.

Carter has hearted the photo, then a message pops up.

CARTER
You're beautiful.

I close my eyes, resisting the urge to kick my feet like a middle schooler getting her first text from a boy she likes.

I heart Carter's message, then switch over to Instagram, trusting the Jaguars' social media crew has posted pictures of the team boarding the airplane. Sure enough, a post went up this morning. It doesn't include photos of every player, but it's my lucky day because there's a great shot of Carter, sunglasses on, looking serious and sexy and perfectly delicious.

I spend an inordinate amount of time thinking about the fact that less than an hour before this photo was taken, he was pinning me against the wall in our kitchen, kissing me senseless.

While I wait for Anna, I fall into a rabbit hole of Jaguars' social media. I skip the highlights of past games—I'm not quite ready for those—but I screenshot photos of my husband with carefree abandon and save them to my phone. When Anna comes downstairs, she leans over the back of the couch and peers at my screen.

"Come on," she says. "Seriously? He's your husband. Just have him text you a selfie."

"But these shots are so good," I say. "Their social media people are great at their jobs." I scroll back up to an earlier post. "Look at this one of Miles. It's such a good picture of him." I hold out my phone, and she leans in to look, but she doesn't seem all that impressed.

"I mean, sure. It's a good photo," she says. "But wouldn't you rather look at the photos you don't have to share with the rest of the world?"

I look back at my phone, noticing the thousands of likes and comments each of the posts I'm looking at have gotten. So many people seeing the same photos, probably *admiring* the same photos. I guess I see Anna's point.

Fiona lets out a little whimper, and Anna circles the couch, coming around to gently scoop her out of my arms.

"She's been a little squirmy the last few minutes," I say, and Anna nods, fighting a yawn. "She probably needs to eat again." She sits down on the opposite end of the couch and takes a minute to get Fiona situated for breastfeeding.

I stand and retrieve Anna's giant water cup from the kitchen, refilling it with ice and fresh water, then I carry it back to her. She always gets thirsty when she's nursing.

"You're a gem," she says, taking the cup and helping herself to a long drink. "You'd think I've never had water before." She sets the water on the side table, then pats the couch cushion in between us. "Come on. Let's do something fun. The girls are asleep, and I really wanna binge the new *Count of Monte Cristo* series and eat an entire half gallon of ice cream directly out of the container. Are you going to help me to do it, or what?"

I retrieve my purse from the floor and tuck my phone inside, suddenly certain that a distraction is exactly what I need. "Yes, and *absolutely yes*," I say. Then I head to the kitchen for the ice cream.

It's after midnight when I finally get home from Anna's. I don't expect to hear from Carter, but after I feed Gordie and get ready for bed, I find a new text waiting for me.

CARTER

Are you still up?

I snuggle under my covers and key out my response.

SARAH

I stayed late at Anna's bingeing a new series with her, so I just got home.

Gordie says hello.

CARTER

He's with you now?

I take a quick photo of Gordie snuggled into the crook of my arm and send it to Carter.

CARTER

I have never been so jealous of a cat.

SARAH

I'm jealous of YOU because now you have two selfies of me…and I have NONE of you…

Seconds later, a photo pops up.

Carter is sitting on the bed in what I'm guessing is his hotel room, a book open on his lap, *annnnd* he's shirtless.

It's not even fair how good he looks. He's not flexing. Not posing. He's just…*reading*. And it's the sexiest thing I've seen all day.

Suddenly, I understand exactly what Anna meant about photos I don't have to share with the general public. This picture of Carter is infinitely better than anything I've seen on social media. It feels intimate, completely private, and meant *just for me.*

Over the next week and a half, Carter and I text every single day. Sometimes, there's only time for a message or two—I'm sure his schedule is grueling—but he always texts before he goes to sleep at night and again when he wakes up in the morning.

Most of what we talk about is completely random, even a little silly. He tells me the story of having an entire interaction with a fan at a pre-game meet-and-greet, not realizing until the very end that she thought he was his brother the entire time. He ended up signing Theo's name when she asked for his autograph because he thought that would be kinder than embarrassing her by telling the truth.

I send him countless pictures of baby Fiona, who is growing and thriving and getting cuter every single day.

We talk about music and movies and books and crossword puzzles.

But there are three things we don't talk about.

We don't talk about my childhood.

We don't talk about why I can't watch hockey games.

And we don't talk about the kiss we shared right before he left.

I know we *will* talk about these things. Of course we will. I don't think either of us wants to have an official *define the relationship* talk over text, or even over a phone call. It makes sense we're intentionally avoiding the subject. But it still makes me antsy, more and more anxious the closer we get to him coming home.

I can't stop thinking about the things I need to tell him that are going to be hard to say out loud.

My therapist, whom I've already talked to twice since Carter left, has made it clear that any successful path forward requires full transparency and honesty. That means I have to tell him why watching hockey is so triggering. Which means I have to tell him about my dad. Miles won't like it, but if I really am falling for Carter, then Miles doesn't really get a say anymore.

The team arrives back in Atlanta just after two p.m. on the day of their final home game. They head straight to the arena, so I don't see Carter before I go to Anna's to babysit. I get there with plenty of extra time, guessing she'll need it since this will be her first night out since Fiona was born.

I find her in her bedroom, flopped onto her bed next to a mountain of clothes. She's wearing a pair of jeans, but only *sort of* wearing them. It doesn't look like she was able to get them buttoned.

Fiona is in the bassinet sucking on a pacifier, and Poppy and Olive are in the bathroom sitting at Anna's vanity. Poppy is giving Olive a makeover that's going to be *very fun* to wash off.

"I'm sensing a fashion emergency," I say to Anna as I drop onto the foot of her bed.

She lifts her head to look at me. "They won't even button." She picks up the sides of her pants as if to illustrate her point.

"Of course they won't button," I say. "You had a baby *three weeks ago.*"

"So what do I do, then?" she asks. "I'm supposed to look cute at games. I can't go in pants with an elastic waist. That's against all kinds of rules."

"No one is going to be inspecting your pants," I say. "Wear your favorite leggings with a pair of boots and the oversized navy sweater you love so much."

She pushes up onto her elbows. "That's actually not a bad idea."

"See? I'm only terrible at fashion when *I'm* having a crisis. Most of the time, I manage just fine."

Anna stands and moves into her closet. "Have you heard from Carter? Did the team get in okay?" she calls from inside.

"They did. They're already at the Vortex. You haven't heard from Miles?"

"Nah, but I usually don't on gamedays," she says. "He says it messes with his focus." She comes back out of her closet with the new outfit on—the one I suggested. "What do you think?" she asks.

"It's perfect," I say. "You look great."

I glance at my watch, all too aware that I'm going to see Carter tonight.

I just have to kill seven hours first.

The girls, at least, make that a lot easier. Anna nurses Fiona right before she leaves, and there's a stockpile of milk in the fridge, but she's still in a fussy mood, so juggling the older girls and getting them into bed while keeping Fiona happy takes all my focus.

I'm upstairs trying to coax Olive into her big girl bed when the game starts. I manage to keep one eye on the score, but I'm still distracted, which only makes the time pass more quickly.

I finally drop onto the couch just before nine and read through the game highlights, scanning for Carter's name. Poppy and Olive are finally asleep, and Fiona is in the swing right next to me, still awake, but not fussing, which I'm taking as a win.

I reach for the TV remote, thinking I can at least try to watch something even if I can't truly focus, but then my phone rings.

"Hey," Anna says as soon as I pick up. Based on the sounds coming through the phone, she's still at the game.

"Hey. What's up?"

"Hang on," she says to me, then there's movement, some sort of shifting, before she says, "I know. I've got her on the phone right now. I will. I'll tell her."

My heart starts pounding, and I sit up a little taller. She'll tell me what? An ache of worry makes my stomach tighten, and I suddenly wish that I *had* gone to the game so I would know, right this second, that Carter is okay.

I need *eyes* on my husband. Not just words coming through a phone.

"Anna," I say, panic clawing at my throat. "What is it? Is it Carter? Please just tell me if my husband is hurt."

"Carter's fine," she says. "Breathe, Sarah. He's okay."

I *do* breathe, and tears inexplicably spring to my eyes. "Is it Miles?"

"Miles is fine too. Sarah, it's Theo," she says. "And it's pretty bad. Carter has to finish the game, but I'm sure he'll head to the hospital as soon as he can. I'm leaving the Vortex now, and I'm coming straight home. I thought you might want to meet Carter there."

26

CARTER

I'VE PLAYED THROUGH A LOT OF DIFFICULT HOCKEY GAMES.

When I was with the Appies, I played an entire third period with a hairline fracture in my shin bone. I've gone onto the ice with fresh stitches on my face and a missing tooth. Another time I had a broken pinky and a couple of bruised ribs.

But all of that was easy compared to tonight's game.

Staying on the ice while Theo was rushed down the tunnel, his hand sliced open in the bloodiest injury I've witnessed in hockey—that was brutal.

But what choice did I have? Contractually, I was obligated to stay. We were only two minutes into the third period, and we were down two goals. No one was going to approve having *two* defensemen off the ice just because I was worried about my brother.

So I played. *Hard.* Channeled my frustration into the game and landed more than one hit against the guy who started the scuffle that ended with Theo's injury in the first place.

It wasn't his blade that cut him. But he's the reason Theo was down.

We manage to make up one goal and nearly grab a second with less than a minute left, but when the game ends, I'm not sorry we didn't tie it up and push it into overtime.

I'm off the ice and down the tunnel faster than any of my teammates, eyes searching for our head trainer, Nico, or anyone else who might know something about Theo. One of our assistant trainers, Jake, is in the hall just outside the locker room. He's on the phone, but he holds up a finger like he wants me to wait for him.

I nod and step to the side, making room for my teammates to file past me. Several drop a hand on my shoulder, a quiet acknowledgement that they know exactly why I'm standing here waiting to talk to Jake.

He finally hangs up the phone just as Coach Kimzey steps up beside me.

"That was Nico," he says. "They made it to the ER at Atlanta General. They've stopped the bleeding, and now they're just waiting for the surgeon to consult—"

"A surgeon," I say. "Jake, I don't even know the extent of his injury. I've been on the ice—"

Coach Kimzey drops a hand onto my shoulder. "Maybe just fill us in from the beginning," he says, and Jake nods.

"Theo was cut from just above his wrist down to the center of his palm. It likely hit the radial artery, which would explain why he lost so much blood so quickly. It looks like he severed several tendons. The goal is to get him into surgery as quickly as possible. The faster they can repair any vascular and nerve damage, the better off he's going to be."

"Nerve damage," I repeat. "Could this impact his ability to

play?" I look over at Coach Kimzey. "He's going to get through this, right? Make a full recovery?"

Coach looks at Jake, his expression solemn, then he lifts both hands to my shoulders. "The most important thing is that we get to the hospital to support him. Get out of your gear. Take a quick shower, then I'll drive you over as soon as you're ready."

The locker room is more subdued than normal, even after a typical loss. We all saw how much blood hit the ice when Theo was cut. It's hard to think of anything besides the fact that he isn't here.

Miles is waiting at my stall, Holly beside him, but I'm spared having to rehash the details because Coach Kimzey comes in behind me and does it for me. Usually I would sit, give Coach my full attention, but I'm too focused on getting to the hospital—on getting to Theo—and I know he'll understand.

Less than twenty minutes later, I'm dressed and on my way out the door. Miles stops me before I make it into the hall. He and I have been locked in a sort of tense standoff since he showed up at my house demanding to see Sarah. I'm not sure it has impacted our play, but the energy in the locker room has definitely been off. But now, the ire I'm used to seeing in his eyes is completely gone. "I talked to Anna and filled her in on what Coach told us. She already called Sarah, and Sarah's getting in touch with your mom."

I nod, a sudden ache pushing through me at the thought of Sarah. Somehow, it feels right that she's the one communicating with Mom. She'll be gentle but reassuring, two things I feel wholly incapable of being on my own. "Good. That's good. Thanks, man."

It takes some maneuvering to get away from the press,

who are understandably hoping to get a comment from me on my brother's injury, but Coach Kimzey is firm and unyielding in his dismissal, telling everyone our assistant coach will handle the post-game presser and will release any updates on Theo's condition as soon as we know more.

I'm as grateful for this as I am for Miles's efforts. The last thing I want to do right now is talk into a microphone.

I've been playing hockey with Theo for twenty-two years. And we've been on the same team, playing side by side since the very beginning. It's hard to wrap my head around the possibility of playing without him.

But even more than that, this game is Theo's life.

What will it mean if he can't play anymore?

I turn Theo's phone over and over in my hand. I grabbed it, along with his wallet, on my way out of the arena.

Coach Kimzey is silent for the ride to the hospital, which I appreciate. I don't feel like making small talk, and we don't know anything about Theo, so what is there to say? I just need to get to the hospital and get eyes on my brother. That's all I want to do.

We finally pull to a stop in front of the emergency room entrance. "You go," Coach Kimzey says. "I'll park, then come find you."

It takes a minute to get through reception, but eventually they figure out who I am and why I'm here, and I'm taken upstairs to a private waiting area. Apparently, Theo is already in surgery.

Nico is alone in the waiting room, his elbows resting on his knees and his head in his hands. I've never seen our head trainer look so dejected.

He stands as soon as I come in.

"How is he?" I ask.

Nico takes a deep breath, hesitating just enough to make me worry.

"Be straight with me, man. How bad are we talking here?"

He sits down and motions for me to sit beside him. "It's bad, Carter. The cut was deep. They're going to do everything they can, but the doctor was honest about the challenges with injuries like this. The possibility of losing fine motor skills, the dexterity in his hand—it's very real."

My mouth goes dry. "So he might not play again?"

"I mean, this is Theo we're talking about," Nico says. "If anyone is stubborn enough to beat the odds, it's him. But his recovery won't be easy."

I drop my head into my hands and fight the urge to cry.

Theo not playing hockey. It can't happen. It *can't.*

"He has to play again," I say, my voice soft.

Nico drops a hand onto my shoulder. "I know, man. Let's believe he will, all right? He's got the best surgeons in the state working on his hand right now. We just have to leave it to them." He glances up as Coach Kimzey enters the waiting room. "And pray for a miracle."

I stay seated as Nico gives Coach the same rundown he just gave me, my thoughts spiraling.

I wish I could have seen Theo. Talked to him. Looked in his eyes and told him he was going to get through this. That I would be *right here* every step of the way.

I want to yell at Nico for not calling me before they took him back.

I want to yell at Coach Kimzey for not getting me here fast enough to see him.

I want to go find Andrei Kiminsky and pound his face in for starting the fight with Theo in the first place.

But then movement at the doorway of the waiting room catches my eye, and I look up.

Sarah.

She's breathing heavy, like she ran here, her eyes scanning the room until they land on me.

I can't explain it. The magnetic pull that lifts me out of my chair and carries me across the room to her. I just know I couldn't stop it if I tried.

Her arms wrap around me, and I melt into the embrace, breathing her in. Over the past nine days, I've imagined a dozen different ways this moment might go. How seeing her again might feel. Being on the road made me all too aware what my feelings for Sarah actually are.

But this moment sharpens that realization even further.

I'm out of my mind worrying about my brother, filled with a desperation that makes me want to rage and cry all at the same time.

But with her arms around me, all of that somehow stills.

She feels like an anchor. Like *home*.

My body starts to tremble, and she tightens her grip.

"I've got you," she whispers. "I'm here." Her hand lifts to the nape of my neck, her fingers tangling in my hair. "Everything's going to be okay."

27

SARAH

THE FIRST HOUR AT THE HOSPITAL, WE DON'T KNOW MUCH OUTSIDE of what Nico first told Carter about the nature of Theo's injury. Now we're just hoping a member of the surgical team will update us as soon as there's more information to share.

Which means the only thing we have to do is wait.

Several of the Jaguars players stop by, and of course Nico and Coach Kimzey are here, but I can't decide if the distraction of extra people around is making things easier or harder for Carter. Because he wants to talk to everyone. Make *them* feel better. Make sure everyone else in the room has everything *they* need.

But is that what *he* needs? I'm not sure rehashing the same information, answering the same questions over and over again, is doing him any good.

I step to the door of the waiting area and look up and down the hall, wondering if there's somewhere else I could take him for a minute of solitude. Long enough for me to look him in the eyes and make sure he's okay.

Across the hall, a nurse in navy scrubs is watching the

347

waiting room. *Really* watching. Not just passing by, but staring like she's thinking about coming in. My eyes drop to her name badge. It reads Rebecca.

Rebecca. Could she be Theo's Rebecca? Carter *did* say she worked on the surgical floor of Atlanta General, so this could absolutely be her, but it's not a super uncommon name, so maybe not?

"Hi," I say when we make eye contact. "I was wondering if you could help me. My husband's brother is in surgery right now, and there are so many people here to support him and wait for news. But I think he might need a minute of privacy. Is there somewhere we could go? Just for a second."

"There's a quiet room down the hall and to the right," she says. "It's usually empty."

I nod. "Perfect. Thank you."

She looks like she might want to say something else, but then she gives her head a little shake and turns and heads down the hall.

I make my way back to Carter, finding him in a conversation with Holly and Jordo. I slip an arm around his waist, and he tucks me into his side, his grip on my shoulder a little tighter than usual. It feels like he's telling me not to go anywhere.

"Hey," I say, as soon as there's a break in the conversation. "Come with me for a sec?"

He nods and I thread my fingers through his, tugging him toward the door. "We'll be right back," I say to Nico, then we head down the hall to the quiet room.

The space lives up to its name. It *is* quiet—we can't hear the low hum of hospital activity at all—with low lighting, comfortable seating, and a tiny water feature in the corner that creates a surprisingly soothing vibe.

"I thought you might need a minute to breathe," I say to Carter.

He moves to the small couch against the wall and sits down, then pulls me onto his lap, wrapping his arms around me and burying his face in my shoulder.

"That was a good thought," he says.

I lift my hands to his hair, gently running my fingers over his scalp. "What do you need? Is there anything I can do?"

"You're doing it," he says. "I'm really glad you're here."

"Where else would I be?" I let my hands slide down to his face, then I lean in and press a lingering kiss to his mouth.

"I missed you," he says, his voice soft. "I feel like there's so much I want to say to you, but..."

"We have time," I say. "We don't have to worry about any of that now."

He takes another deep breath, and I can practically feel the tension leaving his body.

"So, I'm pretty sure I saw Rebecca," I say. "This is her floor, right?"

"Yeah, I guess so," Carter says.

"Honestly, when I said we needed to get Theo back in the hospital to run into her, this is not what I had in mind."

Carter chuckles. "It is very Theo. Nice and dramatic."

There's a slight tremor in his voice, and an ache fills my chest. I wish I could reach in and take out his worry, carry it for him so he wouldn't have to feel this way.

We're quiet for a long moment before I say, "He's going to be okay, Carter."

His grip around me tightens.

"He's strong and stubborn and fiercely competitive. He's not going to let this beat him."

"But will he play hockey again?" he asks, his voice raw, vulnerable.

"He will," I say, hoping against hope that I'm not lying to him. "He'll find a way."

We stay in the quiet room for another ten minutes or so, then Nico texts to say the surgeon is there to give us an update, so we quickly make our way back to the waiting room.

According to the surgeon, everything has gone well so far, but the microvascular team is still tackling the very delicate work of repairing the damaged nerves and blood vessels.

No one needs to say out loud how important this part is. If he *is* going to play again, at the same elite level he plays at now, his dexterity is a huge part of it.

Carter shakes the surgeon's hand. "Thank you, doctor," he says. "How much longer will he be in surgery?"

"At least another hour," he says. "Maybe a little longer."

After the surgeon leaves, Holly and Jordo and the other players who are still around say their goodbyes and head home. Even though they don't have a game tomorrow, play-offs start in two days. They all need to be prioritizing their health, making sure they're getting enough sleep. Coach Kimzey also leaves, promising to return first thing in the morning, leaving just me, Carter, and Nico in the waiting room.

"Listen, if you want to head home and get some sleep," Nico says, "I can call you as soon as he's out of surgery and awake. You have to take care of yourself, man. The team's going to need you now more than ever."

Carter quickly shakes his head. "I won't leave until I see him."

"I won't leave either," a voice says, and we turn to see

Miles standing behind us. He has a to-go container of food in his hands, and he holds it out, offering it to Carter. "I assume you didn't eat after the game. You need to."

Carter takes the food, then he glances over at me. As far as I know, he and Miles haven't talked much since their confrontation on our front porch. I haven't talked to my brother at all, so his presence now is unexpected. Maybe it shouldn't be. He's Theo's team captain, after all. He *should* be here.

Miles makes eye contact with me, then he hesitates the slightest bit, like he's suddenly questioning whether he's welcome.

He clears his throat. "Mind if I sit?"

"Not at all," I say, motioning for him to sit down. He chooses the chair directly opposite Carter, then leans forward, propping his elbows on his knees.

"I'm sorry I'm late," he says. "I had to do the post-game presser, then I waited for the kitchen to box up a meal for you—it's that chicken they said you really like—then I went home to check on Anna, then I wandered around the hospital looking for a microwave where I could heat up your food. Oh, wait. Here." He pulls a plastic-wrapped set of disposable silverware out of his pocket and hands it to Carter.

Carter hasn't opened the container yet—he's probably just as confused by Miles's presence as I am.

"Dude. Eat," Miles says. "You have to refuel after a game."

"Thank you," Carter says slowly, then Miles looks over at Nico.

"Nico, can you give us the room please?" When he's like this, I can absolutely understand why Miles makes such a good team captain. He has a very commanding presence.

Nico quickly stands and steps into the hallway, and

suddenly I'm alone with the two most important men in my life.

Miles is quiet for a long moment, eyes on the floor. "I have something to say to each of you," he finally says. "And I'm bad at stuff like this, so just...let me get it all out before you say anything."

I pull my knees up to my chest and wrap my arms around them, suddenly sensing what Miles is about to do. Carter glances over and must sense my discomfort, because he puts down his food and reaches for my hand, giving it a reassuring squeeze.

Miles looks at Carter first. "When Sarah and I were kids, our father was not a good man. He wanted to be, but then he would drink too much, get angry, and tell me about that anger with his fists. For years, that was my reality. But I took it, dealt with it, because he was still paying the bills. Mom was sick, unable to work, and I wasn't sure how we would survive if we left him."

I tighten my grip on Carter's fingers. I'm not sure I've ever heard my brother speak this openly about our past. Not to *anyone*.

"As soon as I signed my first contract and started making enough money to take care of them, I found a house for Mom and Sarah, told my dad to get lost, and threatened to press charges if he ever talked to any of us again." He takes a steadying breath. "I tell you all that because I need you to understand why it's been so important to me that Sarah stay in the U.S. with me. I'm ten years older than she is—she was only eight years old when I started in the NHL. I have been responsible for protecting her, taking care of her, for a very long time."

"I get that," Carter says, but Miles holds up his hand, stopping him before he can say more.

"Just let me finish."

I shoot Carter an amused look. Even in his apology, Miles is still being very *Miles*.

"My frustration has never been about *you* personally," Miles continues. "It's always been about my own fear and my unwillingness to relinquish control. But then when I showed up at your house and you wouldn't back down, I realized you're exactly the kind of man I want for my sister. Not because you can protect her as well as I can, but because you recognize her strength better than I ever have." Miles finally shifts his gaze over to me. "I'm sorry, Sarah," he says. "I'm not going to tell you what to do anymore. I trust you. And I really do think you're an amazing artist. Anna says I haven't made that clear enough, so I'm going to work on that." He waves a hand in our general direction. "And if the two of you want to just...*be in love* or whatever, then I guess I'm happy for you."

I make eye contact with Carter. We haven't said anything about love—not to each other—but I'm not about to protest when Miles is essentially giving us his blessing. Not just for a marriage of convenience but for a *real* union. A real marriage.

We've done everything out of order. Marriage is usually the thing you build to—work toward for months and months, getting to know each other, learning how to fight, learning how to compromise. We've got the marriage part out of the way, but all that other stuff hasn't happened yet, and there's something scary about that.

Then again, maybe knowing we love each other is enough. Love is what makes you willing to put in the work. I've never been so certain that I'm willing—that a life with Carter is exactly what I want.

I reach for Carter's hand, pulling both of his into mine and capturing his full attention. I tilt my head toward Miles. "That's why I can't go to hockey games," I say. "The fighting triggers panic attacks. I saw one game where someone was punching Miles, and I just...lost it. But I really want to figure this out. I'm already talking to my therapist again because I *want* to come. I want to watch you play and support you as well as you've supported me."

Carter leans over, cradling my face as he kisses me softly, his thumbs wiping at the tears suddenly spilling out of my eyes. "I don't need you to be there," he says. "I mean, of course I'd love for you to be, but...I've been thinking about the possibility of Theo not playing again, and I don't want hockey to be the only thing I have going for me." He looks over at Miles. "We could lose all of this at any moment. Any game. One wrong move and we're out. Finished. I want what I have at home to be important enough that if that happens, I still have a reason to wake up in the morning." Carter pulls his gaze back to me, his expression so earnest, it makes my heart ache in my chest. "That's you for me, Sarah. That's what I want us to have."

He kisses me one more time, this time long enough to make me keenly aware that my big brother is watching.

To Miles's credit, he doesn't joke or comment or tell us to get a room, even though I'm one hundred percent certain he wants to.

Carter gives me a small smile as he pulls back, his hands lingering on my face. "Thanks for telling me," he says.

"I'm sorry I didn't sooner. It's not particularly easy to talk about. Also, *someone* didn't want me to." I tilt my head toward Miles, who holds his hands up defensively.

"Don't look at me like that. You got your apology. And I

did all the extra things Anna said I had to do to make sure you know I really meant it." He points at Carter's still uneaten meal. "I warmed up his food, which, come on, man. It's probably not even warm anymore."

Carter chuckles as he picks up the container. "I don't mind eating it cold. Thanks for bringing it."

"So are we good?" Miles says, clapping his hands on his knees.

I stand and hold out my hand, motioning for Miles to get off his chair and give me a hug. "We're good," I say. "Thanks for apologizing."

"So, talk to me about Theo," Miles says as he sits back down. "What are we going to do to get him back on the ice by next season?"

28

CARTER

THEO'S SURGEON COMES OUT TO TALK TO US JUST AFTER ONE IN THE morning. She looks exhausted, but she's smiling when she tells us that everything went as well as she could have hoped, and she expects Theo will make a solid recovery, despite the extensive repairs his injury required.

Only time will truly tell us what challenges he'll face when it comes to hockey. The surgeon mentions lingering tightness from the tendon repair and potential nerve damage that could have long-term impacts, but overall, we have every reason to be hopeful.

"Theo is still in postoperative recovery," she says once she's gone over everything. "But once he's moved to a regular room, a nurse will take you up to see him."

I breathe out a sigh and sink back onto the couch. "So, more waiting," I say.

Sarah sits down next to me and drops her head on my shoulder. "I don't know how the two of you still have your eyes open," she says to me and Miles. "I barely can, and you're the ones who played a hockey game tonight."

"Yeah, but you put my kids to bed," Miles says from the opposite row of chairs. "I've done both, and hockey is easier."

I lean my head back against the wall and chuckle. "I believe it."

Five minutes later, a nurse walks into the room, and I sit up a little taller, surprised Theo has already been moved. But then I recognize Rebecca.

Something tells me she's *not* here to take us to Theo's room.

She sits down directly across from me, her expression focused, resolute.

"I wasn't going to do this," she says. "I've been trying to avoid coming in here, but then I kept coming up with random reasons to walk by, which is so entirely stupid. I'm over him. It's been *years*. Of course I'm over him. But I think...I just need to know that he's doing better. Not from the surgery. Which... I did hear it went well. I just mean...from before." She meets my eyes, and suddenly, I'm right back in high school telling her that Theo doesn't want to see her again. Rebecca was far too patient with Theo back then. She tried so hard to be what he needed, but he was wrestling with demons that were much bigger than what any of us should have had to handle. He turned so far inward, the only thing he managed *not* to give up on was hockey. And that was only because I didn't give him a choice. It's a credit to her character that after how he treated her, she still cares about him at all.

"Is he doing okay?" she asks. "Is he...happy?"

I consider how to answer. Theo doesn't know she's here, doesn't know she's asking, and I don't want to betray his privacy. But she also went through a lot for him—more than she deserved. "It took a while," I say. "But he's doing a lot better. He's happy."

She sniffs and lifts her gaze to the ceiling like she's trying to fight back tears. "That's good. That's what I want for him—that's what I've always wanted for him." She lifts a hand to her forehead and lets out a little laugh. "I was supposed to scrub in for his surgery," she says. "I mean, what are the odds? That of all the ORs in the country..." She takes a deep breath. "Anyway, thank you for the information. And I'm sorry to barge in on you like this." She looks over at Sarah. "Also, I read about your wedding online and you were such a beautiful bride, and I really hope the two of you are very happy."

"I'm sorry," I say, suddenly realizing I never introduced Sarah. "I should have introduced you. This is my wife, Sarah, my brother-in-law, Miles, and the Jaguars' head trainer, Nico Alvarez. This is Rebecca Bradley. We went to high school together."

She takes a deep breath. "It's nice to meet you all," she says. "I feel like I'm making a really terrible first impression."

"Not at all," Sarah says. "You're totally fine. I know a little something about how these guys can get under your skin." She tilts her head toward me, and Rebecca laughs.

"Ha. Yeah. That's an understatement," she says. "I should get back to work now, but thank you for talking to me. And not making me feel silly for needing to ask."

"No problem," I say. "It really is nice to see you again."

She stands and adjusts her nursing badge. "I was really glad to read about the two of you making it to the NHL. I know how badly Theo wanted it, and I have a feeling he got it because you didn't give up on him. He's lucky to have you, Carter," she says, then she moves to the door. "It was nice to meet all of you."

"Um, just for the record," Miles says as soon as Rebecca is gone, "I don't think she's really over him."

I let out a chuckle. "Yeah. Me neither."

A few minutes later, another nurse shows up, this one fully prepared to take us to see Theo, who is finally out of recovery.

Nico and Miles stay back in the waiting room, and Sarah offers to do the same, probably wanting to give me time alone with my brother. But I quickly dismiss the idea. I want her beside me. She's been my lifeline the past few hours—I'm not about to give her up now.

"Is he awake?" I ask the nurse when we finally reach Theo's room.

"He's still a little groggy," she says. "But he's awake." She pauses, hand on the large wooden door. "He needs his rest, so a short visit would be best."

Seeing Theo in a hospital bed, IV attached, oxygen cannula in his nose, feels like a punch to the gut.

My stupidly strong, annoyingly boastful brother looks terrible. His skin is pale, and he has dark circles under his closed eyes. His left arm and hand are heavily bandaged, resting on a pillow at his side.

Sarah and I hang back while the nurse approaches. "You've got some visitors, Theo," she says, and Theo opens his eyes. He scans the room, eyes finally landing on me, then he smiles.

"Took you long enough," he says, his voice raw and scratchy.

Sarah sits in the chair near the foot of the bed while I step up and take Theo's hand. His grip is stronger than I expect it to be, and it sends a surge of emotion through my chest.

He's okay. He's here, and he's okay.

The nurse takes a second to hang a new bag of IV fluids, then she moves to the door. "I'll be back in a few minutes for another vitals check," she says, then she leaves us alone.

"Way to scare me half to death," I say to Theo, and he gives me a tired grin. "Sarah's here too, and Nico and Miles are still in the waiting room. And Coach Kimzey will be back in the morning."

Theo leans to the right and looks around me. "Hey, Sarah," he says, and my wife stands, moving up beside me.

"Hey, Theo," she says, her voice soft.

Theo drops my hand and points between the two of us. "So...where are we at with this?" he asks, his words slurring the slightest bit like he's still a little bit under the influence. "Have we gotten to the part where you two just admit you're in love with each other? Or...not yet?"

My face heats even as I look over at Sarah to see her pressing her lips together, clearly fighting a smile.

"Seriously?" I say to Theo. "You're just asking right in front of her like it's no big deal?"

"What?" he says. "It's a fair question."

I hold Sarah's gaze for a long moment. She doesn't seem bothered by Theo's question at all. There's no uncertainty behind her eyes, no hesitation. Just warmth and what feels an awful lot like *love*.

I turn back to Theo. "We're working on it," I say. "But *someone* decided to have a big dramatic accident, so we haven't had a lot of time to talk."

"Whatever, man," Theo says. "You've known how you feel for weeks. Don't pin this on me."

Sarah starts to chuckle, and I shake my head. It's not like he's wrong, but I'd rather he not tell Sarah before I can.

Theo clears his throat, wincing, then licks his dry lips. "Is there any water in here?"

"I'll get you some," Sarah says, lifting a hand to my arm and giving it a quick squeeze. "I'll be right back."

I nod, watching her as she leaves the room, then I look down to see my brother watching me. "I'm happy for you, man," he says. "You deserve it."

There's a distance in his tone that makes me think he doesn't believe the same thing about himself, and I think about Rebecca, wonder if I should tell him that I spoke to her.

I'm sure I will eventually, but maybe not tonight.

"Did we win?" Theo asks.

"Nah," I say. "We scored one more time, but they took it in the end."

He huffs out a laugh. "Cause y'all suck without me."

"Yeah, we do. Which is why you'd better heal quick."

He closes his eyes for a long moment before he opens them and fixes his gaze on mine, his expression serious. "Be straight with me, man. Did you talk to the surgeon?" He takes a steadying breath. "Will I..."

I nod, knowing exactly what he's asking even if he can't find the words. "Yeah," I say. "You will. It'll take a lot of work. Rehab. But there's no reason why you shouldn't expect to play again."

He nods, letting his eyes fall closed. It seems like it's getting harder for him to stay awake. "Whose blade was it?"

"Dmitri Isakov," I say. "They'll have an official review, but Fly was right there when it happened, and he says it was pretty obvious it was an accident."

"I'd never blame Dmitri," Theo says. "I love that guy. He probably feels terrible."

"Yeah, he texted already," I say. "Probably messaged you

too, which, come to think of it, I have your phone if you want it."

I pull it out of my pocket and use my own face to unlock it. "Yeah," I say, scrolling through his notifications. "You've got a message from him and pretty much everyone else you've ever met."

"I'll look at them tomorrow," he says. "What happened to Kiminsky?"

"He got a major for boarding," I say. "That was it."

"No game misconduct?"

"The refs ruled the cut wasn't a direct result of the hit."

Theo grumbles. "Did you let Kiminsky know how you felt about that?"

"Two solid hits in the last half of the third," I say. "You know I've got your back."

He holds up his good hand, and I step closer, gripping it with mine.

"I do know that," he says. "I always know that."

"I can't play this game without you, man." My voice cracks, tears springing to my eyes, and I suddenly feel so tired, so completely frayed by everything that's happened.

"You won't," Theo says, like he's the one who's supposed to give *me* reassurance. "I mean, if it was *you* who got cut, you'd probably be done. Career over. But me? I've got this."

I drop his hand and gently shove his good arm. "Shut up."

Sarah comes back in with a cup of ice water and a straw, so I help Theo sit up enough to take a drink while she holds the straw to his mouth.

"Thanks, Sarah," Theo says. "Now, will you please take your husband home and put him to bed? You both look like you need to sleep."

"We'll be back tomorrow, all right? And Mom's flying in first thing. She should be here around nine."

Theo nods, his eyes already closed. "I love you, brother," he says. "Thanks for being here."

"I love you too," I say, then I make my way to the door where Sarah is already waiting.

She slips an arm around my waist. "You okay?" she asks, and I nod, wiping my eyes.

"Yeah. Just tired. Ready to go home."

Home. The word has had a different meaning lately. The new house helps, but it only feels like a home because Sarah is there. She's what I crave, and I'm suddenly intensely aware of how lucky I am that *going home* means having her with me.

29

CARTER

AT THE HOUSE, THERE'S A PACKAGE ON THE FRONT PORCH, ALONG with a stack of our mail. Sarah scoops it up and carries it inside where Gordie very enthusiastically lets us know how happy he is that we're home.

I take him into the kitchen to feed him while Sarah opens the package.

"Who is it from?" I ask, honestly a little curious why she's opening it now when it's the middle of the night and we should both be crashing into bed.

"It doesn't say," she says. "It's postmarked from New York."

So *that's* why she's opening it. I probably would too if I were her.

Once Gordie is eating, I move to the counter where she's standing and look over her shoulder. "What is it?"

"A book, I think," she says pulling it out of the box. It's wrapped in brown paper, and she makes quick work of removing it, then she lets out a gasp. "Oh my gosh! It's Adrienne Vale's monograph."

"In non-art-speak, please."

"A monograph—it's a book of an artist's work," she says. "It's a big deal to have one made because you have to have created a body of work impressive enough to justify it." She flips through the book's pages. "Adrienne Vale is a personal favorite of mine. Her work is incredible."

"You still don't know who sent it?"

"I don't. There's no card."

"Is there an inscription?"

She flips back to the front of the book. "Oh, there is one," she says. Then she reads, "'Sarah, it was wonderful seeing your work at the Second Light. Let's talk about the Rooke. Congratulations on the new addition to your extended family. Calista.'" She looks up at me. "Let's talk about the Rooke," she repeats, a slight tremor in her voice. "Does that mean what I think it means?"

I lift my hands to her shoulders. "I think it means she wants your art in her gallery."

"She wants my art," Sarah says. "Calista Reinhardt wants *me*."

"She wants you," I echo. "And I'm not even a little surprised."

Sarah puts down the book, then she turns and throws herself into my arms.

I lift her up, loving that I get to be here for this moment. That I'm the one who gets to celebrate with her first. "I wish it wasn't so late," I say, as I lower her back to the ground. "We need to celebrate."

"Tomorrow," she says. "After we sleep."

Silence stretches between us, and I wonder if she's thinking the same thing I am. There isn't anything else to do but go to bed, but I've been away from her for nine days, and I don't really want to say goodbye to her yet, even just for her to walk to her own bedroom.

But I also don't want to come on too strong. There are things I need to say, promises I want to make, and I'm not sure I can do the conversation justice at four in the morning.

She reaches up and tugs on the penny that's hanging around my neck. "Penny for your thoughts?" she whispers.

"Are you sure you want them?" I ask, letting out a little laugh.

"That's the rule, isn't it?"

"Only if you give me a new penny," I say. "*That's* the rule."

She purses her lips to the side, like she's really thinking about where she might find an actual penny. Then her expression brightens. "Wait! I totally have one." She tilts her head toward the living room. "Go sit down. I'll be right back."

She disappears down the hall that leads to her bedroom. I kick off my shoes and sink onto the couch, feeling a new wave of exhaustion. But then Sarah comes back, eyes bright, looking stupidly beautiful considering the hour, and drops a penny into my palm.

"Your penny," she says, lowering herself onto the cushion beside me. "Now spill."

"I'm warning you," I say. "There might not be anything graceful about this. I'm too tired to be tactful."

"Consider me warned," she says.

I lean forward and drop the penny onto the coffee table, then I reach over and take her hand, holding it with both of mine. My thumb brushes over her wedding band, and I lift my gaze to meet hers. "I'm thinking...that I love you. That I've probably loved you since before I married you even if I hadn't admitted it yet. I'm thinking that I want a life with you. That even though we did this backwards, I really want to be married for real. I'm thinking that I want to kiss you every single day. That I want us to have a family—not yet. Just…one day. Whenever we feel ready. And…" I swallow against a sudden knot in my throat. The way she's looking at me right now, it's taking everything in me not to pull her into my arms and kiss her senseless. "And I'm thinking that I don't ever want you to sleep in your bed again," I say. "Because I want you in mine."

She smiles, biting her lip in that way that kills me. "Those thoughts are worth a lot more than a penny."

"Are they?"

She nods, then scoots over and climbs onto my lap, straddling me so her knees bracket my hips. She takes my face in her hands, her thumbs brushing over my jawline, and leans down to kiss me. I lift my hands to her hips, content to let her lead, to guide wherever this kiss is taking us. It's languid and slow, tender in all the right ways. Kissing like this is its own kind of intoxication. As tired as I am, I still feel like I could do this all night.

Sarah breaks the kiss, but she stays close, her forehead pressed to mine. "I love you too," she whispers, and something in my heart turns over and clicks into place. "I still can't believe I *get* to love you, that we stumbled into a life that feels this good." Another kiss. "Also, you have the better mattress anyway. So…" Her words send fire racing through my veins, but then her mouth is on mine again, and I'm lost to her. To her taste, to the brush of her tongue against mine, the feel of her hands moving over my arms, my shoulders, my chest.

I slide my hands up to her back, fingers dipping under the hem of her shirt to press against her skin.

She leans back and looks at me, brown eyes heavy. "Take

me to bed, Carter," she whispers. "Make me your wife for real."

~

Dawn has turned the world a hazy blue before Sarah finally falls asleep, her head resting on my chest, one leg hooked over mine.

I should sleep too, but I can't stop thinking about the magic of holding her like this. I was not prepared for the gift it was to love all of her before I knew her body like I know it now.

Love changes everything—*intensifies* everything.

All those years ago, when I was getting the therapy I wish my brother had gotten with me, I learned that if life gets overwhelming, I can change my to-do list into a *get-to* list for a much-needed dose of perspective.

I get to play a hockey game tomorrow night. And hopefully, if we can make it without Theo, a few more games after that one.

I get to share a career I love with my brother. I get to help him get better—both his hand *and* his heart.

I get to learn how to be a great uncle to Poppy and Olive and Fiona and a brother-in-law to my team captain.

I get to build a life with a woman who feels like she was always meant to be the other half of my heart.

I get to.

What an incredible privilege.

EPILOGUE

SARAH

I HADN'T HEARD OF THE AZORES ISLANDS WHEN CARTER SUGGESTED it as a honeymoon destination, but he only had to say "tiny island in the Atlantic where hydrangeas grow wild along the roads," and I was all in.

When we got married in March, we told everyone we were planning a honeymoon for the off-season, mostly so people didn't question why we didn't take one right after the wedding. But we never actually planned a trip.

Until we fell in love and decided maybe we deserved a honeymoon after all.

I haven't been disappointed. This place is magical.

The roads are ridiculously narrow and frequently blocked by herds of cattle. And the beaches aren't particularly beachy. The Azores Islands are volcanic, so the coastline is defined by rocky cliffsides and crashing waves.

But the hiking has been unreal, we've seen at least half a dozen whales, and I've eaten my weight in Azores pineapples which are smaller and sweeter and absolutely perfect.

Not that the location *truly* matters. I think I could go anywhere with Carter and still have a good time.

I said as much to Anna when we talked this morning, and she playfully rolled her eyes, then grumbled something about newlyweds. But I'm determined to soak this up as long as I possibly can. I believe her when she says it won't always feel this perfect. That eventually, we're going to have to work a little to make sure our marriage stays healthy.

But I'm happy to ride this wave as long as I possibly can.

Besides. It hasn't *all* been perfect. We've been fighting over the thermostat in the adorable stone cottage we're renting all week long. I like to sleep with the windows open, feel the sea breeze against my face, and he likes to seal the place up tight and crank the temperature down to sixty-four degrees. Something about optimal sleeping conditions, blah, blah, blah.

He ends up in nothing but his boxer briefs under a sheet while I'm wearing two layers of flannel and wool socks with the comforter folded in half to give me double the warmth.

He thinks my body temperature must be abnormally low. I think he spends too much time on the ice and his perspective is warped.

I do love it that when our room is a little colder, he has to use his furnace of a body to warm me up. There are definitely worse things in life than sleeping in his arms.

Now, on the evening before we're flying home, I'm on the back patio of our cottage, waiting for Carter to take a shower, sending a million texts to my brother.

Right before we left, I finished Carter's painting, and if Miles can figure out how to hang it without putting a hole in my living room wall, it'll be up by the time we get home.

MILES

This thing is enormous. I don't know how to
get it on the wall.

SARAH

Don't try it by yourself. Is there anyone there
who can help you?

MILES

I brought Poppy. She wanted to visit Gordie.

SARAH

Is there anyone older than seven who can
help you? Is Kim around?

Carter's mom has been staying at our house, cat sitting Gordie for the week. We had so many people we could have asked to check on Gordie—his mom didn't need to fly all the way in from Texas—but something tells me she wanted to spend some time with Theo.

He's been seeing a therapist this summer, which he says has been great, but I know first-hand that it's also a lot of work. After a month of bi-weekly sessions with my therapist, I managed to go to exactly *one* hockey game of this past season: the sixth game of the Eastern Conference Finals in which the Jaguars lost to the Warriors and fell out of the running for the Stanley Cup.

It was a close game, and I hate that they lost, though I think a part of Carter didn't mind. When they do win a Stanley Cup—because they will eventually—he wants his brother to be on the ice beside him.

Either way, the night still felt like a win to me. Now that I've gotten the first one behind me, I think next season is going to be a lot easier. In retrospect, it almost feels silly. That I let fear rule so many of my decisions for so long. But therapy has also taught me that I deserve to have grace with myself. I can learn from my past experiences, but I don't have to live in them. I can move forward with intention. Be a better version of myself—for me, for the rest of my family, for Carter.

MILES

Kim is lounging by the pool. I think she's asleep.

SARAH

I'm sure she'd be happy to help. She and I talked about you coming over to hang it for me. Or can you call Holly? I bet he'd come over.

Maybe this is a bad idea. Maybe I can just leave it in my studio and take Carter upstairs to see it. Then *he* can help me hang it and I can be there to make sure everything goes exactly according to plan.

MILES

Stop worrying. I'll figure it out. He's going to love it, Sarah. You did good.

Not exactly the most effusive compliment, but coming from Miles, it means a lot.

"What has you looking so serious?" Carter says, stepping up behind me. He lifts his hands and brushes my hair away from my neck, then leans down to press a trail of kisses over my exposed shoulder.

I quickly scramble to put away my phone. "Nothing. Just looking at new pictures Anna sent over of the girls."

"And they made you frown?"

"Was I frowning?" I say, voice a little higher than it should be. "I was probably just missing them." I spin around, looping my arms around his neck as his hands settle onto my waist. He just got out of the shower after going for a run, and he smells delicious. His sun-kissed skin is warm and soft, the hair at his nape still damp.

"Hmm. Can I see the pictures?" he asks, a teasing glint in his eye.

"Of course you can," I say, and I reach for my phone. Luckily, Anna really *did* send photos this morning, so it isn't hard to pull them up. I scroll through several pictures of the girls splashing in Miles and Anna's pool. Charlie is with them, red hair sparkling in the sun, and all three have enormous smiles on their faces. There's also a photo of four-month-old Fiona, brown eyes wide as she smiles at the camera.

Fiona is the *sweetest* baby. Easy and good-natured. She's a much better sleeper than either of the other girls were, which means Anna is getting better sleep too. She's still had a little bit of depression, which we expected, but awareness and support has made it a lot easier to juggle than it was the last time around.

Carter looks at the photos, his expression softening. He loves his new nieces almost as much as they love him. "Those are fun," he says. "It's lucky you had them so easily accessible." He gives me a pointed look. "Is everything okay with your brother?"

I huff. "Carter Williamson, would you just let me have this secret, please? I only need to keep it for about eighteen more hours, then you'll know exactly why I was texting my brother. But I'm not going to tell you right now."

He grins, then leans down and kisses away my annoyance. "Sorry," he says. "I was really just messing with you. Have you happened to check your email today?"

I lift my eyebrows. "Should I?"

His mouth moves to my jawline, his hands lifting to tilt my head just so, exposing my neck. "They scheduled our immigration hearing," he says, his breath whispering across my skin. "Do you think we'll be able to convince them we're in love?"

I close my eyes, goosebumps skittering across my skin as he kisses his way to my earlobe.

"I don't know," I manage to say. "I'm not sure we have much chemistry."

He chuckles before moving his mouth to mine one more time.

When all of this started, we spent so much time worrying about immigration, trying to make everything look legitimate. It feels silly that we were so concerned when we were already so close to falling in love.

I lean into Carter, deepening the kiss in a way that makes him grip my hips, tugging me against him. It's time for dinner, and my stomach is already rumbling, but asking me to step out of Carter Williamson's embrace is like asking a flower to turn away from the sun. It goes against every instinct. I think a part of me has known that from the beginning. I belong *right here*.

"If I couldn't hear your stomach grumbling," Carter says, his voice low and gravelly, "I'd already have you back in bed."

I smile against his mouth. "Feed me now. We'll have time later."

We have an amazing dinner. Then an amazing moonlit walk along a shoreline trail. Then we come back to our cottage, and Carter opens all the windows so he can make love to me while the sea breeze tickles our skin.

After, I lay cocooned in his arms and fiddle with Carter's wedding band, spinning it in a circle around his ring finger. I lift my head, propping my chin on his bare chest. His eyes are closed, his expression peaceful.

"When did you know you wanted our relationship to be real?" I ask. "Was there a specific moment?"

He opens his eyes. They're a deeper blue in the dim light. In the sun, they look more like the sky right at the edge of the horizon, but right now, they're the color of the ocean outside. I can't decide which shade I like more.

He seems to consider my question, his hand tracing lazy circles across the skin on my back. "I knew I was into you when I wiped cupcake frosting off your nose in Anna's pantry," he says.

"The day we met?"

"I didn't say I wanted to *marry* you the day we met, I said I knew I was *into* you."

"Then why didn't you call me?" I ask. "Or ask for my number?"

"Because you were leaving," he says. "I was still thinking about it. I think I probably *would* have called. But then…"

"Miles asked you to marry me instead," I say, and Carter grins.

"Best decision I ever made."

I shake my head, chuckling as I drop it back onto his chest.

"What about you?" he asks, hand moving to my hair. "When did you know?"

"I think I knew I loved you when you kissed me hello at my art show. But I fought accepting it until Anna called and told me Theo was hurt." I shift, pushing up on my elbow one more time so I can look at him.

"Why then?" he asks, and I shrug.

"When I first answered the phone and I heard her voice, I could tell something was wrong. My first thought was for you. If you were hurt, I just realized there was nothing in the world that would keep me from getting to you. No hockey game. No scary memory. Nothing was more important than finding you, putting my eyes on you, doing whatever it took to make you well again."

"I should send Theo a thank you card," he teases. "If all that came out of his injury."

I roll my eyes. "I would have gotten there eventually. I just needed a little nudge to believe I was capable of being what you need. What you deserve."

He rolls onto his side to face me. "You are so much more than I deserve," he says, and I nod.

"I really am, aren't I?" I lean forward and press a kiss to his mouth. "That's exactly why we're going to sleep with the windows open *all night long*."

THEO PICKS us up from the airport, which is perfect because I need him to be at the house for Carter's surprise too.

When Theo was recovering from his surgery, he and his mom both stayed with us for a few days. It meant that Carter and I had a *very* frantic hour moving everything in my bedroom into *his* bedroom so it didn't look like we'd only *just* spent our first night together as a married couple. But then it meant that I got to spend quite a bit of time with Carter's mom. She loved spending time with me in my studio, chatting with me while I worked.

That's when I got the idea for the painting I wanted to do for Carter. His *Sarah Stone* original. I knew it had to incorporate his relationship with his dad, and there was no way to do that without also including Theo.

Fortunately, Carter was so busy with playoffs that it

wasn't hard to keep him out of my studio. I finished the painting in a matter of weeks, let it dry, then hid it behind a few other canvases and crossed my fingers he wouldn't get nosy.

Theo stops his SUV in the driveway, idling while he waits for us to get out.

"Hey," I say, reaching up to nudge his arm. "Can you come in a sec? There's something I want to show you."

Theo looks at me, then looks over to his brother.

Carter shrugs. "No clue. She's been hiding something from me for days."

I roll my eyes as I climb out, shifting my bag up to my shoulder.

"It hasn't been *days*," I say. "It was yesterday. And it's not that big of a deal."

I hope my words sound convincing, because I'm practically dying on the inside. My hands start to tremble as I climb the front steps, nerves making me twitchy. This is almost worse than my first solo show at the Second Light.

From a technical standpoint, I know the painting is good. And I showed it to Carter's mom on a video call, and she loved it so much she cried. But for Carter—and for Theo, too —it's gonna feel more personal.

"You okay?" Carter asks as he opens the door for me.

"Yep," I say with a nod, not trusting myself to say more.

Inside, Kim is standing in the living room, right by the fireplace, like she's waiting for our arrival.

I maybe wish she wasn't being *quite* so obvious, but at this point, it can't be helped. Also, the canvas is four feet tall. It's not like we can ease into this. The second Carter is in the living room, he's going to see it.

I hang back, waiting, watching as he steps into the room

and notices the new addition. He stops in his tracks, dropping our suitcases at his feet before slowly walking over to the painting.

Theo follows, clearly understanding exactly why I needed him to come inside too.

He had to, because I painted them both.

They're standing side by side, eyes on each other, their faces relaxed but engaged, like they're having an easy conversation. They're outside, the sun shining overhead, casting long shadows behind them, but the way they're standing, their shadows blend into one. If you look from just the right angle, the shadow doesn't look like them—it looks like the outline of a different man altogether.

"That's Dad," Carter says softly, looking over at his brother. "Do you see it?"

"Yeah," Theo says. "Wait, can you see his eyes?"

He *can* see his father's eyes. Only faintly, and only from certain angles, when the light hits just right. There are a lot of little details like that. Places where the edges of the scene dissolve into fragments of shapes that represent some part of Theo and Carter's shared history. If you aren't looking for them, you won't see them. But they're there. A hockey puck and stick. A bundle of bluebonnets, which is the state flower of Texas. An Appies logo, to honor their first pro team.

"I see his eyes," Carter says. "And look—there are pennies on the ground."

I wasn't sure they would notice the pennies. There are only a couple scattered around their feet, but it felt like an important detail to include.

Kim moves up beside me and loops her arm through mine. "It looks even more incredible in person," she says.

I nod, grateful for the compliment and happy to have her

standing beside me. But I can't take my eyes off my husband. He's still standing, staring, and I suddenly hate that I'm behind him, that I can't see his face.

Finally, he turns, eyes locking on mine, and walks across the room. I step forward to meet him and he scoops me into his arms, crushing me in an enormous hug.

"This is the nicest thing anyone has ever done for me," he says.

I bite my lip. "You really like it?"

"I love it," he says. "Almost as much as I love you."

Theo comes over next and gives me a hug. He looks a little raw around the edges, which I expected might happen. Carter's had a lot of practice talking about his dad, but Theo's still getting used to owning his feelings in the same way. "Thanks for including me," he says.

"I actually ordered a print for you," I say. "I don't think it's arrived yet, and it's not quite as big, but I thought you might like to have your own copy as well."

He nods. "I appreciate that."

"Will you stay for dinner?" Kim says to Theo. "I cooked enough for all of us. And Anna and Miles are bringing the girls over too." She looks at me. "I hope that's okay. I asked Miles when he was here yesterday to hang the painting. I thought one big family dinner might be nice before I head back to Texas in the morning."

"That sounds wonderful," I say, but Theo seems less certain.

"Maybe you could run out and grab us some drinks," Carter says to his brother. "Then come back in an hour for dinner?"

Theo nods. "I can do that." He walks over and gives his mom an enormous hug, then lets himself out the front door.

Carter watches him go, then looks back at me.

"Do you think he's okay?" I ask, and he nods.

"He will be. He just needs a minute." He holds my gaze. "It means a lot to me that you did something for us both."

"I love you both," I say. "Theo will always mean a lot to me because of how much he means to you."

After a week away, it's fun to have the whole family together, plus Holly and Charlie, whom Carter invited at the last minute. Theo comes back, seeming more like himself, and becomes everyone's favorite when he's willing to get in the pool with the girls and make sure Olive, who is afraid of absolutely nothing, doesn't drown trying to be just like the older girls.

I stand in the shade, close to the house—summers in Atlanta are brutal—and rock baby Fiona, who has fallen asleep in my arms, her chubby cheek pressed against my shoulder.

As I look around the patio at all the people I love, I can't quite believe this is my life. That I took a gamble marrying a man I barely knew and wound up with this. It feels like a miracle that I get to be so close to Miles and Anna, to watch their girls grow up.

But even that pales in comparison to how it feels knowing that when everyone goes back to their own lives, their own homes, I get to stay here.

I get to go inside and clean up the kitchen, maybe watch an episode of something on TV. Then I get to crawl into bed beside the best man I know and fall asleep with my head on his shoulder.

Carter comes up behind me, wrapping his arms around me and letting me lean against him, my head resting on his chest.

"Penny for your thoughts," he whispers, his voice close to my ear.

I tilt my head up to look at him. "Just that I love you," I say.

He smiles softly, then leans down to kiss me. "Love you too."

Who would have ever thought I'd marry Carter Williamson and finally find *home*.

~

The End

For a bonus epilogue featuring Carter and Sarah, please visit www.jennyproctor.com/fooledmebonus

ACKNOWLEDGMENTS

Thanks so much for reading, friends. Before we go further, I want to say a quick word about the immigration scenario that led to Carter and Sarah *conveniently* getting married. As an author, I have the unique privilege of crafting love stories where I get to sand off the rough edges of life and dabble in circumstances that often feel too good to be true. My goal is to create an escape for you—where things work out, love conquers all, and people always get a happily ever after.

While I love creating books that provide a tiny, temporary respite from real life, the reality is, navigating the immigration system is rarely so simple or smooth, particularly for those in marginalized populations. I hope you'll take this book as it was intended—as a happy escape and a celebration of the love Carter and Sarah were destined to find, with or without a marriage of convenience.

Once upon a time, my critique partner suggested that we work on a hockey series together. You know what I knew about hockey? Absolutely nothing. But I started researching and learning and then I started watching and soon, I discovered a love for a sport I once new nothing about. I'm now a DEDICATED Carolina Hurricanes fan, and my husband is still scratching his head about how I got here. I know stats. I know player names. I pay attention to trade rumors and game strategy and playoff brackets. It makes me so happy, I can't even begin to tell you.

Even when I'm no longer writing hockey romance, I'm positive I will STILL be watching and loving hockey, and I love that. That this job has given me something that brings me so much joy.

I loved creating an NHL team that I could slot into a world I've learned so much about, and I hope you enjoyed the Georgia Jaguars as much as I enjoyed creating them.

For all the people who helped me breathe life into this book, thank you from the bottom of my heart. Kristina, Emily, Kiki, Lucy, AS ALWAYS, your thoughts and feedback were so helpful. You are all such a vital part of my process, thank you feels like such a simple thing to say that will never truly be enough. But it's all I've got so I hope you sense how much I mean it—how truly valuable you are to me.

To my readers, you're the most important part of what I do. Thanks for being on this journey with me. Always, always.

ABOUT THE AUTHOR

Jenny Proctor is an award-winning author of more than twenty romantic comedies and an Amazon bestseller.

She began her career in publishing in 2013; her writing has been a constant since then and is now her full-time focus, but in the past, she spent several years as the owner and managing editor of Midnight Owl Editors and as the chair of the Storymakers Conference. Wired for relationships, Jenny loves public speaking, teaching, and building lasting connections.

Jenny lives in the mountains of Western North Carolina, a place she considers one of the loveliest on earth. She loves to hike with her family and spend time outdoors, but she also adores lounging around her home, reading great books or watching great movies and, when she's lucky, eating delicious food she did not have to prepare herself.

To learn more, find Jenny online at www.jennyproctor.com.

ALSO BY JENNY PROCTOR

The Appies Hockey Romance Series

Absolutely Not in Love

Romancing the Grump

When Alec Met Evie

Midnight Rush Romance

Once Upon a Boyband

One More Made Up Love Song

How to Kiss a Hawthorne Brother Series

How to Kiss Your Best Friend

How to Kiss Your Grumpy Boss

How to Kiss Your Enemy

How to Kiss a Movie Star

The Oakley Island Romcom Series

Eloise and the Grump Next Door

Merritt and Her Childhood Crush

Sadie and the Badboy Billionaire

The Some Kind of Love Series

Love Redesigned

Love Unexpected

Love Off-Limits

Love in Bloom

Other Novels

How to Kiss on Christmas Morning

The Christmas Letters

Her Last First Date

Just One Chance

www.ingramcontent.com/pod-product-compliance
Lightning Source LLC
Chambersburg PA
CBHW011924050726
47591CB00009B/2322